The Lost Boys

ALSO BY FAYE KELLERMAN

Walking Shadows

Bone Box

The Theory of Death

Murder 101

The Beast

Gun Games

Hangman

Blindman's Bluff

The Mercedes Coffin

The Burnt House

The Ritual Bath

Sacred and Profane

The Quality of Mercy

Milk and Honey

Day of Atonement

False Prophet

Grievous Sin

Sanctuary

Justice

Prayers for the Dead

Serpent's Tooth

Moon Music

Jupiter's Bones

Stalker

The Forgotten

Stone Kiss

Street Dreams

Straight into Darkness

The Garden of Eden and Other Criminal Delights:
A Book of Short Stories

With Jonathan Kellerman

Double Homicide

Capital Crimes

With Aliza Kellerman

Prism

The Lost Boys

A Decker/Lazarus Novel

Faye Kellerman

HARPER LARGE PRINT

An Imprint of HarperCollinsPublishers

THE LOST BOYS. Copyright © 2021 by Plot Line, Inc. All rights reserved. Printed in the United States of America. No part of this book may be used or reproduced in any manner whatsoever without written permission except in the case of brief quotations embodied in critical articles and reviews. For information, address HarperCollins Publishers, 195 Broadway, New York, NY 10007.

HarperCollins books may be purchased for educational, business, or sales promotional use. For information, please e-mail the Special Markets Department at SPsales@harpercollins.com.

FIRST HARPER LARGE PRINT EDITION

ISBN: 978-0-06-304056-4

Library of Congress Cataloging-in-Publication Data is available upon request.

21 22 23 24 25   LSC   10 9 8 7 6 5 4 3 2 1

To Jonathan—my coauthor for life
And to our newest first edition—Adeline Grace—
indeed a fitting name

The Lost Boys

Chapter 1

Four decades of detective work had taught Decker a thing or two. One of the delights of Missing Persons cases was that they often had happy endings. But sometimes not. Because people disappear for a variety of reasons.

Some individuals vanished by accident: a wrong turn on a hiking trail or a rogue wave that hit while sailing on otherwise navigable seas. Sometimes lives evaporated by wicked intent—a pickup gone awry or a stranded motorist meeting the wrong type of help. Sometimes souls perished in seemingly innocuous encounters that went terribly wrong, leaving the horrified perpetrators attempting to hide the evildoing, keeping a corroding secret that they were unwilling or unable to confront.

But sometimes people disappeared because they wanted to.

So far, no one was quite sure which reason fit Bertram Lanz—a thirty-five-year-old man with cognitive disabilities who disappeared from a field trip arranged by the Loving Care facility: a residential home. On the trip, there were fifty mentally challenged men and women. Bertram was alive and well when chaperones herded the group back into the bus after a two-hour leisurely hike. But after a one-hour stop at a local diner, while boarding the bus to go home, the supervisors quickly realized that the head count was off by one. And no matter how many times the recount was taken, the Loving Care chaperones came up a body short. It took even more time to discover who was gone from the roster.

That was six hours earlier, and it was now ten in the evening. Since the call to Greenbury Police Station, officers as well as volunteers had been combing the nearby area for Bertram. Nightfall had now blanketed daylight: no moon and an inky sky pierced by a million pinpoints of light. The many forested areas were now as black as pitch and impossible to search. Even in the town proper, street lighting was more for atmosphere than for illumination. Detective Peter Decker had moved from the woods to the residential areas and he had been circling the streets for the last two hours, running into local citizens covering the same blocks. He was worried for the man's safety. Bertram wasn't ill and he wasn't on lifesaving medication, but his limited life skills probably hampered him from negotiating a complex world. Since it was summer, Bertram would at least have the advantage of a warmer night.

Fishing out his cell phone, Decker called his wife, Rina, who had joined the search party. In another life, five years ago, he had been a detective lieutenant with LAPD. He had retired from big-city life, but he still wanted to keep his foot in the door with something. And when a job at Greenbury PD opened up, he welcomed the opportunity to work in a sleepy little college town in Upstate New York. It wasn't that crime didn't exist here, but when it came, it was always unexpected.

She answered after two rings. He said, "Hi, darlin'. Anything?"

"I was going to ask you the same thing."

"No, unfortunately." A pause. "Why don't you go home, Rina? We've got help from neighboring departments now. There's no reason for all of us to keep scouring the same streets."

"Where could he have gone, Peter? The diner is in the middle of nowhere."

"If he's on foot, he couldn't have gone too far. The problem is the woods. If he decided to go for a walk, it's so easy to become disoriented even during the day. Right now, it's too dark to search. We're thinking that he might be holed up in some garage or cabin. You know how this town is. It's filled with part-timers and no one's home. We're trying to get hold of the owners to ask permission to go inside the dwellings. All this takes time."

"What did you mean by 'if he's on foot'?"

"There's a possibility that this was planned. You have to consider everything even if it's unlikely."

"That might make some sense," Rina said. "Otherwise how do you lose a person?"

"We've initially talked to the four chaperones albeit briefly. Once the bus reached the diner, it was a free-for-all. People piled inside, placing orders and looking for chairs. The diner has a maximum seating of thirty-five and there were fifty plus people."

"They were in violation, then."

"Yes, they were. But it's a rural stopover and I suppose the thought of paying dinners outweighed the thought of being cited."

Rina said, "Then the chaperones lost sight of him?"

"They weren't checking off individuals. They were doing head counts. As the residents boarded the bus, they realized they were one short."

"Have you talked to the other residents?"

"Not yet. Too traumatized."

"I can believe that," Rina said. "Are you coming home tonight?"

"I'll be out here until they officially call off the search until morning."

"When might that be?"

"Before midnight, but I might keep searching. I'm a little wired up."

"Is Tyler with you?"

"No. Everyone in the department is riding solo. Don't wait up for me."

"I might," Rina said. "I'm a little wired as well."

"Try to get some sleep, honey. Call me when you've made it home."

"I will. Love you. Stay safe."

"Ditto and ditto."

Pulling into the driveway, Rina was taken aback to find it occupied—surprised but not scared because she recognized the car. A quick look around, then she dashed to the door and let herself in with a key. Gabe stood up when she came inside. "Hey, there."

"Well, this is a treat." Rina walked over and gave her foster son a mama-bear hug. Gabe had been with them since he was fourteen. A decade later, he now stood six two, lean and wiry. His light-brown hair was streaked with dirty blond. His eyes were saturated with shamrock green and peered out from behind rimless glasses. He wore a short-sleeved shirt festooned with cocktail glasses with black jeans and sandals.

Gabe returned the hug. "How are my favorite foster parents?"

Rina laughed. "Not much competition."

"Then how about, how are my favorite set of parents?"

"Still not much competition."

It was Gabe's turn to laugh. "You never age, you know that?"

Rina gave him a skeptical look. She was in her fifties and wavered between feeling like a teenager and feeling like a centenarian. Most of the time, youth won out. She was still trim, and that helped with her energy level. "That's because I'm wearing a scarf on my head and you can't see all the gray hairs."

"All I see are your baby blues and your happy smile."

"You charmer, you." She gave him a gentle slug on the arm. "How are you doing, honey?" A glance at her watch. "When did you get here?"

"I got here about an hour ago. I know it's late. Am I disturbing something?"

"No, of course not."

"Where's the big man?"

"The community is out looking for a lost man. He disappeared near the woods and he's cognitively disabled. I've just come back from searching."

"That's awful. Can I do anything? I've got a car."

"Not at all. I was just sent home. Are you hungry?"

"No, I'm fine. I ate before I came to Greenbury, and then I raided the fridge. I took the rest of the meat loaf. I hope that's okay."

"Of course it's okay. Sit down. Tell me what's going on in your life."

They sat side by side on a blue-and-white print couch. Rina had originally decorated the rooms in multicolored chintz and florals. A year ago, she switched everything to prints in blues and whites. The house looked like a Ming vase with an occasional wood piece thrown in for contrast.

"Nothing much." Gabe sat back into the cushions. "Just thought I'd stop in and say hello. I know it's been a while."

"It has."

Rina smiled and waited for the shoe to drop. When Gabe chose to remain silent, she said, "How's Yasmine?"

"Miserable."

"Oh dear."

"Not with me but with medical school. She's either in class or studying."

"I hear that the first year is the hardest."

"Yeah, absolutely. Her parents keep bugging her to come back to Los Angeles and apply to pharmacy school. There are a ton of Persian girls who are pharmacists."

"I thought her parents *wanted* her to go to medical school."

"I dunno, Rina. Maybe they just want to get her away from me."

"You're engaged."

"We are, but that doesn't mean they're happy about it."

"You converted to Judaism."

"Yes, I did. I even learned a little Hebrew and a lot of Farsi. But I'm not the guy they had envisioned for their daughter." He smiled. "Although they do approve of the ring that I bought her."

"Sparkle always wins them over."

"Who doesn't like bling? Yasmine is thinking about it . . . pharmacy school. I'd support her either way. I just want her to be happy, but I don't suspect she'll be any happier in L.A., living with her parents and away from me. But it's her decision." He looked at his watch. "I shouldn't be keeping you up."

"I'm fine, Gabe."

"How did this man disappear?"

Rina sighed. "He lives in a facility. The residents were on a field trip to hike in the forest. The bus stopped off at a local diner off one of the rural routes. Apparently, it was a lot of people in a crowded space. When the group went to board the bus, he was gone. Peter and other local police departments are still searching. He'll probably be out looking for a while."

"Yeah, of course. Poor guy—the missing guy. Not Peter. Although I'm sure he's working hard."

She regarded her foster son. "What's going on, Gabe? I know you love us, but you don't take a three-hour trip from New York City without a reason. Do you need to talk to Peter?"

"Actually I came to see you, Rina." He looked up at the ceiling and blew out air. "My mother is in the States."

"That's so nice!" A pause. "Or is it?"

"I dunno. My mom and I have a spotty relationship."

"I thought you two had reached a rapprochement."

"Sort of."

"You're on speaking terms."

"We are . . . sort of."

"She took care of you for fourteen years, Gabe. Even when she was destitute, she always made sure there was food on the table and a roof over your head."

"I know, I know. I try to be charitable, but she did abandon me."

"Not exactly. She left you with us."

"Which, in retrospect, was probably the best thing that ever happened to me. But it still hurts."

"Of course. Where is she now?"

"In the city. She called me about two weeks ago when I was working in Chicago, so I had an excuse not to see her. But she must have gone on my website and looked up my concert schedule. She knows I'm in New York now and that I'm teaching a master class." A pause. "She wants to see me. Like sooner rather than like later."

"Do you know why?"

"No idea. But after eleven years of living in India with a man who hates me, it can't be because her maternal instincts suddenly kicked in."

"Do you want to see her?"

"Well . . ." He made a face. "I'd like to see my half sister and my half brother."

"They're with her?"

Gabe nodded.

"What about Devek?"

"He's not with her. That's a plus. The loathing goes both ways." He licked his lips and stood up. "I need some water."

"I'll get it, Gabe. Plain or sparkling?"

"Plain is fine."

Rina went into the kitchen and retrieved a glass of plain water and a cold can of sparkling water. She liked to swig it directly from the container because it was refreshing that way. When she came back, Gabe was standing near the piano, looking at the many family pictures on top of the baby grand. Even though he wasn't at the keyboard, proximity to the instrument seemed to calm him down. He came back to the couch, sat, and drained the water.

He said, "Devek and my mom are having problems."

"Your mom told you that?"

"Not her. Juleen."

"You talked to your sister, then."

"Briefly. Juleen's a stoic kid, but she sounded upset. She told me that her parents barely talk to each other. And she also told me that this trip was very sudden and without her father."

"That doesn't sound good."

"No, it doesn't. My mom ran away from a bad marriage once. I don't put it past her to run away again. Her choices in men are debatable."

"Did your mom say anything to you about her marriage?"

"Not a word. She asked about my dad. She wanted to find out if he was still living in Nevada . . . which he is. She did tell me that if I talked to him not to mention her being here . . . in the States. She's worried that he still carries a grudge."

"Understandable."

"Actually, he's pretty happy in his current life. Chris would never hurt her. He still carries a torch for her. He's told me several times that he'd take her back in a heartbeat. But he'd probably just make her life miserable again."

"He beat her up."

"Yeah, that was bad. Thank God I walked in while he was slapping her. He stopped when he saw me. He was angrier than I've ever seen him."

Rina nodded. She knew what had happened. Chris Donatti had thought that Terry had aborted his child. Lord only knows what would have happened if he had found out then that she was pregnant with another man's child.

Gabe said, "I realize now that she had to leave, but it still hurts."

"I know it does. But that was over a decade ago. Maybe it's time to put it behind you. Both of your parents tried. They just have . . . shortcomings."

"That's a nice euphemism. Chris is a psycho. If he had lived in the 1930s, he would have been executed for a variety of felonies a lot worse than domestic abuse.

I'm his son and he still scares me. *But . . .* at least he's been in my life for the past eleven years. That is way more than I can say for my mom."

"You've been in contact with her."

"A bit, yes." He sighed. "Getting back to the original question, I would like to see my mom in the flesh. But I have a feeling there's more to this than a filial visit. I know she's going to inveigle me into something."

"Like what?"

"Some kind of favor I don't want to do."

"You're not fourteen anymore, Gabriel. You don't have to do anything you don't want to do. And it could be that she wants to see you without Devek. Since there's friction between the two of you, maybe she's being considerate."

"Yeah, maybe you're right. Or maybe you're wrong and I'm right. I suppose there's only one way to find out."

Rina waited.

Gabe said, "Can you be there with me when I visit her? I know that sounds very childish, but if she sees you, she'll act more . . . measured. Less likely to bamboozle me. And if I am getting bamboozled, you can point it out."

"Yes, Terry is good at bamboozling."

"I know. Try not to hate her."

"I don't hate Terry and I don't hate Chris. They're your parents, and they produced a fabulous child."

"Does Peter hate her?"

"Of course he doesn't hate her. He wasn't happy when she left you with us without a forwarding address—for your sake, not for ours. You're part of our family now. Everyone considers you part of the family."

"I know." Gabe bit his lip. "And I do appreciate everything."

"Your appreciation is not necessary. Concert tickets are another thing."

Gabe smiled. "You know, I talk to Hannah almost every day when I'm in the city. When I was telling her about the situation, she told me to ask you what to do. She said you were very wise."

"Funny." Rina laughed. "My daughter has never said that to my face." A sigh. "When are you meeting your mom?"

"I said that I'd call her when I had a free day. What works for you?"

"Next week is okay, but I do want to run it by Peter."

"I figured that. I hope he doesn't try to talk you out of it."

"Peter has never been able to *talk* me out of anything. I suspect that's a husband's lament."

"Husband, boyfriend, fiancé . . . it's a guy's lot in life."

Rina laughed and stood up. "I'll get the guest room ready for you."

"I've already moved in, clean towels and all." He stood up. "I'm really sorry about that missing guy. How could they lose him?"

"Four chaperones for fifty adults. Not a good ratio."

"But you'd think they'd find him right away. I mean how far could he go?"

Rina threw up her hands. "Hopefully, they'll find him in the morning and none the worse for wear."

"Unless he doesn't want to be found," Gabe said. "It can't be fun, being an adult and living in a home. Poor guy. I suppose that even a disability isn't a barrier when the heart yearns for freedom."

Chapter 2

The car in the driveway was a BMW 340i convertible with a black top and custom rims.

What in the world was Gabe doing here?

Decker looked at his watch: 2:28 a.m. He'd just have to wait for morning to find out. Usually Rina parked in the garage and he parked in the driveway, but since the kid's car blocked both spaces, he pulled the car curbside. Luckily, the area was quiet and low crime. He went inside the unlit house, taking care not to wake anyone up.

The bedroom was dark, Rina's shape taking up less than half the bed. She was curled into a ball with the sheet pulled up over her head. Decker picked up the pajamas she had neatly laid out for him and tiptoed into the bathroom to change. It was hard for a man his size to tread lightly. He knew he was a little shorter than his original six-four frame, but he still cut an imposing figure. He had a good head of hair although not as thick as it once was. His mustache was as full as it was five decades ago. But the color had morphed from its natural orange to almost white. He was approaching seventy; he couldn't understand how time had passed so quickly. Try as he might, he couldn't seem to slow it down.

When he got out of the bathroom, Rina rolled over and greeted him with an outstretched arm. "Gabe's here."

"I figured. I recognized his car in the driveway."

"I should have told him to move it." Rina's voice was sleepy. "Sorry."

Decker slipped into bed, took her hand, and kissed it. "No problem."

Rina curled back into a ball. "Any luck with Bertram Lanz?"

"No. We'll try again tomorrow at daylight."

"What time is it now?"

"Around two-thirty."

Rina said, "Dawn is around five-thirty."

"So I'll have either a very short night's sleep or a very long nap."

Rina mumbled something and went back to sleep.

When the alarm went off in the morning, she had already left the bed. Decker exhaled sour breath and trudged to the bathroom. It took him twenty minutes to shower, shave, and dress, but he was rewarded for his effort with a fresh pot of coffee and a smiling wife. How she managed to be so cheerful was beyond his ken.

"Breakfast?" she asked.

"Toast. I can get it."

"I slept last night. You didn't."

"What's with the kid?"

"Your foster son?"

"Yeah, that's what I said. The kid. What does he want?"

"He wants me to come to Manhattan next week. Does that work for you?"

"Of course." A pause. "May I ask why?"

"Terry is in town. She wants to see him. But he doesn't want to see her without backup."

"Why's that? Is she in trouble?"

"I don't know for sure, but she's here with the kids and without her husband."

"Not promising, Rina. You know what happened the last time I tried to help her. We wound up with a son. I don't know about you, but I'm not up to raising any more kids."

"I know. I'm going in with my eyes open."

"How old are they—Terry's children?"

"The girl should be around eleven by now. The boy is younger—four or five."

"What day is this tête-à-tête supposed to take place?" He looked at the date on his watch. "It's already Wednesday. This week is pretty much shot."

"As of last night, we left the date open." Rina brought toast, butter, and jam to the table and sat down with a cup of coffee. "What's the plan for Bertram Lanz? Are you still looking for volunteers?"

"We are. The group is meeting in front of the diner at nine. Actually, the diner is providing pancakes for the volunteers at eight. So whenever you want to show up, that would be great. But if you can't, don't worry. I'm sure there will be a crowd."

"Where could the poor man have gone?"

"I don't know. But if he's anywhere within walking range, we will find him. Kevin Butterfield is organizing several search parties from the various departments. At some point, if we don't find him, I'm going to have to go to the residential facility. Talk to the staff as well as the residents. We need to get a sense of who Bertram is and why he'd go off like that. If he has parents and they haven't been notified, that's got to happen today as well."

"I'll show up at nine to help with the search."

"Thanks. What's Gabe going to do?"

"I suspect he's going back to New York. He's teaching a class, so I know he has some kind of schedule."

Decker took a big bite of toast and washed it down with the dregs of his coffee. "Tell him I said hi. And tell him to call me if he has any misgivings about this meeting. You know I could come instead of you."

"I think he asked me because he knows you're busy."

"Or he doesn't want me there."

"He thinks you're still mad at his mom."

"I'm not mad at all. But Terry turned from this sweet innocent kid to someone who's cunning and manipulative. He needs to watch out."

"I'm sure he's aware of that."

"Yeah, but she's still his mother. Mothers know how to push buttons."

"We had a lovely time with your mother last year."

"We were both on our best behavior."

"Maybe Terry will be on her best behavior."

"That's what worries me. She's a lot more charming than my mother." Decker kissed Rina's cheek. "Thanks for helping out with the search. We're such a small department. We've recruited a few officers from local PDs, but volunteers can make all the difference."

"People helping people," Rina said. "It doesn't make the news, but it gets us through the day."

The morning search proved fruitless. By noon, Decker pulled out his cell and called Tyler, who was searching from another police car. He and McAdams had started out as partners. Now they were friends, although Tyler was much closer in age to Decker's children. Their association had gotten off to a rocky start. But McAdams had proved himself an able colleague. When he answered, Decker said, "Hey, Harvard. Anything?"

"Still dry as a bone. What about you?"

"No luck at all. We don't even have a scent path for the dogs to follow. It could be he was picked up and that's why the dogs aren't smelling anything."

"It was planned?"

"It was planned or he managed to thumb a ride," Decker said. "At this point we need more information. Which means we need to talk to people who were there."

"Everyone has gone back to the facility. Plus, I heard they've contacted lawyers. They might not talk to us."

"Lanz has been missing less than twenty-four hours. It's crucial that we find out as much as we can as soon as we can. Besides, if a big civil suit is coming from the parents, the facility's cooperation will look good. Whether we're wanted or not, I'm going to take a trip to the Loving Care residence and search Bertram's room. Interested in joining me?"

"Of course. And the plan is okay with Mike Radar?"

"I'm going to call him now. I'm sure it's fine." A pause. "Do you have your iPad with you?"

"Always, but I don't have internet. What do you need?"

"Information on Loving Care Adult Residential Home. See if they've had problems in the past. Also, maybe there are comments about them and their level of care."

"Like a Yelp review of adult homes?"

Decker smiled. "I don't know if it's Yelp, but any kind of online reviews. Everyone has an opinion on something."

"True that. How about if I go back to the station house and we can meet up."

"Perfect."

"How far away is the facility?"

"From Greenbury? About a two-hour drive on a good day."

"Have you eaten lunch?"

"Not yet."

"Maybe I'll pick us up something from the kosher deli."

"Good idea. I'll take turkey on rye with lettuce, tomato, mayo, and mustard. You get yourself whatever you want. It's on me. And can you gas my car? I'm just about on empty."

"Sure."

"And map out a route to the home. Get directions from several sites. Better yet, get a paper map."

"Your car has GPS, Old Man."

"GPS is fine but not in rural areas where things are constantly changing. I want backup if their route suddenly leads to a closure that's due to flooding."

"Anything else?"

"Not at the moment. But I reserve the right to dump other assignments on you as I see fit."

McAdams had a picnic precariously perched on his lap. Atop a cloth napkin was a sandwich, coleslaw, potato salad, and a small bowl of fruit. How he had managed to fit so much on his narrow hips' worth of space was a magician's trick. The kid was naturally thin and average height. He was now almost thirty and had filled out across the chest. He had also developed some decent biceps. His brown, curly hair had been clipped short for the summer. His hazel eyes were as sharp as ever, befitting a Harvard man.

He took a bite of his sandwich, and something oozed out from the middle. He licked it up and chewed with vigor. Then he swallowed and said, "Not much to report from what I've read on the Net."

Decker stared out the windshield as he drove down rural roads, heading toward the highway. Green clumps of flora on either side of the asphalt flew by in a continuous verdant band. He was hungry, but the pathway was sinuous and unfamiliar. He had to pay attention to the twists and turns.

"What did people say about the home?"

"Didn't find too much actually. The few reviews I did read reported that Loving Care had clean and attractive surroundings, decent food, good ratio of staff to students, good medical care including therapists, and lots of activities. Residents get single rooms."

"That sounds like all good news. Any naysayers?"

"The main carp was that the place was ex-pen-sive with a capital *E*. The monthly rates are outrageous. If you pay yearly, you get a ten percent discount."

"How much are we talking?"

"It varies but averages out to around ten thousand a month, which pretty much rules out anyone except the very rich. Because it isn't even like rehab, where hopefully, although rarely, it's a one-shot deal. This is year after year."

"Government kick in anything?"

McAdams said, "Probably something, but I suspect not too much."

"For that money, they should be giving five-star service."

"I'd expect nothing less than a Michelin-rated restaurant and an aromatherapy spa," McAdams said. "I'm kidding about the restaurant and spa, but they do give weekly manicures."

"Sign me up," Decker said. "Do they make any exceptions?"

"You mean do they give breaks to the less fortunate? Don't know. There were fifty residents on the field trip. Figure maybe some stayed back. That's around sixty residents at a hundred twenty grand a year. You can give a lot of services with that kind of money and still make a profit."

"There are a lot of very wealthy people in the tri-state area always looking for the best of everything."

"Right you are," McAdams said. "And yet all that money didn't stop them from losing a resident. Or like you suggested, maybe he lost himself on purpose. If he did, he'd have to have help. Anyone would need help. The area is heavily wooded and easy to get lost."

"Maybe he had an escape plan. Do any of the residents have a driver's license?"

"Don't know. Want me to make a call?"

"No, it's fine. We'll be there soon enough."

"You want me to drive, boss, so you can eat?"

"You can drive home. I'll eat then. I don't like to talk to people on a full stomach."

"That's fine, except your sandwich might spoil. It's hot outside."

"I'm sure I can stow it in a refrigerator somewhere."

The two of them rode in silence for a few minutes, McAdams focused on his phone. "No bars." He looked up. "What's new with you?"

"Rina's going to New York."

"Oh, when?"

"Next week probably."

"To visit the grandkids?"

"I'm sure she'll do that, but that's not the reason she's going."

Silence.

McAdams said, "Is it twenty questions, or are you going to tell me?"

Decker said, "Last night we got a visit from Gabe. His mother's in town from India. She's in Manhattan and wants to see Gabe. He doesn't want to see her alone."

"Why not? Is she homicidal like his father?"

"Not homicidal, but she is manipulative. Gabe is afraid that she'll talk him into doing something he doesn't want to do."

"Like what?"

"No idea. Anyway, if Rina's there, Gabe thinks that Terry will be more likely to behave herself."

"O-kay," McAdams said. "Does a twenty-four-year-old concert pianist really need help to say no to Mommy?"

"It's a complicated relationship."

"All relationships with your parents are complicated. And parents are great manipulators. It's nothing unique . . . well, maybe his dad is unique. Even my dad isn't a professional hit man."

"He doesn't do that anymore. He's . . . a psychopath who occasionally kills people when it's convenient." A pause. "I suppose I'm splitting hairs."

"Ya think?"

Decker shrugged. "Long story short, Gabe asked Rina to come, and she said yes. No one asked for my advice. I'm just a bystander."

"Until you aren't."

Decker didn't speak right away. "Do you think I should go with her?"

"You're asking my opinion?"

"I suppose I am."

"There's a first." McAdams smiled. "I guess it depends where we are with Bertram Lanz. If there's nothing pressing, sure, go with her. I am curious as to why Gabe didn't ask you to come in the first place. You know Terry better than Rina does."

"I think Gabe's nervous that I may lose my cool." A pause. "And you're right. I'm better off here until we find Bertram Lanz."

"You think he's still alive?"

"I don't know. If it was an accidental disappearance, I would have thought we'd have found him by now. But it's still early days. We'll keep looking."

McAdams said, "Does Lanz have living parents?"

"Kurt and Mila Lanz. They live in Germany. I looked them up before we left. He's an industrialist—steel and iron. He's not one of the top ten richest men in Germany, but he's still very rich."

"Hence he can afford the hefty price tag of Loving Home. Why would a rich German couple send their kid to a residential program in the States?"

"Yes, that is odd. As far as I can tell, Bertram doesn't have any close relatives in the States." Decker exhaled. "I suspect it's easier for them and their lifestyle if Bertram's far away. But maybe I'm just being unkind."

"Probably not." McAdams paused. "If Lanz is a German citizen, he'd have a passport. He could have taken off anywhere."

"He has cognitive disabilities," Decker said. "Think he could handle airports by himself?"

"Possibly. Especially if he went back and forth to Europe. Wealthy families do that a lot."

"Yeah. Wealthy families are also protected. It might take some maneuvering to get through to them."

"True. The rich are often surrounded with layers of protections. It's like cutting through Kevlar."

"Nothing is bulletproof," Decker said. "You've just got to find the gaps."

Chapter 3

L oving Care Home was situated in Baniff, a small town in western New York halfway between the Finger Lakes region and Rochester without a lot of landmarks to point the way. It was about an hour drive from Senecas—the westernmost group of the consortium. Decker and Rina had driven through the area several months ago for a mini-vacation, visiting different tribal lands, viewing the local arts and crafts, learning about the culture of the native Northeast people. Maybe next summer they'd plan a trip all the way to Niagara Falls and Canada.

After traveling miles of highway, Decker finally found the exit ramp. Within minutes, he hit a place with a main street lined by turn-of-the-century buildings in various states of disrepair. Each structure was painted a different color, giving the avenue the appearance of a patchwork quilt. City Hall was a white two-story domed building surrounded by a green lawn made colorful by mixed flowers in beds. On the side roads, churches were abundant. The only thing that was out of the ordinary was a military museum dedicated to the Revolutionary and Civil wars.

Home styles varied but were primarily wood-sided bungalows with wraparound porches or frillier Victorians fronted with swatches of gingerbread. They were cozy, nestled in small, square lawns shaded by leafy oaks. The main road coiled its way through the town until it was a straight shot through farmland.

The sky was deep blue, still a novelty for Decker, who had plied his trade for so many years in the hot, smoggy summers of Los Angeles. There were times he missed the big city with all its challenges, but Greenbury hadn't turned out to be the sleepy little town he had imagined when he packed his bags. It had unexpected crime and its own issues—lack of funds and little state-of-the-art equipment. McAdams was Decker's first and only partner in Greenbury. Tyler was brash and young when the two of them had started out. The kid's maturity was hastened by two gunshot wounds, and every so often, Decker could detect a slight limp. Why McAdams had chosen law enforcement over a high-powered law practice was a bit of a mystery. Decker suspected it was Tyler's way of getting back at his father—a successful lawyer and financier. In reality, McAdams could do whatever he wanted to do, including nothing. His trust fund was, according to him, enormous.

As they rode southwest, the terrain gave way to wine territory—miles of grapes hanging from trellises.

"How far are we?" McAdams asked.

"About twenty minutes," Decker said.

"Pretty though." McAdams looked around. "New York makes pretty good Riesling and gewürztraminer. I once thought about buying a winery. Then I decided it made more sense to buy the wine rather than make it."

"It's one of those romantic but impractical notions," Decker said.

"Yeah, any kind of agriculture is hard work." McAdams checked his phone. "No word from anyone in Greenbury. You'd think they'd have found something by now."

The wineries soon gave way to empty fields of dry grass. "They should be getting more dogs in the late afternoon."

"That'll only work if there's a scent to follow."

"Maybe the dogs can pick something up in the woods," Decker said. "We have to be able to rule out an accident. He could have tripped and hurt himself. It was dark last night."

"Yes, of course. How far away are we now?"

"Around ten minutes." Decker smiled. "You're like a little kid, Harvard. 'Are we there yet?' You have bars now. Go fiddle with your phone."

"I hate to say this but I have to take a piss."

"Bad?"

"Sooner than later."

"Want me to pull over?"

"Yeah."

"Really?" Decker was surprised, but he eased the car to the curb when he saw a copse of oak trees. "I would think pissing outside would be below your pay grade."

"Certainly, I wouldn't do it in the city, although no one would say anything if I did. But here in the middle of nowhere?" He opened the door. "I'm still a guy, boss. I revel in the marvels of outdoor plumbing."

Built in an open field, the residential facility sat on acreage that held shale reserves. The area had once been used for fracking until it was outlawed by the state in 2014. While the terrain wasn't thickly forested, there was plenty of nature nearby. Decker wondered why the home would choose to bus its residents two hours away for a simple hike in the woods.

The drive up to the entrance led to a guardhouse and a gate. After giving their names to a uniformed man with a black mustache, Decker and McAdams were allowed to continue inside the premises. The parklike space was a deep green lawn, the blades dripping from a recent watering. There were benches placed at strategic spots—near flower gardens or under big shady oaks—but no one was out. It could be the warm weather or it could be that the home wanted to keep a closer eye on its residents.

The compound was anything but institutional. It was a series of low-profile, one-story structures with red-tiled roofs and pink stucco walls more at home in Miami or Los Angeles. The landscape between the buildings consisted of rose beds woven with flagstone pavers. To the left of the driveway was a parking lot. Decker found a space marked VISITORS and angled into the slot.

The two men got out and walked over to double glass doors. They were buzzed into a reception area. The woman behind the desk looked to be in her fifties, with short, straight, salt-and-pepper hair and a pleasant smile. Her name tag said she was Linda

Kravitz, and she asked how she could help. Decker showed identification. "We're here to see Dr. Lewis."

She looked up from Decker's billfold. "Horrible business. Where is poor Bertram?"

"We've got an entire community out there looking for him, Ms. Kravitz."

"Nothing like this has ever happened before. It's so distressing."

"Did you know Bertram?" Decker asked.

"Oh sure. I know all the residents."

"How many are there?" McAdams asked.

"Currently? Fifty-nine."

"What is Bertram like?" Decker asked.

"A quiet, well-behaved man. He was new here. Well, not new. A little over a year. I only say new because some of our residents have been here for years."

"Was he a transfer from some other residential home?"

Linda looked sheepish. "I really shouldn't be talking about him without permission."

Decker was persistent. "I'm just wondering if it's possible that he went back to where he lived before. Would you know his previous residence? It might save everyone time and heartache."

"But how would he get there?"

"I don't know, ma'am, but it's a simple phone call."

"I'll leave that up to Dr. Lewis. Anyway, you can ask him directly." She turned to the phone on her desk and picked up the receiver. Talking softly, she hung up and said, "He'll be with you in a few minutes." She pointed to several plastic chairs bolted to the floor. "Please have a seat."

They sat.

McAdams's eyes followed a pathway to an open space that looked like a lounge. He caught a glimpse of a room filled with couches, chairs, tables set with games, a piano, and the ever-present flat-screen TV. The space seemed to extend beyond his field of vision, but from where he could see, there wasn't a soul.

"Where is everyone?" he whispered to Decker.

"Good question."

A moment later a man came into the reception area, introducing himself with an outstretched hand. "Lionel Lewis." A quick shake. "Please come this way." He walked quickly, glancing behind his shoulder. "This has been just dreadful. How could this have happened?"

"That seems to be the question on everyone's mind," Decker said.

Lewis muttered something unintelligible. He was tall, high-waisted, and long-limbed. Dark, worried eyes peered out from a long face with prominent cheek-bones. His complexion was a warm sepia and his dark hair was cut close to his scalp. He wore navy slacks and a white, button-down shirt rolled up at the sleeves and open at the neck.

He led them past the lounge, through another hall-way, and into a generous-size office filled with natural light from windows that looked out to the still-empty lawn. The furnishings were spare—a desk, a desk chair, and more plastic chairs for guests—but floor-to-ceiling bookshelves were packed with academic texts on health management and hospital administration. There were also books on educational psychology and special education. Any leftover wall space was taken up by diplomas, professional licenses, and certificates of excellence. Lewis was a Harvard graduate. If Decker had to guess an age, Lewis looked to be in his mid-forties.

"Please sit." Lewis pointed to the plastic chairs. His face was very somber.

After the men sat down, McAdams asked, "What house?"

"Excuse me?" Lewis looked confused. McAdams cocked a thumb in the direction of the diploma. "Oh, Lowell."

"I was in the Quad. Cabot."

"When did you graduate?"

"Six years ago."

"Ah." Lewis looked at his diplomas. "As you can see, I was there for a while after graduation."

"He just graduated Harvard Law," Decker said.

"Really." Lewis nodded. "Nice place to be. I wish I was there now . . . anywhere but here." His eyes met Decker's. "And you've had no luck whatsoever?"

"I haven't heard anything." Decker paused. "We were wondering. The lawn outside is empty. The lounge is empty. Where is everyone?"

"We've been holding group therapy sessions all day—ten residents at a time. Our people are shaken up. They're concerned about Bertram, but they were also ill at ease about being interviewed by the police yesterday."

"We didn't actually interview the residents," Decker said. "We mostly talked to the chaperones. A few residents asked questions, and we tried to answer them honestly. Things were very chaotic. We were attempting to get a simple timeline for Bertram. Looking for him was and is our top priority."

"Well, maybe it was just the police presence that made them nervous."

"Perhaps. At some point I would like to interview the residents. Sometimes they know things. Which brings me to another point. The residents are of legal age. Does Loving Care operate as their legal guardians?"

"Well, that is a bit of an issue," Lewis said. "Loving Care is not legally responsible for any of our residents. This is more or less a co-op for like-minded people."

"Does that include Bertram Lanz?"

"Absolutely. Bertram was emancipated. I suppose you could call us de facto guardians, but the walls aren't prison cells. Our people can come and go as they please as long as they check out so we can keep tabs on them—for their safety." The doctor was quiet. "Very rarely does anyone leave permanently. Most of the residents are very happy here. This is their home."

"And Bertram was happy?" McAdams asked.

"Bertram came here around a little over a year ago. From what I could tell and from the feedback, there was some adjustment. I found him polite but quiet. We tried very hard to draw him out. There might have been a language barrier. Bertram was a native German speaker, but he did speak English quite well. At that time we had a woman here—a nurse—who was fluent in German. She, more than anyone else, seemed to have developed a rapport with Bertram."

"Then we should talk to her," Decker said.

Lewis made a sour expression. "She left about two weeks ago." A big exhale. "She got along well with the residents but was a bit of a queen bee. I wouldn't say she sabotaged other employees, but she certainly wasn't a favorite at staff parties."

"Okay. Can I have her name and phone number?"

Lewis looked uncomfortable. "I'm not in a habit of giving out information about employees—past or present."

"We have a missing person," McAdams said.

"And what could Elsie possibly have to do with that?"

Decker said, "In all honesty, Dr. Lewis, we're not sure he's missing or if he may have left with someone."

"Why do you say that?"

"Because the tracking dogs never got a good scent. That sometimes mean that the missing person left in a vehicle. How old is Elsie?"

"Early forties."

"And she was a nurse?"

Lewis nodded. "Yes. And a good one."

"How long had she worked at Loving Care?"

"I have to think about that."

"Just give me a guesstimate," Decker said.

"Maybe three plus years."

"And after three years plus working here, she just decided to leave two weeks ago?"

"As I told you, she didn't get along with the staff."

"But still, she stuck it out for a while," McAdams said.

"We pay very well."

Decker said, "Maybe someone else was paying her more."

"Like who?"

"From what I understand, Bertram Lanz comes from a very wealthy family."

Lewis stared at him. "You're suggesting that Elsie ran away with Bertram."

"I'm considering everything," Decker said. "There's an easy way to answer this. Could you give Elsie a call? What's her last name, by the way?"

A long hesitation. Then Lewis said, "Schulung."

Decker wrote it down. "Can you give her a call?"

"She's probably not home."

"Only one way to find out."

Lewis paused, then picked up the phone and depressed a button. "Linda, can you please get me Elsie Schulung's phone number." A beat. "Cell and landline, thanks." He hung up. "Linda is my right arm. I don't know what I'd do without her."

Decker said, "Anything else I should know about Elsie Schulung."

Lewis said, "She was competent at her job. I never had problems with her. But I was her boss. I know she had her own way of doing things, but I can't see her kidnapping Bertram. That would be pure idiocy."

"Who said anything about kidnapping?" McAdams said.

"Well, why would he leave *here* with *her*? There is no way she could provide the services we have."

"Maybe they ran away together," McAdams suggested. "A man has needs."

Lewis wrinkled his nose. "He's a fine person, but he's cognitively disabled."

"So what? He's still a man."

"And a man with very wealthy parents," Decker said. "You told us he came here about a year ago?"

"That's correct."

"Where did he transfer from?"

"A residential facility in Connecticut."

"Okay," Decker said. "And do you know why he came here to Loving Care?"

"Loving Care is light-years ahead of any of the competition. We have more activities for our residents—more classes for those who want to further their education. We have job training, more interaction with the outside world, and more freedom than any other place around."

"Is dating allowed?" McAdams asked.

"We discourage one-on-one activities, simply because it leads to drama."

"By 'one-on-one activities,' do you mean sex?"

"We discourage sex, but we also discourage romance period. Someone always gets hurt. But despite our best efforts, people pair off. And if we know there are couples who are engaged in sexual activity, we do have sex education. But as far as I know, Bertram was not involved with anyone."

"What was the name of Bertram's prior residential home?" Decker asked.

"I'd have to look that up."

Linda came in and handed a slip of paper to Lewis. "These were the numbers on Elsie's application, Doctor. I don't know if they're current."

"Thank you, Linda." When she didn't immediately leave, he said, "There's nothing else, thank you." Lewis picked up the phone and dialed the top number. It rang twice and then he was given a message that the number had been disconnected. He hung up. "That one's no longer working. From the prefix, it was probably a landline that had been canceled." He tried the second set of digits. It rang and rang until voice mail kicked in. Lewis left a brief message and hung up. "No answer."

McAdams said, "Try texting her."

"That's a good idea." Lewis sent the message off with a swoosh. "I don't know if she'll answer or not. She was angry when she left."

"Did she leave or was she fired?"

"She was reprimanded after several years of people complaining that she didn't follow the channels of communication. I had a talk with her. I thought things had smoothed out, but she decided to leave. That's certainly her prerogative."

"And two weeks later Bertram Lanz is missing," McAdams said. "It's also a little coincidental."

"Not really. I don't see what one has to do with another despite the fact that the two of them got along." A pause. "Bertram could have left anytime. He didn't have to fake a disappearance."

"But you said yourself he had to sign out," Decker said. "I'm sure you would have made sure that his destination was a safe place."

"Of course. I'm just saying he wasn't a captive."

"But in a way, he was." When Lewis was silent, Decker said, "Bertram is mentally challenged and possibly easily swayed. Checking up on him is just common sense on your part. And if you would have found out he was going to a rendezvous with Elsie Schulung, you might have stopped it."

"I *would* have stopped it," Lewis said. "To tell you the truth, I was surprised that she quit. There aren't a lot of professional jobs in a town this size."

Decker said, "We'll need Elsie's address."

"I'll see what we have on file," Lewis said.

Decker said, "I hate to do this, but at some point, we are going to need to talk to the residents one by one."

"Can it wait? A lot of our residents are traumatized."

"I'll take that into consideration," Decker said. "But Bertram is missing. I wouldn't do it unless I thought it was urgent."

"You're right," Lewis said. "I'll arrange it."

"Thank you. And we'd also like to take a look at Bertram's room."

"Maybe you can do that first while I ask the staff to prepare the residents."

"That would work."

"I'll take you to his room." Lewis opened his desk drawer and pulled out a ring of keys.

Decker said, "Have you notified Bertram's parents? Even if he was emancipated, it's the moral thing to do."

"Of course," Lewis said. "I was hoping it wouldn't be necessary."

"Maybe this will resolve today. But the longer you wait, the harder it will be to make the call. And the call is better coming from you than the police."

Lewis said, "Have you checked in recently to see if there have been any developments?"

McAdams stood up and said, "I'll call Captain Radar. It's a dead zone here. I'll have to go outside."

"Thanks." Decker got to his feet. "When Detective McAdams is done, we'll take a look at Lanz's room."

"Of course." Lewis got up to lead the way. He looked at his watch. "It's late in the evening across the pond. If nothing new happens, I'll call the Lanzes first thing in the morning." He looked at Decker. "Nothing like this has ever happened before. In the main, we really are one big happy family."

"I'm sure that's true . . . in the main," Decker said. "But as the saying goes, Dr. Lewis: you're only as happy as your least happy kid."

Chapter 4

Hands on hips, McAdams looked around Bertram Lanz's personal sanctuary. Not large, not tiny—around 180 square feet of tidy space with an attached bathroom. "The guy is neat."

"We have housekeeping service," Lewis said.

Decker said, "What do they do?"

"Make the bed, sweep the floor, clean the sink, toilet, and tub in the bathroom, empty all the garbage, pick up the dirty laundry, and drop off the clean laundry."

"How often?"

"Every day."

"Then his garbage has been emptied recently."

"The room was done yesterday—the day of the field trip."

"Okay." Decker was quiet. "If you're busy, we can take this from here."

"You are going through one of our residents' rooms. Someone should be here supervising—for your protection as well as Bertram's."

"Stick around," Decker said. "But I don't know how long this will take."

He turned to McAdams. "You take the bathroom, and I'll go through his living area."

Lewis's phone rang. He listened and then sighed. "I have something that needs my immediate attention."

"Do you want us to stop and wait for you to come back?"

A long pause. Then Lewis said, "Just leave the door open."

"Thank you, Doctor," Decker said. "I appreciate the cooperation."

"We've all got the same goals: a safe outcome for Bertram." Lewis jogged off.

When he left, Decker said, "Ready?"

McAdams hesitated. "We must spend half of our energy looking through people's crap. And most of the time it gets you nowhere."

"Sometimes it pays off." Decker thought of their most recent case a year ago. "Like with the photos in Jaylene Boch's wheelchair."

"Margot Flint is still at large."

Flint was responsible for the old woman's death, although she was miles away when it happened. She was the prototype of the femme fatale and had master-minded several other homicides. She'd been a fugitive for years. "The noose is tightening. Authorities know that she's in Mexico. She's being watched while the paperwork is being filed. An arrest should come soon."

"If you say so," McAdams said. "Speaking of old times, have you heard recently from Lennie Baccus?"

Decker waited a few moments before he spoke about the young rookie cop, thinking about how naive she was when she had first been assigned under his watch. She had done a tough hostage negotiation, putting herself in the line of fire. Decker thought for sure that she would fold afterward, but she didn't. She had proven herself, but at what cost? "She moved to Redlands, California. She's a detective with the police department there."

"How'd you find that out?"

"She asked me for a reference letter."

"Ah."

"It was a wise choice. The town is intermediate size, it has a small but good university, and there's enough crime to keep her busy."

"Do you talk to her often?"

"We exchange emails. She'll call me if she has a question, and we'll talk shop. I suppose that means she still trusts me. Anyway, let's get going on the search."

Just then a woman stopped in front of the open door. She appeared to be in her thirties, small in stature, which was often typical of Down syndrome. She had blue eyes, shoulder-length brown hair, and a pale complexion except for the blush on her cheeks. Her lipstick was pink and shiny. She had pearl studs in her ears. She said something, but Decker couldn't understand her speech. McAdams, on the other hand, seemed fine with it. He said, "How do you know we won't find anything?" When she answered, he replied, "Bertram had an iPad with him on the bus?"

The woman nodded.

"What about a cell phone?" Decker asked.

She nodded again.

"Do you have his cell phone number?"

"Yes." She recited the digits and McAdams wrote them down. He said, "Are you allowed to have cell phones here?"

She smiled and said something.

McAdams repeated, "It's not a jail." She talked for a few seconds. "You've called his cell phone and he doesn't answer. You must be worried."

"Yes."

"Then you and Bertram are friends?"

"Yes," she said.

"Girlfriend?"

She answered McAdams, but Decker had difficulty understanding her slurred words. McAdams said, "What was his girlfriend's name? Did he tell you?"

"Kathrine." She added a sentence.

McAdams said, "He hasn't seen her since he left his old place, and he's sad about that. What's your name, by the way?"

"April."

"Pretty name," Decker said. "What's your last name?"

She said something and McAdams said, "K-E-L-L-Y?"

She nodded.

"Hello, April Kelly. And, may I ask, how old are you?"

"Thirty-five."

"Where is your room?" She pointed and answered. McAdams said, "Down the hall. Is there a room number?"

"Thirty-eight."

Decker said, "April, could Bertram read?"

She nodded.

"Write?"

She answered, and McAdams said, "He typed words on his iPad."

"Yes." April looked down. "I gotta go."

"Of course," Decker said. "Thank you for your help. And you're sure he took his cell phone and iPad with him on the field trip?"

When she answered, McAdams said, "He showed you the iPad while you were waiting to get on the bus to leave here?"

"And the phone," she added.

"Do you know if Bertram has an email address?" Decker asked.

"Yes." When she recited it, McAdams wrote it down. She said a few more words. "But he's not answering your emails?"

"No." She frowned and looked down. "I gotta go. Therapy." She rolled her eyes.

"You don't like therapy?"

"No. And I don't like the therapist."

McAdams said, "What's wrong with the therapist?"

"She's stupid."

"What's her name?"

"Mary. She's stupid."

"Is she Bertram's therapist as well?" Decker asked.

She spoke and McAdams said, "There are three therapists. Do you like any of them, April?"

"James." April smiled. "He's cute." A frown. "I gotta go."

Decker said, "Thank you, April. You've been a big help."

She looked down. "Find Bertram. It's scary that he's lost."

McAdams said, "We're doing everything we can to find him. Please don't worry." She nodded, waved, and took off. "Poor girl. They all must be traumatized."

"I'm sure that's true." He dialed Bertram's cell phone. There was a garbled message. Decker spoke slowly and clearly as he left a message with his phone number. "Straight to voice mail. I'll see what I can do about getting his phone records and his IP correspondence."

McAdams was writing on his iPad. "Eventually, I'll need a password. I should have asked April about it. Maybe he told her."

"Try *Kathrine*."

"Good idea."

Waiting a moment, Decker said, "Have you worked with people with Down syndrome before, Harvard?"

"Nope."

"You understood her speech very well."

"There's a rhythm to it if you've heard it enough."

A pause. "Okay. I won't pry."

"I'm the only child of my two parents." McAdams gave a sad smile. "But I do have half sibs. My father has a daughter and a son from his second marriage. My sister, Danielle, just got into Harvard. My brother's name is Charles. Chucky, but he likes to be called Chuck now that he's a teenager."

Decker smiled. "Burgeoning adulthood."

"That is true." McAdams looked around the room, but his eyes were focused far away. "One thing I'll say about my stepmom. She insisted on keeping the baby when my dad wanted to give him up. Chucky has had the same nanny for fifteen years. She's the primary caretaker, and she's a good one."

"How often do you see them?"

"My sibs?" McAdams shrugged. "When I go to New York I'll drop in on them—my mother's kids as well. When I was in boarding school I saw Chucky in the summers." A smile at the memory. "He's a great kid. My stepmom ignores him, but she ignores my sister too. My father . . . well, you know my dad. He's either absent or overinvolved. At least that's how he is with me."

"I now understand why he's so invested in you."

"Yes, but he should take some of that investment and give it to the son who really needs him." McAdams shook his head. "But that's not going to happen." A pause. "*Kathrine* as a password doesn't work. I'll go check out the bathroom. Wonder where Dr. Lewis went."

"With any luck he forgot about us and we can take our time without someone looking over our shoulder."

McAdams said, "What do you think about him?"

"Haven't spent enough time with him to form an opinion. I'm sure he's worried about Bertram, but I'm sure he's also worried about a lawsuit if we don't find Bertram alive and well."

"If we find Bertram and he's fine, the parents won't sue. I think they're happy he's in a good place. There aren't a lot of them around."

Decker nodded. "What do you think about Bertram having a girlfriend from his old place?"

"You think they decided to meet up?"

"We can't rule it out. Like April said, the place isn't a prison. He could go anywhere especially if you're right about his owning a passport."

McAdams said, "But like you said, it might be hard for Bertram to travel without help."

Decker said, "In the photos we've seen, it doesn't look like Bertram has Down syndrome. But the pictures aren't very good."

McAdams said, "There are a lot of other things that can qualify for being disabled. Sometimes it's a syndrome, sometimes it's a birth defect, sometimes it's someone on the spectrum, sometimes it's just one of those things where the wiring just doesn't work properly. Chucky's school is filled with different kids with different issues. Talk about diversity."

"I'm sorry if this is painful for you to talk about," Decker said.

"It's not, really. I don't feel sorry for my brother. I feel sorry for people who feel sorry for my brother. Chucky is loving, kind, and funny. And he's deep. Over the years, we've had some very interesting conversations. Chucky has a rich life. He appreciates everything. Unlike my dad, who has everything but appreciates nothing."

Talking to April was productive; searching Bertram's room, not so much. It took less than thirty minutes to go through everything. A look at the bedding and under the mattress revealed nothing. Decker checked the closet neatly hung with button-down shirts, T-shirts, polo shirts, and jeans. Bertram's dresser held pajamas, underwear, and shorts, and an empty patch in the back of the bottom drawer where, at one time, he might have stowed something personal.

Sometimes a room was just a room. Decker called out, "How are you doing?"

McAdams emerged from the bathroom. "Everything seems intact."

"Lots of clothing," Decker said. "If he left voluntarily, I don't think he was planning on going far. Or he left in a very big hurry."

"I'll agree with that. He didn't even take his toothbrush."

"That says something," Decker said. "Does he have a hairbrush?"

"A comb."

"Take that as well."

"DNA?"

"We have to plan for any outcome."

"Are we waiting for Lewis?" McAdams said. "He seems to be taking his time."

Decker said, "He's probably downstairs. He's got his hands full."

"Next step?"

"For Bertram? Follow the electronic trail—phone calls, texts, emails, social media," Decker said. "Let's find the doctor. We still need to talk to people."

Lewis was in his office and on the phone. He looked up, brown eyes bright and alert. He motioned Decker and McAdams to chairs across from his desk, his long graceful fingers massaging a forehead creased like a brown paper bag. He was doing more listening than talking. At the end of the conversation, he made an appointment over the phone for the next morning at ten. He placed the phone back in the cradle.

"The lawyers." Lewis shook his head. "They want to be in the conference call when I phone the parents—even though the Lanzes have indemnified us and hold us harmless against any liability where Bertram is concerned. I've sent them the paperwork, but you know how lawyers are. Anything to make a few extra bucks." He regarded McAdams. "I'm sure there are a few idealists in your profession. I'm just talking my experience."

McAdams smiled. "I think your representation is doing the job properly."

"Perhaps." A sigh. "Did you find anything in Bertram's room?"

Decker said, "Nothing that gives a hint to his whereabouts. We did take a toothbrush and comb."

"Toothbrush?" Lewis noted. "It must mean he was planning on coming back."

"Maybe," Decker said. "We also found out that Bertram Lanz has a phone, an iPad, and an email address."

"Who told you all of this?"

"A resident named April," McAdams said.

"April spoke to you?"

McAdams gave him a look.

Didn't I just say that?

Lewis said, "What did she tell you?"

Decker said, "That Bertram has a phone, an iPad, and an email. Did you know?"

"Of course. We've been trying to contact him since he disappeared. And since he hasn't answered, I've assumed that he's lost in the woods where there is no electronic communication available. Because if he could contact us, I'm sure he would."

"It would have been helpful if you had told us that in the beginning." Decker didn't bother to hide his annoyance. "We would have put in an order for a phone and text log hours ago. As well as an ISP search for his email activity."

"Would you like me to call that in, boss?"

"Please." Then, to Lewis: "April gave us a phone number for Bertram. Would you please verify it? And his username and password if you happen to have it."

Lewis clicked his keyboard. He said, "I can give you the phone number. It'll take a little more time for me to dig up his computer information, but I suspect we have it in some file."

"We can wait."

After a minute passed, Lewis took out a Post-it and wrote a number on the yellow square.

McAdams took the digits. "Same number April gave us. I'll be right back."

"Check to see how the search is going as long as you're making the phone call." When Tyler left the room, Decker took out a notebook and said, "And you're positive that he didn't disappear because he wanted to disappear?"

"I'm not positive of anything, but I shouldn't think so," Lewis answered. "Where would he go?"

"Lots of places," Decker said. "April said he can read. April said he writes on his iPad. The internet has probably given developmentally disabled people freedom previously unavailable to them."

"Just because it's out there doesn't mean they know how to access it."

"I bet we'd both be surprised. What is Bertram's disability?"

"He has cerebral palsy."

"Cerebral palsy is a garbage-can term," McAdams said as he came back into Lewis's office. "It means something happened during birth and no one knows the specifics. Do you have any more details?"

"He's mildly affected physically, but cognitively, he's more impaired," Lewis told him. "It might be better if you talked to the professionals who worked with him. They could give you better information than I could."

"The residents went on a hike," McAdams said. "He must have been fit enough to walk in the mountains."

"It was a gentle walk. We've done it before." Lewis paused. "If you're asking me whether Bertram Lanz could hike, the answer is yes. He had a limp, but he was mobile. Talk to his therapists."

"You must have done batteries of tests when he got here. What can you tell us about that?"

"Psych major, were you?" When McAdams didn't answer, Lewis said, "His testing shows him to be equivalent to a fourth grader mentally."

"A lot of savvy fourth graders out there," Decker said.

"Just because he tested at fourth grade doesn't mean he's like an average nine-year-old. He's more sophisticated in some areas, less in others." To McAdams: "I take it he hasn't been found?"

"You are correct."

The administrator sighed.

"The point is, Dr. Lewis," Decker said, "if he could chat on the internet, he has the possibility of getting himself into trouble. We need to talk to the other residents, and the most advantageous way to do it is in a group. Once one talks, it'll spur the others to talk. It's a good way to weed out who knows what."

"What makes you think that any of them know something? What if Bertram is simply lost?"

"Okay, let me spell it out for you. Option one: he is lost in the woods. If he's lost, we'll eventually find him. What the outcome will be, I don't know. It depends how long it takes us to locate the poor man. The woods can be inaccessible, disorienting especially in the summer when everything is thick with foliage. And it's chilly at night. Animals are out, animals are active, and they're always looking for food. It could go bad in a lot of different ways, so our best option is to soldier on until we're sure we can't find him.

"The second option: he got lost, found the main road, and picked up a random ride. Less likely because there were cops all around the area within an hour after he disappeared. We'd be more likely to spot him than a random stranger, but it could happen. That could also go bad really quickly.

"The third option? He isn't lost at all but he arranged to meet someone when the field trip stopped at the diner. If that's the case, we need to find out what was going on in his life. And the last option is . . ."

A hesitation.

"He was kidnapped for ransom. His parents are rich and money is always a good motive. We're looking into all of the possibilities at the same time. I understand there's a group meeting going on right now. Detective McAdams and I would like to attend and address the residents. It would be good to answer their questions. I'm sure they have a lot of them. Make sense?"

Lewis didn't answer. He placed his hands on the desk, then tented them and brought them to his face, fingers grazing his chin.

Decker said, "What's the problem?"

"They're traumatized. They may be hesitant with the police."

Decker said, "I worked Juvenile and Sex Crimes for many years. I'm not saying I am a licensed psychologist, but I do have experience with trauma. Talking to the residents will not only help us, it'll help you when you talk to Bertram's parents."

"I'm not sure about that, but we'll give it a try." Lewis stood up. "I'll take you to the auditorium. Give me about fifteen minutes to talk to Dr. Mannet and fill her in. She'll set something up."

"What's the doctor's training?" McAdams said.

"Why do you ask?"

"Do you find that question an odd one?"

"A little, I suppose. But then again, you're a detective, so maybe it makes some sense." A pause. "She's a licensed clinical psychologist. She's been with us for four years."

Decker stood up. "Bertram has been missing for about twenty-four hours. That's disturbing. Right now, every minute counts. We need to move."

"What is it that I've heard? If you don't solve something within forty-eight hours, your chances of solving the crime deeply diminish?"

"We don't know if a crime has been committed," Decker said. "Let's go."

The auditorium was two tiers of seating with a large flat area in front to accommodate residents with walkers and wheelchairs. The participants seemed between the ages of twenty and sixty with an equal distribution of males and females. They ran the gamut of phenotypes—from syndromed faces to those whose outward appearance would blend into any population.

Dr. Georgia Mannet, the house psychologist, was thin, with a wrinkled face and a prominent chin. She had short gray hair cut helmet style and watery blue eyes. Her doctor's coat was light blue and she wore her ID on a red rope around her neck. Decker and Mc-Adams sat on the stage with Mannet between them. There were two microphones in the middle and glasses of water for all of them. Dr. Mannet introduced Decker and Tyler as police officers, and Decker noticed apprehension in some of the eyes.

Empathy was necessary to gain trust. And indeed, Decker really felt bad for them. He started out with how frightening Bertram's disappearance must be for all of them. The unknown was always scary. That was why the police had assigned many people to go out and look for Bertram. But the police needed their help. For instance, was Bertram lost, or did he run away on purpose? That was why it was very important for everyone to tell the police anything that they knew or heard about Bertram. Any information—no matter how small. And no one would get into trouble no matter what they told the police.

"Please," Decker said. "Does anyone here know what happened to Bertram Lanz?"

He was met with resounding silence. In any audience, this was usually the case. Starts were slow until someone got the ball rolling.

"Okay, let's start again. Who are Bertram's friends?" Looks all the way around, but no one said a word—not even a whisper. "Did he have friends?"

No response. Of course, no one wanted to be a tattletale. Better to start on neutral ground.

"Does anyone know what Bertram liked to do?"

A moment passed and a reticent hand inched upward. It belonged to a man with Down syndrome who looked around forty. Gray was creeping into his dark hair. He was dressed in a short-sleeved plaid shirt and jeans. He sat in the middle of the second row.

Decker said, "Yes, thank you. What's your name?"

"Ross."

"Hi, Ross. Do you know what Bertram liked to do?"

Ross stood up. Decker couldn't understand him. Georgia Mannet was about to speak, but McAdams stepped in. That was good. It was helpful for the residents to know that the police literally understood them.

McAdams answered, "What did he do on his iPad, Ross?" The man shrugged. Silence ensued. Tyler stepped into the void. He said, "I like to play games on my computer. Did Bertram play games on his iPad?"

Another hand came up: a man in his thirties who sat in a wheelchair. His fingers looked knotted as if he had arthritis. "Space Mission: Combat Control."

Decker said, "What's your name, please?"

"James."

"Nice to meet you, James," Decker said. "Bertram played Space Mission: Combat Control on his computer?"

"iPad."

"Sorry. Bertram played Space Mission: Combat Control on his iPad," Decker said.

"Yes."

April, the resident from this morning, shouted out something. McAdams repeated, "Martian Invaders Five."

"Thank you, April," Decker said. "See, this is very, very helpful. You all know so much about Bertram."

Ross raised his hand again. Decker acknowledged him and the man said, "I'm Bertram's friend."

Decker said. "I'm sure you're a very good friend to have." Whispering to McAdams, "We'll talk to him later."

Ross said something and McAdams said, "I am sure you have a lot of friends, Ross." He looked at the group. "Was anyone else Bertram's friend?"

Another hand came up—a woman in her early to mid-thirties. Wearing a yellow sundress with a white sweater, she had blond hair that fell to her shoulders. She had studs in her ears, and a gold chain graced the notch of her throat. "My name is Colette. Bertram was lonely."

"Nice to meet you, Colette," Decker said. "Why do you think Bertram was lonely?"

"He sat by himself."

Ross said, "Not all the time."

"But some of the time."

April said something. McAdams said, "He missed his girlfriend?" When she nodded, he said, "This is Kathrine?"

Another nod.

Colette said, "He liked Nurse Schulung. But she's not here anymore."

Ross said something, and McAdams said, "She talked to him with funny words?"

James said, "She talked in German. They talked in German. Bertram knew German."

"He did know German," Decker said. "Did he tell you he lived in Germany, James?"

"Once he said it."

The conversation stopped. Decker licked his lips and smoothed his mustache—a habit he often fell back on when he was trying to buy time. "Were they friends, Nurse Schulung and Bertram?" When he got no response, he turned to Ross. "What do you think? Were Nurse Schulung and Bertram friends?"

The man looked lost in thought. "Maybe."

Colette said, "I think they were friends."

April said, "But he missed Kathrine."

A few moments passed, and then James said, "I'm hungry."

Dr. Mannet looked at her watch. "Break time was forty minutes ago."

Decker said, "I understand."

Dr. Lewis said, "You're done, then?"

"For the time being, yeah. Let's get everyone fed. No one works well on an empty stomach."

Chapter 5

As soon as they walked out of the auditorium and into the hallway, Decker said, "This is the number we have for Elsie Schulung. If she's still not answering, call up the local police and ask them to stop by her house just to make sure she's okay. We need to talk to her."

"How far does she live from here?"

"About a half hour away."

McAdams regarded his watch. It was almost five in the afternoon. "We still have some daylight. When do you want to leave?"

"Around six. I want to talk to the residents who spoke up. See if I can get more one-on-one. Oh, and call up Bertram's phone carrier. Ask if someone there can pull up Lanz's records."

"What about the paperwork?"

"It'll come. Sometimes the company will accept verbal requests from the police when the MP is a compromised adult. Bertram's email access will take longer. But call up the service provider anyway even if they won't do it without paperwork. Tell whoever you talk to that there is exigency."

"No prob. Where should I meet you when I'm done, boss?"

"Try the dining hall first. If you don't find me, ask around. Do you have a Tylenol?"

McAdams dislodged his backpack from his shoulders. "I could use something myself. I might be dehydrated." He pulled out a plastic bottle of Tylenol followed by a blended coffee drink in a can. "I could probably use a little caffeine. Want one?"

"Any water?"

"Just a thermos that I drink from directly. Sorry."

"I'm sure there's water in the dining hall." Decker swallowed the tablets dry and rubbed his forehead. "I know that most Missing Persons cases end up all right. But the ones that don't . . . there's always that pressure to get there before it's too late. Constantly asking yourself, are you overlooking anything that might save a life? At least with Homicide, you have a little time to think. Or maybe it's just my age finally catching up with me."

McAdams put his hand on Decker's shoulder. "I still think you've got a lot of professional time left in those old bones of yours."

Decker smiled. "See you in a bit." Waiting for the pills to kick in, he headed off to interview some very scared people.

The dining hall was abuzz with conversation. The room held about fifteen round tables, each one big enough for four to six cushioned folding chairs. Some tables were completely occupied. Others were empty. Afternoon sunlight filtered in through enormous picture windows shaded with transparent mesh, but the room lights were also on. There was a long buffet table filled with hot snacks—anything from soup to mini-pizzas. There were also big bowls filled with power bars, bags of potato chips and pretzels, packets of cookies, and small individual containers of mixed nuts. Decker grabbed a water from the cooler, looked around, and found James and Ross, seated by themselves and in intense conversation. He walked over to the table and the talking stopped.

"Mind if I join you?" Decker sat without waiting for permission. "Thank you for your help, gentlemen." No answer. "Is there anything else you might want to tell me about Bertram?"

After a silence, James finally said, "He didn't like it here."

Decker uncapped a water bottle. "He told you that?"

He nodded. "He didn't play any of the games or go to group time or bingo or movie night."

Ross said, "I like group time."

"You do?" Decker said. "Why do you like group time?"

"Snacks." Ross let go with a smile that lit up his face.

"Snacks are good." Decker turned back to James. "Colette also thought Bertram was lonely."

"Yes," James said. "He was lonely."

Decker said, "But he talked a lot to Nurse Schulung."

"Sometimes."

Ross said, "He was sad when she left."

"How so?"

"He told me: 'I'm sad that Nurse Schulung left.'"

Decker gave a small smile. Direct was the best. "I understand that Bertram had a girlfriend from where he used to live before he came to Loving Care."

"He did." James nodded. "He said they wanted to get married, but they said no."

"Who said no?"

"His parents."

"Yes," Ross told him. "They're rich."

"Who's rich? Bertram's parents?"

Ross nodded.

"Who told you Bertram's parents were rich?"

"Bertram did."

Decker said, "Did you ever meet Bertram's parents?"

"No," Ross said.

James said, "They live far away."

"That's why he was sad," Ross said.

"He was sad being away from his parents?" Decker asked. When there was no response, he said, "Did Bertram ever talk about leaving Loving Care?"

"Where would he go?" James asked.

"Maybe he'd go visit Nurse Schulung?" Decker said.

Both men gave back blank stares. James said, "How would he get there? He didn't ride a bike."

Decker decided that this line of questioning was a dead end. He veered in a different direction. "You told me that Bertram didn't like to participate in group time or movie night. Is that right?" Two nods. "But he went on the field trip to the woods. Did they make him go, or did he want to go?"

James said, "They couldn't make him go on a trip. That's against the rules."

"Then he wanted to go?"

"I dunno."

"Was he excited to go on the trip?"

James screwed up his body in a shrug. "He sat with Colette on the bus. I saw them talking."

"Thanks for telling me that." Decker looked for Colette, eyes scanning the dining hall. "I don't see her. Do you know where she'd be if she didn't come in for snacks?"

"In her room," James said.

"Okay. I'll check for her in her room."

"Boss?" At the sound of McAdams's voice, Decker turned around. The kid crooked a finger in his direction.

"Excuse me, gentlemen. And thanks for your help."

"You're welcome," they replied in unison.

Polite men. Someone had taught them well.

"No answer on Elsie Schulung's cell," McAdams said. "It goes to voice mail. I gave local police the address and asked them to take a look around. I gave them your phone number and mine as well. They said they'd call me as soon as they checked out the property."

"Good. What about the phone records?"

"A supervisor told me to scan over the paperwork and she would help expedite the process. Radar said he'll take care of it."

"Thanks. Good work. I want to talk to Colette."

"The blonde wearing the sundress?"

"Yes. She was sitting next to Bertram on the bus. James said they were talking. Let me see what she has to say, and then we'll interview Elsie Schulung when we find her."

"We'd better make it quick, boss. We're needed back in Greenbury."

"Why's that?"

"They found a body."

Decker's heart sank for a second. Then he said, "'A body'—meaning it's not Bertram."

"Old bones but with some desiccated flesh and clothing on him."

"It's a him?"

"That's what Butterfield called the remains. He thinks it may be related to a cold case that happened around ten years ago."

"I wasn't at Greenbury ten years ago, but I did read up on all the local cold cases when I arrived. The only one that sticks out in my head was a camping trip. Three guys went out to the woods and never came back. They were students at the Five Colleges."

"Right you are. They attended Duxbury. They were sophomores."

Decker looked upward, trying to jog the memory. "One was Anderson. First name was Zac?"

"Zeke Anderson. I'm impressed."

"Don't be. There weren't that many open files here. I don't remember the names of the other two students."

McAdams checked his notes. "Bennett McCrae and Maxwell Velasquez."

"Do you remember anything about the case? You've been at Greenbury longer than me."

"I came a year before you arrived. But I do remember talk about it—how three people could just disappear. The details were fresher back then. Radar wants us back—ASAP."

"Right. But as long as we're here, I do want to talk to Colette. Bertram's still missing. If the bones have been there for ten years, they'll keep another hour."

The door was wide open. Decker peeked inside. Colette's room was as neat in appearance as the woman herself. There was a desk with a pen, a pencil, blank paper, and a vase holding a single red rose. There was a green-and-pink chair on which a stuffed panda sat. A bookcase held candles, several photographs inside sunflower frames, and a variety of small stuffed animals. She was sitting on a floral comforter on her bed, nestled between mounds of brightly colored pillows, studying her laptop. She had changed from her yellow sundress to a green-and-pink striped long-sleeved T-shirt and jeans. Her feet were bare. She looked up when Decker knocked on a yellow wall. She gave them a wide smile and leaped off the bed. "Come in, come in."

Decker crossed the threshold. "What a pretty room you have."

"Thank you." She beamed. "I did it myself."

"It's really lovely!" Decker gave her a thumbs-up. "Can I ask you a few more questions, Colette?"

"Of course." She was wearing clear lipgloss and had patches of blush on her cheeks. "About Bertram?"

"Yes."

Removing the stuffed panda from the chair, she said, "Sit down."

Decker sat on the floral chair; McAdams took the desk chair and brought out his tablet to take notes. Colette sat on the edge of her bed, hands folded in her lap. It was obvious that she took great pride in her excellent manners.

"What's your last name, Colette?"

"Bailey. B-A-I-L-E-Y."

"Perfect," Decker said. "How long have you lived here—at Loving Care?"

"A long time."

"Five years? Ten years?"

"About ten years."

"Okay. Then you probably know a lot about things around here."

Another smile. "I know some things. Not *everything*! No one knows *everything*!"

"That is true. Do you remember when Bertram came here?"

"Of course."

"What do you remember about him?"

She looked down. "I have to think."

"Take your time."

About a minute passed. Then she said, "He didn't want to talk. Even though everyone said hello."

"He was shy?"

"I guess."

"But later on he talked to some of you. I know he talked to April. And I know he talked to you." She nodded gravely and Decker said, "What did you talk about?"

A shrug. "He told me he missed his girlfriend. I thought he wanted me to be his new girlfriend. But I don't want a boyfriend. We're just plain friends."

"It's good to have friends," Decker said. "Is that why you sat with him on the bus to the nature field trip? Because you were friends?"

"Yes."

"What did you two talk about on the ride over?"

"That it was good to go on a trip. That's what we talked about."

"Then Bertram was happy to go on the field trip."

"Well, he didn't say 'I'm happy.' But I think he was. He wasn't sad."

"Do you like going on trips?" McAdams asked.

"Yes, I do. I like it here. They are very nice. But I like to see other things sometimes. I like the walks in nature that we do. And I like the museums. I don't like so much the water parks. They're hot and I don't like the sun."

"Yeah, I'm not much for sun either," Decker said.

"I like art museums," Collette said. "I don't draw. But I like looking at the paintings."

"I don't draw either," McAdams said. "But I really admire those who can do it."

She nodded. Then she turned grave. "It's sad that Bertram got lost."

"It is," Decker said, "and we're trying very hard to find him. That's why we need your help. Did Bertram say anything to you about Nurse Schulung on the bus ride over?"

"I have to think." Seconds passed. "No."

"Okay. The only thing you remember is you two talked about how it was good to go on trips."

She wrinkled her nose. "He talked about video games. He liked video games."

"Right," Decker said. "Do you like video games?"

"No. But I didn't tell him that. I didn't want to make him feel bad." Her eyes widened. "Oh. I remember one thing. I bet it's important."

"What's that, Colette?"

"He was following the bus on a map."

"He had a map?"

"On his phone," she said. "It showed all the roads and there was an arrow and it moved when the bus moved."

"He had nav on his phone," McAdams said to Decker.

Decker nodded. "So, Bertram could see the bus move on the phone."

"The bus wasn't on the phone. Just the arrow."

McAdams said, "I know this is a funny question, but do you remember the color of the arrow?"

"I think it was blue."

"Probably Waze."

Colette looked at the clock. "I need to be in the library to stamp the books."

Decker said, "That's an important job."

"No, it isn't. But I like the library. I like books. I can read, you know."

"It's excellent to read," McAdams said. "Best way to learn about things."

The woman pinkened. "Thank you."

Decker stood up. "Thank you, Colette. You helped us a lot."

"I'm glad." She got up from the bed and put the stuffed panda back on her chair. A smile. "Bye."

"Bye," the men said in unison. They walked a few dozen feet down the hall and then McAdams said, "To use any kind of nav, you have to know how to open an app."

"First, you have to have the app. Why would a developmentally disabled man who didn't drive—who didn't even ride a bicycle—have Waze on his phone?"

"Someone put it there. The question is for what purpose? To teach him how to escape?"

"Don't know," Decker said. "Whatever the reasons, the intentions don't look good."

Chapter 6

S eated shotgun, McAdams had a cup of coffee in one hand and a phone in the other. The ride was going to take a little time. He had plugged his cell into an adapter that fit in the cigarette lighter charger. No chance of running out of juice, but Decker's car was antiquated. "Know what this car needs? Wi-Fi."

"In my car?"

"Yes, Rabbi, it is now possible to have Wi-Fi in your car."

"It'll probably be as useful as my home Wi-Fi—which is always going out."

"Why don't you upgrade?"

"I'm not paying more for something I rarely use. If it's work-related, I use the computers at the station house."

"Well, you're not at the station house, so I repeat. Get Wi-Fi for the car."

"What on earth for?"

"For things like right now. My phone is using towers, which eats up battery life."

"But you're charging your phone, so what do you care about battery life?"

"You're always asking me to look stuff up. I could use my pad instead of my phone. It's easier to read things on my tablet."

"I'm not getting Wi-Fi for a car."

"Your grandkids could watch Netflix on their pads if you had it."

"Bringing my grandkids into this inane discussion is a low blow. Look up the case on your phone. Or don't look it up. It'll keep until we get to the station house."

"No need to get peeved, Old Man, it was just a suggestion."

Decker was silent. McAdams shrugged. Within a few moments he found what he needed and read from his phone. "The missing boys—Zeke Anderson, Max Velasquez, and Bennett McCrae—they lived in the same dorm and went missing in mid-October during Parents' Weekend ten years ago. There was a massive search." He continued scanning the article. "The rest is filled with quotes from students and friends, a couple of TAs and several professors."

"That's good. It gives us a start on who to interview."

"It was ten years ago."

"I'm sure they remember the incident. Anything illuminating in the quotes?"

"Not really: they're shocked, they don't know what happened, they don't know why it happened, they weren't the types to attract bad people, whatever that means."

"Any quotes from girlfriends?"

McAdams kept reading. "Don't see anything."

"Call Kevin at the station house and ask him to search for TV footage."

"Sure. Want to see a picture of them?"

"I have to pull over. Any distinguishing features?"

"Zeke Anderson was Caucasian with a beard. Max Velasquez also looked Caucasian. He wore glasses and looked stunned in this head shot. Bennett McCrae was Black—good-looking. I don't know if any of them were tattooed, but if they were, it's no doubt in the file along with dental records."

"Any description of the clothing that they wore on the day of the disappearance?"

"Nope. The only detail related about the case is *when* they left—late Thursday afternoon. They told people they'd be back for class on Monday. By the following Wednesday, people started getting concerned." McAdams thought a moment. "Who camps in these woods at that time of year? It can dip below freezing at night in mid-October."

"Yeah, it could be a cover story," Decker said.

"I'll call Kevin. That way we'll have the footage when we get back." It was a ten-minute conversation. McAdams disconnected the line and said, "Update. Kev thinks the remains belong to Zeke Anderson from a fabric remnant: red-and-green plaid. Anderson had several red-and-green plaid shirts. Plaid is pretty much a staple item of clothing in Greenbury. But there were handfuls of coarse hair around his mandible."

"Facial hair that fell off when his flesh decomposed."

McAdams nodded. His phone rang. Tyler listened and said, "Sergeant, can I put you on speaker so Detective Decker can hear what you have to say? Thanks." He pressed a button. "Okay. You're on speaker."

"This is Sergeant Quay from the Baniff Police Department."

"Detective Peter Decker here. Thanks for calling back. We were in Baniff investigating a Missing Persons case: a man named Bertram Lanz who lives at Loving Care. He disappeared in our jurisdiction in Greenbury, New York."

"Yes, I understand."

McAdams said, "Could you please repeat what you told me, Sergeant, about Elsie Schulung's house?"

A low, raspy voice said, "Everything appeared to be in order. We looked through windows, checked the doors, and did a once-over around back. Nothing seemed out of place. There's mail in her outdoor box. About four days' worth, I'd say. A few local flyers were left at the front door. There's a window in the garage, and it's covered. I could peek under the bottom of the shade, but I couldn't see enough to tell if a car was parked there. I'll get the make and model from DMV. I will say this. It's a nice time of year to take a little time off, especially if you recently quit your job."

McAdams mouthed, "I told him that."

Decker nodded. "Of course. And since she had mail, she obviously didn't forward it anywhere. But she didn't stop delivery either."

"Not that unusual. Most of it is bulk stuff. It looks to me like she took off for a little R and R."

"Nothing else seemed suspicious?"

"Other than the mail, no. We called out, announced ourselves, but no one answered. No lights were on, and the AC appears to be turned off. There were no weird odors coming from the inside of the house. No flies buzzing around. I don't have any reason to break down a door and do a welfare check."

"I agree," Decker said. "Only thing weird that I've found is her disconnected landline."

"People are doing that more and more. Save on expenses. Do you know when it was disconnected?"

"No. It could have been months ago."

"I'll drive by the house in a few days and see if more mail is piling up. We can reevaluate at that time. How old is she?"

"Forty-three, I believe."

"Okay. Vacation is looking like an option. Anything else?"

"No, I think you about covered it, Sergeant. Thank you very much."

"We'll talk again. I hope by then I have news for you. Bye."

McAdams hung up his phone. "What do you think?"

"Who knows?" Decker shrugged. "I do hope that Bertram Lanz and Elsie Schulung have better outcomes than our missing campers."

"Yeah, right." McAdams looked out the passenger window. "That's really our job, boss. We deal in awful outcomes. We pick up the shattered pieces of broken lives and try to make some sense of the unfathomable. Most of the time all we really do is shove the pieces back in place, but nothing is ever whole again. The lives still remain in tatters."

The car was silent. Decker said, "Feeling overwhelmed?"

"Maybe, although I shouldn't be. I'm done with law school. I am studying for the bar, and it's going well. This case is just hitting close to home. I could imagine Chucky out there by himself . . . not good."

"When was the last time *you* had a vacation, Harvard? As far as I remember, it's been either school or the job. Maybe you can use a few days off."

"Not with Bertram missing."

"Tell you what, Harvard. I'm going back to the station house to look up the camper cold case. You go to the Zeke Anderson's crime scene and let me know what's happening there. Or . . . you can help the team scour the woods for Bertram Lanz."

"I'll go to the crime scene. From what I understand, the two are roughly in the same area." McAdams was quiet for a moment. "I'm at loose ends. I don't know where I'm going after I pass the bar."

"Do you have to make a decision right away?"

"No."

"Then don't worry about it. This job is open for as long as you want. You're a big asset to the department. That's not pressure, that's just a fact. It's never a bad idea to take your time to think about major decisions. And empathy is always a good thing."

McAdams gave a brief smile. "I've traded my life-long sarcasm for deep introspection. I think that's a mistake. Being bitter and angry feels a hell of a lot better than crying in my beer."

Decker laughed. "Harvard, you can be a schmuck with me anytime you want."

"Thank you, boss. Kinder words were never spoken."

It was dusk when they returned to Greenbury, tired and road weary. The ride home had taken longer than expected and now there was little reason to make a stop at the crime scene. The bulk of the remains had been disinterred and were on their way to the morgue. Decker's plan for tomorrow: a stop at the crime scene and a visit to the coroner's office.

What a job he had chosen for his lifelong profession. Most of the time, he was impervious to the gruesome aspect of his work, intensely focused on bringing justice to the families. But then there were the days where it really got to him.

As soon as he arrived at the station house, he poured himself a strong cup of coffee and called his wife. Her voice made him smile. "Hey there."

"Hey there, yourself. Are you back or calling from the road?"

"We're back. No luck finding Bertram, but while the cops were out in the woods looking for him, they came across some buried remains."

"'Remains.'" A pause. "Not a recent case, then."

"About ten years ago three male college students went camping and never returned. We may have found one of them, judging by remnants of clothing. We'll know more if we get a positive identification."

"And this happened ten years ago?"

"Yes."

"Do you know the date? I'll look it up."

"Mid-October."

"Who goes camping around here in mid-October? The woods can get very cold."

"A few hearty souls."

"Was it an exceptionally warm autumn?"

"No idea. I suspect that back then there were lots of marijuana farms hidden in the woods. Our climate isn't the best for growing things, but if it was a warmer October, there still could be some plants to harvest. If you were a local dealer ten years ago, when marijuana was illegal in the state, hidden farms would have been one way to get material without going through a middle-man."

"Any indication that the boys were dealers?"

"I haven't read the files, so I don't know. I'm going to spend a couple of hours reviewing the case. You don't have to wait up for me, but if you do, I won't yell at you."

Rina let out a small laugh. "I think I can manage to stay up until ten. Did you eat?"

"I'll manage."

"Nonsense. I'll bring you some dinner at the station house. What about Tyler?"

"He could use food. He seems hangry. Or a version of depressed-hungry. We can call it dungry."

"He's depressed?"

"He just finished law school. He's a little lost."

"He has a lot of options."

"Sometimes it's better not to have so many options," Decker said. "But I'm not shedding tears over his plight."

"You're going to be busy with this case. Ten years old and a lot of material to cover." She paused. "Maybe it's a good time for me to go to New York and deal with Gabe's issues."

"Sure."

"How about if I leave on Sunday?"

"Fine with me. Is Gabe still holed up with us?"

"No, he left this morning, almost as soon as you left. I'll call him and let him know my plans."

"Good luck."

"I don't mind going. No sense being home by myself."

Decker felt a pang of guilt. "I'll take some time off as soon as I catch my breath."

"Oh, for goodness' sakes, Peter, I'm perfectly fine going to the city, visiting our kids and grandchildren, and taking in a little shopping. Hannah can always use some help with the baby."

Their youngest now had a baby of her own. It made Decker smile . . . and feel a little old. "How's my princess doing?"

"Sleep deprived. She sounds like the walking dead. If time permits, I'll go to Philadelphia and visit Cindy the next day."

Decker's daughter from his first marriage. It was lovely that she and Rina were friends. "She has time off?"

"Well, like her father, she's always working on a number of big cases. I'll give her a call. If she can make it, fine. If not, another time."

"Where will you be staying?"

"If it's overnight, I'll bunk down with Sammy and Rachel and the kids. There are more bodies in their apartment in Brooklyn, but it has two bedrooms. Hannah and Rafi are still in a studio."

"It's a big studio."

"It is. But when baby makes three and you have all that infant paraphernalia, no space is big enough."

The cases had been archived. The room that held the files was dim and dusty, but the boxes were organized properly. Four of them—one for each student plus a box for anything that the three had in common. There were no coroners' reports or crime-scene photos in the notebooks because there had been no bodies. There were long lists of interviewed people and artifacts belonging to each boy for DNA purposes. While there was a great deal of overlap, some names appeared on one list and not the others. Or some names appeared on two lists but not the remaining one. Lists of relatives, friends, teachers, interests, and anything else that may link the three boys.

There were also multiple photographs of each of them.

According to the health records from the school and the drivers' licenses, Ezekiel Anderson was caucasian, five eleven, and 175 pounds. His face appeared wide, but that could have been because of the beard. Brown eyes, bushy eyebrows, and a mop of unruly brown hair. Although no one could tell the police what he was wearing when he left for camping, his usual dress was a plaid shirt under a sweater with jeans. Often he wore high-top sneakers. He was an English major with a political science minor and had made remarks to quite a few people about joining the Peace Corps when he graduated. He was an excellent student and a committed member of several socially active campus associations. He was fond of physical activity. More than a few interviewees had stated that he worked out almost every day. He was described as an intense man who wanted to make the world a better place.

Maxwell Velasquez was five six and 180 pounds. He had an olive complexion with a round face and dark eyes that peered out behind dark-rimmed glasses. He was doing a double major in math and bio. and he had hoped to go to medical school, carrying on his father's family tradition. He was an excellent student, but not much for extracurricular activities. People described him as very smart but shy, especially in a crowd. He didn't appear to have a lot of friends or even many acquaintances. While no one had a bad word to say about him, most didn't have a good word either. He had come across as a nonentity. His usual dress—as far as anyone could remember—was a collared shirt under a sweater, jeans, and sneakers or Vans. The few people who did seem to know him—even a little bit—had been surprised that he had gone camping, especially in mid-October. His activities were sedentary—reading or playing video games. But college was all about experimentation, and the camping might have been his stretch from his comfort zone.

Bennett McCrae was six one, 160 pounds. From the photos, he appeared to be a light-skinned Black man with a lean face, dark eyes and a narrow nose flared at the nostrils. In this picture he wore a wide, white smile. His major was still undeclared, but McCrae favored classes in African studies as well as political science. He and Anderson had been members of some of the same associations, and people often saw them in the gym together. People described McCrae as outgoing, charismatic, and very opinionated. He was the first one to join in discussions and often played devil's advocate for the fun of it. He, like Velasquez, also came from a medical family, but his class choices suggested that he was charting a different course from his father. Some of those interviewed recalled Bennett as meticulous in his appearance and dress. His closet, when the prior detective had checked it out, contained everything from workout garb to a tux and, unlike Zeke, he didn't favor any particular type of clothing.

The boys were last seen on October 15. The temperature was mild—sixties during the day, forties at night—but it was often colder in the woods and colder still at the higher elevations. The boys had to have packed warm clothing, which made Decker think about what might have happened to Zeke Anderson's jacket. No one had mentioned any outerwear with the remains. Anderson's car—a two-year-old black BMW 3 series—was missing from its parking spot near his dorm. It was found later at the trailhead. An exhaustive forensic search of the vehicle yielded nothing: no leads as to where the young men might be.

There were a few students who had suggested that the camping trip was a ruse and the car had been left to throw the police off the track. That didn't make a lot of sense to Decker. No one wastes a good Beemer. But neither did it make sense that three strapping young males would suddenly vanish utterly and completely. And if the boys hadn't gone camping, why were Zeke Anderson's remains—well, possible remains—found in the woods and his car near the trailhead?

The files gave addresses for each of the students' parents. As Decker wrote them down, he noticed that all three of them were from New York. Zeke lived in Brooklyn, and McCrae and Velasquez were from Queens. Not exactly a big coincidence in a city whose population was over eight million, but a closer look revealed that McCrae and Velasquez had gone to the same high school. Were they friends before college? Did their fathers—both of them in health care—know each other professionally?

Decker loaded up the boxes, carted them upstairs, and dropped them on his desk. The noise made McAdams look up from his computer. "Need help?"

"You can go home, Tyler. I'm about ready to quit anyway."

"You sure?"

"Positive. It's been a long day. See you tomorrow."

"*Lila tov*, Rabbi. Get some shut-eye yourself." He picked up his jacket and left.

Shut-eye sounded like a bully idea. But he wanted to organize the material as well as his thoughts before he went home. Ten minutes later, he felt a tap on his shoulder and looked up. Rina placed a cooler at his feet. She wore a white shirtdress with tan espadrilles on her feet. Her rich, dark hair, drawn into a ponytail, was covered on top by a pink bandana. "Sorry to distract you." She handed him the paper cup of coffee from a cardboard tray she was holding.

"You're never a distraction." Decker took the coffee

and sipped deeply. "That's way too good to be station-house coffee."

"It's from across the street." She set another paper cup on his desk. "For Tyler. Where is he?"

"Sent him home." He looped his foot around the leg of a chair and dragged it over. "Have a seat."

"How's it going?"

"Lousy."

"Sorry to hear that."

"I'm utterly frustrated. It would have been nice to follow up on Bertram Lanz before opening up a ten-year-old cold case. And if the remains don't belong to one of the campers, then we're really in the dark."

"Have you stopped looking for Bertram?"

"Not at all. But it's been over twenty-four hours and we've gone over the area meticulously. We haven't found so much as an errant hair follicle. My opinion? He had arranged to be picked up by someone when the Loving Care bus stopped at the diner."

"Do you have a suspect?"

"A person of interest, as we now call it. Bertram was very close to a nurse named Elsie Schulung, who worked at the home. She spoke German. Bertram was German. She quit two weeks ago. She doesn't appear to be home—hasn't been for around four days. She's not answering her cell. The house doesn't look tampered with. It's not a crime to go away on vacation. Since Bertram's a legal adult, it's also not a crime for him to go with her."

"He's a legal adult?"

"Yes. All the residents of Loving Care are emancipated. That way, if they do something illegal or disappear or whatever, the home isn't held liable for their actions. But that doesn't mean Bertram isn't susceptible to nefarious influences even if he is responsible for his own welfare. If he and the nurse ran away together, fine and dandy. I just want to make sure he's safe and he's with her of his own free will."

"Have his parents been contacted yet?"

"I believe the director, Lionel Lewis, is calling them as soon as the time zones mesh because the parents live overseas. Thanks for reminding me. I'll follow up."

"Police don't contact the parents?"

"There's no evidence of a crime. The news is better if it comes from Loving Care since they're the ones who've lost track of him. Anyway, what did you bring me?" He lifted the lid of the cooler. "Smells good."

"Grilled chicken breast," Rina said. "It's warm enough to use the barbecue. I made enough chicken and side salads to pass around the station."

"You spread goodwill wherever you go. Are you joining me?"

"I already ate." A pause. "I looked up the cases on the internet: the missing boys."

Decker unwrapped the foil, picked up the whole breast with his fork, and took a bite. "Wow, good eating."

"Peter, there are plates and utensils in the cooler."

"I like playing caveman." He took another bite. "Find anything interesting about them?"

"It's all interesting, but the information's probably in your case files. Peter, can you please use a plate?"

He took out a paper plate and put it on his head. Then he speared another chicken breast the same way as the first.

Rina laughed. "Okay, you win."

Decker took the plate off his head and smiled. "What's the spin in the newspaper?"

"The boys seemed to have disappeared into thin air. No sign or trace of them except Zeke's BMW. It was warm when they left for the woods, but a few days later the weather turned. It rained and then snowed."

"Which means if there had been evidence, it might have been washed away by weather by the time the search was underway."

"Exactly. Nothing of any importance was found in the car."

"Right."

"I told you it's probably in your files." Rina took a sip of her coffee. "There was a one-year follow-up human-interest story. It implied that the police were still baffled. Even with modern databases—like AFIS and CODIS—nothing has ever been connected to the missing boys. The police never got anywhere past the basics."

"What basics do you have?"

"They interviewed people associated with colleges. The students were obviously very bright, because Duxbury is the most competitive college of the consortium." Rina looked at a notepad. "In the follow-up article, they interviewed a few people who had known them, specifically a boy named Jack Carlson. He was the fourth suitemate. I don't know this for sure, but it sounds like there were two guys in two rooms."

Decker rifled through the common file for the three young men. "Here he is. Jackson Carlson." He read out loud. "Okay, they all came from different freshman housing. Zeke, Bennett, and Jackson—he was called Jack—chose to room together in their sophomore year." He kept reading. "Okay, here's the deal. The three of them were short a guy needed to complete the foursome required for their second-year housing." He looked up. "I'm not sure how Max figured into the mix."

"Interesting," Rina said. "Odd man out, but it must have turned out okay since he went on the camping trip with two of them."

"I think Bennett McCrae and Max Velasquez knew each other before college. They went to the same high school. Both of their fathers are in health care—one is a doctor, the other is a hospital administrator."

"Family friends? They took him in as a favor?"

"Don't know, but it's plausible."

Rina said, "In the papers, Jack Carlson made a point of saying that they all got along."

"Then why didn't Jack go on the camping trip with them?"

"It was Parents' Weekend. His folks were the only set that came in."

"Then he was at the college the entire time."

"I suppose."

"I'll check that out." Decker rifled through Zeke Anderson's case files. "Here it is again . . . ten pages long." He looked in the boxes of the other two missing boys.

"The same interview with Jack Carlson is in all three files. I'll need to read this carefully." He continued shuffling through the papers. "I can't see any follow-up interviews." He looked up at Rina. "Do you know what happened to Carlson?"

"Actually, I looked him up. He works in Brooklyn. His social media feeds say he's married and he and his wife just had a baby boy."

"Anything else on him?"

"No," Rina said. "Should there be?"

"I don't know. I'll interview him once we have a positive ID on the remains."

"How long will that take?"

"A day or two."

McAdams strolled over to his desk and sat down with a plop.

"I thought you went home," Decker said.

"I forgot my wallet." He took it out of his desk. Then he sniffed. "Why didn't you tell me that Rina was bringing dinner? Or did you want to hog it all yourself?"

"Chicken breasts," Rina said. "There's plenty to go around. I also made coleslaw."

"Thanks, Rina. I'll take it home. I really am tired." McAdams glanced at his watch. "I take it there's no news from Kev?"

"He's still in the field. The crew searched for forensics in the general area, but they can't do much until all the remains are packed up. The area is cordoned off. He'll try again tomorrow at dawn's early light. He's assuming we'll be there."

"Sure, I can come," McAdams said. "Oh, by the way, boss. While you were in Archives, I spoke to the coroner."

"And?"

"He said you can come by the morgue tomorrow afternoon. He should have things sorted out by then."

"The crypt is in Hamilton?"

"Your favorite place."

"We all get along now," Decker said. "Who's the coroner?"

"Oscar Kahn. Do you know him?"

"Nope," Decker said. "Does he have any idea how long the bones have been there?"

"There is some flesh, but not much of it. Ten years maybe—within the time frame of the boys' disappearances."

"The boys all had parents who lived in New York. Plus, there was a fourth roommate—Jack Carlson. He didn't go camping because his parents came for the weekend. He still lives in New York. Rina is going to Manhattan on Sunday for Gabe. If I can set up some interviews, I'll think I'll go down as well."

"Actually," McAdams said, "I was planning to go into the city on Saturday. Call me when you get there, and we can interview everyone together."

Rina said, "What's the occasion?"

"I want to pay my siblings a visit."

"That's very nice of you, Tyler. I'm sure your siblings would love to see you."

McAdams smiled sadly. "Maybe." He picked up the coffee cup on his desk. "For me?"

"Yep," Rina said.

"Thank you." McAdams helped himself to food from the cooler and put it in a paper bag. "This looks great, Rina."

"Take whatever you want."

"I'm fine." McAdams smiled. "See you tomorrow, Rabbi."

"See you tomorrow." After he left, Decker said, "Did you know that Tyler has a brother with Down syndrome?"

"I did know. Chucky. I suppose this case is getting to him personally."

Decker wrinkled his brow. "When did he tell you?"

"About two years ago."

Silence. "He told you and not me?"

"It wasn't like that. I was going down to visit the family, and Tyler asked me to bring Chucky some Boston Celtics paraphernalia from the NBA store. Chucky is a big Celtics fan."

"Unbelievable."

"Not really. It's better than rooting for the Knicks."

"No, not *that*. I meant unbelievable that he told you and not me." A pause. "Did he ask you not to tell me?"

"Yes."

"*Why?*"

Rina sighed. "I asked him why. He couldn't answer. Want to know my opinion?"

"Lay it on me."

"Tyler didn't want you feeling sorry for him."

"Why would I feel *sorry* for him?"

"Because maybe that's how people have reacted when they found out about Chucky. It doesn't take much to light Tyler's fuse. He's an angry young man."

"Okay." Decker kissed her forehead. "We never had this conversation."

She returned his affection with a kiss on the lips. "Mum's the word."

Chapter 7

Since Decker never slept with blackout shades, he often awoke with the sun, and at this time of the year dawn was early. No matter how quiet he was, Rina stirred as soon as he swung his legs over the mattress and planted his feet on the floor. By six-fifteen, coffee was brewing and bread was toasting and there was background music courtesy of one of the many streaming services. They had yet to install any communication assistant and probably never would. Having worked law enforcement, Decker knew all about spy bots, even those that were coded under cute names.

Mozart's delicate notes were coming from the iPad as Decker sat at the kitchen table and buttered his toast. Rina sat down opposite him and placed a cup of coffee in front of his plate. He said, "Thanks. What's going on with you?"

"Today's my teaching day."

"Ah, right. It is Thursday. How many classes are you doing this summer?"

"Two—Hebrew Language and Chumash. Actually, it's Tanakh. I'm starting Melachim Alef."

"Kings 1," Decker said. "That's a good one. Full of juicy stories. How many students?"

"Hebrew is twelve, Kings is twenty-five. The classes are open to the public, and there's lots of interest in the Bible studies from all sorts of people. What are you up to?"

"First, I'm going to the crime scene. Also, I should pay a visit to the coroner's office."

"But?"

"It's an old murder, so time isn't urgent. I'm really concerned about Bertram Lanz. It's going on two days. I don't think he's in the woods, Rina. We've scoured the area. I think someone picked him up. I think it was prearranged. I just hope . . ."

"What?"

"Nothing."

"An abduction?"

"The thought crossed my mind."

"Ransom note?"

"Not that I know of. But parents could have gotten something and haven't involved the police."

"Or the director of the facility?"

"That too. Dr. Lewis was going to call the parents. I'd like to talk to them myself."

"What's stopping you?" Rina asked.

"If Bertram was abducted and the parents don't want the police involved, I don't want to mess anything up."

"Isn't it always better to involve the police in something like this?"

Decker nibbled on his toast and thought for a moment. "If it was my kid and the kidnappers said no police, I might try to handle it myself."

"But you are the police."

"You know what I'm saying."

"I do."

"I feel like I'm missing something. I want to go back to Loving Care and reinterview people. Yesterday, I didn't have time to do everything I wanted, including a visit to Elsie Schulung's house. We're just in the dark with this case."

"What about CCTV from the diner and on the main road? Did that turn up anything?"

"Most of the cameras were broken. That's not unusual. Stores put them in and forget about it. Butterfield did get a few tapes from the highway, but if someone took the back roads, we're sunk."

"The diner doesn't have CCTV?"

"Just one at the front entrance. The quality is poor. And the place was overcrowded with all the residents. Kevin and McAdams will go through what we do have. Maybe we'll get lucky."

"What about the nurse's car? Has anyone spotted it?"

"I don't think anyone has put out a BOLO because she isn't a suspect. For all we know, it still could be in the garage. The police haven't done a welfare check."

"Why not?"

"No evidence. Just some mail piling up."

"How much?"

"Nothing alarming. She's a grown woman. She could have gone anywhere." Decker shrugged. "The thought of an abduction is so depressing. I'm really worried about Bertram. I'm hoping to find out more about him. Yesterday, we just scratched the surface."

Rina looked at the kitchen clock. It wasn't even seven. "It's super early and traffic is light. If you leave now, you'll make good time."

Decker took a big swig of coffee. "Do you mind?"

"Do I mind? Why would I mind?"

"Cutting our breakfast short?"

"Oh please. I'm used to you leaving on a moment's notice. But it's nice of you to ask."

Decker got up and opened the refrigerator. He took out a plastic container: lasagna from a week ago. He sniffed it. "This looks pretty good."

Rina snatched it from his hand. "I meant to throw that out. I'll get you something fresh." She opened the freezer. "I've got individual containers of meat loaf. It's frozen but it should thaw out by lunch. How does that sound?"

"Great."

"Go get yourself ready, and I'll put together a care package."

Decker said, "Want to go out tonight? Veggie Thai. Seven o'clock?"

"That sounds fine. If you show up in time."

"I promise I'll make it."

"Don't make promises you can't keep."

"I do it because I choose to give you hope."

"Ah, hope: it inevitably disappoints." Rina laughed. "Pandora really shouldn't have messed with that box."

"I don't know what more I could possibly say to help you." Lionel Lewis unlocked the door to his office and swung it open. He motioned for Decker to step inside, pointed to a chair, and sat down behind his desk. The administrator was dressed in a tan jacket over a green plaid shirt and a solid red tie. Jeans and slip-on shoes with no socks rounded out the attire. "You're the one in charge of finding him."

Decker sat. "It's harder than it looks on TV."

Lewis was quiet. He folded his hands. "I'm sorry if I appear rude. I'm dealing with everyone here, trying to calm down frightened people. We're all upset. I just don't understand why you can't find him."

"We've scoured those hills," Decker said. "I'm beginning to wonder if he's out there. We've searched a huge perimeter. So thoroughly that we found another set of remains."

"*Remains?*"

"We think the bones might be from a ten-year-old case."

"And you're positive they're not Bertram's?"

"They are not Bertram's bones," Decker said. "By mentioning that, all I'm saying is we went over the area inch by inch."

"Obviously better than you did ten years ago."

"I'll ignore that."

"Maybe whoever did that to your remains, did . . ." Lewis didn't finish his sentence. "You know—the proverbial bogeyman in the hills."

"I haven't discounted that idea that Bertram may have encountered someone harmful. But first I'd like to rule out planned abduction."

"*Abduction?*" Lewis shook his head. "Why would you say that?"

"His parents have money. Why wouldn't I say that?" Decker paused. "When you talked to them last night, how did they sound?"

Lewis looked upward. "I didn't talk to them. They were out of town, and their private secretary—the one I spoke to—said they'd be hard to reach."

It took several moments for Decker to integrate the words. "Their son is missing. If that doesn't constitute an emergency, what does?"

"He said he'd pass along the message once they were in reach of communications."

"'Reach of communications'?" Decker made a face. "Are they at an ashram in the Himalayas? I betcha even ashrams have cell phones."

"I don't know, Detective. I'm just as confused as you are. But I can't *make* him tell me where they are." Lewis bit his thumbnail. "It's anxiety provoking. I have to have this conversation sooner rather than later. Anyone would assume that the parents would want to know." A pause. "I've seen this before. Issues come up and the parents just don't want to deal with them."

"This is more than an issue. Did you deal with the parents when planning Bertram's living arrangements?"

"No, just a series of secretaries and caregivers," Lewis said. "We hadn't been informed of any problems from Bertram's prior facility, so we took him in."

"He was in love with another woman there. A woman named Kathrine? Did you know that?"

"Yes, I did know. How did you find out?"

"Some of the people I interviewed yesterday told Detective McAdams and me all about her. Could he have run away with her?"

"Not without someone else's help."

"How about Elsie Schulung? She's not home and there's mail in her box." When Lewis didn't answer, Decker said, "Can I have the name of Bertram's previous residential facility?"

"Why?" Lewis asked. "Ah, you want to find out if Kathrine's still there."

"Exactly. Because if Kathrine isn't there, that gives me an avenue of inquiry. Maybe they ran away together. Can I have the number of the facility?"

"I have to get the number. And I'll make the phone call." Lewis buzzed his secretary, asked her for what he needed, then hung up the phone. "Say you call Bertram's old facility and Kathrine is there. Then what?"

"I have to consider abduction." Decker leaned forward. "Do you think it's possible that the parents have received a ransom note and don't want the police involved?"

"Being as I haven't had any communication with them, how would I know?"

"Can I have your contact number for them?"

"You cannot. It's private information." Again, his thumbnail went to his mouth. "And why would you get any more details from the secretary than I did?"

"Sometimes police involvement makes it more official."

"Let me think about it."

"Do that," Decker said. "In the meantime, I'd like to talk to your staff. I didn't have a chance to interview them yesterday. Maybe they know something. I'll keep it short."

A frustrated exhale. "Who do you want to talk to?"

"Anyone who dealt with Bertram on a regular basis. Just a few questions."

"It's clear you're not going to leave me alone unless I do what you ask."

"Mea culpa," Decker said. "I care."

"I'll see what I can set up." Lewis stood. "I don't know what's taking Linda so long to get a phone number."

"And I'd really like the name of the previous residential care house. I really need to find out about Kathrine."

"Let me call first, and if something is a problem, I'll tell you. Fair?"

Decker didn't answer. Then he said, "I'd like to look at any files you might have on Bertram. I know he's a legal adult, but he has been missing for almost two days."

"The files would be in another room. I'll see what I can do." Lewis stood up. "Just wait here. And no snooping."

Decker gave him a Stan Laurel smile. "God forbid."

"Leave the door open."

"Of course." As soon as Lewis left, Decker quietly got to his feet and started rummaging through Lewis's desk drawers. He pushed a few items around but didn't find anything that looked consequential: no stacks of cash, no hidden valuables, no weapons, and no practice ransom notes. There were patient files, but nothing with a heading of Bertram Lanz. He thought about doing some electronic rifling, but Lewis would surely catch on to his spying. A computer search dumped evidence that was hardware retrievable. What Decker did was copy down the names of many of his computer files even if he didn't open them up. To a cop, an order of "no snooping" was a direct invitation to do the opposite. If Lewis didn't realize that, the man, despite his degrees, knew nothing about human behavior.

While Linda was photocopying Bertram's file and while Lewis was making phone calls, Decker was given a list of staff members who routinely dealt with Lanz. The first one was a physical therapist named Gray Mathers. He appeared to be in his late twenties, with sharp features, a big chin, and strong arms. He wore a gray tee and gray sweats and was working with a client when Decker walked into the gym, a roomy space aired out by open windows. It was equipped not only with standard exercise machines but with specialized devices. Mathers was finishing up a session with a woman who was walking on a treadmill, holding on to the rails. She had short brown hair and wore glasses. The machine slowed and stopped. The woman waited while Mathers helped her off. He handed her a cane and a towel. Mathers said, "Good job, Anna. See you tomorrow."

Anna wiped her face, handed him the towel, and balanced on her cane. "See you tomorrow."

"Do you need help?"

"No, no." Slowly, Anna headed for the door. "Thanks."

"Thank you." Mathers waited until she was out the door. "Marvelous progress. When she came here three years ago, she was in a wheelchair. Then a walker. Now a cane." He faced Decker. "One of my success stories."

"Must be rewarding," Decker said.

"It is. You're the detective?"

"I am. Peter Decker."

"Gray Mathers. How can I help?"

"I understand you worked with Bertram Lanz regularly?"

"Twice a week we'd do some weight lifting." Mathers sat down on a bench and looked up at Decker as he talked, a towel draped around his neck. "Bertram had some noticeable physical impairments. We were working on some balancing exercises because his right side is more affected than his left. He had a broad chest, so there was something to work with. For his size and his condition, he's strong. His gross motor coordination is decent to good."

"Interesting. Mind if I sit?"

"Not at all." Mathers moved over on the bench and looked him up and down. "Football, right?"

"Yes, but it was more perfunctory than anything else. I was never deep into sports. My height was wasted on me." Mathers smiled and Decker said, "Tell me about Bertram's progress. What did you do with him besides balancing exercises?"

"Strength training, isometrics, and aerobics. I dealt with the gross physical impairments, but he had an occupational therapist for fine motor. Bertram functioned pretty well. And he was more than capable of carrying on a good conversation."

"Is it fair to say that you and Bertram talked a lot?"

"Not a lot but enough to get to know him a little. I talk to all my clients."

"Anything personal?"

"Nothing too deep. I'm really upset about this. Why can't you guys find him?"

Again, with the accusations. Decker tried not to act defensive. "We're all wondering the same thing. I'm also wondering if he doesn't want to be found. Was he close to any staff member here?"

"Elsie Schulung took him under her wing. When she left a couple of weeks ago, it was hard for Bertram. He didn't complain, but he became more withdrawn. Not that he was that social to begin with. He liked doing solitary things. Like you heard yesterday, lots of residents enjoy video games. They measure their success against themselves and not the outside world."

"Probably why games are popular in general," Decker said. "Anyone else besides Elsie Schulung?"

Mathers gave it some thought. "Not really." A pause. "You think he ran away with her?"

"I don't know."

"What other possibilities are you considering if he isn't lost?"

"The usual. He could have run away with someone else. He could have been taken. Then there's the obvious. Most people are good. But a few are very bad."

Mathers was quiet. "The thing is that Bertram could bench-press about 150. He could dead-lift even more than that. It's not weight lifter territory, but even for the average Joe, that's strong. I think he could fight off an attacker."

"Unless he knew who kidnapped him and went into the car voluntarily."

"Sure, that could have happened."

"Did Bertram ever talk to you about his former girl-friend?"

"Kathrine? Yes. In his mind she was his active girl-friend."

"Could they have run away together?"

"It's possible. It might be hard for them to do that without help."

Decker said, "Did he tell you anything specific about her?"

"Just that he missed her. And she'd be proud to see how strong he was." A brief smile. "The lifting was good for his mental state. Exercise usually is." Mathers looked at Decker. "We talked, but not most of the time, Detective. The steps I put them through demand concentration."

"And yet he told you about Kathrine."

"I think he told anyone with ears about her. She was important to him." Gray shrugged. "Why don't you call up Elsie Schulung? I think she still lives in the area."

"She's away at the moment."

"Ah, too bad."

"Do you know why she left?"

"She was very caring to the residents but she wasn't one for rules. I think it finally caught up with her."

"Was she angry when she left?"

"I don't really know. I didn't hear of any drama. It was probably a mutual decision between her and the administration."

"What rules in particular didn't she like?"

"Her most egregious errors were her house calls. Or room calls. Protocol says the residents come to her office. Not the other way around."

"That doesn't seem so terrible unless she was doing more than checkups."

"I really don't know what she did. Take it up with Dr. Lewis." Mathers stood up. "My next appointment is here."

April Kelly had walked into the gym. She was wearing yellow yoga pants and a floral sleeveless workout top. "Hi, Detective. Any news?"

"Sorry, April. Not yet."

"Dang!" Her eyes watered.

Decker patted her shoulder. "Don't give up, April. We haven't."

She wiped her eyes on the hem of her shirt.

Mathers said, "Ready to sweat?"

The woman nodded and muttered something while she clasped her hands together, brought them to her chest, and bowed her head.

"She's praying for him," Mathers whispered. "We're all praying for Bertram. It's not much, but right now it's the only weapon we have in our meager arsenal."

Chapter 8

The office was adorned with diplomas and professional certificates. Bertram Lanz's therapist,
Belinda Adreas, had a PhD in clinical psychology
with a specialty in adults with intellectual disabilities.
She was in her early forties with a square build. Her
face was round as were her blue eyes. Blond hair was
pulled back into a ponytail. A badge was pinned over
the pocket of her bright pink doctor's coat. Decker
thanked her for taking the time to see him.

She said, "You haven't found Bertram?"

"No, we haven't."

A glum smile. "I keep thinking, did I miss something? He was a bit unhappy when he first came here,
but he seemed to be adjusting well."

"That seems to be the consensus, although I've also heard from others that he wasn't very social."

"He has a few friends—the ones you talked to yesterday. Did they elucidate anything for you?"

"Just that he played video games."

"A lot of the residents here play video games. It's encouraged as therapy. Mastery and fine motor coordination."

Decker nodded. "Some people mentioned that Bertram talked a lot about his girlfriend, Kathrine. Did he mention her to you as well?"

"He's not dead, so he still has confidentiality," Belinda said. "If he talked to other people about it, you can extrapolate."

"Can you give me an idea of what you two spoke about?"

"Sorry, no."

"Could you at least tell me if he ever spoke about running away?"

"He never spoke to me about running away. If we didn't talk about it, I'm not breaking confidentiality. If he decided to leave, it was something impulsive."

"Okay. That helps," Decker said. "Any idea where he'd go if he ran away?"

"Probably back to his old facility, if I had to guess. As you can tell by your conversations with others, he probably missed Kathrine and his old friends. It doesn't take deep psychological insight to figure that one out."

"I heard he left his former residential facility because people thought it would be a good idea if he and Kathrine were separated."

"There are a lot of rumors going around. I heard that one as well."

"Do you give it any credence?"

"All rumors have a kernel of truth."

"Do you know if sex was involved?"

"All rumors have a kernel of truth," she repeated.

"Poor guy." Decker thought for a moment. "He had cerebral palsy or some sort of birth defect, right?"

"Right."

"CP doesn't necessarily equate with mental disability, right?"

"Correct."

"But in Bertram's case, he had cognitive disabilities."

"Yes."

"In your opinion, how mentally disabled was he? Could you give me an age equivalent?"

"No, that whole thing is fallacious. I can't tell you anything about Bertram specifically. But I'll speak in general terms. Adult mentally disabled might be more advanced than let's say a ten-year-old at some things and less advanced than a ten-year-old at other things. The delays become more pronounced as the individual moves on to more abstract learning."

"Then let me ask you a general question. Do you think someone like Bertram could navigate his way back to his old home?"

A pause. "If someone gave him explicit instructions, he could probably follow them. But as I told you, he never talked to me about making an escape." She regarded her watch. "I have someone in five minutes. It would be rude for you to see my client coming in. We try to keep things private."

"Thank you, Doctor. You've been helpful."

The sad smile reappeared. "If I have been helpful, then maybe you can find him."

"We're doing whatever we can."

"We all do our best," Belinda said. "That's the problem, Detective. Insight doesn't always equal success."

It was after two in the afternoon when Decker stepped outside to call Sergeant Quay at the Baniff Police Department. A few minutes later, the raspy voice came over the line. "Hello, Detective. What's going on?"

"I'm at the Loving Care facility, interviewing staff. If Bertram Lanz left on his own, he'd probably need help. Elsie Schulung would be the logical person for him to go to. He seemed closer to her because she was German speaking. I think we should do a welfare check to make sure Bertram isn't there."

"If he left on his own and he's a legal adult, there's no grounds to go in."

"The second option is she abducted him."

"If you think that's a possibility, I'd be inclined to break a lock and explain it later." A pause over the line. "Any ransom notes?"

"No, but I don't think he's lost in the woods. We've gone over the area inch by inch. We've brought in dogs. We haven't found anything. I think he had a planned rendezvous."

"Why would he want to leave the home? Is there evidence of abuse?"

"Not at all. But he did have a girlfriend at his old residential-care facility. I'm thinking he ran off with her and Elsie was the go-between."

"Why would she do that? Put herself at risk."

"Bertram came from money."

"Oh. Okay. You're now saying that she helped him because he promised her money."

"It's a theory. I just want to make sure he's not there."

Quay said, "I can meet you at her place in an hour."

"See you then." Decker disconnected the line. Then he called McAdams. "Hey. Any luck with CCTV?"

"No sightings of Bertram, unfortunately. We got a little footage from CCTV at gas stations and rest stops along the main highway. But most of the area is rural. Plus, the images we did get are poor quality. But we'll keep at it. I think there's a truck stop ten miles away. I might try there. Anything on your end?"

"I'm going to swing by Elsie Schulung's house. First thing I'll do is look inside the garage and see if her car is there."

"Did Quay get the make and model of Schulung's car?" McAdams asked. "You said he was going to do that. Our next step is to go through the CCTV again and look for her car."

"I'll find out the information for you," Decker said.

"If not, I can look it up." McAdams paused. "Do you really think she's involved?"

"I can't think of anyone else who would help Bertram. She's a long shot, but it's all I have right now. What's going on with our remains?"

"The lab is doing a complicated DNA replication test because the biological material is degraded and might be contaminated. Everyone's being careful about an identification. But some preliminary results should come in this afternoon."

"Great. I'll be back tonight at around six, maybe seven. We're thinking Thai."

"Are you inviting me?"

"I am."

"Then I'll come."

Baniff was a rural town consisting of a hundred-year-old city hall, small, individually owned shops, several schools, and a church on every corner. Schulung lived in a residential area not too far from Main Street, which cut the business district in two. Most of the houses were one story with brick and white-clapboard siding and a single brick chimney that peeked out from wood shingle roofs. The lots were small, and while some lawns were dewy green, others were turning yellow in the heat. Elsie lived on a quiet street shaded by oaks and elms in full leaf.

Decker parked in front of the address and got out of the car. He checked the mailbox. It was getting pretty stuffed at this point.

Lots of the houses had been planted with shrubs and flowers. Elsie's hadn't gotten the memo. The abode was a plain Jane with a walkway that bisected the lawn and led to a step-up front porch. The outside furniture included a broken swing and a beaten-up sofa. A solid front door flaked red paint, and the screen door was hanging off of its hinges. No car in the driveway, and the shade over the window in the one-car garage prevented him from seeing inside. The garage blocked off the backyard on the left side, but there was a metal gate on the right that allowed access to the rear.

Retrieving his phone from his coat pocket, Decker was internally debating whether to have a look around when a Baniff Police black-and-white pulled up to the curb. The middle-aged man stepping out of the driver's side wore a short-sleeved tan uniform and tan brimmed hat. There was a police belt strapped around his waist. He was tall and thin with a big Adam's apple. His eyes were brown, his face deeply tanned and weathered. When he saw Decker, he touched the brim of his hat. "Detective."

"Pete's fine by me. Thanks for doing this." Decker held up his phone. "For photographs in case there's something in the house."

"Let's hope not." Quay paused. "You know, even if you didn't ask me, I probably would have checked it out in a couple of days." He knocked loudly at the door, announcing himself. Did it several times. "Let's go around the back and knock there."

Quay went up to the side yard metal gate and lifted the latch. The two men walked into the backyard. There was a small patch of brown lawn, an old Weber barbecue, and pieces of white plastic furniture: a dinette set on a patio, and two lounge chairs, sans cushions, on the lawn. The area was fenced off by brown two-by-fours, and two trash bins were shoved into a back corner. After putting on gloves, Decker went over to the containers, shooed away flies, and pulled off the lids. The bins were empty. "If she took a vacation, she emptied the garbage before she left."

"People usually do that." Quay rocked on his feet. "My time's limited. Let's go inside." He banged several times on the back door but got no response.

Decker said, "I've got a set of lock picks in my pocket. Neater than breaking a window."

Quay said, "Go for it."

The lock was substantial. Decker took out the tension wrench and turned it to the left. The time-consuming part was moving each pin into alignment. By the time he was done, beads of sweat had formed on his nose and forehead.

"Nice," Quay said.

"Thanks." Decker pocketed the lock picks. "You take the lead?"

"Sure. Doesn't seem to be anyone home, but we should probably clear the place before we look around."

Decker took off his gloves and unsnapped his shoulder holster. "I'm a good shot. I'll cover you."

Quay nodded and slowly pushed open the back door, which led into the living room. Within five minutes, it was clear that the house was empty. Both men returned their firearms to their holsters. Decker had a quick look around.

An old house with an old interior decorated with old furnishings. But the place was relatively neat, considering all the junk outside. The floor was not only free of debris, it had been cleaned with bleach and lots of it judging from the strong chemical smell. The living room was small with minimal furniture. The bookshelf had been recently dusted. It contained knickknacks and around a dozen old paperbacks. Schulung favored romances.

Quay said, "I'll check out the bedrooms. You can do the kitchen."

"Perfect," Decker said.

The kitchen counter was clean. There were no dirty dishes in the sink, and the floor's white tiles appeared recently scrubbed. Here, the odor of bleach was even stronger, and it didn't take a genius to realize that someone had been intent on scouring something. He looked inside the refrigerator. There were some condiments and some cans of soda and beer but nothing perishable. The freezer was a bottom-drawer pull-out. Nothing in there to warrant alarm.

His eyes went to his shoes and he knelt down. He swept a gloved finger under the appliance, and it came back rust-colored and sticky. A quick sniff revealed what he thought it was. Since the freezer was on the bottom, it was possible that he was looking at animal blood from meat, but that combined with the bleach smell was adding up to a more nefarious conclusion.

"Quay! I need your help." The sergeant appeared within moments. "Could you help me move the fridge?"

"What did you find?" Quay sniffed the air. "Wow, that's strong."

"Yes, it is." The two of them positioned themselves and carefully slid the refrigerator off to one side, revealing a sizable pool of the same sticky stuff that was on Decker's gloved finger. "Do you have a presumptive blood test in your cruiser?"

"No," Quay answered. "But with the smell and this . . . I'll call the techs from Scientific Investigation Division." His breathing became shallow and his complexion tinted yellow. "That's a lot of blood."

"And I'm betting we'll find more blood evidence with luminol. Bad accident—we are in a kitchen—or something way worse." Decker waited as Quay made his phone calls and stowed the mobile in his police belt.

"While we're waiting for a forensic team, I have something to show you." Quay took in a breath and let it out. "I'll be right back." He returned thirty seconds later. "These photographs were in her nightstand drawer. Take a look."

"Photographs? That's old school." Decker regarded the first one, then the next one and the next one. The snapshots of Bertram that he'd be given at the beginning of the case had been pretty blurry as far as features went. He was now looking at a clear picture. The man had deep-set eyes, a round face, and sandy-colored hair. He had a wide smile that bespoke of some hidden secret. His arm was around a short woman—she looked short compared to the man—with blond hair and dark eyes. She was smiling as well. She looked to have Down syndrome if Decker had to guess. Both of them were photographed from the waist up.

Decker said, "This might be Bertram."

"You don't know what he looks like?"

"I was given poor-quality snapshots," Decker explained. "I'm betting the woman he's with is his girlfriend, Kathrine."

"Why would Elsie have pictures of them?"

"Don't know." Decker scanned through the other photographs. There were several of a woman in her mid-to-late thirties—long face, long, straight hair, and round eyes. Her mouth was halfway between a sneer and a smile. He showed the picture to Quay. "Any idea who she is?"

"Not a clue."

"I'd like to show this to Lionel Lewis from Loving Care Home. Could I keep them for a day or so?"

"I don't know how my captain will feel about that"

"How about if I keep the one of Bertram and his girlfriend, and the one with this thirties-plus un-identified woman." He handed back the rest of the photographs.

Quay said, "I suppose it's fine."

"Thanks," Decker said. He looked at the sticky stuff under the fridge. Now that it was exposed to the air, and without the appliance on top of it, the edges were seeping outward. "If the pool is a leftover amount from a good cleaning, there was a lot of blood originally. We should cordon off the area."

"I have some crime-scene tape in the car." Quay again rocked on his feet. "I'll go get it."

"I have the gloves," Decker said. "Do you have any paper shoe covers?"

"Sorry, no."

"It's fine." Decker smiled to himself.

An old cop joke came to mind.

What does a dog park and a crime scene have in common?

In both places, you need to be careful where you step.

The red pool was tested and determined to be human blood. Then the floor was sprayed with luminol. Previously white tiles became streaked, smeared, and spotted with electric blue. As the techs dusted for prints and took numerous samples of the rusty pool, detectives from Baniff were busy searching the house for other potential evidence of a crime as well as canvassing the area, talking to neighbors. Whatever happened occurred days ago, which complicated the situation. One thing that the discovery allowed them to do was check the garage. Elsie Schulung's car was gone, which prompted an immediate BOLO. Decker had finished his statement and went outside for a breather. After inhaling stale smells and the metallic odor of blood for the last hour, he welcomed the fresh air. His first call was to the stationhouse—to McAdams specifically.

"Awful," the kid said. "Can the techs tell you anything about the makeup of the blood?"

"It's human. They're waiting to get a DNA profile before they say anything else. We have Bertram's toothbrush and comb, but they're back in Greenbury in the evidence room."

"I'll get them for you," McAdams said. "Want me to run the items to the lab in Hamilton?"

"Yeah, at this point, I think we need Bertram's DNA. Deliver the items in person"

"Sure thing. So right now, we don't know if Elsie Schulung is the cause of the blood or the victim."

"That is correct. The only thing I can tell you is that the place was cleaned up—which takes attention to detail. I don't see Bertram scrubbing it down without guidance. Elsie's car isn't in the garage, and Bertram can't drive. I looked up her license and registration. Elsie drove a six-year-old silver Ford Focus."

"Yes, I know. I looked it up as well."

"Any luck with CCTV?"

"No." A silence across the line. "There are lots of back roads around here. If she knew the area, she could avoid the main highway pretty easily."

"Why do you think she knew the area?" Decker asked.

"If she was planning on escaping with Lanz, she must have done some homework."

"True," Decker admitted. "It would be super if we had evidence that the two cases are related."

"That's a good point, boss," McAdams said. "I've been thinking. You said there was about four or five days' worth of mail in the box. Bertram's only been gone a couple of days. It sounds like her disappearance could have predated his disappearance."

A valid point. Decker said, "Why would Elsie drag Lanz into a situation like this?"

"She had a friendly relationship with Bertram. Maybe she called him in a panic."

Decker said, "You would think she'd have other friends that she'd call first, right?"

"Maybe she called him because her other friends might go to the police," McAdams said. "She probably had more control over Bertram, especially if she did something criminal and needed money in a hurry."

"His parents are wealthy, but that doesn't mean that Bertram has a lot of money in the bank." Decker paused. "Lionel Lewis called Bertram's parents in Germany yesterday. He got their assistant, who said they're not in communication reach."

"That's strange."

"I thought so, too," Decker said. "I suppose there are a few places left on earth where cell phones don't reach. According to Lewis, the assistant was evasive. At that time I thought maybe Bertram's parents received a ransom notice and were told not to involve the police. I think I need to call them myself."

"Sure. Maybe you'll have better luck than Lewis." McAdams waited a few moments. "We need like a timeline."

"It would help. Any thoughts?"

McAdams said, "First something bad happens at Elsie's house. In a panic, she contacts Bertram. He comes over and helps her clean up the mess and dispose of the body."

Decker said, "Then you're thinking that Bertram is *not* the victim in the kitchen?"

McAdams paused. "Good question. Assume that he's not the victim. He is an accomplice after the fact. I'm thinking that he and Elsie cleaned up the mess together."

"And buried an anonymous victim's body?"

"Maybe."

"Where?"

"No idea," McAdams said. "I'm just working through a timeline."

"Go on," Decker said.

McAdams said, "Okay. At some point during the cleanup, Lanz tells her about the field trip. Something starts percolating in Elsie's brain. She knows she needs money. But she also knows that if she escapes with Lanz that night, it'll raise suspicions. Both of them disappearing at roughly the same time. So, she takes Lanz back to Loving Care. That gives her a few days to think. She hatches an escape plan and that involves picking up the one person who knows what she did."

"Okay. She arranges to pick up Bertram from the diner. Then what do they do? Does she kill him since he knows about the body? Does she take him with her?"

"I'm assuming that if she needs money, Elsie would want Bertram alive," McAdams said.

"Then you are assuming she more or less kidnapped him for ransom."

"Let's go down that avenue," McAdams said. "They make a phone call to Bertram's parents—a plea for money. Maybe that's why the parents are not talking to Dr. Lewis. *And* that would also explain why her disappearance predated his."

Decker said, "It's a theory that explains all the moving parts except for the identity of the victim and where the body is."

McAdams said, "Did you find any other evidence of the crime?"

"Like blood or biological matter elsewhere in the house? Not so far. We're still checking the backyard and the garage." Decker thought a moment. "I've got some snapshots from Elsie's place. I think one of them is Bertram and Kathrine. The other is an unidentified woman who appears to be in her mid-thirties. She may be our missing link. I'll show you the pictures when I get back."

"Okay."

"What's going on with our remains in the hillside . . . which—unlike this one—is in our jurisdiction."

"What time is it?"

"Around five."

"It might be too late, but let me call the coroner and see if he's made an identification," McAdams said. "Want to hold?"

"Sure." Decker checked his email while the line was silent. Harvard's voice punched through five minutes later. "We've got a prelim match with Zeke Anderson. But it's not solid yet. The tech wouldn't go to court with it."

"Meaning?"

"The extracted sample was degraded and contaminated: everything from soil to bugs. But there were a few strands that seemed to match Zeke's DNA in the sample. The lab tech wants further purification before making a positive ID. That could be ready as soon as tomorrow. We've already started searching for the other two students."

"Good," Decker said. "I've pulled the original files. All of the folders have lists of names, including a couple of lists of names common to all three boys. I'd start with the fourth roommate, Jackson Carlson, and then branch out to the other names. I'll try to reach him by phone. Maybe I can set up a face-to-face interview when we're in New York on Sunday. It's getting late. You can go home."

"I don't mind taking a peek at the files," McAdams said. "I'm not doing much anyway. Between you and me, I've got the easier job. At least I know who the victims are."

"Thanks, Harvard. I'll see you tonight for dinner."

"Thank you for the invitation. It certainly sounds better than what I planned: sugary cereal with sour milk and a bag of chips."

"Don't you ever shop?"

"Why should I? I'm a spoiled brat, and you and Rina are enablers by always inviting me over."

The kid was making a good point.

McAdams said, "When we get to New York, I'll take you out for a great meal."

"It'll be kosher and it'll be expensive."

"No problem. I'm flush."

Since the case was in Baniff Police Department's jurisdiction, there wasn't any real detective work for Decker. Jake Quay told him that he'd keep him in the loop, but his own captain wanted his department to investigate without help—meaning without interference from him. Decker was fine with that. He started up his car, heading for the residential facility, hoping to show the photographs to Lewis.

He called Rina while he was on the road. Recounting the details, he tried to keep emotion out of his voice.

"You've found a murder scene, then," Rina said.

"Maybe. I'm going to be a little late for dinner."

"A little late? Sounds like an all-nighter."

"I'm not the lead, and Baniff wants to give this a crack without my expertise."

"That's stupid. Why wouldn't they want your help? You've probably worked more homicides in a month than he has in a lifetime."

"Some people just don't know a good thing when it looks them in the eye. Right now, I'm going back to Loving Care. At Schulung's house, we found a photograph of Bertram Lanz with a woman. I think she might be Kathrine. I also have a photograph of an unidentified, mid-thirties woman."

"Any idea who that is?"

"Not a clue. I want to show them to Dr. Lewis and see if he knows who they are. If all goes well, I'm hoping to be home by nine."

"Promises, promises."

"Yeah, I know. I'm not good at keeping them. Sorry."

"Nature of the beast. I'll get the takeout and wait until nine. If you're not going to make it, give me a call and I'll eat by my lonesome."

"I invited Tyler over for dinner."

"Then I'll call him and see if he wants to join in the feast. On another note altogether, Gabe called me. I told him we'll be in Manhattan on Sunday. Are you still planning on coming with me?"

"Yes, definitely. The lab has tentatively found Zeke Anderson's DNA in the remains. We'll be reopening the case, and once the ID is confirmed, I'll make the death notice."

"Poor you. Where do the parents live?"

"Brooklyn. The other two boys were from Queens. They went to the same high school, but the boys appear to have little in common. From the interviews I've scanned, Velasquez seemed to be bookish and into math and biology. McCrae was a social activist of sorts and a jock. But I'm figuring that maybe they knew each other before they went to Duxbury."

"Drugs make strange bedfellows."

Decker paused. "Why do you think it was drugs?"

"Three college students in the woods in mid-October? Sounds like a front for something illegal."

"I'd agree with you, but we found Zeke's body in the woods."

"Maybe they went to buy drugs and stepped on someone's toes." Rina waited a beat. "The woods are a good place for a hidden meth lab."

"Meth labs . . ." Decker paused. "I was thinking marijuana farms, but meth labs could work. They were really abundant ten years ago."

"Meth is easier to produce."

"If you don't blow yourself up," Decker said.

"Maybe that's what happened. How far are you from the Loving Care Home?"

"About twenty minutes. Maybe a little longer because the roads are dark."

"I don't want to distract you. Call me when you've landed."

"Roger." Decker chuckled. "I love you."

"Ditto, handsome. It's a crazy world out there. Keep yourself safe."

Chapter 9

Lewis was at a staff conference when Decker arrived. He spoke to his receptionist, Linda. They were becoming fast friends. "Do you know when Dr. Lewis will be free?"

"No one tells me anything, Detective. I suspect the meeting can't be too much longer. Most of us leave at six, and it's already ten after. I was just waiting around."

"Can you buzz him for me?"

"I shouldn't even be here." Linda opened a drawer and placed a pile of papers inside. She closed the drawer and then stood up. "If you want to call him, it's this button on the intercom. It'll go directly to his phone. But he might not answer." She put on her sweater, even though it was still warm outside, and slung her purse over her shoulder. "If the desk phone rings, don't worry about it. The answering service kicks in at six-fifteen."

"Have a good evening," Decker said.

"Thank you, Detective. FYI, I could use a good one. What happened to Bertram has thrown everyone into a tizzy. It would be good to have some answers."

"I know. We're working on it."

"I didn't mean to imply . . ." Decker was still standing. Linda said, "You're welcome to sit down, you know."

"Thank you." Decker smiled and sat in a chair across from her desk. But as soon as she left, he stood up and began to rifle through her things. Opening the drawer, he took out the mess that Linda had stowed away. It included a phone message book. The original messages were probably on top of Lewis's desk, but the book made copies of each message that Linda had written down, albeit they were hard to read. Decker took out his phone and started snapping pictures of the ones that had today's date. What he didn't see was any sort of a message from Kurt or Mila Lanz.

He moved on to a stack of mail and quickly took in the return addresses. None were familiar names, but he took pictures of the envelopes as well.

The desk phone rang. Decker picked it up before the service could get to it. "Loving Care Residential Home."

"Is this Dr. Lionel Lewis?"

It was a female voice. Decker said, "This is his assistant. Who am I speaking to?"

"Dr. Forrester. Dr. Lewis left a message yesterday about Kathrine Taylor."

"Right," Decker said. "Dr. Lewis wanted to make sure Kathrine was all right. Where are you located? In Connecticut, right?"

"Yes. Why do you think Kathrine isn't all right?"

"She had a boyfriend who used to live at your facility. Bertram Lanz."

"Of course. I know Bertram. What about him? Is he all right?"

"He's missing. We're thinking that he went to visit Kathrine."

Another long pause. "I don't want to be rude, but could you please put Dr. Lewis on the line?"

"Dr. Lewis is in a meeting. We're all frantic about Bertram. Whatever you tell me, I'll pass along to him."

"Bertram's not here."

"Okay. Thank you very much. And what about Kathrine? Is she all right?"

"Why shouldn't she be all right?"

Decker paused. "It's a simple yes or no answer."

There was a long pause over the line. "*Who is this?*"

It was time to come clean. "Actually, Dr. Forrester, I'm Detective Peter Decker from Greenbury Police in

Upstate New York. I'm in charge of the Bertram Lanz Missing Persons case. I'm waiting for Dr. Lewis to come out of his meeting, and that's why I answered the phone. I knew that Dr. Lewis called you, and I was hoping you had some information for me. Is Kathrine all right?"

"She left here two days ago, and she was fine when she left."

A beat. He said, "Was the departure unexpected?"

"We got a call from her mother, saying she was needed home—family emergency."

"Did you phone up her parents to make sure it was actually Kathrine's mother who called?"

There was a long pause. "Detective—if you are one—please ask Dr. Lewis to call me."

"Doctor, I need your help."

"I shouldn't be talking to you."

"On the contrary, I'm the one person you should be talking to."

"So you say." She hung up.

Decker looked at the desk phone and was about to press redial when Lewis came through the door. His face was not happy. "What do you think you're doing?"

"I was about to press redial because Dr. Forrester hung up on me. She's the head administrator from Bertram's former home in Connecticut."

"I *know* who Dr. Forrester is. I called her." A pause. "Did you answer Linda's phone? That's totally inappropriate!"

"Your righteous indignation is going to have to wait because we have more important things to worry about." Briefly Decker told him about the blood at Elsie Schulung's house. "We found some photographs there, Doctor. I'd like to show them to you. Perhaps you can identify the people in the snapshots."

"Fine, fine." Lewis snatched the pictures from Decker's hands. "This is Bertram. I'm sure you knew that already." A pause. "I don't know the woman he's with."

"What about the other one?" Decker asked.

Lewis spent a little more time with the woman in her mid-thirties. "No . . . No, I don't know her."

"You're sure."

"I'm not holding back on you." He sat down at Linda's desk chair. "I do hope you're not planning on showing them around to the residents."

"Residents, staff. Why not?"

"Because it'll upset them."

"These aren't morgue pictures. They're just plain photographs."

"Even so."

"Dr. Lewis, something happened at Elsie Schulung's house. Her car is missing. I find pictures of Bertram with a woman that's probably Kathrine. And she's most probably missing—"

"How do you know that?"

Decker waited a few seconds. "Dr. Forrester told me that Kathrine Taylor was called home by her mother for a family emergency a few days ago—around the time Bertram went missing. Did you know that?"

"No, I didn't know. How could I know? I hadn't spoken to the woman yet."

"I'm pretty sure that no one from Kathrine's residential home called her parents to verify that it was actually her mother who phoned. I just left a crime scene and now have Kathrine Taylor's safety to worry about." Decker pressed redial and handed Lewis the phone. "Find out the details and ask for Kathrine's phone number, okay?"

Lewis took the receiver. When the line clicked in, he said, "This is Dr. Lionel Lewis from Loving Care Adult Residential Home in New York. Is this Dr. Renee Forrester?" Decker couldn't hear her answer. "Yes, this really is Dr. Lewis. The man you spoke to— Detective Decker—is legitimate as well. One of our residents—Bertram Lanz—went missing in Upstate

New York, and Detective Decker was assigned to the case."

Decker put the phone on speaker. "Hello."

Lewis sighed. "Detective Decker would like to speak to Kathrine's parents just to make sure that she's okay."

A voice squawked over the speaker. "How do I know you're both legitimate?"

"Dr. Forrester," Decker said, "I can find out where Kathrine Taylor's parents live. That won't be hard for me. And when I do find the phone number and address, I'll call up the local police department and ask for a welfare check. I don't mean to frighten you . . ." A lie. "But what started out as a Missing Persons case has potentially turned into something more serious. We found blood."

She gasped. "Bertram's?"

"We don't know yet, but we're investigating all possibilities. If Kathrine's parents don't know that their daughter left your home, they're in for a rude awakening. Her disappearance might be better coming from you. And if Kathrine's all right, then there's no harm done. All I want to do is make a phone call."

"Who are you again?"

"Detective Peter Decker—Greenbury Police Department. Here's the number." He recited the digits to the front desk. "Call them up. You can verify that it matches Greenbury PD. Ask for anyone. They'll let you know that I'm on official business."

"I'll call you back." She hung up.

Lewis said, "I know you are dealing with Bertram's disappearance, so I'll excuse the intrusion into someone else's property—this time. But you know that you just can't simply barge in here and run your own show."

"Apologies."

"I'd like to call up Baniff Police and find out the situation at Elsie Schulung's place," Lewis said. "Who do I ask for?"

"Detective Jake Quay. He's handling the investigation."

"Are you involved in it?"

"Right now, only peripherally. That may change as the cases progress." Decker looked at his watch. "What's taking so long?"

"Perhaps you don't realize this, but a situation like this has to be approached delicately."

Decker didn't comment. Instead, he said, "No matter what Dr. Forrester tells us, the police will need to talk to the parents. Even if Kathrine is home and safe, she might know something about Bertram. And there's always the possibility that they received a ransom note that says don't involve the police."

The phone rang. Lewis picked it up. "Yes?" Slowly,

his complexion lost color. "Yes, I see . . . hold on. I'll put you on speaker again." To Decker: "Kathrine is *not* at home. Her parents are now in a panic." Lewis pressed the phone button. "Go ahead, Dr. Forrester." The speaker announced, "Are you there, Detective Decker?"

"I'm here."

"This is a horrendous situation. What do I do next?"

"The Mangrove police need to be notified. That is where she was last seen. Where do Kathrine's parents live?"

"In Pittsfield, Massachusetts. Do you know where that is?"

"I know it's in the Berkshires. I'll call them up as soon as I'm off the phone with you. I need a number and an address."

Forrester recited the information. "It's all my fault. I should have verified."

Yes, you should have. "Did you see Kathrine leave?"

"Yes. And when the car pulled up, Kathrine hopped right in. She definitely knew the driver."

"Dr. Forrester, do you have any kind of CCTV at the front entrance?"

"We have a camera at the doorway. I don't know about the driveway. I'll find out right away."

"Leave the CCTV to the police, but tell them about it. In the meantime, what can you tell me about the car?"

"I'm sorry." She sounded deflated. "It was white or maybe light silver. That's about all I can tell you. I'm not a car person."

Lewis said, "Elsie Schulung's car?"

Decker shushed him. "Was the car a sedan? A coupe? An SUV?"

"Not an SUV."

"Compact? Subcompact?"

"I don't know. The car wasn't tiny."

"Two or four doors?"

"I don't know."

"Did you watch Kathrine get in the car?"

"Yes, I was standing right outside. I waved to her and she waved back. Nothing untoward at all. She got in and the car drove off."

"Did she get in the front or back seat."

"Uh . . . back."

"Did she open the car door herself?"

"Yes, she did." A beat. "It must have been a four-door."

"Could you see how many people were in the car?"

"I wasn't paying attention."

"Was there a front-seat passenger? Why else would she get into the backseat?"

A pause. "I think there was someone in the front seat."

"Man or woman?"

"I couldn't tell you."

"Young? Old?"

"Not a child . . . probably not a teenager if I'm remembering correctly. Honestly, I may be making this up. I'm not observant when it comes to those kinds of things."

"And you talked to someone who told you she was Kathrine's mother?"

"Yes."

"What did the voice sound like?"

"A regular woman's voice."

"Any accent?"

Exasperation. "I don't remember," Renee said. "I think the parents are expecting a call from you."

"It helps to have information first. You're doing fine, Doctor."

"No, I'm not."

"Yes, you are. Let's move on to contents. Someone told you that Kathrine was needed home for a family emergency."

"Yes. It was a five-minute conversation, mostly me saying 'I hope everything is okay' and the woman saying 'I'm sure it will be.' Then I hung up and went to Kathrine's room. I told her that . . ." She didn't finish her sentence.

Decker said, "What?"

"There was a suitcase on her bed. I thought that was odd, since I hadn't told her she was needed home yet. I figured her mother must have called her cellphone." A pause. "I didn't say anything. I was intent on getting her ready because the car was coming soon."

"You think, in retrospect, that Kathrine was expecting this phone call?"

"I don't know if she was expecting it, but at the time I thought it was odd. Her suitcase was on her bed— open."

"Were there any clothes inside?"

"I'm pretty sure there was clothing."

"Then she was already packing up?"

"A dresser drawer was open. She could have been packing."

"All this helps," Decker told her. "I'll call Mangrove police, Dr. Forrester. As far as we are concerned, Kathrine is now a missing person."

"Oh my God! I can't believe this."

"Her disappearance could have nothing to do with my missing person."

"You don't believe that, do you."

"Right now, I'm just trying to get the lay of the land. In any case, I'll coordinate with Mangrove."

"Thank you. Will you be meeting with the parents?"

"Yes, probably tomorrow if they can make it early in the morning. Fridays are hard days for me."

"Give me a time and I'll try to be there. It's over an hour away and I've got a busy schedule—"

"You don't have to come, Dr. Forrester. But you should give them a call to find out how they're doing."

"Of course, I'll call them."

"And at some point, I'll want to visit your facilities and look through Kathrine's room."

"When will that be?"

"Ideally, I'd like to cram everything in tomorrow. Where exactly are you located?"

"Mangrove is just below the Massachusetts line, slightly north of Salisbury," Renee said. "Could you call me back after you've spoken to the police?"

"No problem," Decker said. "And you'll call the parents as well? I'm sure they'll want to hear from you."

"Yes, of course I'll call."

"Thank you." A pause. "I'm sure you're better at handling this kind of crisis anyway, being a psychologist and all."

"Social psychologist," she said. "I never had a great knack for clinical work. But I've got good executive functioning and I am a good administrator." A pause, then a sigh. "Or so I thought." Her words were followed by a click.

Decker decided to make his calls from the road, starting with the local police of Mangrove, Connecticut. He spoke to a detective sergeant named Michael Rand, explaining who he was and giving him the reason why he was calling, laying out the details as succinctly as he could. He finished up by saying, "I don't know if the two cases are related, but my person disappeared two days ago and so did Kathrine Taylor. They were once a romantic item."

"You think they ran off together."

"Possibly, yes."

"So what does that have to do with the nurse?"

"Elsie Schulung worked at Loving Care Home until two weeks ago. While she worked there, she befriended my missing person—Bertram Lanz. When Bertram disappeared, I thought he may have gone to her house.

I called up Baniff PD, and Sergeant Quay went over there to help me out. All he found is an unoccupied house. Today, we did a welfare check. That's when we found the blood under the refrigerator. Kathrine Taylor's disappearance may not have anything to do with my case. But her sudden departure needs to be looked into, since the emergency phone call wasn't from her mother."

"Got it. I'll get someone down."

"I'd like to go through her room at her facility. See if it relates to my case. The director has given me permission, but I don't want to step on your toes."

"When were you thinking of doing this?"

"Tomorrow."

"Okay. How about if you give me a time and I'll meet you there."

"Can we make it in the early afternoon? I'd like to talk to Kathrine's parents first."

"Our department should be doing that."

"I know. I promise to share."

A pause. "You know it's over an hour from the Berkshires to Mangrove."

"I know. I could probably make it to headquarters about noon."

"Fine."

"Thank you, Sergeant Rand. I'll see you then."

Decker hung up. He knew he should be concentrating on cases within his jurisdiction, especially a ten-year-old cold case now that he had identified a set of remains. Two other campers were still missing. But as long as there was a chance that Bertram was still alive, even a small chance, a warm case outweighed a cold one.

Chapter 10

"No sighting of Elsie Schulung's car from the CCTV we've gone through." McAdams shuffled through his notes. He was at the station, talking to Decker via speakerphone. "She could have taken back roads or changed cars. If I was involved in something bad, I would have changed cars."

"If she changed cars, then we've got to approach this a different way."

"Meaning?"

"Call up car-rental services." For Decker, hope of finding Bertram was draining—not like a gush of water from a burst pipe, more like from a hissing radiator. "What's new with our bones? Heard from the coroner?"

"The more sophisticated DNA test says it's Zeke Anderson. Do you want me to call the parents?"

"I'll do it. I had planned to set up an appointment just to talk to them. Now that I have definite news . . ." He sighed. "I'm sure this call has always been in the back of their minds, but it's always a shock to hear confirmation. Do you want to come with me for the interview?"

"I'll be there, pad in hand." A pause. "Poor people."

"Yes." Silly him for thinking that police work was happy work even in small towns. "Anything else?"

"Yeah, actually," McAdams said. "We got the full coroner's report. Anderson's ribs were shattered—front to back. Something blew a hole in his chest. Probably a through-and-through gunshot wound."

"Any bullets recovered at the dig site?"

"No."

"Shell casings?"

"No. He was probably shot elsewhere."

"What about his skull?"

"What about it?"

"Bashed in anywhere? Any signs of a fracture?"

"I don't think . . . hold on." He shuffled through the report. "No, the skull was intact."

"What about arms and legs?"

A pause over the line. "The skeleton wasn't complete. There were femurs found intact with scratches on them. The coroner thinks the most likely explanation is gnaw marks from animal activity."

"And his arms?"

"The left ulna and radius are intact. The right arm bones were in pieces."

"He stuck his hand in front of his chest when he saw the gun?"

"Could be. We found scattered finger and toe bones as well."

"Any idea of the caliber that shattered his ribs?"

"Something big and probably a close-range shot."

"Any pellets?"

"Nope."

"You said Forensics dug up his shirt, right?"

"No, they dug up pieces of plaid fabric that look like a shirt he commonly wore," McAdams said.

"Do any of the remnants have something that might be a bullet hole?"

"I didn't see anything like that at the time, but I'll check again as soon as the stuff comes back from the lab. We also found bits of denim material—probably his pants."

"Any blood on the fabrics?" Decker asked.

"I don't know. They're still being tested."

"And the search didn't find any personal effects?"

"Nothing in the way of ID—no wallet, no driver's license, no student ID card."

"What about other kinds of things? Business cards from a restaurant or a shop. Any kind of credit card receipt? Or maybe something handwritten like from a dry cleaner or a specialty shop?"

"Not yet. Forensics is still searching."

"This question goes to the fact that the kids were up there in late October," Decker said. "I'd like the area searched for abandoned drug labs. I'm thinking that maybe the kids saw something bad and paid for it."

McAdams said, "I thought you were thinking of marijuana farms."

"Any marijuana farms in existence ten years ago would be long gone." Decker paused. "They may have left behind a greenhouse or growing lights and a dryer for plants. Yeah, sure, check for that as well. Take people with you. And some vests and guns. Those kinds of people don't like trespassers."

"We'll poke around, look for anything associated with labs. When do you want this search to be conducted?"

"How many people do we have?"

"Two or three maybe. The rest are still on Bertram Lanz."

"Coordinate with Butterfield and set something up for next week. I don't want to spend too much man power looking for labs on a ten-year-old case when Bertram is still missing."

"Understood. What else?"

"Tomorrow, I want to talk to Kathrine's parents first. I'm headed out to Pittsfield, first. I told the Taylors I'd be there at around nine. I'll need an early start to visit the Taylors and make it out to Kathrine's residential facility. I'll have to do all this and then make it back home before sundown."

"What time does Shabbos start?"

"Late—around nine. I should be okay. You're invited for dinner."

"I'll be there. I'd like to come with you to interview the Taylors. My experience might be helpful."

"Sure. I'm starting out at around six-thirty in the morning."

"I'll bring the coffee. What time tonight are you due back in Greenbury?"

"Around nine. Just tell Rina you're coming for Shabbat."

"Nice of you to include me." He laughed. "The man who came to dinner—and breakfast and lunch. Like I said, I'll treat you guys to dinner in New York. Least I can do for all the meals you've fed me. Thank you very much."

"What got into you, McAdams? You're being down-right gracious."

"Dunno, boss. I get in these moods every so often. But not to worry, though. Like a kidney stone, it'll pass."

The Berkshires bloomed glorious in the summer, the highlands dotted with villages and towns and beautiful geography. The region was noted for mild tempera-tures in the summer, historic buildings, music and art festivals, fine museums, and lots of tourists taking up the roadways. The main highway from Greenbury to Pittsfield would take Decker northward and out of the way. The closest route was scenic but could become congested, as much of it was two-lane strips of asphalt. Starting out early allowed Decker to go through the back roads without too much traffic. It was turning into a warm day with a brilliant sun and a deep-colored sky. The air was clear and crystalline as only nonindustrial towns could boast.

Kathrine's parents lived a mile past highway 7, where the foliage was thick and green. Their house was a bungalow with sky-blue wood siding, white trim, and a red door. The living room was small but tidy, with comfortable furniture. Tea and coffee were waiting for them when Alison Taylor invited them inside. She appeared to be in her sixties, tall with a thin build. The lack of subcutaneous fat was evident in her wrinkled face. Her hair was silver and cut just above her shoulders. She was wearing a gray gym suit, as was her husband. He was also trim and about two inches shorter than his wife. Guy Taylor had curly salt-and-pepper hair with a bald spot and a round face with blue eyes. They sat on the couch huddled together. Both of them appeared drained.

Renee Forrester hadn't called Decker back. He didn't know if she was planning to show up, but he certainly wasn't going to wait around for her. He was anxious to get started but waited with a relaxed posture as Alison poured coffee and offered them a plate of homemade scones. McAdams shook his head. Decker took one but placed it on his napkin. "Tell me about Kathrine."

The woman sat and was quiet for a moment. "We couldn't have children of our own. We were going to adopt—had all the paperwork and everything. The birth mother seemed cooperative, but . . . she changed her mind. It was devastating."

"It was hell," Guy remarked quietly. "For me, the hardest thing was watching Alison go through all that agony."

"I was inconsolable." She looked at Decker. "Do you have children?"

"I do."

"How many?"

Guy said, "Alison, that might be personal."

Decker smiled. "One daughter with my first wife, one daughter with my second wife, two stepsons from my second wife, and a foster son."

Alison smiled. "A real blended family."

"Except they're more like individual components on a dinner plate than a stew."

"I wanted lots of children, but Guy was right. I couldn't go through that again. I gave up and decided to become a dog breeder—Cane Corsos. They're Italian mastiffs."

"Hence the deep barking we heard coming up the steps," McAdams said.

Guy said, "We've got an acre property that bleeds into the woodlands. If Kathrine would have been here, no one could have gotten close to her without my knowing. How could this happen?"

Decker said, "From what I understand, she appeared to know the people she went with."

"Maybe. Kathrine could be trusting." Alison wiped her eyes. "She was five when we got her. Her biological mother had five other children from three men and just couldn't cope with a child with special needs."

"I was not in favor of taking on a child with Down syndrome. The work and responsibility were enormous. But . . ." Guy's lower lip quivered. "Kathrine won me over. She was so sunny and enthusiastic about life. She's very high-functioning. She was the one who pushed for independent living. I didn't want to let her go."

Alison said, "Kathrine can be quite stubborn when she wants something."

"It goes with her high IQ." Guy smiled. "She can read and write. She has computer skills. She's a very extraordinary person. When we met with Dr. Forrester, it was as if she were heaven sent."

"Kathrine was homeschooled," Alison explained. "This was not only her first venture on her own but her first venture with other adults with special needs. In retrospect, we should have been more prepared."

"Don't blame yourself, Ali. We did everything we could." Guy got up and brought back a picture of a woman with deep blue eyes and coiffed blond hair. She wore makeup and had a thousand-watt smile with perfect teeth. "Kathrine's a beautiful girl. It should have been clear to us that she would attract attention."

"Bertram won her heart. I do believe they were truly in love. But they were just moving too fast."

Alison swiped a tear away from her right eye. "We should have never separated them."

"It's a hindsight call," Guy said.

"Maybe, but we saw her grow depressed." Alison looked at Decker. "We told her to give it some time."

"She seemed to be doing better lately." He turned to his wife. "Am I right about that?"

"Yes, I thought so, too." Alison looked up at the ceiling. "Maybe she was happy because she was planning her escape." Her eyes went to Decker's. "I know I said that Kathrine was trusting. But she would have never left the residence with someone she didn't know."

"Do you think she's safe?" McAdams said.

"I don't know. Just because she knew someone doesn't mean that someone was a good person. She was still naive."

"Do you think she ran away with Bertram?" Decker asked.

"I *hope* that's the case," Guy said. "But I do know that Bertram can't drive."

"He could have learned," McAdams said.

Alison didn't answer. Just gave out a deep sigh.

"I spoke to the Mangrove Police Department," Decker said. "They've gone through the video from the outside camera on that day. It didn't catch much, but she left in a light-colored car. Could be white or it could be silver. The images were black and white, so we can't tell. We're looking for a missing woman who drove a light-colored Ford Focus."

"Who?" Guy asked.

"Her name is Elsie Schulung. She worked as a nurse in Bertram Lanz's residential facility. She was German-speaking, and from what people at the residence told us, she got along well with Bertram. She had a snapshot of a couple in her home." Decker saw several photos of Kathrine in the Taylors' house. Same face, but he needed confirmation. "The man is Bertram. Do you recognize the woman with Bertram?"

He handed the picture to Guy, who shared it with his wife. They leaned toward each other until their shoulders touched.

Alison's eyes got wet. "That's Kathrine. Not very recent, though. It's about a year old. Kathrine's hair was long back then. She cut it very short after Bertram left."

"Her rebellion," Guy said.

"She was in mourning, Guy." A look to Decker. "And this photograph was found at the nurse's house?"

"Yes."

"And *she's* missing? The *nurse*?"

"Yes."

"What is her role in all of this?"

"I don't know."

McAdams said, "You haven't had any communication with your daughter in the last couple of days?"

"No, but that's not unusual," Alison said. "We don't call her every day. Her wishes."

"Nothing like a ransom note?"

"A *ransom* note?" Guy was stunned. "You think she was kidnapped for money?"

"Unfortunately, that's usually the motive behind kidnappings."

"But look at how we live!" He shook his head. "I'm a retired college professor. My wife works in a flower shop. Do we look like the ransom type?"

"Guy, they don't know that."

"Excuse my asking," McAdams said. "But how do you afford to send her to a residential facility?"

"There are government programs that help out," Guy said. "And Kathrine was provided for in my mother's will. She adored her."

"We manage." Alison looked at the detectives. "Doesn't Bertram come from money?"

"He does," Decker said.

"Did you ask Bertram's parents about a ransom note?"

"We haven't been able to get hold of them."

"You can't get *hold* of them?" Guy was aghast. "Do they know that their son is *missing*?"

"I've called them, the director of the residence has called them. According to their private secretary, the parents are not available."

"What!" Guy was outraged. "I can't believe that."

"I can." When the detectives looked at Alison, she said, "When this romance started up between our children, I tried calling them. I wanted to hear their opinion, ask them did they have any insight they'd like to share. I, also, got a secretary, who said they'd call me back. They never did. For all I know, they're just names. Maybe they're not even real people."

"Mila and Kurt Lanz are real people." Decker looked at McAdams. "Did we ever do a background check on Bertram's parents?"

"Yes, I did a search on the internet. They're private people. Anything made public has to do with Kurt's professional accomplishments."

"Let's do a little more digging." Decker's brain was whirling. "See what you can find out about the family. It's always possible that Bertram went back to Germany with Kathrine." A pause. "Would you know if she had a passport?"

"She does," Alison said.

"We took a trip to Europe three years ago," Guy chimed in. "Kathrine loved it. We had such a great time."

Decker said, "Would you know if the passport is still current?"

"We got a new one for the trip," Guy said. "I think they're good for ten years."

"And she's in possession of it?" McAdams asked.

"She asked for it a while back," Guy said. "For ID purposes."

McAdams said, "Is there anyone else that Kathrine felt close to at her residence?"

"No one she mentioned." Alison's eyes leaked tears. "She and Bertram wanted to get married." She looked at her husband. "In retrospect, maybe that would have been for the best."

Guy said quietly, "At the time we did the best we could."

Alison regarded Decker. "Do you think that the nurse took them both away?"

"It's a possibility," Decker said. "What I've been told, she appeared to like Bertram very much. And then we found this photo in her house. Maybe she thought it was the right thing—for them to be together—and she facilitated that."

"Let's hope that's the case." Alison nodded. "At least that way they're both safe."

"Does Kathrine have a phone or an email address that we might be able to tap into?"

"We've called her phone over a dozen times," Guy said. "It goes straight to voice mail."

"Same as Bertram Lanz," Decker said. "Their phones are probably off. But we can get a lot of information from the phone company and her ISP server. It takes time to process things so if we could get the paperwork started, that would be helpful."

"I understand." Alison supplied him with the information.

Decker said, "And you will tell us if you hear from Kathrine."

"Of course. Right away."

"We just want to make sure she's safe. If you hear from her, tell us. Even if she asks you not to tell us. You don't want to waste police time."

"I understand," Guy said.

But Decker knew that if Kathrine asked them not to talk to the police, they probably wouldn't say anything. Parents are parents first. Good citizenship was way overrated. He said, "I really hate to ask you this, but do you have an old toothbrush or hairbrush of Kathrine's?"

"DNA," Guy said.

"We've done the same for Bertram—and for the nurse we're looking for. We have to be prepared for anything."

Silence in the room.

"I haven't given up. I'm still assuming that they're very much alive. Right now, I'm trying to piece together a timeline. I'm sorry I can't be more specific, but as the facts come in, I'll let you know."

"I appreciate your honesty," Guy said. "A rare thing in this day and age."

Decker nodded. "Thank you. I've always found that honesty works well. To me, lying is hard work."

Chapter 11

It was close to eleven in the morning by the time they were on the highway to Mangrove, Connecticut—approximately an hour and change away. McAdams could feel his stomach rumbling. He reached over into the backseat and retrieved a paper bag inside a cooler. "There's tuna or what is this . . ." He stared at a wrapped sandwich. "I think this is egg salad."

"Go for it," Decker said.

"Thanks." McAdams tried the egg salad. "Like the dill mayo. Good touch."

"I'll tell Rina."

"Renee Forrester crapped out," McAdams said. "Wasn't she supposed to meet us at the Taylors' house?"

"She said she'd try."

"A resident is missing. You'd think she'd do more than try."

"You'd think."

"You're a man of few words."

"Just thinking. If you're bothering to kidnap someone whose parents have money, why take along another person to worry about? The only thing I can come up with is maybe Elsie figured that having Kathrine along would make Bertram more cooperative and more willing to deal with his parents."

"Sounds like a reasonable assumption."

"We really need to contact Bertram's parents. I'm wondering about that number that was given to us. It might be fake."

"Do you want me to call up Interpol or something like that?"

"We have no crime so Interpol isn't an option. How about the local police?"

"That can be done. Do you speak German?"

"No," Decker said. "Do you?"

"No," McAdams answered. Silence. "I know Rina's parents were Holocaust survivors. Does she speak German?"

"Her parents are Hungarian. She does speak a little German. And she doesn't mind helping me out. But interviewing police officers in a foreign language is too much for her to take on."

McAdams agreed. He took another bite of his sandwich and popped the top on a can of Perrier. "Good stuff."

"When are you leaving for New York again?" Decker asked. "Tomorrow?"

"That's the plan."

"You're renting a car?"

"Yes, boss, I know how to do that."

"And you're up for a long drive by yourself?"

McAdams smiled. "Yes, Dad, I've done it dozens of times. You didn't grow up around these parts. Los Angeles is its own island. You fly everywhere because nothing's close. Unless you have a private plane or a helicopter, everyone around here drives from one city to another. From one state to another."

"Florida is on the East Coast."

"I mean those of us from the original thirteen colonies," McAdams said. "Florida is an interloper."

"McAdams, you are such a snob."

"And I wear it proudly."

Kathrine's residential facility was located in the rolling hills of Mangrove, a town about the size of Greenbury, with its own police department. The brick two-story building was nestled between leafy trees under a blue sky intermittently whitewashed with clouds. The weather was warm, and the air was humid and perfumed with the blossoms of summer. Decker pulled into a visitor's space in an open parking lot. He had called Detective Rand from the road, and they decided on a meeting time of twelve-thirty. Since Decker had arrived forty minutes early, he pondered the question swirling in his mind: wait, or go in and risk the wrath of the local law. Nearby he had passed a town with loads of cafés and a few restaurants. For once he decided to slow himself down. He turned to McAdams. "We're a little early. Want to grab some coffee?"

"You don't want to go inside?"

"Problem is, I told the local police I'd wait for them."

"Yeah, but they don't have a long drive home facing them. Let's just look around. No harm in that."

Decker smiled. He had trained McAdams well. "We might as well introduce ourselves to Dr. Forrester. That'll eat up some time." He got out of the car. McAdams followed.

Double glass doors made up the front entrance, which was shaded by a green striped awning. Inside, they found a good-size lobby with floral couches and wood tables resting on a terrazzo floor. Toward the back was a U-shaped reception desk. Several people were behind the counter. One woman looked up and smiled. Garbed in a deep-blue uniform, she appeared to be in her early forties, with short brown hair and small brown eyes.

"May I help you?"

"We're looking for Dr. Renee Forrester?"

"To the left down the hall. Her office is on the right side."

"Thank you." No curiosity about who they were and why they were there, but Decker didn't complain. It was nice not to have to explain yourself.

Forrester's office was open. A woman, with a phone at her ear, sat behind a large desk and looked up. Decker showed her his badge, and she nodded and pointed to a couple of chairs. Her expression was weary—wrinkled brow and a frown. She was raking her hair with red painted nails.

"I hear you, Derrick. We'll work these issues out but I can't do it now. I have the police in my office as we speak." She listened patiently. "I'm fine . . . totally. No worries . . . I hear you . . . we'll handle it, no problem . . . no prob. Derrick, I have to go. I'll talk to you later. Bye." To the men: "That guy needs a cane around the neck to exit stage right. I can't tell if he's just overly loquacious or trying to jack up the bill."

"Your lawyer?" Decker said.

"Yes, he is. I called him regarding Kathrine. Obviously, he doesn't want me talking to anyone about what happened until everything is sorted out."

"We're all on the same side."

"Yes, we are," Renee said, "but I understand where he's coming from. Kathrine left on her own accord, that much I can tell you. She's a legal adult even though she has special needs, so liability isn't an issue."

"Then what's with the lawyer?"

"CYA time." The woman sighed. "Enough of me. How are the Taylors holding up?"

McAdams said, "All right, considering."

"I was planning on being there, but then I had an emergency and then Derrick said it would be a bad idea to meet them at their house. I did talk to them on the phone an hour ago. We made an appointment for them to come in tomorrow. They wanted to see her room. She didn't have a whole lot and there's not much left."

"What is left?" McAdams asked.

"Some clothes, some books, some frilly things like a blanket and a few stuffed animals. Her phone is gone. Her laptop is gone. No diary that we could find. There are some papers in her desk. Maybe you guys can get a clue. Do you want to go up there now?"

"I'd first like to see the closed-circuit tape from the day she went missing."

"*Missing* is a strong word. She left of her own free will."

"On the day she left, then," Decker clarified.

"Mangrove PD took the original disc."

That made perfect sense. "I'll talk to them about it," Decker said. "They should be here in about twenty minutes."

McAdams said, "Your CCTV is digital?"

"Yes."

"Then you must have a backup disc besides the original, right?"

"Probably."

"Could you check?" McAdams said.

Renee exhaled, then picked up the phone and dialed an extension. "Hi, it's Renee. Is Sendra around?" She waited about a minute. "Hi, Sendra. Technical question. Do we have backup discs of our CCTV system? We do." She gave a thumbs-up. "Okay, could you get it? I have some detectives in my office, and they want to take a look at Kathrine Taylor getting into the car. You have it, great! Thanks." She hung up. "She says ten minutes. Can I get you coffee or water in the meantime?"

"I'm okay, thanks." Decker looked at McAdams.

"I'm fine."

"Let me know if you change your mind." She shook her head. "I sure hope this can be resolved soon. Any luck with Bertram Lanz?"

"We're still investigating."

"What about that blood in that nurse's house?"

"Still investigating."

"Is it Bertram's?"

"I don't know. We took toothbrushes from Bertram and Kathrine for DNA purposes. Maybe I can also pick something up in her room?"

"Like I said, there's not much, but maybe you can see something that we missed." Renee stood up. "I'll walk you over to Sendra."

Decker stood up. "Thanks."

"God, what a mess." Renee shook her head. "Everyone here is a mess."

"So are the Taylors," McAdams added.

Renee continued walking and didn't respond. She kept her eyes glued to the terrazzo floor.

There was nothing on the disc to identify the car's make and model, but it wasn't a total bust. The computer tech, Sendra—a twentysomething woman with multiple piercings and multiple tattoos—printed out three images that showed the car's hubcaps. Sometimes hubcaps were as unique to the car as the badge itself. By the time Decker and McAdams climbed the steps to Kathrine's room, two people from Mangrove PD were already poking around. One of them was tall and Nordic looking with blond hair, blue eyes, a jutting chin, and a florid complexion. He introduced himself as Michael, spelled Mikael, Rand. His partner was Sergeant Amy Rosner—short and compact, with blue eyes and curly dark hair. After Decker made introductions, he asked, "Have you found anything?"

"We came here about ten minutes ago," Rand said. "Someone said you were checking out something on the computer downstairs?"

"I was looking at a copy of the disc from the CCTV that showed Kathrine leaving," Decker said. "Trying to see if I could get anything distinguishing on the car."

"And?" Rosner asked.

"Nothing on the car, but we saw parts of the hubcaps. Maybe they're associated with a specific make or model."

"Clever. What else?"

"From the disc?" Decker asked. "Nothing. Why? Did you notice something?"

"Me, no. I didn't even think about the hubcaps. What did you learn from the Taylors this morning?"

"They didn't know anything about the phone call or even much about Kathrine's life once she left home. She tried to be independent, like Bertram. There is a possibility that they ran off together with the help of Elsie Schulung, the nurse who worked at Loving Care, where Bertram lived. We found a year-old photograph of Bertram and Kathrine in Elsie's house." Decker shook his head. "Maybe Elsie thought of herself as a modern-day matchmaker."

"Why do you say that?" Rand asked.

"Well, for one thing, she had a picture of these two in her home. That says she had a relationship with them."

"Could be she was planning on kidnapping them and wanted a picture."

"Then why a year-old picture?"

"How do you know it's a year-old picture?"

"Because Kathrine's hair was very long in the picture. Her parents told me that she cut it short after Bertram left here. It wouldn't have grown back that quickly."

"Clever," Rosner said. "What about the blood you found in the nurse's house?"

"Baniff PD will do a DNA profile," Decker said. "They promised to share."

Rand said, "Well, we haven't found anything of use—no phone, no laptop, no tablet."

"Her parents told me she had a phone and an email account," Decker said. "I've already been in contact with the phone company and her server, but it'll take time to get the information."

Rosner said, "I've checked social media—Facebook, Instagram, Snapchat, and WhatsApp. Nothing."

"Bertram isn't on social media either," McAdams said. "I suspect that many residential homes don't allow it because it would expose their charges to all sorts of predators."

Rosner said, "Her two bottom desk drawers are stuffed with papers."

Decker walked over. "Anything interesting?"

She pulled out a wad of papers from the middle drawer and sifted through them. "Pencil drawings. A lot of happy faces. One after the other."

Rand said, "Her maturity was like a kid, right?"

"Yes and no," McAdams said. "Can I see some of those?"

Rosner handed her the pile, and McAdams glanced through the drawings. There was a slew of happy faces. He said, "Can I look through the drawers for a moment?"

"Knock yourself out," Rosner said.

McAdams bent down and started at the very bottom. He scanned through the papers and noticed that one pile featured mostly sad faces. Tears from the eyes and a big frown. "Huh!"

"What?" Decker asked.

McAdams pulled out another group of papers and sorted through them. "You know, most of the faces are unhappy until you get to the very top of the middle drawer. The last, what, thirty or forty pages are happy faces." He held up a finger. "You know what these are. These are mood indicators that a psychologist might give the residents to determine how they feel. If I'm right, Kathrine was very upset until forty pages ago. Which would mean that if she saw a therapist every workday, her mood abruptly changed about two months ago."

Rosner nodded. "Clever."

"We should talk to her therapist," McAdams said.

"Who won't say anything because Kathrine still could be alive," Decker said.

"I bet I can get *something* out of her."

Decker concurred. "Then go find her therapist, Tyler. I'll catch up with you."

"Sounds good." He gathered up the pages and left.

Rand said, "How'd he figure that one out?"

"I guess college wasn't wasted on him."

"Psych major?" Rand asked.

"I have no idea," Decker said. "I'm going to start to pull apart her bed."

"I'll do the closet," Rosner said. "Mike, you want to do the bathroom? Or do you want to switch?"

"I'll do the bathroom."

"Great." Rosner started checking out the built-in structure, examining the walls and drawers for hidden compartments. She worked quietly for a few minutes. Then she said, "I got it."

"Got what?" Decker had folded the sheets back and was checking the mattress for anything hidden.

"The mood faces," she said. "Your partner's got a sibling or a kid with emotional problems, right?"

Decker pulled the mattress onto the floor to examine the box spring. He looked at her and smiled. "Clever."

She smiled back. "Which one is it?"

"I said clever." Decker laughed. "Beyond that I plead the Fifth."

Opening the cooler in the trunk of the car, Decker pulled a soggy tuna sandwich from a paper bag. He immediately put it back and hunted around. There was a thin pool of cold water at the bottom. The ice packs that Rina had made with quart-size zip-up plastic bags must have leaked and turned everything wet. The sandwiches were supposed to be for the ride home. It was either soggy tuna or nothing.

McAdams was looking over his shoulder. He said, "There must be a bagel place somewhere. Bagels are ubiquitous." He consulted his phone. "Aha! There is a coffee place that sells pastries and bagels about three miles from here. Let me call and see what they have at this time of day."

"Sure." Decker rolled his shoulders. "I suppose I can use a cup of coffee anyway. The thermos is just about empty."

"Just let me dump this out in the garbage." McAdams hoisted up the cooler and looked around for a trash can. "No sense smelling up the car. I'll save the drinks."

Decker got in the driver's seat and turned on the engine and AC. He waited until McAdams was back and seat-belted in, then took off. Ten minutes later they were parked in a lot and eating in the car. It didn't take long for Decker to polish off his lunch.

"You still hungry?" McAdams said. "I am."

"I'll go for round two."

"Another coffee?"

"No, when they say a large coffee, they mean large."

McAdams went inside and emerged five minutes later with the grub. He slid into the passenger's seat and doled out the food. "Are we going to talk about the case or just stuff our faces?"

"Does it have to be either/or?"

"Kathrine left voluntarily," McAdams stated.

"And Bertram?"

"My opinion? Him too. But that doesn't mean it didn't turn into something bad. I'd feel better if you hadn't found blood in Elsie Schulung's kitchen. Any news on that?"

"Not yet." Decker took another bite of his bagel. "I keep coming back to what you said a couple of days ago—that Elsie took off before Bertram went missing. Maybe she's using Bertram and Kathrine as shields. Who would think that a woman with two dependent adults would be hiding something sinister? She's not old enough to be their mother, but she could pass them off as her sister and brother."

"Escaping with two dependent adults would slow Elsie down if she was running away from something. And all that blood makes me think that she is running away."

"No argument from me."

McAdams said, "Baniff should be looking for her. I hope they know what they're doing."

"I'll call up Jake Quay when we get home. I should have a few hours before Shabbos. I want to write up a few notes. There are a lot of tentacles, and I want to make sure we're not missing something." Decker wiped his mouth, threw the napkin into a bag, and started the car. Driving off, he said, "Are we all set with Zeke Anderson's parents?"

"Sunday at three in the afternoon."

"Has Kevin found anything else in the woods?"

McAdams checked his phone log. "He hasn't called. Let me give him a ring." A pause. "Straight to voice mail. Maybe that means he's still in the woods."

Decker said, "I forgot to tell you. We're going out to dinner with the family before we leave the city Sunday night. You're invited. But I'm warning you. It's going to be disorganized and loud with the children, their spouses, and the grandchildren."

"Yeah, how many are you up to?"

"Five. Hannah had a baby a couple of months ago."

"Wow. Amazing!"

"Yes." Then Decker said, "What's amazing? Do I look too young?"

"You don't, but Rina does." McAdams grinned. "Am I still invited even after the snide comment?"

"Yes. But now the invitation is given begrudgingly."

McAdams patted his shoulder. "Rina is meeting Gabe and his mother, correct?"

"Yep."

"Is she staying with Gabe?"

"No, Terry's at a hotel."

"And you don't know what the meeting between Gabe and Terry is all about?"

"I don't know the specifics, but I'm sure Terry wants a favor. Probably a big one. The last time we did her a favor, we ended up with Gabe for four years."

"How old was Gabe at the time?"

"Fourteen."

"How old are Terry's current children?"

"I think around eleven and five. It isn't going to happen again for us. I think Terry knows that. But Gabe is their brother. She might be hitting him up."

"Why do you think she's dumping her kids on Gabe? Maybe she just wants money."

"That request can be made with a phone call. And Gabe would give her money. He has plenty of it. I think she's escaping something and she doesn't want the kids with her. Call it a hunch."

"Is her current husband as bad as Donatti?"

"Devek? Don't know a thing about him other than his name. But Terry's *in* New York with the kids and *without* Devek. If she is running from him, it wouldn't surprise me. The girl is a doctor; brains aren't the issue. Her heart is another thing. And the heart can lead to some very poor choices."

Chapter 12

About fifteen minutes after the start of the sabbath, Decker's cell buzzed. It was Kevin Butterfield. Decker had spoken to him an hour before, regarding progress on the search for the two other missing college boys. There had been nothing to report on that front, but obviously something had changed.

"What's going on, Kev?"

"One of the uniforms just found Elsie Schulung's car. You don't need to come down, Rabbi. I'll have it towed and brought in for processing. I've got someone out here taking pictures. I'll send them to your phone when she's done."

"Where was it found?"

"About a mile and a half from the diner."

Decker's stomach dropped. "How'd we miss that?"

"According to the officer—it was Bill Jensen—the vehicle was parked behind a big clump of brush and not visible from the road. But in answer to your question, I have no answer except that we're looking at a very overgrown area."

"Of course. Did you have a chance to look it over?"

"For forensics, not yet. But Bill did a once-over check including the trunk. No bodies, so that's hopeful."

"Yes, it is." Decker gathered his thoughts. Let's keep going with a search crew and make sure we didn't miss anything else."

"I'm on it, Deck."

"Any luck with residences or businesses in the area?"

"No, not really."

"I know. It's rural. I just keep hoping."

Kevin said, "There are some trailers, but no CCTV that I could spot except for the rest stops, which so far haven't yielded anything."

"I think McAdams said something about a truck stop about two miles away?"

"I'll check it out. We'll be out there again at daybreak, canvassing the woods and knocking on doors of any structure in the vicinity. I'll call if we find anything important. If we don't, I'll call you after the sabbath."

"Do you have enough people? Between this and searching for the lost boys, we're getting stretched.

Should we ask for more people from neighboring departments?"

"I think we're okay for now," Butterfield told him. "Lucky for us that there's not much crime in town. Enjoy a little peace, Rabbi. Isn't that what you say? Shabbat shalom?"

Decker smiled. "It is indeed what we say. Shabbat shalom to you as well."

Eight o'clock Sunday morning, they hit the road for the big city. Rina said, "I'm going to try to relax a little."

"Tired?" Decker asked.

"A bit."

"Close your eyes and rest, honey."

"Thanks." She leaned back the seat, put on earbuds, and listened to music on her phone. Every so often she'd open her eyes and glance at her husband. He stared straight ahead, his thoughts unreadable. At ten, Decker's cell sprang to life through Bluetooth. It was Kevin Butterfield with the latest update. "A whole lot of nothing."

In some ways disappointing, in other ways a big relief. That meant no new bodies. Decker said, "Any details on your nothing?"

"The car is still being processed. It's Sunday and things are slower. We did find lots of crap inside—food wrappers, cans of Coke, empty drink cartons, empty water bottle, an empty jar of nuts, several boxes of raisins. Everything pointing to a trip to a convenience store."

"You can get more wholesome food at a convenience store," Decker said. "It sounds like they stopped at a convenience counter at a gas station."

"We're checking out the fuel stops in the area."

"My guess is that she drove toward the diner in her own car and had another car waiting at a designated spot."

"She swapped them out," Butterfield said. "Which means we've been looking for the wrong car." A pause. "This must have been set up a while ago. How did Elsie Schulung find Bertram in the woods? Did the two of them have a meeting place? I mean, how well could Bertram follow a map?"

"The woman who was sitting next to him on the bus said that Bertram was following the bus on a map app like Waze. Maybe Elsie had programmed something into his phone."

"That's possible," Kevin said.

Decker said, "How did Elsie get a second car? Bertram doesn't drive."

"Another person was involved?" Kevin said.

"It's beginning to look that way." Decker shook his head. "Are you sure you have enough people? I can send

McAdams back. I have to interview Zeke Anderson's parents, but he doesn't have to be there."

"I take it he's not with you in the car?"

"No, he's in the city already. But he can return to Greenbury if you need him."

"Tyler is a good cop," Butterfield said. "Life and a few gunshots have humbled him to the point of nobility. But in my frank opinion, he's better at desk work than fieldwork. Let me get a little further along. When there are calls to be made or CCTV to check out, I'll let you know. Tyler's good at that stuff. He's got a sharp eye."

"Fair enough."

"I really do like the kid. I'd appreciate it if we keep this conversation between you and me."

"Fair enough as well."

Rina told Decker to drop her off in front of the Carlyle at Seventy-Sixth and Madison. Before she could get out of the car, Gabe flagged them down. Decker slowed and Gabe got into the backseat. "Change of plans. She's on the West Side now near Columbia. Do you mind driving us?"

"Of course not."

"Thanks." Gabe got in and slumped in the backseat. He wore a white open-necked dress shirt and a pair of jeans. High-tops on his feet. "Leave it to her to change plans. She must be in trouble. Husband trouble most likely."

"Do you want me along?" Decker asked. "I have about an hour."

"No, but thanks, Peter."

"You're coming tonight?" Rina asked.

"Right. The dinner." He slapped his forehead. "Yes, Yasmine and I will be there. Mom has me totally discombobulated mentally. I can fend off a gang of armed thugs, but I can't face my mother."

Traffic was crawling on Madison but eased up as they went north. Decker turned left on Central Park North, which turned into 110th.. He went west until he hit Broadway, then turned right.

Gabe said, "It isn't much farther."

Rina said, "Why don't you let us off here? I really could use a little walk to clear my head." She turned to Gabe. "Is that all right?"

"Yeah, of course."

Decker pulled over and they both hopped out.

Gabe stuck his head in the driver's window. "I'll see you tonight, Peter. And thanks again."

"Whatever your mother wants, Gabe, you can say no," Decker told him. "You are an independent adult."

"You're right. But it's hard for me to say no to my mom." He looked at Rina. "Will you say no for me?"

"Sorry, Gabriel," Rina said. "I'm your support system but not your mouthpiece."

She opened the door to the hotel room, and her face fell as soon as she looked past Gabe and saw Rina. Terry's gold eyes wavered between disappointment and anger, but she had no choice but to be gracious and let them both in. "Hi, there." A big smile. "I didn't know you were in town, Rina."

"Peter had business. I decided to tag along."

"Not true," Gabe said. "I invited her to come. Well, that's not true either. I *asked* her to come."

Terry's cheeks pinkened. "I thought we might enjoy a little alone family time."

"Mom, she is *family*."

"Of course." Terry looked at Rina. "I apologize."

"No need, Terry. We're all friends."

"I wonder." Terry looked at Gabe. "How about a hug?"

Gabe regarded his mother. At forty-two, she was beautiful and lithe with long auburn hair that had been kissed by the sun. Her complexion was pure porcelain. If she had aged, Gabe couldn't detect it. Usually, she was mistaken as his sister. No miracle there because she had given birth to him in her teens. Even so, she looked young for her years. The passage of time had been kind to both his parents, probably because they never gave a damn about anything other than themselves. He gave a smile and a hug, and she clung on longer than she needed to. When she finally let go, her eyes were wet. The woman always did know how to turn on and off the emotional faucets.

"Looking good, Mom," Gabe granted.

"You look . . . like a man," she told him. "I still have this image in my head of you as a teenager."

"You just saw me last year in Mumbai."

"I know," Terry said. "But it was a brief encounter and I still have this idea of who you are that's out of date with reality. Sit down. Both of you."

"I'd rather stand, if you don't mind." Gabe looked around the hotel suite. It was done up with brown silk walls, a red couch, black lacquer chairs, and Asian vases with silk flowers spilling out. A wall of mirror framed by gold and some minimalist art hung on the walls. There was a small kitchenette and a view of the Hudson's whirling gray-green waters. Soft music was playing from a Bose radio system. It was quiet, considering that her children were eleven and five. They were nowhere to be seen. "Where are Juleen and Sanjay?"

"In the bedroom watching TV."

"I want to say hi."

"I thought I could talk to you first while they were occupied. Once they see you, it'll be like trying to put toothpaste back in the tube."

Gabe shrugged. "What's up?"

Terry looked at Rina and then back at her son. "I don't know where to begin."

A moment later a door opened and a little boy ran out, an ear-to-ear smile on his face. Sanjay was dark complexioned with big brown eyes and black hair. He was built thick and short and was the image of his father. He ran to Gabe and threw his pudgy arms around his knees. Gabe picked him up under his shoulders and planted a kiss on his forehead. "How's my boy?"

"Are you staying?"

"For a little bit." He turned and faced his sister. Juleen's complexion was halfway between his mother's and Devek's skin tones. She was a delicate little thing, thin and waifish, with dark hair and eyes a shade darker than gold. She seemed aloof and reserved, standing near the doorway. Gabe said, "You've grown."

Juleen gave him an appraising look. "You haven't."

"Ha ha and ha." Gabe walked over to her and gave her a peck on her forehead. "How have you been, beautiful?"

"Fine." A glance at Rina. "And this is your other mother?"

Terry winced. Rina said, "Foster mother. It's nice to meet you, Juleen." She offered her hand and the girl took it.

"Gabe speaks highly of you."

A pointed comment, to be sure. Rina said, "The feeling is mutual. He often talks about Sanjay and you. He misses you very much."

"Perhaps."

"Not fair, girl," Gabe said.

She returned the comment with a sad smile. Then her eyes welled up. Gabe knew there were problems in the marriage, but he felt he was witnessing a tipping point. His heart bled for his sister. "We'll talk later."

"Perhaps."

Sanjay said, "Can you play Firefox with me?"

His favorite video game. "Sure, but first I have to talk to Mom."

"Why?"

"Sanjay," Terry said. "Go back to the bedroom and finish your TV show."

"Why?"

"Because I said so!" Terry was kneading her hands.

Juleen took his hand. "Let's go, Sanjay. We'll have time with our elusive brother later."

"Thank you, Juleen," Terry said.

"Of course."

After the two children went back into the bedroom, Gabe said, "Where's your husband? Or is he the reason you want to *talk* to me."

Rina said, "Gabriel, let her get her story out, okay? I want to hear what she has to say."

"I'm just helping her find a starting place."

"No, you're not. You're being sarcastic."

Gabe smiled. "A little."

"Thanks for the help, Rina," Terry said. "You and the lieutenant have always been so kind." She lowered her head as tears fell down her cheek. "I'm sorry."

"No apologies necessary," Rina said. "Did you leave your husband, Terry?"

"Of course she did." Gabe looked at his mother. "Did he beat you as well?"

"Gabe, stop!" Rina called out.

"Just stating fact."

Terry snapped. "Okay, Gabriel, you win. I've made lousy choices in men. Now, do you want to hear me out, or do you just want to rub my nose in my idiocy? Which, by the way, you don't have to do because no one feels as idiotic as I do."

"Spare me your righteous indignation."

"It's not for me." Terry's eyes overflowed with tears. "I asked you here because of the children."

"Such a caring mom," Gabe muttered.

"But you're not bitter," Rina told him. "Stop sniping at her."

"She just makes it too easy," Gabe said.

"You're just like your father!" Terry shot back.

"You mean the one who's been supporting me the last decade?"

"Stop it, both of you." Rina sighed. "Terry, honey, you know how angry he feels. He's never been subtle. You must have expected this when you asked him to come."

"You're right." A pause. "And he has every right to be angry. I deserted him. But I was truly afraid. He beat me up!"

"I know, I was there, remember?" Gabe sighed. "I don't mean to be so harsh . . . well, maybe I do mean . . . just a little." He sat in an armchair with black lacquer arms. The cushion was rock hard.

Rina looked at Terry. "Go on."

Terry looked at her son. "You know as well as I do, I had to get away from Chris. He would have *killed* me. I was pregnant with another man's child!"

"He wouldn't have killed you. He would have killed Devek, but not you."

"We're Catholic. I would've had the baby. Then he would have made me give her up for adoption. I wanted my baby. At least I knew you were in good hands."

She wiped her eyes. "You tell me. What should I have done?"

Gabe said nothing. Terry was breathing hard. "Devek isn't Chris. When I met him here—in America—he was kind and sympathetic. He was courtly and gentle and soft-spoken. He's not a cruel man, but he is weak. And like all weak people, when he's backed into a corner, he turns ugly. Self-preservation and all that."

Gabe closed his eyes and opened them. "What happened?"

"I'll try to keep it short. When I moved with him to India, everything was fine up until maybe four years ago." Tears continued to run down her cheeks. "It was like a light switch, Gabriel. He turned controlling and demanding. Not unusual in his entitled family. But it was distressing because he had been very loving. Suddenly he becomes this harsh taskmaster especially with the children. You've seen Juleen. Do you think she behaves like a normal eleven-year-old?"

Gabe's face hardened. "He isn't hurting her, is he?"

"No, no, no," Terry said. "Nothing physical. He's just so *stern*. She can't move without his permission. I've tried to talk to him, but something happened with the way he sees her now that she's on the verge of puberty. His family is old-fashioned. Lots of Indian fathers are obsessed with virginity. I'm worried that he's thinking about an arranged marriage for her."

"You can't allow that," Gabe said.

"Why do you think I'm here?"

There was silence. Rina said, "Do you know what brought on the change of personality?"

Terry sighed. "Devek had a big gambling problem. Apparently, he's always had a problem. His family knew it but I didn't. He was able to abstain here in America. The casinos weren't at his fingertips in downtown Manhattan. He was a well-respected man here, and he wanted to make a good impression on everyone. He was able to stop for a while. Then, four years ago, he got a job in Goa as head of Cardiology in a very prestigious hospital. Goa is about three hundred miles from where we were living. He used to leave Sunday night by train and come back on Friday."

"That couldn't be easy on either of you," Rina said.

"It was *horrible*," Terry said. "It was hard on me, but honestly, it was worse for him. He was in a pressure cooker. Family pressure, professional pressure from the hospital, pressure from the community. He had so much responsibility to so many people. I think he cracked."

"Why didn't you move to Goa with him?" Gabe asked.

"I offered a hundred times," Terry said. "He didn't want us to move. He said it would destabilize the family. I thought it was really odd but I didn't argue." She rolled her eyes. "Then I found out the real reason. Goa is the gambling center of India. I caught on when the calls started coming from the bank."

Gabe got up and started pacing. "Are you broke?"

"Worse than broke. He's in heavy debt. Really heavy debt. In the past his family had bailed him out." She shook her head. "Not this time. He swears to me he won't do it again. But he's broken his promises in the past. And his swearing won't do anything about the money he owes."

"And you're *sure* that his family won't help him out?" Rina asked.

"Positive. They've had it. *I've* had it." Another exhale. "In order to pay off his debts, he's borrowed *some* of it from a prominent family. But he still owes plenty to some very unscrupulous people. It's a total mess. I know that Devek is worried about his safety foremost, but also about our children. We're all at risk."

"I noticed you didn't say he's worried about your safety, Terry," Rina said.

"Rina, we are *done*," Terry said. "I also found out that he's been keeping a woman there—in Goa. He confessed to the affair, assured me it's over and has begged my forgiveness. He's also promised to give up gambling for good. But I simply don't have any charity left in me." Tears continued to fall. "Still, I don't want anything bad to happen to him."

"Then why don't you all move to America?" Gabe said.

"Because Devek cannot move out of India until he's paid back the money."

"Why can't he pay back money if he lives here?"

"It'll look like he's running away. They'll hunt him down."

"Then *you* move."

"Devek will not allow me to move to America with the children."

"Who cares what he wants? Divorce the guy and come back here."

"That's exactly what I'm doing, Gabe. Except that I'm not supposed to leave the country with the kids until custody is decided."

"You fled without his permission."

"Of course I did. He's going to fight me for full custody, and he'll win. His family has the money to battle this out. His father won't pay off Devek's debts but he's not going to let his grandchildren leave the country. And despite what the law says, the courts are biased."

The room turned silent. Rina appraised the woman. "What else, Terry. I feel like you're holding back on us."

Terry bit her fingernail. "It's not just custody, it's because of Juleen. Normally when a couple gets married in Hindu tradition, it's the bride that gives a dowry. We have no money. Devek is considering an arranged marriage where Juleen won't need a dowry."

"Shit!" Gabe said. "You are *kidding* me!"

"I wish I was."

"She's eleven! Isn't that against the *law*?"

"Of course it is. Marriage at that age is forbidden, but not betrothal. And please keep your voice down."

"Does Juleen even know about that?"

"Sort of."

"You didn't agree to this, did you?"

"Why do you think I'm here? I came here to protect her and to clear my mind. I'm trying to figure out a game plan."

No one spoke. Then Rina said, "You think that's why he's been so strict with her?"

She nodded. "With her father's consent, Juleen can marry as young as sixteen. I know he's already spoken to a few older men who are widowed. Not bad men. I know one of them. He's very wealthy. In exchange for Juleen, he would help pay off *some* of Devek's debts.

He's a nice man, but he's almost sixty. I can't do that to my daughter."

Gabe said, "Does she *know* about this?"

"Please lower your voice!" Terry said. "Yes, she knows. No marriage will take place unless she complies."

"She hasn't *agreed* to this, has she?"

"It's not like America, Gabriel. Kids do not defy their parents. That's why I'm here." Terry wiped her eyes. "I don't know what to do."

"Why Juleen?" Rina asked. "I'm sure there are lots of young and beautiful girls willing to marry rich old men."

"The man I know . . . he is a family friend. I truly think he wants to help. But she's a child. She deserves the right to make up her own mind. But that's a very American way of thinking. Devek, of course, probably wants an agreement signed yesterday. It is very shameful to owe that much money."

"How much are we talking about?" Gabe said. "A hundred thousand?"

"More." Terry shook her head. "Much more."

"A million?"

"Maybe even more than that."

"How did his debts get so out of control?" Rina asked.

"He kept on using his family credit. He's an idiot! And I'm an idiot for having an affair with him twelve years ago. God, what on earth was I thinking?"

Gabe said, "Do you want me to ask Dad for the money?"

"He hates me."

"He doesn't hate you. He's mad at you, but I know he still has feelings for you, Mom."

"You know what taking money from Chris would mean?"

"It would mean you'd be in his debt forever. Better you than Juleen."

"I agree."

"Then what's the problem?"

"Even if Devek were to become debt free, there is no guarantee he won't gamble in the future. Then we'd all be in the same situation. I need to remain here where the children will be acquisitional citizens. I need a lawyer. I have to get the paperwork done. But even with all that, there's nothing to prevent him from kidnapping the children and taking them back to India."

"You're their mother," Gabe said.

"Yes, but a case could be made in India that I kidnapped the children and brought them here."

Rina said, "Does Devek even know where you are?"

"I'm sure he knows that I'm in America. He's probably figured out that I'm in New York because Gabe's here. And yes, he will come after them once he realizes I'm not coming back. I need the children safe and hidden, so I can figure out my next move."

No one spoke.

"I know. I've gotten myself into another real mess."

Gabe said, "Mom, I love you. I truly do. But I can't take them. I've got a visible career, and I can't ask that of Yasmine. Furthermore, I can't protect them."

"I know."

"Rina can't take them either. She's already done enough." When Rina started to speak, Gabe said, "No, you will not take them, Rina! Enough is enough!"

Terry said, "Then what do you suggest I do?"

Rina said, "Let me ask Peter."

"No!" Gabe insisted. "We're not having a repeat of what happened over a decade ago."

"I agree, Gabe. When I said let me ask Peter, I mean if he had any advice." Rina looked at Terry. "As much as we love Gabe and don't resent what you and Chris did, both Peter and I are too old to foster the children. And it's not the same situation as it was with Gabe. There wasn't a custody battle."

Terry's face drooped. "You're right. Totally right."

"Let me ask Peter what he thinks should be done."

"What do I do with the children in the meantime?" Terry said. "If Devek finds me, he will take them and I will never see them again."

Silence.

"I'm not asking forever, Rina," Terry pleaded. "Just please take them until I can sort this out legally."

Gabe felt his anger rise. "You know that's not going to happen! Even if she agreed, I wouldn't let her."

"Would you rather Juleen go back to India and be subjected to an arranged marriage?"

"I can't help you every time *you fuck up!*"

"Gabe, I appreciate you coming to my defense, but let's try to dial it down," Rina said. "Terry, can you lie low for a bit? I'll ask Peter if there are options for you. But this will take time."

"And what do I do if he finds me?"

"Stop putting her in this position," Gabe said. "It's so unfair to ask her."

"He's right, Terry," Rina said. "We can't take the children. Even if we did, we can't protect them. When we took Gabe, no one was threatening to kidnap him."

"Quite the opposite—you both were very happy to let me be someone else's responsibility."

"Was that really necessary?" Terry shot back.

"Apparently yes, 'cause you're doing the same thing over again."

Rina said, "I hate to say this, Terry, but . . . you're missing an obvious person."

"She means Chris," Gabe said.

"No, no, no, no." Terry looked horrified. "He'll kill them."

"He wouldn't kill them," Gabe said.

"He'll sleep with Juleen just for spite. He'll turn her into a whore."

Gabe said, "Yeah, that could happen." A pause. "*I'm kidding.*"

Rina said, "He certainly could protect them. Devek wouldn't stand a chance against Chris."

"I'm not going to be anyone's punching bag." Terry had turned angry. "You two may have a relationship with him, but I don't."

"It's a valid point, Terry," Rina said. "It was just a thought."

"I know that you're only trying to help, Rina. And I know you can't clean up my messes. Peter and you have been my heroes. It's wrong for me to expect more and ask Gabe for help, but I don't know where to turn."

Rina said, "So where do you go from here, Terry?"

"For one thing, I'm getting out of New York. It's a big city with lots of places to hide, but Devek knows the city because he's lived here. I'll go back to Los Angeles. It's also a big city, but I know it and he doesn't."

"Do you need money?" Gabe said.

"I'll be okay."

"Stop it, Mom. I do want to help, but I can't take the kids." Silence. Gabe said, "Please let me do something for you. I have money of my own. You wouldn't even be taking Dad's money."

Terry's eyes began to water. "I'll pay you back as soon as I find work. I'm still a licensed physician—"

"Stop it, Mom," Gabe said. "How much? Five grand? Ten grand?"

"Just make out the check for whatever you want to give me." Terry looked down. "I guess I'll start packing, then. I'll let you know where I am once I settle in the West Coast."

"How about if I take the kids for ice cream and a trip to the toy store while you start making arrangements?"

"Gabriel, I don't know if I'm being watched. I don't want the kids out of my sight."

"Can I order up room service?"

"As long as no one comes inside the room."

"Okay." Gabe turned to his foster mother. "Thanks, Rina. You're always helpful."

"It's fine, honey. And Terry, I will ask Peter for some advice if you want it."

"No thank you, Rina. I'll manage. Gabriel is right. You two have done enough."

Rina said, "Do you really think that you're in danger?"

"Not from Devek. He wouldn't hurt his own kids." Terry sighed. "I don't know much about the men he borrowed from. While I don't think they'd hunt me down here in the States, I do know that they're bad people."

"Maybe you should hire a bodyguard."

"It's a thought, Mom," Gabe said.

"It's a thought and a good one." She nodded. "Let me get to L.A. first and then we'll talk strategy."

"Maybe Peter can recommend something," Rina said. "He knows a bit about Los Angeles."

Terry smiled. "Those were the days." A sigh. "Man, I was really stupid."

"You were young and naive."

"That, too."

Rina stood up. "Good luck, Terry. I hope this all works out."

"Thank you."

"I'll walk you out, Rina. As a matter of fact"—Gabe turned to his mother—"tell the kids I went to buy them a surprise. I'll be back in an hour."

"Will you *really* be back?"

"Of course, Mom." Gabe shrugged. "I love my *siblings.*"

The barb thrown Terry's way was processed with more sadness than anger.

Chapter 13

In their hearts, the Andersons had known for years that Zeke wasn't coming back. Even so, finality, whenever it knocked, still brought a current of shock. Keith Anderson was in his fifties. He was average height and held a little extra weight around the middle. His eyes were brown, his gray hair was thick and unruly, and his silver beard was little more than stubble. He wore an open-necked white dress shirt and jeans with sandals on his feet. Mary Anderson was petite, and her sloped shoulders seemed to further decrease her diminutive size. Blond hair from a bottle framed a face that held sad brown eyes and a downward mouth. She was painfully thin, with veined, trembling hands. She wore a short-sleeved dark green dress that hung on her bony frame.

The couple invited the detectives into their home in Brooklyn.

It was a generous apartment with a view of the East River. The furnishings were modest, and scattered throughout the shelves were lots of framed pictures of a boy and a girl. The girl had turned into a woman with kids of her own. The boy stopped at twenty. Decker and McAdams were shown a seat on a cream-colored couch. Keith sat opposite in a leather chair, feet up on an ottoman. On the coffee table was a plate of cookies and several bottles of water.

Mary was still standing. "Coffee anyone?" When the answer wasn't immediate, she announced that she was having some, so it was no trouble.

Decker said, "I'm fine with water, Mrs. Anderson, thank you."

McAdams said, "I'll take coffee."

A fleeting smile. "There's an honest man." She disappeared.

Keith fiddled with his hands, eyes on his lap. He took a pen from his pocket and clicked it several times. Then he stowed it back. He remained silent.

Decker said, "I'm so sorry for your loss."

"He was lost to us years ago," Keith mumbled, eyes on the floor. "You would think that knowing would be better." Eyes upward. "It's not better, it's not worse. It's all hell."

"I'm so sorry." Decker took a water bottle and opened it.

"Why are you here? Surely your sympathies could have been conveyed by phone."

"I'd rather do this face-to-face," Decker said. "Also, we'd like to ask you some questions about Zeke. Get to know him."

"You think you can solve this after sitting on your hands for ten years?"

Decker said, "We now have Zeke, and that's a big deal."

"Meaning he was murdered."

"Meaning he didn't die of natural causes."

"Then what else is there, if it's not murder?"

"An accident. I'm not saying it was an accident. We just don't know yet."

"He was buried."

"The two other boys could have done that if there had been an accident."

Keith stared at him. "You think those boys are *alive*?"

"We don't know. But since we haven't found their bodies, we keep an open mind."

"Are you looking for more bodies?"

"Yes. We're actively looking." A pause. Decker said, "Do you keep in touch with the other missing boys' parents?"

"Not anymore. Both families moved away from the East Coast." Eyes redirected to his lap. "In the beginning we'd call, ask if they'd heard anything recent. After a while, we stopped calling."

McAdams nodded. "You called them."

"Yes."

"Did they ever call you?"

"Occasionally," Keith said. "The other parents knew each other. We were the odd ones out. Then you figure what difference does it make anyway?"

Mary came back with four cups of coffee. Keith said, "They asked if we kept in contact with the Velasquezes and the McCraes."

"Not really." Mary distributed the cups. "In the beginning yes, but as time went on what we had in common was not a foundation for a friendship. They moved away about six years ago. Did Keith tell you that?"

"He did," Decker answered. "Thanks for the coffee."

"Just in case." Mary sat down on the leather ottoman next to her husband's feet. "Have you found the remains of the other boys?"

"They're still searching," Keith said. "The detectives are entertaining the thought that the other two might still be alive."

Decker said, "Until we find their bodies, anything is possible."

"What do you really think?"

"More than likely, they are deceased as well."

"Then why can't you find them?" Keith said.

Mary said, "Be nice, darling."

"Why?"

"Because they are trying to help." When Keith just looked down, Mary said, "It's a legitimate question. Why can't you find them? And why didn't you find our son sooner?"

McAdams said, "The area is heavily wooded. It's easy to overlook something because the terrain is so similar. I'm not making excuses. Just telling you what's going on."

Decker said, "There could be a dozen reasons, Mrs. Anderson. And incompetence could be one of them. I am sorry about your loss and very sorry it's taken this long to find your son. But now that he's come to our attention, we will work the case as hard as we can."

"And you think you'll solve it?"

"We're hoping."

"How?"

"There's no set answer to that. I've worked hundreds of homicide cases and quite a few cold cases. I know what I'm doing."

No one spoke.

"I'd like to ask you a few questions."

"He was a good boy," Mary said. "Idealistic. Passionate. He wanted to join the Peace Corps, for God's sake."

"I'm sure he had his heart in the right place," McAdams said. "But college is weird. Sometimes things happen. What do you know about his friends there?"

Keith said, "He didn't talk about his friends; he talked about ideas."

"How about his roommate, Jackson Carlson?"

"You mean Jack?" Mary asked.

"Yes, Jack."

"We met him once. We were going, he was coming. It was a two-minute conversation."

Keith said, "After Zeke went missing, a lot of attention was focused on Jack. He was supposed to go camping with the boys. I thought he was cleared."

"He was," Decker said. "He was with his folks at Parents' Weekend."

"Oh, yes, that's right. So why are you asking about him?"

"Just getting a feel for his friends."

Mary said, "The truth is, when we asked about friends . . . or more directly, girlfriends . . . Zeke said that wasn't his focus. We only know about his social life from what was dug up by the two private eyes we hired."

Decker sat up. "Would you have their reports?"

"Of course we do," Mary said. "It's in our over-bloated files that take up almost all our storage bin downstairs."

"You have a trove of information," McAdams said. "Probably more than we do. Mind if we take a look?"

"Well, that's a sad comment on your competence." Keith looked McAdams up and down. "Maybe not you. You look fresh behind the ears. Probably weren't there when it all happened."

"I came to Greenbury PD five years ago. Detective Decker arrived a year later." McAdams shrugged. "Together, we've got a good track record."

"We'll look at this case from a fresh perspective," Decker said. "Your files will be very helpful."

"You'll never go through everything we have in one day."

"I heard that New York City has a few hotels," Mc-Adams said.

The remark brought a fleeting smile to Mary's face. "Come on, I'll take you down to the basement." She opened the front door, led him into the hallway, and pressed the elevator button. "Tell me about yourself. Did you always want to be a cop?"

"No, but once I discovered what being a cop was, I was hooked."

"I'm betting your mother wanted you to be a lawyer or doctor."

"You win the wager."

The elevator dinged and they were gone. Decker was left alone with Keith. The man had trouble making eye contact.

Keith said, "I didn't know anything about his college friends."

"What did the PIs find out about his social life? Friends are usually the first thing they look into."

"I don't remember everything. The reports said that Zeke spent a lot of time working out."

"You mean working out—as in a gym?"

"Yes. That's where he met Bennett McCrae. They were workout buddies."

"How about Max Velasquez?" Decker asked. "Where did he meet him?"

"I think through Bennett. Apparently, Bennett was a force of nature. An opinion on everything."

"Do you think he got Zeke into trouble?"

"How should I know? I never met the boy."

"The boys told people that they were going camping for the weekend. Did Zeke like to camp?"

"We went camping when he and his sister were kids."

"Often?"

"Once a year."

"Then Zeke would be pretty self-sufficient?"

"I wouldn't say we had survival skills, but we knew how to pitch a tent." Keith thought about the question. "It wasn't something foreign to him, if that's what you're asking."

"Okay," Decker replied. "Mid-October can be cold in the woods, but if they were experienced campers, maybe it makes sense."

"I wouldn't say experienced, but he wasn't a novice."

"Okay." Decker redirected his questions. "Did Zeke work when he was in high school?"

"Why do you ask?"

"Kids need money. I'm wondering how Zeke got his pocket change."

"He had a job in the athletic department," Keith told him. "He'd do whatever the coaches asked him to do. Tutoring some of the players who needed a little extra help. Sometimes he led warm-up sessions for the JV teams. When he asked for money, we'd give him some. His requests were always reasonable. But he worked because he liked the feeling of being independent."

"Was this high school or college?" Decker asked.

"College," Anderson said. "In high school, he did some typical summer jobs. Nothing out of the ordinary."

"What kind of friends did Zeke have in high school?"

"Mary would know more than me."

"Nice kids?"

"I liked some better than others. He was buddies with a kid named Leo Novis. He's now a lawyer. Moved out of state."

Decker took out his notepad. "Anyone else that you remember?"

"Let's see. Leo and . . . Josh something."

"Girlfriends?"

"A few dates here and there. Mary would know better. Zeke wasn't interested in being tied down. He wanted to travel the world." At that moment, Mary walked back into the apartment. "He's asking if Zeke had a girlfriend."

"In college? I wouldn't know."

"High school, Mary."

Mary said, "He went out with the Kelton girl for about six months."

Decker said, "What's her first name?"

"Sally. Last I heard she married and moved out of state."

"Where are her parents?"

"Probably around. Why do you ask?"

"And what was the last name of his friend Josh?"

"Oh wow, this is memory lane. Josh Freed something."

"Freelander," Keith said.

"Yes, you're right," Mary said. "Freelander."

"And where is he?" Decker said.

"I have no idea." Mary shrugged. "When Zeke came home from college, he didn't hook up with his old friends."

"He outgrew them."

Mary's eyes watered up. "He was so excited about seeing the world, helping to make the globe a better place." A pause. "Like I told you, he wanted to join the Peace Corps."

Decker nodded. "He sounds like the kind of son every parent would want." A pause. "I hate to ask you this, but had Zeke ever been in trouble?"

Mary said, "Every kid gets into trouble."

Keith said, "He means trouble with the law. No. Never."

"Do you know if he took drugs?"

Mary sighed. "We found pot in his bedroom in his junior year of high school. A very small amount."

Keith said, "He said he smoked when he was nervous—to calm him down before a big test. I didn't see the harm in that. My main concern was not the smoking, it was where he was getting the drug. I didn't want him to associate with dubious people."

"And?"

"He said he bought it from friends. Now it's a different world. Who cares about pot?"

Some people do, Decker thought.

"He didn't smoke all the time," Mary added. "Just occasionally. Which made sense with the small amount we found. We didn't see the necessity of making a big deal out of it."

Decker said, "And that's the only drug he ever admitted to using?"

"That's the only drug he did use." Keith turned angry. "What difference does it make what he took? He's the victim here."

"Of course, he's the victim," Decker said. "But just like you, I want to make sure he didn't associate with dubious people."

Mary said, "He didn't."

You knew nothing about his college friends, so how do you know who he hung out with? Out loud he said, "I'm sure you're right. He's your son. You know him better than anyone else."

Keith said, "Besides, what happened to our boy didn't happen here."

"Absolutely."

"Go talk to people at the colleges. He was there, not here."

"Of course," Decker said. "You've been gracious. Again, I'm so sorry."

Mary said, "You said you've worked hundreds of homicides. Is Greenbury rife with crime?"

"I was with Los Angeles PD for over twenty-five years."

"Ah, that explains it. And you were a homicide detective?"

"I retired as a lieutenant actually. I ran the detective squad. When I hung up my badge in L.A., I didn't want to work in a busy city but I still wanted to keep my foot in the door. Hence Greenbury."

"So how are you going to solve this?" Keith wanted to know.

"Patience and doggedness. But unlike L.A., where I had stacks of incidents, I can make this one of my top priorities."

"What other priorities do you have, if I may ask?" Mary said.

"We have a missing person . . . two actually. We're trying to locate them just to make sure they're all right."

"And?"

"No luck. But they may have left on their own accord. Anyway, Detective McAdams and I are now concentrating on that case and Zeke's case. It's more than enough to keep us both busy." Decker paused. "This may sound odd, but do you know if Zeke owned a gun?"

"A *gun*?" Mary was aghast. "He was *shot*?"

"His hand was shattered."

"If *his* hand was shattered, why would you *assume* that Zeke had a gun?" Keith was angry. "No, he didn't have a gun. He *hated* guns."

"He was philosophically opposed to guns," Mary said.

"Okay," Decker said. "Now I know. When I interview the other parents, I'm going to ask them the same question."

"Are you going to interview the other parents?" Mary asked.

"Of course. Now that we found Zeke, I have to do that."

"You think a bullet shattered his hand?" Keith asked.

"We didn't find a firearm or casings when we found Zeke. Someone could have used a revolver that doesn't eject the casings. Or maybe the injury wasn't caused by a bullet. We're keeping all options open. That's why I asked about a gun."

"He didn't own a gun," Mary said.

"Okay, that's fine." Decker got up. "I'd like to join Detective McAdams and to go through your files." He took a couple of bottles of water. "We may be there for a while."

"The light isn't very good," Mary said. "You're welcome to work here. We have an office in the back."

"We wouldn't want to intrude."

"It really would be better than explaining to the super what you're doing down there.

Keith stood up. "Mary, set them up in the back room. I'll go down and fetch the boxes."

"And you're sure it's all right if we work here?" Decker asked.

"It's more than all right." Mary wiped her tears from her cheeks. "At last, someone is looking into my baby's death. At last something's being *done*."

Choosing a coffee shop close to his condo in the Upper West Side, Rina didn't have to look at her watch to know the time. Punctuality was Gabe's forte. If he said two o'clock, Rina could be sure that the church clock would peal out two bells.

"Thanks for meeting up with me," he said. "I know you must be anxious to see the grandchildren."

"I'd be lying if I said no." A smile. "How'd it go with your mother once I left?"

"Once business was out of the way, it was fine. I actually remembered why I liked her. Mom can be a lot of fun. What can I get you?"

"Cappuccino is fine."

"I'll be right back." It took around five minutes, but he was back with coffee and a muffin and her cappuccino. He lowered his head and blew out air. "It was nice. Seeing her was nice."

"Good to hear."

"I know she was in a bad way when she abandoned me. But she could have reached out more. I'm sure that Devek didn't want her to have contact with me. I know he doesn't like me."

"How do you know that?"

"Once he walked in when we were Facetiming. He told her to get off, that he needed her right now. He sounded angry. She told him she'd be off in a minute. She sounded weary—like it wasn't the first time he was angry with her." A pause. "She sure can pick them."

"Poor woman."

"Yeah, a victim of her own poor judgment. Anyway, with Devek gone, I guess she's more comfortable with me. Do you want some of my muffin? It's kosher."

"I know. I saw the certificate. This is fine for now." She took a sip. "Delicious."

"Yeah, they make good coffee." He looked at Rina. "We lost over ten years, Mom and me. I grew up into an adult, and she missed it all."

"She did, Gabe, but from what you've told me, she always treated you as an adult."

"True." He nodded. "I suppose that's why our relationship is pretty much where we left off. I do feel bad for her. I hate to see her in distress. First with Dad, then with that jerk. I just can't help her now."

"It is unreasonable for her to expect you to help her."

"I still feel bad. I would hate for anything to happen to her or my siblings. Do you think she's exaggerating?"

"I don't know. When is she moving back to Los Angeles?"

"I think as soon as she can make arrangements to get out of here. I hope we can spend some catch-up time together in the future. I go to Los Angeles pretty often."

"Gabriel, if what she is saying has any truth, be careful you're not being watched."

"I know. I'm cautious to the point of paranoia. I did learn a few tricks from Chris."

"Yes, I know. But you're only one person, and who knows what her husband is up to. And tell Yasmine to be careful as well."

"I will. She's studying all the time, so it's easier for her to live on campus."

"You two don't live together?"

"No. Her parents would never approve. She'll spend the night occasionally, but I'll tell her not to come over to my place until this thing with my mom is resolved." Gabe wolfed down the muffin. "I've got to teach a master class in about twenty minutes. Thanks so much for coming and meeting up with me. You and Peter are always there when I need you most. Don't think I'm not aware of that."

"You're welcome. We'll see you tonight?"

"If I don't get kidnapped, yes."

"Don't joke, Gabe."

"Who's joking?"

Chapter 14

Making the phone call outside the apartment, away from prying ears, Decker called Leo Novis, Joshua Freelander, and Sally née Kelton now Goldberg. The conversations lasted five to ten minutes each and were not very illuminating. He went back up to fetch McAdams, who had made himself a pop-up office in the Anderson study.

Decker said, "Let's go for a cup of coffee."

McAdams rubbed his eyes. "Good idea."

They found Mary in the kitchen, standing over the marble counter, slicing vegetables for a salad on a plastic cutting board. Decker said, "We'll be back in about a half hour."

"Where are you going?" she asked.

"Just out for coffee."

"I can make you coffee."

"I need to stretch my legs," McAdams said. "Thanks all the same."

"You don't want me to hear." She put down the knife and looked them in the eye. "Nothing you can tell me is worse than that initial phone call telling me Zeke was missing."

"There's nothing to tell," Decker said. "If I find anything new, you'll be the first to know. I really do need a bit of fresh air."

"I suppose I'll accept that. I have no choice." She went over to a wall and took a key off of a rack. "Keep this. You're free to come in anytime and look at our notes. I'll give you the alarm code."

Decker said, "Thank you for your trust, but we'll be back in about a half hour. Will you be home?" When she nodded, he handed her the key. "We'll ring in."

She closed her hand around the key. "You will keep going with this, right?"

"We will." Decker smiled. "See you in a bit."

As they rode the elevator, McAdams said, "That's weird, handing over the key."

"It creates an intimacy. The more connected I feel to them, the more I'll want to solve the case. What she doesn't realize is I always feel connected. I take these things very personally."

"They gave up at some point," McAdams said. "Otherwise why relegate the files to the basement?"

"I agree." They walked several blocks until Decker saw an espresso machine through a glass door in a storefront. "This okay?"

"Fine."

They sat at one of the four tables and ordered two coffees. Decker said, "By the accounts of his former friends, Zeke seemed like a very nice kid. If he was a big doper, they didn't know about it. If he was a dealer, they didn't know about it. If he had any weird preoccupations with the occult or the dangerous, they didn't know about it."

"Okay. Nothing in high school. But like I said, in college kids change. They experiment—drugs, alcohol, and sex."

"Yeah, the triad." Decker paused. "The only thing I found out is that he *might* have been gay."

"Hence no college girls."

"Or sex just wasn't his thing," Decker said. "The girl he dated in high school, Sally Kelton, told me he was respectful, maybe a little too respectful. Her words, not mine. But nothing she could pinpoint. He just was a solid kid—idealistic and excited to be out in the world. Right now, I'm baffled as to a motive for a murder."

"If it was a murder."

"Why? What did you find out?"

"I only got through one PI." McAdams took out his notebook. "Selwin Barnaby. He was on the case for two months. He started with the college, naturally, since that's where Zeke disappeared. Barnaby spoke to people he knew there. He interviewed Jack Carlson."

"And?"

"Barnaby's report indicated that Zeke and Jack had different interests. Jack liked to party, Zeke was a perennial cause person: global warming—now it's called climate change—the homeless, third world poverty, third world sickness, police brutality, racism, sexism, elitism . . . lots of isms."

"Idealistic." Decker took a sip of coffee. "Nothing wrong with that. His parents said he most certainly would not own a gun."

"So, the gun—which may or may not exist—didn't belong to him."

"Something blew a hole in his chest." Decker thought a moment. "Zeke was really keen on working out. That's kind of a narcissistic thing—perfecting your body."

"Yeah, it fits more with what the PI learned about Bennett McCrae."

"Did he work for the McCraes?"

"No, but in investigating Zeke, he looked into Bennett, who seemed to be quite the party guy," McAdams said. "He and Jack knew each other well because they went to the same bashes. Bennett came alive with people. He was the more usual college guy—he drank, he smoked, he hooked up."

"Was he known to camp out a lot?"

"Bennett? No idea. But it seems to me that it wasn't a natural fit for his busy social life. The PI didn't say a whole lot about Max Velasquez. He didn't have many friends, he was really shy, he didn't date. Most of his classmates said he was kind of nerdy—which must mean real nerdy because most of his classmates were probably on the spectrum."

"Tut, tut." Decker smiled. "Isn't that being a bit . . . mathist?"

McAdams smiled back. "Stereotypes grow up for a reason. I'd be your typical aggressive asshole attorney if I practiced law. Instead I'm your typical aggressive asshole cop."

"I'm a cop," Decker said. "I am not an asshole."

"Depends who you ask."

"Low blow."

McAdams smiled. "I was referring to felons, not colleagues."

"Most of my felons and I got along. We all knew where we stood. Anyway, is there anything in the notes to suggest what *might* have gotten Zeke in trouble?"

"No." McAdams finished his coffee. "I'm hungry. You want a pastry? I think the place might be kosher."

"Why would you say that?"

"There's a certificate in the corner saying it's kosher." Decker laughed and then McAdams said, "There are sandwiches. How about mozzarella, tomato, and basil on a French roll."

"Sure."

McAdams placed the order and came back to the table. "From my reading, if anyone would be involved in funny business, it would be Bennett."

Decker said, "First, let's read through all the material we have on Zeke Anderson and see if we missed anything. Then we'll read through it again. And then a third time. Because no matter how many times we read it, we'll overlook something. Then we start looking at the others."

"Why can't we do them all simultaneously?"

"It'll increase our odds that we'll miss something with Zeke. Besides, we have his body, and that gives us justification to work the case as a homicide. For all we know, the two other men could still be alive."

"Right," McAdams said. "What time is our appointment with Jack Carlson?"

"Five."

"We'll have to tell him that we found Zeke's body."

"I think he sensed it when I called him up for an interview," Decker said.

"Of course," McAdams answered. "When are we going to visit the other sets of parents?"

Decker thought for a moment. "Soon. I was hoping that once they heard about Zeke—once it's common knowledge—they'll call us."

"If they don't call us, that'll tell us something." McAdams got up and retrieved the sandwiches. When he got back to the table, Decker was on the phone. By the conversation, it was clear he was talking to Kevin Butterfield at the station house. After he hung up, McAdams asked, "What's up?"

"Still processing Schulung's car. We'll know more on Monday. The good news is that if something bad did happen, it didn't happen in the automobile. Kevin and a few uniforms are going down the back roads, checking to see if there are any workable cameras in any of the houses or businesses. They're also checking out service stations with convenience stores. Her car was littered with junk food."

"What about that truck stop?"

"Yeah, right," Decker said. "Kev paid it a visit, looked over the CCTV. Nothing promising so far."

McAdams said, "At some point Elsie switched cars with someone, right?"

"Or she could have been murdered and is buried somewhere in the woods." Decker seemed frustrated. "Butterfield's looking for tire tracks. It hasn't rained. Maybe we'll get lucky."

"To make it into that terrain, it must be a four-wheel drive."

"Elsie's car wasn't a four-wheel drive, but I see your point."

McAdams said, "Has anyone heard from Bertram's parents?"

"I don't know." Decker checked his watch. "I'll give Dr. Lewis a ring. Maybe he's had some luck." He stood up and placed the call, then left a message. "Not answering. Or maybe he's not answering me."

"Or maybe he has the weekend off."

"Lewis shouldn't be relaxing with a resident missing," Decker snapped. "I'm wondering if he might be in on Bertram's disappearance."

"Why?" McAdams made a face. "What would be his motive?"

"Bertram's parents aren't being cooperative. Maybe he's doing something for them."

McAdams said, "Like what?"

"Maybe Lewis is helping Bertram fake a kidnapping for money. We got the parents' phone number from Lewis. Maybe that's a fake too. Because I sure as hell can't get hold of them."

"That is very odd," McAdams agreed. "If Lewis is involved, he's hiding it well."

"I agree with you there," Decker said. "I will say, from what we've seen so far, he runs a pretty good ship. The residents do look happy. The place is clean, the employees don't seem censored. I don't get the feeling that there's any underlying tension."

"I'll go along with that," McAdams said.

Decker opened his sandwich and took a bite. "Thanks. It's good. Going back to Zeke Anderson and the other students, do we have DNA on them?"

"No DNA. But we have dental records."

"Fingerprints?"

"Actually, we do have fingerprint cards," McAdams said. "I think Duxbury has a policy of fingerprinting incoming freshmen. Why do you need fingerprints? We're dealing with bones."

"We need to run them through AFIS. Maybe something will pop up."

"I think that was already done," McAdams said.

"How long ago was that?"

"No idea."

"Ask Kevin to do it again. See if the men have re-surfaced."

"I'll do it now." McAdams stood up and pulled out his cell. "I'll just step outside. Reception's better."

"Thanks." Alone, Decker took another bite of his sandwich and stared at the wall, trying to clear his head. The photographs that hung were black-and-white pictures of narrow alleys lined with old doors inset into stone buildings. It could be Paris, it could be London, it could be Rome, it could be Jerusalem, it could be down-town Manhattan in some small enclave—somewhere antique, untouched from centuries ago.

Wherever it was, Decker wished he were there.

There was something magical about being alone in the city without work and responsibility on the brain. The noise and congestion never bothered her: it settled in her head as a background hum. Rina was uptown, walking south on Madison, making her way back from the Jewish Museum on Fifth with a bag of Russ & Daughters mixed rugelach in her hand—truly a treat for the family if the bag ever made it there. She was desperately trying to limit herself to one cinna-mon and one chocolate, but the aroma and the sugar were calling her name.

After she passed Eighty-Sixth Street, her phone sprang to life with a blocked number. She almost let it go to voice mail but then she figured that it might be Peter calling from a police station. She slid her finger across her phone and answered the call.

The low, menacing voice said, "I hear you've been talking to my wife."

Ex-wife, actually, but she didn't correct him. Chris didn't mean to sound menacing. It's just the way he was. "Did Gabe call you?"

"He did not."

"Then you just have ears everywhere, Mr. Donatti."

"I won't argue with that." Donatti paused. "Is it windy over there? I'm getting static."

"It is windy. Hold on." Rina stopped walking and stood under an awning. "Better?"

"Yes. What was the conversation about?"

"Pardon?"

Donatti sounded impatient. "Your conversation with my wife."

"Why don't you call up Terry and ask her?"

"I would except we haven't been in contact for over a decade."

"Why the sudden interest in her?"

"Could you answer the question? What was the conversation about?"

"Call your son if you want information."

"He lies. You don't."

"I don't lie," Rina said. "But that doesn't mean I'll break a confidence."

"Is she all right?" His voice softened. "Really, that's all I want to know."

Rina paused. "Why wouldn't she be?"

"Is she all right, Rina? Yes or no?"

"She's okay." *For now.*

"You don't sound convinced."

"She's okay," Rina repeated.

"Does she need money?"

"Ask Gabe."

"How much did he give her?"

"Ask Gabe," Rina repeated. "Chris, what's going on? If you haven't spoken to Terry in over a decade, why are you suddenly worried about her?"

"Who said I was worried?"

"When you ask if a person is all right, that means you're concerned."

"I am concerned, but I'm not worried. If I get to the point where I'm worried, I'll surface."

"Where are you now?"

"Here and there."

"Are you more here or more there?"

"I'm not in New York, if that's what you're asking. If you see my wife again, tell her to call me. I could be useful for her."

"How do you mean 'useful'?"

"Rina, we've known each other too long to play games," Donatti said. "So I'm just going to lay it all out. I don't know what bullshit she spun you, but her idiot husband has a gambling problem. He's in debt up to his eyeballs to some very unsavory people. Terry is the mother of my son, and I don't want her hurt. Furthermore, I don't want her kids hurt. They're nothing to me, but they are Gabe's siblings. Something is *off*. Now, *what* did Terry tell you?"

"Chris, I'm not trying to be difficult, but I'm not going to break a confidence. Why don't you call her up? I'm sure you have her number."

"I haven't phoned her in years. If I suddenly call her, she'll get nervous and I don't want to alarm her for no reason. I've tried to call Gabe, but he's not answering. I'm a busy man. I don't have spare time to keep calling people. You're seeing Gabe tonight. Pass my message along."

"How do you know that?" Rina asked. "Do you have a tap on my phone?"

"Just pass the message on." A pause. "If I say please, will it help?"

"I'll let him know." Rina paused. "Chris, what aren't you telling me?"

"I'm not holding back. It's just what I told you. Her husband is in trouble. He borrowed money from the wrong people."

Rina's heart was now racing, and she had to take a deep breath. "How do *you* know that Devek owes money to bad people? Did someone threaten *you*?"

"Nobody threatens me and lives to tell the tale," Donatti said. "I just know that the idiot is in deep, deep trouble. I also know that bad things can be avoided if you approach the situation with a little finesse and some reasonable recompense. Terry doesn't have the money, but I do. Just tell Gabe to call me. I'll tell him what he needs to know."

"If you really think that Terry's in trouble, it's un-ethical not to say something to her."

"Terry knows the situation. And she knows where to find me. If you talk to her, tell her that."

She exhaled. "Fair enough."

"Good. How are you?"

The question took her by surprise. "I'm okay." A pause. "Why do you ask?"

"It's weird for your little brother to ask about his big sister?"

Rina shook her head. It was a ruse they had once used with a very bad man whom she shot in the chest. The action was completely justified and the man survived. But she still had residual anxiety. She said, "I'm not your sister, Chris."

"You don't have to be related by blood to be spiritually connected. And once you pulled the trigger, that's all I needed to claim you as one of my own."

Then the line went dead.

Rina stowed the phone in her purse.

She kept walking.

But the mood was ruined.

Chapter 15

Jack Carlson worked for the Public Defender's office in Brooklyn. When Decker first called, Carlson said that he had to prepare for an important trial on Monday and he'd be buried in work over the weekend. Eventually, he agreed to spare fifteen minutes in the late afternoon. The meeting place was a small green space a few blocks away from Jack's office: a disc of flat grass with a half dozen black iron benches placed around the perimeter. When Decker and McAdams arrived, the circle was empty except for a man sitting on a bench, eating out of a Chinese take-out carton. Now, in his thirties, Carlson had thinning dark hair and a slim build and wore a blue shirt and dark pants. On his feet were worn black oxfords. He stopped eating as Decker and McAdams got closer, then stood up and pitched his food into a trash bin. Introductions were made, hands were shaken, and then the trio sat down.

Up close, it was evident that Carlson could use a shave. His cheeks and chin had too much unshaped stubble to be a statement. His brown eyes were puffy, even more inflated because his face was long. He looked down at his lap. "I . . . don't know what to say."

"We realize it must be a shock."

"No, it's not a shock. I knew this day would come. They had to be dead. But having it hit you in the face. It brings up all sorts of bad memories that I've tried to not think about." He looked up at Decker. "I don't know how I can help you any more than I could help the police way back when. I wasn't there."

"It was clear that you were with your parents over the weekend."

"I was. About a thousand people saw me." A beat. "An exaggeration, but you know what I'm saying."

"I do," Decker said. "You were all sophomores when they disappeared?"

"Yes. I was Zeke's roommate. Max and Bennett lived in the other bedroom. The four of us shared a suite."

"If I can ask, why did your folks come for Parents' Weekend? Isn't that usually for freshmen?"

"Any grade in Duxbury can participate in the weekend. Some parents come all four years. But yes, the majority of the parents are mothers and fathers of freshmen. I didn't want my parents to come. You go to college to get away from your parents. I wanted to go camping. Afterward, I felt guilty. Like I dodged a bullet. But I also felt relief."

"At the time, did you suspect that something bad had happened?"

"All sorts of things were flying through my head, and bad was certainly at the top of the list. When we first made plans, it just seemed like a cool weekend."

"You were planning on going, then," McAdams said.

"Yes. I was pissed at my parents for coming up. I tried to dissuade them, but my parents are stubborn people. Thank God for that."

"What had been the plan?" Decker asked.

"As I recall—this was ten years ago—the plan was to drive to the woods in Zeke's Beemer and spend a weekend doing hikes and rock climbing. Getting back to basics: no phones and no laptops. But we had camping equipment and fire starters and a compass and a trail map. We were also bringing food and water, although Max wanted to forage. He was into mushroom hunting, which I thought was stupid because most mushrooms are poisonous. All he had was a book. We shot that idea down pretty quickly. Max was always a tool."

"You didn't like him," Decker said.

"No, I didn't. He was normally shy, but with us, he always trying to be the man—an expert on something or other."

"What about Zeke and Bennett?"

"Zeke and I were good friends. It wasn't hard to be friends with Zeke. He was a nice guy. Bennett was all right—kind of a braggart, but at least he had a good sense of humor, some of it self-deprecating, which softened his arrogance. We were into physical fitness: the three of us. Not Max. He was soft and weak and lazy. Sorry to be so blunt, but it's the truth."

McAdams said, "He seemed like a poor fit for your trio."

"He was a friend of Bennett." A sigh. "Maybe *friend* is too strong a word. He knew Bennett growing up. That was the connection."

"Did Bennett like him?"

A pause. "I guess it doesn't make a difference now, but the truth was that Bennett used him. Max bought his friendship. He gave Bennett cash and things for the privilege of hanging around him."

Decker said, "How much cash and what kind of things?"

"He paid for the majority of the expenses—the groceries, the cable and internet. He bought the refrigerator and stocked it with beer. He paid for dinner whenever he and Bennett went out. He paid for dinner when the *four* of us went out, although Zeke asked for separate checks. Whenever we went to the movies, Max paid. We would offer to pay him back, but he refused."

McAdams said, "Sounds like all of you benefited."

"Not like Bennett, but yes, that is a valid point. At least Zeke made an effort to be fair. But Max would usually insist, and we didn't argue. Furthermore, Max would kind of flaunt it. Make a show of whipping out cash or his credit card." Jack shook his head. "I thought it was pathetic: he was trying so hard. He was totally clueless as to how stupid he looked. I'm ashamed to say that I wasn't very nice to him, but I wasn't the nicest person back then. When they disappeared, that sobered me up very quickly."

Decker said, "How did Max and Zeke get along?"

"They didn't have much to do with each other. Bennett was the common link."

"I've heard that Bennett went out a lot, dated a lot of girls."

"More like screwed a lot of girls." Jack looked upward. "But that was college. We all bed-hopped. That's just what you did."

"Did Max have a girlfriend?"

"Not that I remember."

"What about Zeke?"

Jack thought a moment. "No one special."

McAdams said, "Did he date?"

"Yeah, of course." Another pause. "I just can't re-member anyone specific."

"It sounds to me like Max was not only trying to buy Bennett's friendship but also maybe he was trying to buy his affections."

Jack bit his bottom lip. "Max could have been gay."

"What about Bennett?" Decker asked.

"Not a chance." Carlson smiled. "Although I suppose if he were drunk enough, which was often, he'd take it from anyone."

"What about Zeke?"

"No, I don't think so." Carlson appeared to be thinking hard. "Truth is, I can't remember him with a girl or a guy. He was into his studies." He shook his head. "No indication of him being gay, and we roomed together. Then again, I didn't keep tabs on his social life." He stood. "I've got to get back to work."

"Important case?" Decker asked.

"More than my usual DUI."

Decker said, "What do you think happened to your buddies, Jack?"

"No idea. Not that I haven't thought about it a mil-lion times." He sat back down and looked at the hot, blue sky. "I had lots of theories. Maybe they got lost and starved to death. Or maybe something attacked them. Or *someone* attacked them. Which, in hindsight, is probably what happened because didn't you say that Zeke was buried in a makeshift grave?"

"Yes, he was buried."

"Then you know more than I do about what happened."

"Did any of you boys have any enemies?"

"We weren't the nicest people around—well, Zeke was a nice guy. I was rude and a wiseass, but I can't think of anyone who'd want to kill me. Max could be annoying, but not enough to inspire that level of hatred. Bennett? Who knows? He had a lot of contacts, so a few of them could have been unsavory. But following them from the college to the woods to kill them? I just can't see anyone I knew back then doing that."

"Camping in late October can be cold," McAdams said. "Why then?"

"For one thing, it was a three-day holiday because of Parents' Weekend. Actually, I recall the weather being nice. It was cold a few weeks before but then it had warmed up. You can look up the temperatures."

"We did. It was warm, but you didn't know it was going to be warm."

"Like I said, we planned it because it was a three-day weekend. I was really pissed about not going. Who wants to hang around Mom and Dad when you can have a cool time in the woods?"

"By 'cool time' do you mean drugs or drinking or both?" Decker said.

"Yes, part of it was getting ripped. Maybe it was a regular occurrence with Bennett, but not me. School was demanding. Even on weekends I didn't party all the time because I had to study. This was an opportunity to just unravel. Like a Burning Man thing."

"Did you guys pack up anything stronger than weed?"

"I don't know, Detective. I didn't wind up going."

"I'm just wondering if they met someone in the woods and something went bad."

"Like a drug dealer?"

"You tell me."

"I can't tell you because I don't know. I wasn't there." Carlson checked his watch. "I really have to get back. I'm married, I've got a baby. I need this job."

"One more question," Decker said. "Did any of you own a gun?"

"A *gun*?" Carlson made a face. "I didn't. I don't know about the others." A pause. "Was Zeke *shot*?"

"We're still waiting to hear on the coroner's report," Decker said. "But his hand was shattered."

"And that's why you're thinking about a drug dealer? Someone who might have a gun?"

"We have to consider everything. Zeke could have been shot. Or maybe he accidentally shot himself. Or it could have been something else." Decker thought a moment. "Is it possible that Max might have brought a firearm to show off that he was a tough guy?"

"It's possible, but I don't know if he owned a gun or not." He stood up again. "I really have to leave."

"Thanks for your time," Decker said.

"Sure." Carlson hesitated. "You haven't found the other two yet?"

"No."

"Could they possibly be alive?"

"Until we've got remains, that's always a theory."

"How likely is it?"

"Jack, I don't postulate. I just go wherever the evidence points. It's not glamorous. But it usually gets the job done."

The lawyer nodded, got up, and left. Afterward, Decker turned to McAdams and said, "What do you think?"

"What do I think?" McAdams looked straight ahead. "I think you have a theory even though you don't postulate."

Decker smiled. "And what's my nonpostulated theory?"

"You're thinking Max shot Zeke because Zeke and Bennett were buddies and Max was jealous of their friendship."

"It's possible," Decker said.

"Or even a lover's triangle. That Max was crushing on Bennett. But instead Bennett and Zeke had something going. And Max got jealous."

"We have no evidence that any of them were gay," Decker said. "Quite the contrary, Bennett seemed to be a player with women."

"But according to Jack, if he were drunk enough, he might try anything. We know Bennett was a horndog. What better time to experiment than in college? And there they were, ripped, stoned, high, whatever. Why not experiment—away from all your judgmental peers?"

"Maybe."

"Zeke and Bennett were gym buddies," McAdams went on. "Both of them were into being strong, buff, and looking good. Gyms are notorious pickup places for men coming on to women and also for men coming on to men. Furthermore, if Max did get jealous over Zeke's friendship with Bennett, it would explain why we found Zeke but not the other two. Both of them took off. They still could be alive somewhere."

"Maybe yes, maybe no," Decker said. "One theory is as good as another, because we don't know anything. Finding Zeke was an accident. Now we're actively searching for evidence. Let's give it more time."

McAdams said, "You must be thinking of Max as the bad guy."

"Why do you say that?" Decker asked.

"You asked about a gun."

"I'm going to ask all the parents about a gun. If there wasn't a firearm, I am wondering how Zeke got a gaping cavity in his chest. It's time to contact the other parents. I'd like to find out if they put a private investigator on their sons' disappearances. If they did, I'd like to see what the private investigator uncovered. If they didn't hire a private, that tells us something."

"I'll see if I can set up interviews. Both the McCraes and the Velasquezes have moved from New York." McAdams paused. "Don't you find that odd? Both sets of parents moving after their sons disappeared?"

"Not really," Decker said. "Maybe they were escaping bad memories. Me? I find it a little strange that Keith and Mary Anderson have stayed put all these years with the ghost of their son lurking in every room and hallway. It would make me depressed." A pause. "Do we know where the McCraes and the Velasquezes are currently living?"

"Not off the top of my head, but both families are in the Midwest."

"In the same city?"

"Don't think so," McAdams said. "I'll call Kevin and get an exact address."

"I'll call him," Decker said. "I'll also call the coroner and see if he's written up his finalized report on Zeke Anderson."

"Boss, it's Sunday."

"Kevin is still working."

"Yeah, we're a pretty dedicated bunch," McAdams said.

"Pat yourself on the back, Tyler."

"No biggie. I just learned from the original work-aholic."

"I'll accept the title with honor," Decker said.

McAdams smiled. "I'd like to look up some stuff on my tablet. I'll need Wi-Fi. That's a problem. You certainly don't want me working on a case in a public place."

"What about your step-grandmother's place?"

"I would except she's out of town. No one is there."

"What about your mother?"

"She's also out of town. My father is in town, but it's very distracting at his place. There's plenty of room but also plenty of drama. Danielle is home for the summer, and she doesn't believe in closing doors unless she's slamming them. Chucky is distracting in a different way. He loves to see what I'm doing. He wants to help me, and I find it hard to tell him that I don't need his help."

"You don't have your own room where you can close and lock the door?"

"No, I don't have my own room, because it's not my childhood home." McAdams seemed to turn sour. "I could probably use my dad's office if he's not around. No one dares to come in when the door is closed."

"It's better than a coffee shop where someone could see what you're doing," Decker said.

"It is, but not by much. I hate being there. You know who the nosiest of all of them is? My dad." McAdams stood up from the iron bench. "I'll figure it out."

"Okay. Let's meet up at dinner. You are coming to dinner with us, aren't you?"

"Yeah, you guys are a family I can get behind: invitations to all the parties with no expectations. Well, none socially. You've laid plenty of expectations on me professionally."

"Of course I have expectations," Decker said. "Most of our work is monotonous, but the few times it is dangerous, I want a professional at my back."

"I've proven my worth."

"That you have."

"Then no complaints."

"None." Decker smiled and added, "So far."

He couldn't be sure, but he thought he heard Mc-
Adams mutter a *fuck you* under his breath. He wasn't
offended. Instead, he stifled a laugh.

Chapter 16

Everyone made it to dinner on time. Thirteen adults, three children, two babies, and a hundred opinions. The Decker clan was not shy about voicing views on politics, religion, science, medicine, economics, music and art, and anything involving anyone else's work. Advice was given freely. Advice was discarded freely. By the time the meal was over, everyone was sated and talked out. Long good-byes, great hugs and kisses, and a lot of see-you-next-times. As they were breaking up, Rina took Gabe aside.

"Your dad called me. He's trying to get hold of you."

"I reached him. He just wanted to pump me for information about Mom. I think he's concerned about her safety."

"I think you're right."

"That really makes me nervous. He knows about Devek's gambling problem."

"And?"

"He confirmed what Mom said, that Devek owes a lot of money. He didn't say how much but when Dad used the term 'a lot,' he meant a *lot*. Chris is crazy but he's not prone to exaggeration. I'm nervous. Plus . . ."

Gabe looked at the ceiling. "I can't get hold of my mother. She's not at the hotel, she's not answering any of my calls or texts. I don't know what's going on."

"Is her phone disconnected?"

"No. I left messages." Gabe looked at his foster mom. "She said she'd leave a forwarding number. Why does she *do* this to me?"

Decker said, "What's going on?"

"Terry seems to have disappeared." To Gabe, Rina said, "Let me know if you hear from her, okay?"

Gabe kissed her cheek. "Sure."

Decker said, "Why do you think she's disappeared?"

"She's not answering her phone."

Rina said, "Terry said that she's moving back to Los Angeles, Gabe. She was packing up when we left to get toys for your sibs. Maybe she's on her way to the airport."

"Then why would her phone would be off?"

"Maybe she's afraid of being tracked," Decker suggested.

"By Devek?"

"By Devek or by the men to whom he owes money."

"Yeah, of course." Gabe hit his forehead. "That's it. You're probably right."

"Call us in a couple of days if you're still concerned," Decker said. "I know she has your siblings with her. That's reason enough for you to want to know where she is."

"Will do," Gabe said. "Thanks, Peter."

"No problem. Keep in touch."

The prospect of a peaceful long ride home sounded delicious. Rina relinquished her shotgun seat to Tyler, hoping to curl up in the back and fall asleep.

A few minutes into the ride, McAdams said, "Are you sure you're all right?"

"I'm fine." Rina stretched to the side and put her legs up. "I'm just bummed that Cindy couldn't get off work tomorrow."

"Like father, like daughter," Decker chimed in.

"In all the good ways," Rina said.

"You could have stayed overnight."

"Thanks, but I'm tired. I don't mind going home." A pause. "It was nice that she and Koby came into town. I know it's a schlepp for them."

"It was lovely seeing all the kids." Silence. Decker then said, "I'm curious, Rina. You spoke to Terry. Why do you think she bailed on her husband? Is it that bad?"

"Is this really what you want to hear after spending two hours in the Situation Room?"

"You're one voice, not many," Decker said. "Unless you don't want to talk about it."

"It's fine with me. In a nutshell, Terry is divorcing her husband because he is a gambler and he's in hock up to his eyeballs. He owes a lot of money, but according to her, Devek has an out. A friend of the family—a widower—is willing to give him money to pay off some of his debts in exchange for marrying Juleen. She's eleven. Terry, not surprisingly, objects to the arrangement."

"Hmm . . ." Decker said. "That doesn't pass my smell test."

Rina nodded. "In the cold light of day, it does seem a little far-fetched." She sat up in her seat. "Terry is also worried that when she and Devek divorce, she won't get custody of the children. She claims Indian courts are biased toward Indian parents."

"That's more believable," Decker said. "Courts like consistency and stability when it comes to children.

While India is a big country and the law takes into consideration all kinds of circumstances, she may not have the money for a drawn-out court battle where the odds are probably not in her favor."

"Her husband does have a gambling problem," Rina said. "And he does owe money. I'm sure of that."

"Maybe that part is true. And I can believe that Terry wants a divorce. But Juleen being betrothed at eleven? To me it sounds contrived and a little convenient."

Rina thought about that. "You think she told me a story so I would take her children like we did with Gabe."

"Maybe. I don't trust Terry. And I don't trust *anyone* in the middle of a divorce and a custody battle. My advice is, don't get involved. It's not an order. It's a request from your husband who loves you very much."

"I think you're right." A sigh. "Chris called me up. He knew that I saw her this morning. He asked me about her."

"What did you tell him?"

"I told him to call Gabe if he wants answers."

"Good girl." Decker paused. "Then Donatti must be your informant regarding Devek's gambling problems?"

"Yes."

"Hardly an unbiased source of info."

"How would Donatti know about all this?" Mc-Adams asked.

"He's always kept close tabs on Terry," Decker said.

Rina said, "He's a bit of a stalker."

"That should be the worst thing about him," Decker said.

"Chris is concerned about her, Peter," Rina said. "I could hear it in his voice."

Decker said, "Maybe Terry is escaping something. You didn't agree to take the kids, did you?"

"No, of course not. I would never make that decision without you. Besides, Gabe wouldn't allow it. But it does sound like she's in trouble. And now Gabe says that she's not answering her phone."

Decker said, "If what you're saying is true, she's probably gone into hiding. Again."

"Poor Gabe."

"If Chris wants to handle her mess, let him deal with it. If Devek really does owe money to the wrong people, stay clear of Terry as well. I know your heart is soft, but you can't get involved every time the world bleeds."

"I am a little naive, aren't I?"

"You're a trusting soul. You think everyone's like you. They're not."

"Why would Chris want to help his ex-wife who dumped him?" McAdams asked. "Last I heard, he isn't the forgiving type."

"That's prototypical Donatti," Decker said. "He's waiting until she's truly desperate. Then either he'll take her back on his terms or really stick it to her." To Rina: "If Donatti does call you again, tell him to call me instead. I know he admires you. I know he thinks of you as the big sister he never had, but you are my wife and I need to protect you. Please. I'm asking you. Stay out of it."

"You're right," Rina admitted. "I'm done with this whole affair." She took out a can of club soda from the cooler and popped the lid. "Your turn. What did you find out about Zeke Anderson?"

"That he was a nice guy by the accounts," Mc-Adams said.

"No skeletons in his closet?" Rina asked.

"He might have been gay. But even ten years ago, that wasn't an issue especially in a place like Brooklyn. Besides, it's irrelevant. He went camping and wound up dead. No one has a clue as to why that happened."

"What about the other two lost boys?" Rina asked. "Did they have secrets?"

Decker said, "We're just starting to investigate. Next stop is speaking to their parents. The McCraes live in Saint Louis. The Velasquezes live in Cleveland."

"When are you going?"

"Sometime this week. We'll fly to Cleveland, drive to Saint Louis, and then take a plane back to Kennedy. Do you want to come, Rina?"

"What would I do in Cleveland and Saint Louis?"

"Visit the Rock & Roll Hall of Fame and the Gateway Arch."

She smiled. "No. I'll probably come back to the city and do a proper visit with the grandkids while you're gone."

Decker said, "Did Elsie Schulung's car produce anything?"

McAdams said, "Not beyond what Kevin told us. Like I said, it's the weekend. We're the only two idiots working on Sunday."

"Welcome to Homicide," Decker said. "Murder doesn't respect days off."

Rina sighed. "I hope Gabe is okay. He would be just devastated if she abandoned him again."

Decker said, "What can you do?"

"Nothing," Rina said. "Sometimes heartbreak leaves scabs. Sometimes it leaves scars."

Monday afternoon, they boarded a one-and-a-half-hour flight from JFK to Cleveland, Ohio. The city's population had been dropping steadily since the 1950s, although its decline was now leveling off. As with most places in the Northeast, less cramped housing seemed to equate to more green space.

When they landed, they rented a car with Decker behind the wheel. As he drove from the airport into suburbia, they passed verdant parks and long stretches of wild foliage. If there was suburban decay around, he had a hard time seeing it. GPS led McAdams and him to an area where the homes were mostly two story, with well-tended frontage that displayed plenty of pride of ownership. Henry Velasquez was a thoracic surgeon: his wife, Wanda, was a social worker. They resided in a well-appointed, wood-sided home that backed up into forested greenery.

It was Wanda who answered the door: a stout woman with short, straight dark hair dyed blond at the tips. She had smooth brown skin, a prominent nose, thin lips, and dark, sad eyes. Wearing jeans and a T-shirt with espadrilles on her feet, she stepped aside to let them in, into a living room that was tidy and generic. She offered them coffee.

"Only if you're having," Decker said.

She managed a weak smile. "I'll be right back."

While they waited, they settled into a gray sofa that had little give. Decker looked around, noticing that the photos on the walls ranged from two small children—a boy and a girl—to a young woman with two girls of her own. Wanda returned within a minute with coffee and cookies and placed them on a glass sofa table. She poured the coffee from a porcelain pot.

Decker said, "Thank you for seeing us."

Wanda smiled. "It's my day off." She sat down on a wingback chair. "The doctor is working. I told him I'd write everything down." She held up a pad. "You haven't found Maxwell, have you?"

"No, we haven't," Decker said.

"I figured if you had, you would have told me over the phone." She sighed. "How are the Andersons holding up? Probably better than me." She shook her head. "What happened to Zeke?"

"Still being determined," Decker said. "There were some shattered bones."

"From what?"

"A number of possibilities. Unfortunately, things aren't always neatly wrapped up, especially when so much time has passed."

"Okay." Wanda took a breath in and let it out. "May I ask why you're here? I told the police everything I know when it happened."

"The disappearance occurred ten years ago, Mrs. Velasquez. Police officers come and go. Memories fade. Detective McAdams and I are new to this case and we want to look at it with fresh eyes. Which means starting at the beginning."

"I don't know what I can tell you." A pause. "I suppose I should be happy that someone is doing something after all these years."

"Now that we have Zeke's remains, we can reevaluate," Decker said. "I'd like to talk about that weekend. Did you know that Maxwell was going camping?"

"I knew he was going away for the weekend. He called and told me, but he didn't tell me where. I had no idea he was going camping."

"Was he a big camper?"

"I don't think he'd ever gone camping in his life. No one was as shocked as I was to find out that the boys were lost in the woods. We looked for them for days. I didn't sleep for months afterward, years actually."

"Where did you think he might be going if he didn't say he was camping?"

"Boston maybe. It was close by. He said they were still making plans. Camping was so unlike him. Max was a studious boy. The other two—Zeke and Bennett—they must have talked him into it."

"Why would they do that?" McAdams asked.

"I don't know, Detective."

Decker said, "Did Max have something specific to offer them on the trip?"

"Like *what*?"

"Did he offer to buy the food or bring the equipment?"

"What *equipment*? He wouldn't have equipment. He'd never been camping!" She had turned angry. "All I know is Maxwell wouldn't have done this without some prodding. I didn't know Zeke at all. But I knew Bennett. He was a troublemaker."

No one spoke for a moment. Decker then said, "How so?"

"He was always talking Maxwell into doing things he didn't want to do."

"Like what?"

"Like camping, for instance."

McAdams said, "Why would he talk Max into a camping excursion?"

"He just would."

"Okay, let me rephrase the questions," Decker said. "What benefit would Bennett get out of having Maxwell along on a camping trip?"

"Bennett took advantage of Max every opportunity he could. I told Maxwell to stop hanging out with him."

"How did he take advantage of him?"

"For one thing, he was always borrowing money from him. I told Maxwell that it had to stop. I wasn't supporting Bennett through college. I was supporting *him*!"

"Did it stop?"

"They weren't around long enough for me to know." Wanda's lip trembled. "I suppose it is possible that Max paid for the camping equipment—for Bennett. Another so-called loan!"

"I understand that Max and Bennett knew each other prior to college. That they went to high school together."

"They were in the same high school but weren't friends. We did socialize with the McCraes a few times. Henry and Barney worked in the same hospital. Barney was a hospital administrator. They moved out of New York as well, you know."

"Saint Louis," McAdams said.

"Yes."

"Are you still in contact with them?"

"No." She looked down. "The way I saw it, the boys never seemed to hit it off. Bennett was outgoing. Maxwell was reserved. They knew each other, but there wasn't much of a connection."

"Do you think it's possible that Bennett did something harmful to Max?"

"I don't know!" She threw up her hands. "All I'm saying is that if something bad happened, Bennett was at the forefront."

Decker digested her words.

If something bad happened.

Something bad definitely *did* happen.

She seemed to realize what she was saying. "I mean, I know that Maxwell is probably gone." Tears welled up in her eyes. "I guess Bennett is a convenient scapegoat. He's probably gone too." Wet trails were falling down her cheeks. "Maxwell didn't have a lot of friends. He was different. What you'd call today on the spectrum. But he was a good, solid boy." She wiped her eyes with her index finger. "He just wanted to fit in . . . to be liked."

"Nothing wrong with that," Decker said.

"Not at all." Wanda stood up. "Excuse me."

She left the room, and they could hear her weeping. There was nothing to do but wait her out. She came back about five minutes later and sat back in her wing chair and dabbed her eyes. "Sorry."

"Nothing to be sorry for," Decker assured her.

"I've tried to move on." Her voice clogged up. She pointed to a picture of the young woman with two little girls. "They're my reasons for everything, I guess."

"Is your daughter older or younger than Maxwell?"

"Older by three years. Arianna was the golden child. Good student, good athlete, good social skills. When Maxwell came along, we were both thrilled to have our boy and our girl. It was pretty clear early on that he was a different kind of child."

"Can I ask what he was like as a child?" Decker asked.

Wanda looked upward. "He had a great attention span. He could stick with a task for hours. But it also made him temperamental. If we needed to go somewhere and he was engaged in something, it was hard for him to stop and to change directions. He was a slowpoke. Getting him ready for school was a chore. Getting him to bed was a chore. He seemed unable to refocus on what needed to be done. In school he had similar issues. You know how it is. When math is done, you put away the book and take out the English folder. He had a hard time going from subject to subject. We put him in a private school where he could move at his own pace, but even a freer school has some schedule. The thing that saved him was that he was very bright."

"Duxbury is a very competitive school. He must have been very intelligent," McAdams said.

"He had a very high IQ."

"Then college must have been better suited to his needs."

"In some ways, yes. His professors really appreciated his intelligence. But socially, he didn't seem to do much better." She was quiet for a moment. "I hated that Bennett took advantage of him. But—if I'm totally honest with myself—at least he was including Maxwell in some capacity, even if it was for his own benefit. Which is why when Maxwell said he was going away for the weekend with Bennett and Zeke, I was actually glad that he was doing something social."

Decker said, "Did you know Zeke Anderson well?"

"No. I met the Andersons when we went to Duxbury to search for the boys." Her face darkened. "It was a hellish, horrendous, nightmarish week. Of course, the three of us—the three sets of parents—never stopped looking even after the police gave up."

"Did you hire a private detective?" Decker asked.

"Of course we did," Wanda told him. "We all did. We compared notes." A headshake. "Nothing ever came of it."

McAdams said, "Do you still have the notes?"

"I think somewhere. I haven't looked at them in years."

"Is it possible to retrieve them?"

"I have no idea where they are. They could be in the attic. They could be in the basement. It's a real mess in both places."

"What's the name of the PI that you used?" Decker asked.

"Oliver something."

"You don't remember the last name?"

"Mendall or Mendal or something like that." A beat. "He might be dead."

"We could probably contact him, but we'd need your permission to look at anything he might have found on your case."

"He didn't find anything," Wanda said. "I could probably dig up the files, but it may take me a week or so."

"That's a long time," Decker said. "We wouldn't put you out unless we felt it was important."

Wanda gave out an angry sigh. "It'll take a while for me to find them."

"We can wait," McAdams said. "Or better yet, we can look with you."

A pause. "I'm not being obstinate on purpose. It's just bringing up all sorts of bad memories, but that's not your problem." Wanda stood up. "We'll start with the attic."

Decker said, "How about if I go down in the basement and Detective McAdams and you search the attic?"

"No offense, but we stick together. I don't want you poking around into my things." Wanda crossed her arms over her chest. "Those are the rules."

"Lucky for you, we're good at following rules." Decker smiled and stood up. "One more thing. Did Max own a gun?"

"A *gun*?" A look of horror. "No! Was Zeke shot?"

"We don't know. But as I told you, he had some shattered bones."

"Oh Lord!" She shook her head. "All I can tell you is that Maxwell never owned a gun! He hated guns."

"Could Bennett have talked him into buying one?" Decker asked.

"No." Her lip quivered. "Shall we get on with it?"

Decker nodded. "You lead and we'll follow."

"He did not own a gun!" Wanda muttered.

"I believe you," Decker said.

He thought: *The question is, Wanda, do you believe you?*

Two hours of searching produced a very thin file with a cover letter and a two-page synopsis report. Decker looked the papers over while sitting on the living room couch. McAdams was reading along with him, looking over his arm. Wanda was sitting across from them, stoic and silent.

The synopsis said the following:

Oliver Mandella had contacted the police and questioned them about the case.

He had contacted the school and had spoken to some of Max's professors.

He had spoken to the parents of the two other missing boys.

He had talked to search crews.

There was nothing in his conclusion that would further this case. But without his field notes, Decker didn't know exactly what he did or didn't do. He said, "Would you mind if I contacted him? This file is sparse."

Wanda hesitated. "I think Mandella is dead." A beat. "Actually, I know he's dead."

"Okay," Decker said. "Do you know if someone took over his business?"

"No, I don't."

"If we could locate his files and notes, do we have your permission to look at them? Sometimes details that don't seem important might become very important."

"Sure, but don't hold your breath. We expected a lot. We got nothing." Wanda looked at the ceiling. "The truth is, about five years ago my husband got fed up and threw out everything that Mandella had sent us during the course of his investigation. Henry wanted to move on, and this was the best way he could do it. Not a thought about how I felt. I managed to save what I've given you. My husband is a surgeon and has a surgeon's practicality—if it's bad news, cut it out." Again, her eyes grew moist. "Don't think poorly of him. It's just his way of dealing with this horrible situation."

"We're not here to judge," McAdams said.

"Henry would not approve of your digging around."

"Even if it helped us find out what happened to your son?" Decker said.

"Maxwell is gone, Detective. No amount of knowledge will bring him back. Henry has washed his hands of it."

"And you?"

"I'd love to give my son a proper burial. So please . . . go ahead and search. Just talk to me if you call, okay?"

"Fair enough."

"Are you going to talk to the McCraes?"

"Yes."

"Send them our best." A few seconds passed. "I didn't like Bennett. But he seemed to be the only friend that Maxwell had. For that, I'm grateful to him."

Chapter 17

They walked to the car. Once behind the wheel, Decker hesitated before turning on the ignition. Instead, he made a call to what once was Oliver Mandella's office. He hung up after a five-minute conversation. "The man is indeed dead."

McAdams was playing a game on his phone. "Sorry, I didn't hear you. What?"

"The private eye that Wanda Velasquez hired. He's dead."

"Too bad." McAdams logged out of the game. "What happened to his old files and field notes?"

"All files five years or older were destroyed by the PI who took over the practice."

"Then we have nothing except the synopsis, which is useless."

"At least we know the Velasquezes hired a private detective. That says to me that they were trying to find him at some point. Then Dad wants everything thrown away. He wants to move on. I'm not judging but parents never move on." Decker started the motor. "What do you make of Wanda's statement that *if* something bad happened, it was Bennett's fault?"

"Yeah, I caught that. Her blaming Bennett for whatever happened." McAdams paused. "Could be she knows more than she's letting on."

"Her son is still alive and he told her everything?"

"It's a theory," McAdams said.

"It's a theory based on nothing," Decker said. "But the thought did cross my mind."

McAdams said, "Both families moved from Queens at roughly the same time. Here's another theory based on nothing, but maybe *both* boys are still alive and the families have relocated to get away from prying eyes."

"Sure, that's possible. After all, we know that someone buried Zeke." Decker shrugged. "Hopefully, we'll get a better feel after we visit Bennett's parents."

McAdams said, "Max may not have liked Zeke. But why would Bennett kill him?"

"No idea." Decker paused. "We can hint at the boys being alive to the McCraes and see how they react."

McAdams said nothing.

After a few seconds, Decker said, "Okay, Harvard. What gives? You looked bothered."

"It's a little perverse to hint to grieving parents that their son might still be alive."

"We're not telling them that. We're just saying that we haven't found Bennett's body. So without further evidence, there's a slim possibility that he's still alive."

"It might give them false hope. Especially coming from the police. If you think he's really alive, then go for it. If you're not sure, I wouldn't hint at anything."

"You're right," Decker said.

"Are my ears actually hearing correctly?"

"Harvard, I'm actually saying that you are right. We'll do the interview straightforward. We found Zeke, we haven't yet found Bennett or Max. We're looking for whatever information the parents can provide."

"I think it's more sensitive," McAdams said.

Decker let out a small laugh. "What happened to you? You're suddenly Mr. Humanitarian?"

"And that's bad? What's wrong with realizing how vulnerable survivors of crime are?"

"Nothing. Take it easy." Decker put the car in park and drove off. "I was just wondering what brought about all the change?"

"I'm not a total boor."

"Never said you were."

"Although I've had my boorish moments," McAdams admitted. "People do change. In my case, it's been a slow evolution."

"Maybe it's realizing you're not invincible?" When McAdams didn't answer, Decker said, "Sorry. That was out of line."

"No, it's fine. The truth is, Peter, it's more like realizing that *Peter Decker* is not invincible. That was really scary."

The car went silent.

"More for you than for me," Decker said. "I barely knew what was happening. Just that all of a sudden, I was knocked down. You're the one who got shot."

McAdams said, "Better me than you, boss."

Decker jerked the steering wheel to the right and pulled the car over to the curb. "Listen, Harvard, and listen up good. If it's ever a choice between you or me, you choose you. I've lived most of my life. And it's been a great one. You're almost young enough to be my grandson. Besides, I'm not living with survivor's guilt, okay?"

"I don't know, Peter. I don't think I could take the survivor's guilt, either. What would I tell your wife?"

"Since we're both among the breathing, how about we both don't go there," Decker said.

"You brought it up."

"Yes, I did. I needed you to hear me. Now let's change the subject."

"Whatever you want, Old Man."

"Very funny. FYI, you little punk, I'm not ready for the glue factory."

"I concur." McAdams smiled. "You still have many more years to make my life miserable."

They ate sandwiches in their room at an airport motel. Depressing atmosphere that befitted a depressing morning. Decker thought about the case, how there were so many victims in a single crime. He was deep in thought, his brain barely registering McAdams's voice as he spoke to Kevin Butterfield over the phone. Finally, Tyler hung up.

"Kev just returned from SID in Hamilton. He met up with a tech and they had a look at Elsie Schulung's car. The problem isn't going to be collecting evidence, it's sorting the wheat from the chaff."

"Did they find anything meaningful?"

"Everything's meaningful. It's filled with hair, fibers, a couple of blankets, food wrappers, papers, receipts, dirt, blood—"

"Blood?" Decker looked up from his papers. "How much blood?"

"More like from a cut than a stab wound—Kevin's words, not mine. One thing he did say is that the car wasn't a crime scene. SID will analyze the samples tomorrow. Kev also said he'd coordinate with Sergeant Quay at Baniff PD to see if the blood in the car is a match for the blood found at Schulung's house. There are also a ton of prints that need to be looked at."

Decker said, "Both Kathrine and Bertram have print cards on file with their residential homes. Elsie's prints were taken when she got the job at Loving Care. Let's run hers through AFIS, see if she ever went by another name and did something criminal."

"That's a good idea," McAdams said. "Want me to have Kev do it now?"

Decker said, "Sure, he can run it through what we have on file, but the data is limited. We might need a bigger base. We should also ask Butterfield to look for blond hairs."

"You're thinking that Kathrine Taylor has been in the car?"

"Maybe."

"Boss, if the car was dropped off at the same time that Bertram went missing, how would Kathrine's hair be in the car? She was picked up at her residential home *after* Bertram went missing."

"Right," Decker admitted. "You know, it could be that Kathrine had been in Schulung's car before she went missing. Remember, Elsie had a photograph of the two of them. Did they check the trunk?"

"It was as dirty as the rest of the car, but no obvious signs of something bad."

Decker nodded, deep in thought. "Maybe that's why Kathrine went with Elsie willingly. She knew the nurse from before."

McAdams agreed. "Is Quay investigating Elsie's private life?"

Decker said, "He wouldn't be much of a detective if he didn't."

"Has he contacted you at all?"

"Nope. Could be he hasn't found much. Or he's not a good sharer."

McAdams didn't speak for a moment. "I'm still trying to figure out how two disabled adults might figure into this mess at Schulung's house."

"Maybe Bertram was there when it happened," Decker said. "Bertram saw Elsie arguing with someone and was scared for her. He came to her rescue and went overboard."

McAdams said, "Or maybe Elsie called him up for help after the fact. She picked him up at Loving Care and brought him to the house. Together, they cleaned up the mess."

Decker said, "Except that we figured that the mess at Schulung's place preceded Bertram's disappearance from the diner."

"Yes, of course." McAdams shrugged. "Then we're back to our other theory. Elsie picked Bertram up from Loving Care in the middle of the night, took him to her place, and together they cleaned up the mess. For helping her out, Elsie offered Bertram a reward."

"Kathrine."

"Exactly. But Elsie knew they couldn't take off together that night. Too many fingers pointing in her direction. Besides, vanishing would take careful planning. So, Elsie brought him back to Loving Care and told him to go on the field trip. They planned to rendezvous when the group stopped at the diner."

Decker furrowed his brow. "This is what I'm having trouble with. Why would Elsie leave her car so close to the diner, knowing that there was a good chance we'd find it? It would immediately throw suspicion on her."

"Good question," McAdams said. "And if she wanted to exchange vehicles, there are many easier spots to have a rendezvous. Leaving her car in the woods just doesn't make sense. Unless you had to bury a body in the woods before you took off."

"Whose body?"

"The body that left all that blood in Elsie's house—Bertram or Kathrine or maybe both. Or someone else altogether."

"Didn't Kevin just say that the car wasn't a crime scene?"

"Maybe it wasn't the primary crime scene, but if the body was wrapped well enough, there wouldn't be evidence immediately discernible to the naked eye. The car hasn't been fully processed yet."

Decker paused. "I have no evidence for this, but my intuition tells me that Bertram and Kathrine are with Elsie and they're alive. So if there is a body buried in the woods, it doesn't belong to either one of them."

"You think that because . . ."

"Right, I think that because . . ." Decker said.

McAdams made a face. "If they're not dead, Elsie would have to feed them, clothe them, house them, make sure they don't talk to anyone. My brother would usually get stares from people. But they usually address their questions to me. Most of the time, adults averted their eyes. Keeping them quiet wouldn't be a challenge."

"Where the hell is Elsie? She changed cars. Her phone is off, so there's no way to track her."

"What about credit cards?"

"Quay told me that no charges have been made on Elsie's cards since Bertram disappeared. People usually surface when they need money."

McAdams said, "If Bertram has enough cash on him, that wouldn't happen for a while. Do we know if Bertram or Kathrine has a credit card?"

"Bertram has one," Decker said. "His records haven't come in so I don't know if it's been used."

McAdams said, "Kev said he'd coordinate with several police departments near Mangrove to see if they can get a sighting of them."

"It's worth a try but the odds are slim." Decker said, "I'm not usually an optimistic person in kidnapping cases. Within the first six hours, the victim is dead. For some reason, I feel they're still alive."

"I agree. Having those photographs . . . Elsie has to be emotionally attached." McAdams looked out the window. "What's our next step?"

"We keep doing what we always do," Decker said. "Plug away and hope for a break."

The cell chimed and Rina looked at the window while rocking the stroller. The baby was taking a long nap, God bless. She tapped the green button. "Hi, Gabe. What's up?"

"It's official. I checked with their hotel. She's gone. They're all gone."

"Why are you surprised? Your mom said she was leaving for California. She'll probably call you when she gets there."

"She didn't even bother to say good-bye."

Poor kid. Abandonment all over again. Rina said, "If Devek really does owe that much money, it's certainly possible that she went into hiding again."

"That could be. Her phone is dead." A pause. "Rina, I can barely hear you. Are you outside?"

"Yes, I am," Rina said. "Where are you?"

"Home. Why?"

"I'm in New York. Do you want me to come over?"

"Sure." A pause. "What are you doing in New York?"

"Peter's out of town for a couple of days. I thought I'd come back and spend some time with the grand-children."

"Where are you?" Gabe asked.

"In Brooklyn. At the moment, I'm at a park."

"I need to get out. I'll come to you."

"Are you sure?" Rina said. "I'll be in Manhattan later on to visit Hannah."

"It's not a problem."

Rina said, "It's almost naptime. Let me drop the kids back off and we can meet somewhere in about an hour. I can use a little break as well. There's a bakery about two blocks from Sammy's apartment. I think it's called Breadstuff. I'll text it to you."

"Perfect."

Sixty minutes later they sat facing each other, Gabe nibbling on a croissant and Rina breaking apart an almond bear claw. She picked off the icing as she regarded her foster son. He looked despondent. He was even dressed for depression: gray T-shirt, gray linen pants, gray Vans. Rina understood his feelings, although Terry's disappearance was not unexpected. She came and went by whim.

Gabe sighed. "I just wish she wouldn't call me anymore. She only calls when she needs something." He looked up. "I'm probably not being fair. But why should I be fair? She's a pain in the ass. I should cut her loose, but I'd miss Juleen and Sanjay. Not that they'd miss me much. We don't have much of a relationship."

"Not true," Rina said.

"I only see them over the computer."

"How often?"

"Once a week maybe."

"Often enough," Rina said. "You know, when I was young, I had first cousins who lived out of state. Hardly ever saw them, but when I did, it was like we forgot gation298 • FAYE KELLERMAN

about the passage of time. That's the way it is with relatives." Rina sipped coffee. "I've seen the way they look at you. You're their big brother. They idolize you."

"Well, now they're gone. And my closest living blood relative is a hit man who runs his own little village of brothels. Actually, I own them. He can't own them because he's a felon. If that ever got out, I'd lose everything. No one wants to associate classical music with sex workers."

"People are pretty tolerant."

"Not that tolerant."

"I wouldn't worry about it. Your ownership is buried under a sea of shell corporations and DBAs."

Gabe looked at her. "How do you know?"

"Because Peter and I set it up that way with your dad. When you turned eighteen, the ownership was passed from Terry as your guardian to you. Peter and I knew it might be a problem. We weren't about to let you be dragged down. The whole thing went easier than expected. Your dad wasn't anxious to ruin your career either."

"If it came to him or my career, he'd choose him."

"I'm not so sure about that."

"I am." Gabe shook his head. "You guys are such nice people. Much better than blood."

"You know, it could be that your mom cut contact with you because she's worried about your safety. Her husband is in deep trouble."

"I think she's more worried about *her* safety than mine. She had no problems dragging me into the mess in the first place."

"For sure," Rina said.

"I wouldn't even believe her story except that Chris told me the same thing: that her husband is in deep debt from gambling."

Rina said, "He seems genuinely worried about your mother. You'd think after all this time, he wouldn't give a hoot about her."

"You'd think. He always told me that he'd take her back." Gabe shrugged. "We're two of a kind. No matter what she does, I still want her in my life."

"She's your mother, Gabe. That's not weird. But carrying the torch for a woman who ran off with another man? That's a little weird."

"Who can explain love?"

"Is it love or just a desire for revenge?"

"Maybe both." Gabe became lost in thought. Then he said, "Chris has this gigantic office where he works— more like a living room. With leather sofas and chairs with a desk and an office for his secretary."

"Talia."

"Yeah, Talia. That's where he meets rich clients and people from the casinos and from the banks. He has a stocked bar. He's always entertaining people there— parties for the rich and famous with his sex workers milling around."

"You've been to them?"

"I attended a few when I turned twenty-one. Chris does everything by the book now. He kept me well hidden until I was of age. Then, all of sudden he wanted me to meet some people—impress them that he has a classically trained pianist as a son. You know, cart me out as a prop. Actually, I didn't mind. The women . . ." He blew out air. "Unreal. Chris thought I was an idiot for not taking advantage of his generosity, but I'd never do that to Yasmine. Never."

"You've got a good moral compass."

"Yeah, it's amazing considering where I come from." His eyes were far away. "You know, my dad actually pays them for sex whenever the mood hits him. I guess it's like paying himself. But they do get their percentage and a tip. He drills it into them. You're a sex worker, emphasis on the worker part. Never ever give it away for free. Not even to the boss. To him, even sex is a business."

"He's done very well for himself."

"That's an understatement." Gabe returned to earth. "Anyway, the party office is Dad's public space. He has an equally gigantic private office that's only accessible from a private elevator that has fingerprint and pupil recognition as well as a punch code. His own personal Fort Knox. He has a vault in there. A big one. My dad always has a lot of cash on hand."

"I'm thinking that brothels might be cash business."

"For sure, but the private office is more than a big safe. It's all done in black and white. Not an ounce of color. He has his gym area with equipment that looks like a torture chamber: weights and straps and God knows what else. He also has a regular desk there. But mostly he spends his nights with this Captain America set of video monitors that shuffle through all the rooms in his brothels. You'd think it would be lurid, him staring at people having sex for six hours, but it's not. It's his way of keeping tabs on everyone, making sure that his girls and boys are okay, making sure the clients are not trying to bargain or cut deals behind his back, making sure no one gets too rough, making sure the rooms are properly cleaned afterward, making sure that the workers are tipped properly. It's all business. Like I said, Chris is all business. Despite the parties and the sex and all the fun and games, Chris is eagle-eyed. Nothing escapes him."

"I don't doubt it."

"His private suite is basically a bunker with a view of the mountains. No one goes into that office except him. He posts a guard outside to make sure that he gets privacy. I've got my own private suite one flight up when I visit. I confine myself up there. The one thing I don't want to do is get in Chris Donatti's way. I keep quiet until he's ready to talk or to go to dinner or whatever. When he's ready, he focuses on me. Laser eyes. He has the capacity to listen when he wants to. Until then, I stay in my suite. It's fine. He bought me a Steinway. I'm happy."

"You know how to handle him."

"Absolutely. Over the years, I've come to like my dad. But in the back of my mind, I know what he is. The point of all this rambling is I've been to his private office twice. Once I was there because I cut my leg on a rusty nail that was poking from my bed frame. I was bleeding pretty badly. I called him up and told him what happened. He came up and got me and brought me to his suite until the doctor could see me in *my* suite. The other time was when I got terrible food poisoning and I thought I was going to pass out. Finally, I called him and he took me to his private space, just to keep an eye on me.

"When I cut myself, I was sitting on this big black leather couch waiting for the doctor, watching him as he did his monitoring. But when I had food poisoning, I was actually in his bedroom, lying on his ginormous bed. The walls were bare except for this beautiful, detailed pen-and-ink drawing. Only drawing there, only drawing in his private space period."

He looked at Rina.

"It was Mom. I think he drew it from a photograph right after she left him. You don't keep that in your private space unless you love the subject of the drawing."

Rina thought a moment. "Then maybe he does see this as a chance to get her back. And maybe that's good, Gabe. No one could protect your mom and your siblings better than Chris."

"Yes, he could protect her—if he didn't kill her first." Gabe was the picture of dejection. "Why didn't she call just to say good-bye?"

Rina said, "I don't know, but I do know that she will contact you when she's ready. In her own way, she loves you very much."

"Yeah, in *her* own way. It's got to be her way."

"No sense getting mad."

"You're right." Gabe threw up his arms. "I've got a great fiancée. I've got a foster family that has accepted me as one of its own. I've got a great life without her. Why do I care?"

"She's your mother."

"She's whacko."

Rina patted his hand. "Gabe, you made yourself a good life—you were blessed with great genetics and a superior talent, and you've made the best of it. Your career has taken off. Enjoy your success."

"And yet I'm still sulking. What is wrong with me?" He paused. "She's okay, right? I mean, my mother is a ridiculous person, but I wouldn't want anything to happen to her—or to my sibs."

"Terry is a survivor," Rina said. "She'll do whatever she needs to get by."

"Do you think Chris was lying when he said that he doesn't know where she is?"

"I have no idea."

Gabe stared at her. "Why was it his first instinct to call you and not me?"

"He said he did try to call you."

"I didn't see any missed calls from him. He didn't call me until way later in the day."

"I don't know, Gabe. Your dad uses me as a sounding board in much the same way you do. Please don't kill the messenger."

"Sorry." Gabe took a bite of his croissant. "I guess I'm still resentful of both of them."

Rina said, "You know that your mom had a really hard upbringing. She practically raised her half sister single, and her parents used her like household help. When she got pregnant, they kicked her out. She lived with her grandparents for a few years, but then they moved to a retirement home in Florida and again she was left on her own. Even when she didn't have anything, she always made sure you had a roof over your head and food in your stomach."

"A lot of peanut butter and jelly and macaroni."

"Exactly what kids like to eat. And through it all, she somehow managed to go to college and get into medical school."

"Chris was supporting us by then."

"Do you know how desperate she must have been to go back to him?"

Gabe looked sheepish. "I see your point. And I do love her. That's why I'd like to know that she's safe."

"She'll call you when she's ready." Rina touched his hand. "I'm having dinner with Hannah and Rafi at their house. Want to come over?"

"No, I've got a rehearsal at eight in the city. Afterward, maybe Yasmine will take a break and we can spend a few minutes together. Medical school hasn't been easy for her. Being with me hasn't been easy for her. I'm always gone—traveling. And her relationship with her parents is not what it used to be. She was so close to her mom, and now they don't talk like they used to. I try to be supportive, but I know she feels alienated. That can't be good for her."

"She's a determined girl. She'll get through it."

"Yes, she will." He smiled. "Sounds like someone we both know, so please don't tell me I'm marrying my mother."

Rina smiled. "The thought never entered my mind."

Chapter 18

Initially, Decker had planned to keep the car and drive to Saint Louis. Upon learning it was an eight-hour drive, they opted for a nine a.m. flight out even if the tickets came out of their own pockets. Since the appointment wasn't set until eleven-thirty and they gained an hour, they had plenty of time to rent the car and get their bearings. The address put them in Clayton, Missouri, an area bordering western Saint Louis. As they drove, they followed GPS in a circuitous route, because a public park, miles long, kept interfering with streets. It was a beautiful, verdant area, encompassing the zoo, museums, a planetarium and science center, and sports areas, all of it abutting a major college.

"Washington University," McAdams said. "It's a great school. No Harvard, but then again what is."

"That's the Tyler I've come to love." Decker grinned. "Snob."

"Definitely." McAdams looked out the window. "I wonder why Bennett McCrae decided to go to Duxbury rather than Wash U."

"The McCraes were living in New York back then."

"Ah. Right." McAdams nodded. "Not that Duxbury isn't a great college, but New York has some excellent universities."

"Like most teens, he probably wanted to get away from home," Decker said.

"That is understandable." McAdams looked at the multitudes sunbathing on the grass. He didn't understand the appeal of basking. It was hot outside. He turned up the fan a notch. "Brutal out there."

"It's the humidity. I hated Florida in the summer. But at least it was training ground for 'Nam. We were in long sleeves and pants and boots. In the jungle, it's a necessity because of all the bugs and other creepy crawlies. Sweat pouring out of you. You had to drink even if you didn't feel like it because of the climate. You became dehydrated so quickly. The enemy wasn't as problematic as the weather. Those poor northern boys— they'd never felt heat like that. It's all-consuming."

He turned left and into an enclave of brick houses. Some were in the Federal style, but others were two-story Arts and Crafts bungalows with wraparound porches. Retail stores included boutiques and little cafés and vegan restaurants. As they wended through the area, the lots grew bigger, the homes became statelier, and the lawns went from patch size to sports fields.

Barney and Harriet McCrae lived in a Georgian-style house replete with pillars and a double-door front entrance. The lawn was green, with leafy white oaks, maples, dogwood, and sweet gums blocking the fierce sun. The driveway was circular, and one lane was taken up by a black Land Rover. Decker parked behind it and killed the motor. He stepped outside, and the heat was one big, wet slap on his face. He could already feel his clothes drooping. They walked up to the front door and rang the bell. It seemed like ages before it opened, and that welcome gust of cool air kissed their cheeks. A well-dressed woman was at the doorway. She had on a white short-sleeved shirt, denim pants, and jeweled sandals. Her brown hair was short and shagged, and her ears were adorned with gold hoops. Her skin was smooth, her complexion was chestnut-colored. Her eyes were brown and sad, and when the detectives identified themselves, they turned even sadder.

"Come in." She moved to the left to let them in. "I'm Harriet McCrae. I suppose you know that. Would you like some water or lemonade?"

McAdams said, "Anything with ice."

A small smile. "It's hot outside." She led them into a parlor that looked out past the driveway and the front lawn. The furniture was sixties modern—slung-back sofa, brightly colored wing chairs with wire bases, a mirrored coffee-table top held up by a giant ceramic hand.

McAdams said, "I like how you did the room."

"Clean lines, nothing fussy," Harriet said. "I've had enough fuss in my lifetime. Please sit. Is it too hot in here? I hate frigid air-conditioning. My husband always complains that I keep the register too high."

"Keep it however you're comfortable." Decker sat on the sofa. "But I will take off my jacket."

McAdams took up an aqua chair. "Same."

"Give them to me, gentlemen. I'll hang them up."

"Is your husband home as well, Mrs. McCrae?"

She turned around to face them. "No. Should he be?"

"No breaking news, sorry," Decker said. "I was just curious."

A long sigh. "He's working. I'll be right back."

After she left, Decker made a face. "I think I inadvertently raised her expectations."

"Expectations are all she has left."

Decker regarded the parlor. Not many pictures in the bookcase: a portrait of her husband in black and white; a wedding picture with the same man in a tux standing next to a woman in a lace, long-sleeved gown with a high neckline and a big veil; a snapshot of two middle-school-aged boys; another of two teenaged boys next to a house; and one more wedding picture, this one with a man in his late twenties or early thirties and a young woman in a strapless gown.

Harriet returned with three glasses and a pitcher of lemonade and ice. She poured half a glass into each tumbler and distributed them before she sat down on the opposite arm of the sofa from Decker. "Thanks for letting me know about Zeke Anderson."

"I thought you'd prefer to hear about it from the police."

"Of course." A pause. "I called your police department earlier this morning to see if you had any more details. I spoke to a man named Kevin Butterfield. He was nice enough but didn't tell me much." Harriet looked intently at Decker. "I'm hoping you can be more forthcoming."

"There's not much to report, unfortunately," Decker said. "We found Zeke's remains several days ago and we're still looking for any others."

"How can that be?" Harriet exclaimed. "They all disappeared at the same time."

"We realize that. We have people out there scouring the woods. We're hoping that something will materialize."

She sighed loudly. "Have you talked to Wanda Velasquez yet?"

"We were there yesterday," McAdams said.

"What does she say about all this?"

"Not much."

"They hired a private detective. So did Zeke's parents, and so did we. We figured we could compare notes and come up with some ideas." She dismissed the outcome with a wave of her hand. "Waste of time and money. More than that, it was a waste of hope. So where are you in the investigation?"

"At the beginning," Decker said. "We're going over everything from page one. Now that we have Zeke's remains, we have an actual case to look at."

McAdams asked, "Did you keep the notes from the private investigator?"

"We threw them out. Like I said. Waste of time and money."

"You threw out everything?"

"We did . . . about five years ago. Doesn't matter, Detective. Ask me any questions. I had his notes practically memorized. Not that there was all that much. He wasn't very good."

"Anything you want to share?" McAdams said.

"If there was, I would have called you a long time ago." She took a sip of lemonade, and the others followed. "Ten years, Detective. A whole decade has come and gone with no resolution."

"And I'm very sorry for that." Decker put his glass down on a pink glass coaster. "I'll do whatever I can to move this forward. In that spirit, do you mind if I ask you a couple of questions?"

"Of course not. I mean why else would you come here."

"I understand Bennett and Max knew each other before Duxbury."

"They went to the same high school. They were nothing alike."

"Friends?"

"Hardly. Bennett used to say he didn't need a pet because Max was his puppy dog. Not the nicest thing to say, but the boy was a nuisance. I think Max applied to Duxbury because that's where Bennett wanted to go. Once there, Bennett, being social and witty, made lots of friends."

"And Max? Did he have a lot of friends?"

"I wouldn't know. I didn't keep track of him." A shrug. "Bennett said he was as socially inept in college as he was in high school. Sometimes Bennett found him a pest. Other times he took pity on him. Like when the boys needed a fourth roommate to complete their suite. Bennett asked Max. I think he just felt sorry for him."

"Any reason why Bennett would put himself out there for a guy he felt was a pest?" McAdams asked.

"Because he was a *nice* boy!" Harriet's eyes moistened. "I know people thought he was full of himself, but they were jealous because Bennett had the world at his fingertips." The tears were stronger. "He had his whole life ahead. He could have been a wonderful, productive member of society—the kind of person this world needed. And now he's *gone!*" She was sobbing.

Decker said, "We will keep at this case until we have some answers."

"No, you won't," Harriet shot back. "You'll look for a while, and then newer cases will push my son to the back of the line. I'm not blaming you, but I know how it works."

"I am sorry you're frustrated," Decker said. "But it's different this time, Mrs. McCrae."

"Harriet."

"Finding out what happened is our top priority." Decker paused. "Harriet, was Bennett an experienced camper?"

"Not from us. We're not campers, but he went to sleep-away camp for five years. Maybe he got a taste of it there."

McAdams said, "Did he tell you he was going camping that weekend?"

"Not specifically. He phoned me and said he wouldn't be on campus over the weekend. Naturally, I asked him where he was going. He said he had a three-day holiday because of Parents' Weekend and he was deciding between several places. He was thinking about Vermont or Canada. He also mentioned camping. He said the weather was going to be nice and he wanted to be outdoors. None of us knew how much colder it was in the forest until we got to Greenbury. That's when I really started to worry."

"I'm sorry I have to ask these questions," Decker said. "I know it's hard, but if you can think back a little. When Bennett told you he was going camping, did it strike you as odd?"

"No. Like I said, he told me the weather was going to be nice. He was a strong boy. He was athletic. Why not go camping?"

"Did he own camping equipment?"

"I don't know, Detective."

"No gear stored away at your house?"

"No. Like I told you, we didn't camp."

Decker said, "And there was no specific reason why he went camping that weekend other than he wanted to be off-campus and in nature."

"I would think that would be enough of a specific reason."

"Yes, you're right," Decker said. "Getting away from campus is always a good reason."

She nodded her head. "Zeke was found buried in the ground. So his death wasn't accidental."

"His death could have been accidental, but burying him was not," Decker said.

Her lip quivered. "How did he die? Or can't you say after all these years?"

"Still investigating, but he had a shattered hand."

"He was shot?"

"We haven't found evidence of a firearm yet," Decker said. "We've asked this question to Zeke's parents and to Max's parents. Please don't be offended. Did Bennett own a gun?"

Harriet's lower lip was still quivering. She bit it with her front teeth. "Not when he lived at home."

"Okay," Decker said. "How about at college?"

"I don't think you're allowed to have a gun in your dorm room."

An idea suddenly popped into Decker's head. "There's

an indoor shooting range up there—at the Five Colleges. Did he ever go to it?"

She didn't answer.

McAdams said, "If you don't know, we can check it out. They're required to keep a logbook."

She looked sheepish. "I believe he said something to us about going to the range."

"Okay," Decker said. "Thanks for being honest—"

"I told him that whatever he did up there, that was his business. But he was *not* to bring a gun home. I was adamant about that."

"Then he did own a gun?"

"I don't know if he did or didn't. He did mention that he was learning to shoot. There wasn't a gun when we got his things back from his dorm room. That much I can tell you."

McAdams turned to Decker. "It's possible that he kept a gun in a locker at the range."

"It wouldn't be there after all this time, but we could find out if he kept a locker." Decker turned to Harriet. "Did you ever get any kind of a bill from the gun range? Perhaps a storage fee or membership bill or anything like that?"

"Not that I remember." She wiped her wet eyes. "Bennett was into a million activities. I'm sure shooting was just one of many things he tried out. Are we done?"

She was reaching her limit. No sense pushing her when Greenbury PD could check the gun range's records. Perhaps they'd make some headway. "Thanks so much. I'm sure it's been difficult."

"You have no idea."

She was right. He didn't have any idea. Thank God for that. Decker said, "We'll show ourselves out."

Harriet stood up. "I'll show you out. Least I can do since you came all this way for nothing."

"Not for nothing," Decker said. "Getting background is important. Meeting you . . . looking you in the eye, that's important. It reminds us why we work in Homicide. There is justice to be done and someone's got to do it. Who better than me?"

Driving to the airport. This time McAdams was behind the wheel. Decker said, "What do you think about Harriet throwing away all the PI files?"

"Same as Wanda Velasquez."

"At least Wanda kept something—a synopsis."

"A meaningless synopsis, but I see your point. There was something about both of them that said, 'I really don't want to talk to you.'"

Decker said, "Wanda seemed to blame everything on Bennett, who, depending who you talked to, ranged from being a nice guy to an arrogant user of people."

"Yeah, Wanda really didn't think twice about throwing Bennett under the bus. And Harriet didn't think twice about portraying Max as a pest. It's odd. All three boys were victims."

Decker said, "Maybe Harriet and Wanda just want someone to scapegoat."

"Or Max and Bennett could still be alive," McAdams said. "They were both a little evasive."

"Leery. I'm sure they've been disappointed many times and they don't want to get their hopes up." Decker opened a bottle of water. "On a whole other topic, what do you think about Bennett taking shooting lessons?"

"Totally plausible. Everyone has portrayed him as an adventurous guy."

"I think that's important," Decker said. "Everyone we talked to said Max followed Bennett like a puppy dog. It's conceivable that once Bennett started with shooting lessons, Max imitated him."

McAdams said, "But even if Max did kill both of them, do you see him as capable enough and strong enough to bury two guys like Bennett and Zeke?"

"If he had enough time. Desperate men do desperate things."

"Bennett, on the other hand, would have no problem."

Decker said, "I'm just trying to work out a motive. Why would Bennett kill Max and Zeke?"

"I don't know. Why would Max kill Bennett? He idolized him."

"Maybe he just got tired of being the butt of everyone's jokes."

McAdams said, "He snapped. Something trivial might have finally gotten to him."

"Possibly," Decker said.

"He snapped and took it out on whoever was around," McAdams said to himself. To Decker he said, "We should check the range to see if Max was taking shooting lessons along with Bennett."

Decker said, "We should check out all three of them. We'll do it first thing tomorrow morning."

"Yeah, we have to get back to Greenbury first. We're going into Kennedy?"

"Yes, Rina will meet us with the car. We'll drive back tonight."

"You're not eating dinner with the kids?"

"We'll get in too late. Rina will pick something up for the car ride back. I think she's getting sandwiches from somewhere. I'll ask her to pick you up something."

"Thanks," McAdams said. "What are you having?"

"Probably a chicken breast sandwich."

"I'll take pastrami on rye with mustard."

"The ironclad stomach of youth."

"You're just jealous."

"Damn right, I am. My blessing to you is thus: may it be many years before you learn the joy of heartburn."

"Amen to that."

Chapter 19

The Five Colleges of Upstate New York were spread over considerable acreage, each institution with its own land, its own specialties, its own dorms, and its own character. The oldest school, Duxbury, was founded about 150 years earlier and had a reputation for excellence. It boasted Beaux Arts architecture, which translated into stately buildings of limestone, weathered to a perfect patina. Its curriculum emphasized liberal arts and had a strong core in the classics and seemed like a perfect fit for Zeke Anderson. It was also a good fit for Bennett McCrae who had a variety of interests, although Decker pictured him more as a Morse McKinley guy. MM College was a wheeler-dealer school, noted for its classes in government and politics both domestic and international. Many of its alumni went on to do things in DC and all over the world.

Clarion was a hundred-year-old women's college that had consistently voted to stay a women's college although the definition of a woman had changed over the past ten years. It accepted biological women, transgender women, and biological women who transitioned to men during their stays at the institution. The fourth college, Littleton, was a funky, artsy school that preached social action with an emphasis on sustainable living. Life was, by its very definition, sustainable until it morphed into death, which was anything but sustainable.

Although smart and gifted, Max Velasquez didn't seem particularly curious, which made Duxbury an odd choice. He never showed signs of being interested in the world around him socially or politically, which excluded MM and Littleton as ideal institutions. And he wasn't a woman either by choice or biologically, so Clarion wasn't an option. The last and most recent college, Kneed Loft, emphasized the STEM subjects and, in Decker's mind, would have made the best fit for the kid. But from what Decker had learned, the young man seemed more interested in proximity to Bennett McCrae than a specific college.

What all five colleges had in common were disaffected teens who, on numerous occasions, found outlets to vent their spleens. There was much to protest in an imperfect world, and outrage on campus could be

324 · FAYE KELLERMAN

found in almost anything. What wasn't a stretch was to rant against a gun range on campus. Decker had never been to this building, precisely because there was a constant cadre of protestors, and to him it was worth the extra fifteen-minute drive into the more gun-tolerant town of Hamilton.

But the kids had a point.

While it was true that people kill people, guns seem to be the destruction of choice to carry out the mission most efficiently. And while it was also true that most gun owners are balanced people, the few unbalanced ones do horrible damage. Decker had witnessed unspeakable mangling and mutilation over the years. The images never completely left his mind. It was a pain in the ass to deal with the protestors, but he wasn't offended when twenty-plus sneering, hot-faced students met McAdams and him in the parking lot. They swarmed the car like a funnel of angry bees.

"Dedicated group," Decker said. "To take the time to do this during summer classes."

"What's more fun than rousting police?"

"They don't know we're police." Decker turned off the motor.

"They'll know as soon as we come out."

"Yes, they will." Decker opened the door.

They were immediately engulfed by screams of "murderers," "sickos," "psychos," and a lot worse. All this without having shown their badges. But as long as it stayed at the verbal level, Decker was fine. He, being tall and remarkably strong for his age, could have forged through the group, but instead he turned to address the irate mob.

"We're detectives. We're investigating the disappearance of three students who went to college here ten years ago. We found remains up in the hills, and one of them may have practiced shooting at the range. We're trying to find out what happened to these poor guys. If it was one of you, we'd do the same thing. All we're trying to do is give the parents some answers."

One of the women—a curly-haired redhead with a mass of freckles who appeared to be about nineteen—spoke. "Zeke Anderson?"

"Exactly," Decker said.

"We spoke to his parents on Sunday," McAdams said. "They've been wondering about their son for ten years. Think about how your parents would feel if it was one of you."

"Two other students that went missing with Zeke," Decker said, "we talked to their mothers yesterday. They'd like to bury their children, but first we have to find them. We're still looking in the woods for bones, but it's a slow process. We're here because we're following up on a lead."

The redhead put down her sign. "Good to see the cops doing jobs other than shooting unarmed African Americans."

"Thanks, I guess." Decker smiled. "If you'll excuse us, please."

The attitude disarmed them, and the group parted like the Red Sea to allow them passage. The gun range was housed in a brick building—rectangular and big enough to accommodate indoor shooting. The entrance was two double glass doors—bulletproof—and once inside, Decker could hear the muted *pop, pop, pop* of discharging weapons.

McAdams paused before walking up to the front desk. "I understand what's going on with the kids. I'm still a student myself, and college is an angry time. But all this protesting is a colossal waste of time. It has nothing to do with the outside world."

"At least they're protesting weapons instead of words."

"Yes, you're right about that. Man, you should see the babying the administration does, even at the law school. Great legal minds shouldn't need grief counselors when the candidate of their choice loses. It's appalling."

"Life will thicken their skins. Either that or they'll be perpetually unhappy because no one gets their way all of the time."

"Some people do," McAdams said. "It's called 'to the manor born.' And yes, I'm speaking about myself."

"You could have coasted."

"I still do, actually. In the recesses of my mind, I always have that safety net. That privilege of 'I really don't have to do this.' Not like some of these working-class kids who go into the police academy as their career to put bread on the table. I've had opportunities that most people can't even fathom. Specifically, how it feels to not need money."

"Self-awareness is good, but I'll tell you this, Harvard. Wealth doesn't mean you haven't paid your dues. A bullet doesn't know the difference between rich or poor." When McAdams colored, Decker laughed. "I've embarrassed you. That's a feat."

"You didn't embarrass me," McAdams said.

With that, Tyler turned and walked away. Decker smiled, shook his head, then followed him to the front desk, which was enclosed with glass except for a metal grate where sound could come in and out. The young man behind the partition was blond with a sunburned complexion and a short haircut. He had a thick neck, thick arms, and a broad chest. He could have come directly from a farm in the Midwest, except he had a British accent that made him sound aristocratic. "I see you made it past the mob." He rolled his brown eyes. "Every day they hassle me. I'm a student just like they are. This is part of my work-study for my scholarship. I need a job to satisfy the school visa, or else I get sent back. I once tried to explain that to their leader, but to Neda I'm just a stupid, dumb hick from the hinterland. Not that she knows what the hinterland is. Instead, she keeps telling me to go back to Iowa. I'm not even sure where Iowa is."

"It's in the middle of the country," Decker said.

"Do I *sound* like I come from Iowa?" He exhaled. "Anyway, you're not here to listen to my woes. How can I help? I'm Boyd Evans, by the way."

"Nice to meet you, Boyd." Decker introduced McAdams and then himself. "We're working on a ten-year-old cold case. We think that one of our victims may have practiced shooting here. He may have kept a gun locker. We know you keep records. We're wondering if they go back that far."

"I'm not sure. Most of the entry and exit logs are handwritten into binders, but the gun-locker rentals are computerized. I don't know if they go back ten years. What's the name?"

"Bennett McCrae." Decker spelled it and gave him the approximate date.

Evans pressed some buttons on the keyboard. "I don't see it . . . but it's a long list of names."

"Mind if I take a peek?" Decker asked. "I know what I'm looking for."

"You'll have to sign in."

McAdams said, "Happy to do that."

"I'll need ID. Your badge numbers will do." The men took out their IDs. "Do you have weapons on your person?"

"We're police, Boyd."

"Sorry. You still have to check your weapons in through the steel box. You can pick them up in the gun-locker room."

"No problem." Decker took out his Glock. McAdams carried an S&W .38 snub-nosed revolver. After stowing their guns in metal boxes and getting tickets for the pieces, the men passed through the metal detector until they were on the other side of the glass. Looking down a long list of names, Decker didn't see Bennett McCrae's name. But Max Velasquez had rented a locker. Three months after the boys disappeared, the box and its contents were seized for failure of payment.

330 · FAYE KELLERMAN

McAdams said, "Wither you go, I will go."

Boyd looked up. "Excuse me?"

"He's quoting the Bible," Decker said. "This student—Max Velasquez—what kind of paperwork do you have on him?"

"I don't have the slightest idea."

"Do you know what they might have done with the contents of the box?" Decker asked.

"Not specifically, no," Evans said. "I know when a locker is seized, the lock is broken and an inventory is taken. I think they try to contact the owner."

"How? By phone or mail or . . ."

"I don't know."

"What about the entry and exit logbooks? How far do they go back?"

"Not a clue." Evans brightened. "Stella would know. She's been here forever. Hold on." He pushed a button on a landline phone and waited. "She isn't answering. I can't leave my desk. I have to make sure everyone who enters goes through procedure."

"Why don't you just point us in the direction of Stella's office?"

"I would except I would incur Stella's wrath. She hates to be disturbed."

"We're seasoned cops, Boyd," Decker said. "We're excellent at handling wrath."

As it turned out, Stella was in a shooting booth, prac-
ticing with a Glock 22, a bigger, more versatile version
of the 19 that Decker carried, as it could shoot 9 mm
as well as S&W .40 ammo. Since there weren't a lot of
calls for drawn weapons in Greenbury—violent crime
was virtually nonexistent—he packed the 19. It was
easily concealed and made for less intimidation when
he was in the field.

The range had six indoor lanes separated by par-
titions and the usual red lines running down the lane
to denote the specific firing area. Stella had on headphones, and her stance was that of a pro. She was tall
and had an Olive Oyl frame with stick arms and bony
hands that belied a deadly aim. She wore a gray T-shirt
over jeans and ankle boots on her feet. When she was
finished with target practice—five rounds on or near
the bull's-eye—she holstered the firearm and pressed
the button to examine her handiwork.

In her own glass box and looking over the lanes,
a manager provided shooters with headphones and a
handout with a long list of dos and don'ts while in the
range. She was in her mid-forties with a weathered face,
and she kept a sharp visual on all six shooters. In front
of her was a console with buttons for verbally commu-
nicating with the shooters in the booths. While Stella

was looking over her target, the manager depressed a button. She said, "Stella, you have visitors."

"In a minute" was the response.

The manager said, "You can wait for her in the gun-locker room. We don't allow people to congregate out here. It's through that door on the left."

The man in charge of the gun-locker room also sat behind a glass partition.

No one was taking any chances.

He appeared to be in his fifties, with a broad chest and sleeve tattoos on both arms. He had long hair streaked gray, wore a black sleeveless shirt with a red, sequined Harley logo to match the red MAGA cap.

Decker went over to him. "Excuse me." The man lifted his face. "Boyd told us that we can pick up our guns here."

"Tickets." When presented with the stubs, the man said, "Slide them under the glass."

Decker cooperated. A moment later, a small glass door on the side of the partition opened and out came the metal boxes. "Thank you."

"Cops?"

"We are."

"How about arresting those cretins out there?"

"They're allowed to be there."

"They're allowed to protest. Not to hassle me every time I come in and out."

Decker smiled. "Somehow I think you can take care of yourself."

The man smiled back. "Plead the Fifth on that one."

"I like your shirt," McAdams said. "It sparkles."

"Represents my feminine side." When he smiled, he bared teeth—a complete set but yellow. "Got all this shit at Sturgis."

"My wife and I made it as far as Keystone on our way to see Rushmore," Decker said. "But it was during Sturgis. There were women who could have whopped my ass, and I'm not a small man."

"Don't surprise me. We're the true outlaws. Not those punk-asses out there—about as tough as a noodle."

At that moment Stella walked in. "You two wanted to see me? You look like cops."

"We are cops."

"Greenbury PD or the colleges?"

"Greenbury." McAdams pulled out his badge.

"Real police. As much as this place has real police. Mostly just a bunch of young nothing officers and old men for detectives." She winked at Decker. "No offense."

"None taken," Decker said.

"He worked Homicide in L.A. for over four decades," McAdams said. "Does that qualify as real police?"

Stella turned her steely blue eyes back on Decker's face. "What division?"

"I wound up a lieutenant running the detective squad. But here I'm just an old man looking for information. With that in mind, we're wondering if you've kept old logbooks of people who came in and out of the range."

"How old?"

"Ten years back."

"We have old logbooks. You looking for someone specific?"

"Max Velasquez," Decker said. "He's on your computerized list of locker renters."

"If he rented a locker, he must have come in and out of the range," Stella said.

"Not necessarily," Decker said. "He could have rented the locker for someone else."

Stella wrote down the name. "Anything else?"

"Do you keep records of the contents of lockers?"

"Only if the person who rented it was delinquent in payment. And I take it the information you want is also from ten years ago?"

"Yes, ma'am."

"You're looking for a gun?"

"Possibly."

"Okay, Mr. Cagey Lieutenant, let's deal with the gun first," Stella said. "If payment is delinquent, we first try to contact the owner. Even after we empty a locker, if it has a firearm, we still try to contact the owner. If there's no owner, we turn in the firearms to the authorities."

"Which authorities?" McAdams asked. "Greenbury or the colleges?"

"Greenbury. If the locker you are seeking had a weapon, go search your own backyard."

"We will do that," McAdams said. "But if you have *any* information about what was in the locker, that would help."

"I'll see if we have any contents lists. If we did, they'd be in my office. You two have guns?"

Decker said, "We just retrieved them."

"Give them back to Casey. We don't allow guns anywhere except on the range and in the gun-locker room."

"How do we get from the gun-locker room to the parking lot without going through the front door?" McAdams asked.

"It's called a back door." She pointed to a door cut in the wall of the gun-locker room. "Pretty ironic that a gun range has to protect itself against crazies with guns."

The windowless office had four walls of metal file cabinets. The interior was a desk, a desk chair, and two folding chairs. On top of one of the cabinets was a coffeepot, a bag of coffee, and a pile of artificial sweetener packets. Two mugs sat side by side: one was a red emblazoned with the gold MAGA logo; the other said DEPLORABLE AND PROUD OF IT. There was also a water machine sandwiched between two cabinets. Stella started opening and closing drawers.

"Nope." Slam. "Nope." Slam. "Nope." Slam. A pause. "Here we go. Got the year. What month?"

"September and October."

"And the name is Max Velasquez?"

"Yes."

She stopped looking and turned abruptly. "Does this have to do with the bones you found in the woods?"

"Yes," Decker said.

"They're saying the bones belong to one of the Duxbury students who disappeared around ten years ago."

"Zeke Anderson," Decker said.

Stella sat down and looked at the wall. "So that's why you want to go ten years back."

"Yes."

"Their faces were in the local papers for months afterward," Stella said. "Velasquez was one of the names, wasn't it?"

"Yes." Decker pulled out a picture from his wallet. "This is Maxwell Velasquez."

"Don't recognize him as a user," Stella said. "And I'm good with faces. Matter of fact, I'm pretty sure that one of them did some target practice here. He was Black."

"Bennett McCrae," McAdams said.

When she shrugged, out came the picture from Decker's wallet. "Him?"

"That's the one," Stella said. "Always wearing an Obama cap. Occasionally we'd talk politics."

"Different sides of the aisle?" McAdams remarked.

"What do you think? No, I wasn't a fan, but I told him I could understand why he was a fan. We don't get a ton of Black kids who like to shoot, but he sure did. He came to the range pretty regularly."

"And not this one?" Decker showed her the picture of Velasquez again.

"Nope. If he came, it wasn't on my watch."

"When is your watch?" McAdams asked.

"From opening till closing."

McAdams smiled. "We used our badge numbers as IDs to sign in. What do you usually ask for? Driver's licenses?"

"That or school IDs."

"Does the school ID have a photograph?"

"Yes."

Decker said, "Probably easier to doctor a school ID than a driver's license."

Stella said, "You think this Bennett guy was using Velasquez's school ID."

"Possibly."

"Why bother? We don't check who rents the locker. If the person has a key, that's enough."

Decker thought a moment. "Could be he didn't want to use his real name in case the gun was used in something illegal. Or maybe he didn't want anyone to find out he liked guns."

Stella made a face. "None of that makes a lot of sense."

"Just ideas," Decker said. "Never said they were good ones."

Stella smiled. She put down the file. "Give me a little time, and I'll go through everything around those dates, Detective. It's better than me looking piecemeal."

"How long do you think it will take you?"

"Don't know. Give me a phone number and I'll call you back."

"Are you sure?" Decker asked. "We can wait."

"Nah, I'll call you. Be careful making your way back through the throng."

"They don't bother me."

"They don't bother me, either," Stella said. "Sometimes, when I'm in a benevolent mood, I even bring them water on a hot day. They don't drink it." A smile. "They probably think it's poisoned."

"It's still nice of you."

"No biggie." A pause. "I once batted for the other side. Then my brother—who was twenty at the time—was murdered over his sneakers. The bastards who did it were juveniles. They were out after serving six months." Her face turned rabid. "I can't forget and I don't forgive. I know that's not the Christian way. But it's my right to hate. And hate I shall."

Chapter 20

As soon as they walked into the station, Decker's desk phone jangled. It was Kevin Butterfield, who was still in the field, directing the search in the mountains for additional remains. Reception was spotty at best. It took a few moments before the parties could hear each other.

"When did you get back?" he asked Decker.

"Last night. Kev, I'm putting you on speakerphone so Harvard can hear."

"Hey, kid."

"Hey, Kev."

"How did it go with the parents?"

McAdams said, "They're grieving."

"Learn anything?" Butterfield asked.

"Maxwell Velasquez was obsessed with Bennett McCrae."

"As in sexually?"

"Maybe, but however Max felt, it was one-way. McCrae took advantage of Velasquez. Max gave him money without any expectation of being paid back."

Decker said, "We were at the school's gun range this morning. Max Velasquez was on the range's locker rental list ten years ago, but the woman in charge who has been there forever doesn't recall ever seeing Max's face. However, she remembered a young Black man using Max's ID. I showed her Bennett McCrae's photo, and the rest is history."

"It matches up with what Harriet McCrae remembers," McAdams said. "Bennett used to shoot at the school range, although she claims she never saw him with a gun."

Butterfield said, "We still haven't found any signs of a firearm near the remains."

McAdams said, "The range empties gun lockers that are delinquent for payment after three months. If there's a firearm inside and they can't find the owner, they hand it over to Greenbury PD. We're waiting to hear back to see if the range has any written records of handing the gun over to Greenbury."

"If the gun was turned in that long ago, it was probably destroyed."

"No doubt," McAdams said. "What's up with you, Kev?"

"We got a DNA profile from the blood at Elsie Schulung's house. It's not hers, it's not Kathrine Taylor's, but it is female."

"That narrows it down by fifty percent."

"It gets more interesting. I just got off the phone with Jake Quay from Baniff PD. It seems that Elsie Schulung had a girlfriend named Pauline Corbett. The police were at Pauline's apartment. No answer at the door, so the management let them in. The place wasn't emptied, but it was bare bones. Baniff canvassed the neighborhood, and Pauline hasn't been seen in a while. She doesn't seem to have a job. Neither does she have a criminal record. Their forensics team took several things from her place that should yield DNA."

"What specifically?" Decker asked.

"A toothbrush and a nail file . . . maybe a hairbrush. They're going into the lab tomorrow for testing."

Decker thought a moment. "Kev, how much blood was found in the kitchen?"

"You tell me. You were there."

"It was more than a nosebleed, that's for sure. Quay was going to pull up the tile to see if even more blood seeped through. I'm wondering if it was enough for ex-sanguination of a human body?"

"Quay didn't say."

"I'll give him a call," Decker said. "Does Pauline have a car?"

"She does and it's gone. We have a BOLO on it." Butterfield gave him the make and model.

"Great." Decker's cell buzzed. "I need to take this. It's the lady from the gun range."

"Sure. I'll talk to you later."

Decker hung up the landline and depressed the cell's green button. "Hi, Stella."

"Hello, Detective," she said. "There was a gun—an S&W M&P—registered to Max Velasquez at the time he rented the locker. He was required to register it. But when the locker was closed out—in May of 2010—there was no record of a gun being inside the locker."

"Okay," Decker said. "Then whoever had access to the locker could have taken the gun."

"Absolutely," Stella concurred. "You know, there is also a small chance that we messed up and the gun was sent to Greenbury and we just didn't note it. You should check your own records."

"We will."

"One more thing," Stella said. "I was going through the gun-locker registrations. Zeke Anderson also rented a locker, but he closed it out about eight months before he went missing. I went back and looked at our sign-in sheets. According to the logs, he came here about a dozen times in the year preceding the students' disappearances. I don't know if it's significant, but there it is."

Decker was writing as fast as he could. "Could you give me the dates?"

"I'd have to go look them up again." Stella paused.

"Do you remember if he came into the range with anyone?"

"Show me a photograph and I can tell you yes or no. My memory isn't *that* good. I can look up his name in the sign-in sheets and see if there's another name that was frequently next to his."

"That would be great, Stella. Thanks." After she hung up, Decker turned to McAdams. "Zeke Anderson also rented a gun locker. He used to shoot at the range."

"I thought his parents said he despised guns."

"Guess his parents don't know everything."

McAdams shrugged. "They rarely do."

At the station house Decker made about twenty minutes' worth of calls before he finally hung up the phone. He looked across his partner's desk at McAdams, who was checking gun records in Greenbury PD. "Any-thing?"

"If we received the gun registered to Zeke or Max, it wasn't recorded here." He lifted his head. "The more likely explanation is that the boys emptied their lockers when they stopped paying. As far as Zeke Anderson goes, I don't see any record of a gun license for him. He could have purchased it at a gun show and just never registered it. Things were much laxer back then. Who were you talking to? Baniff?"

"Yes. Jake Quay brought in a blood-pattern expert two days ago because he was wondering the same thing as me. If the amount of spilled blood was consistent with death."

"And?"

"After applying luminol, the expert did not see any evidence of spray, back spatter, or castoff. Not a likely slash wound, either, because there would be back or forward splatter."

"Meaning the victim wasn't shot, stabbed, slashed, or beaten. What's left?"

"Well, probably not shot or beaten or slashed," Decker said. "Stabbed is still possible. The place was thoroughly cleaned. We could smell the bleach. But usually something telltale is left on the walls or ceil-ings if the wounds were mortal. She posited that the amount of blood remaining might be consistent with a stab wound—a deep stab wound. A kitchen accident where something sharp sliced into the skin, but didn't hit an artery. If the wound was deep enough, the blood would drip down and pool under the fridge. SID also found droplets near the sink."

McAdams said, "If you get a bad cut, your first instinct would be to wash it off."

"Exactly," Decker said. "It could have been an accident. But the expert also qualified that the injury could have been fatal and the person bled out elsewhere, especially if that person wasn't given proper medical care. Quay told me that Elsie had a knife block and nothing was missing from that. He did a visual check on all the knives he could find. That was also a negative."

"That much blood would need attention," McAdams said.

"Of course," Decker said. "Quay has checked with local urgent care centers as well as hospitals. Negative."

McAdams said, "Boss, Elsie was a nurse. She could have tended the wound herself."

It was a good point. Decker told him so.

McAdams said, "Suppose Elsie and Pauline got into a fight and Pauline got injured. Elsie might be hesitant to go to a hospital. She'd get arrested. And maybe Pauline wouldn't want her to be arrested. You know how domestics are. Love-hate-love-hate."

"Okay. I understand that," Decker said. "Then where does Bertram fit in?"

"What we've been saying from the start, Rabbi. Maybe it was too much for Elsie to care for Pauline *and* do all the cleanup. She calls Bertram for help. She picks him up from Loving Care and tells him to clean up the blood while she tends to Pauline's wound. As a reward, she'll reunite him with Kathrine."

"It's about a half hour from Loving Care to Elsie's house. Would she just leave Pauline to tend to a bleeding wound while she goes to pick up Bertram? Caring for the injury is more important than the cleanup of a house."

McAdams said, "She tended to the wound and then she picked up Bertram?"

"But that wouldn't explain why Elsie would abruptly leave town with two adults with special needs. If Pauline turned out okay, no harm done. Why skip town?"

"Maybe Pauline threatened to go to the police."

"If it was an accident, why would she do that?"

"Maybe it wasn't an accident," McAdams said. "Maybe Pauline was attacked."

Decker said, "That makes more sense to me. Given the strong bleach smell, someone was hiding something. How Bertram and Kathrine fit in is anyone's guess."

McAdams thought a few moments. "We know the blood isn't Elsie's. Let's assume it is Pauline's blood."

"We're back to that?"

"Just hear me out. What if Elsie and Pauline had been planning to take off with Bertram and Kathrine? The accident or stabbing just delayed everything. Then instead of taking off that night, they wanted to give the wound time to heal. So, they waited a few days. Then they picked up Bertram from the diner during the field trip and picked up Kathrine a day later at her facility."

"All right," Decker answered. "That scenario makes a modicum of sense and it explains some of the moving parts. But why the massive cleanup if they were leaving anyway? And why would Elsie take off with Bertram and Kathrine? What did those two bring to the table?"

McAdams said, "Bertram promised Elsie money if she could convince Kathrine to come along with them. Or maybe it's a kidnapping for ransom. Bertram's parents have money."

"Right now, kidnapping is the only thing that makes sense," Decker said. "That Elsie is trying to extort money. And that's why she needed Kathrine—to keep Bertram under control. How Pauline would fit in is anyone's guess."

"Maybe Elsie and Pauline planned the kidnapping together," McAdams said. "To me, that makes more sense than Elsie killing Pauline. And if Pauline was dead, they wouldn't be traveling in her car. That would be stupid. Then, Elsie would have to get rid of two cars—hers and Pauline's. Bertram doesn't drive. To me, that points to Pauline being alive."

Decker said, "Just to muddy up the waters, what about suicide? Slashing your wrists produces a lot of blood, but you have to cut pretty deep to get an artery. It's a good theory to explain what we found at the scene."

"Pauline cut herself, and Elsie had no choice but to take her with them."

Decker shrugged. "I suppose if Elsie did a good enough job of bandaging, Pauline could still drive her car. That would at least explain why both cars are gone. Actually, both cars aren't *gone*. We found Elsie's car."

McAdams said, "This is getting very complicated."

"Way too complicated. I like our Pauline as a homicide victim better. It explains why Elsie would need Bertram's help and why she'd take off immediately. If that's the case, Pauline's body should be out there somewhere."

"And we should be looking for Pauline's car, don't you think?"

"I do think," Decker said.

The station-house phone rang. Decker picked up the receiver and listened intently. "Where?" More listening. "Okay, Kev, we're on our way." He hung up and looked at McAdams. "The cadaver dog sat on a spot about two miles from Zeke Anderson. The crew started digging and stopped when they found a human tooth. Coroner is on his way."

"Two miles?"

"Yes."

"All righty dighty. Let's go."

"Pull a half dozen waters from the fridge, McAdams. It's hot out there and we'll be camping out for a while."

It took them almost an hour to find the exact spot because GPS is useless in uncharted areas. By the time they parked, SID was in full operation. There was a white forensics van parked next to a pop-up tent enclosing the affected area—standard procedure in Greenbury for remains in remote locations. It prevented unwanted animal activity and detritus from falling into the hole as Forensics unearthed the bones. A large flap had been rolled up and tied at the top, probably to allow some air inside. Kevin was walking out just as they were coming toward the tent. He pulled off his cap and gloves and wiped his forehead. His bald head was dripping sweat. His naturally thin frame probably had lost a couple of pounds in water weight. Decker and McAdams stopped at the open flap. Butterfield said, "Fucking hot in there."

"You want some water?" McAdams asked.

"Yeah, that would be great." Butterfield downed the contents of the plastic bottle in three gulps. "Scientists are digging carefully. They've found two more teeth and an intact mandible with some teeth in the bone. No cranium yet. SDI has just finished setting up. Coroner should be here momentarily."

"What's the plan?"

"I've laid out a grid," Butterfield said. "Most of it is ground we haven't covered. I wanted to be as organized as possible. We've got bags, gloves, and metal detectors in the van."

"Still got the dogs?"

"A dog, yes. And its handler. I'd like to head up the search team, but someone needs to stay close to the diggers."

"I can do that," Decker said. "I'll have to suit up."

"There are suits in the van as well. I'm warning you, it's hot and dusty inside."

"I've handled worse." Decker shielded his eyes from the glare of sunlight as he glanced around. "Has anyone searched the area *around* the tent?"

"Not yet."

"I can do that while they're working inside. I'll do like a fifty-foot radius, and you and your crew can go out from there. Sound good?"

Butterfield nodded. "How about if you take Mc-Adams and search a hundred-foot radius? If you do that, my crew will be out of the way."

"Okay with me," Decker said.

"Want a tape measure?"

"I'll just pace it off from the four corners with a string."

McAdams said, "That might be more of a rectangle than a circle."

Decker crooked a finger in Tyler's direction. "The kid knows geometry."

Butterfield smiled. "Nice to know that elite universities still have some standards."

The leftover scrub sets were too short for Decker's long limbs. The shoe covers barely fit over his oxfords. But it was enough protection for Decker to take a peek at the remains inside the tent. Digging was still going on. Inside the hole—as with Zeke Anderson—there was hair around the skull. The locks weren't as plentiful, but what was there was dark and curly, scattered over the cranium like a halo. There was a neat hole in the forehead but no sign of a weapon. He'd ask Kevin Butterfield about it. The thorax had been removed but not the limbs. There were fibers near the body—possibly denim. No jewelry on the fingers or around the neck. SID was working to expose the legs. The femurs seemed intact, but that's where it stopped. Below the knee of both legs were splintered fragments of tibia and fibula, indicating the area that took the brunt of the damage. The ankle and foot bones on the right were intact; the left foot was shattered.

On the table, the coroner was arranging the thorax. Decker walked over, hoping to get more information. The doctor was burly and barrel-chested. He had a round face with a double chin and thick black glasses that were fogged in the heat and the humidity. He promptly pulled them off and cleaned them with a wipe. He smiled at Decker.

"Craig Vitello. I don't think we've ever met." He extended his hand, and Decker shook it.

"No, I don't think we have. Pete Decker. Thanks for coming down."

"Not a lot of calls in your department for my profession?"

"Thankfully not too many."

"Not a local accent." Vitello wrinkled his fleshy nose as he thought. "Slight drawl. Can't tell if it's southern or western."

"Born in Orlando but lived in Los Angeles for over thirty years."

"The accent is a little bit of both, huh?"

"People have told me that I have a twang, although I don't hear it." Decker smiled. "Not hard to hear where you're from."

"New England through and through."

"Can you tell me anything?"

"I just got here ten minutes ago. First glance, the remains look like they've been interred for a while. I know you're investigating a ten-year-old cold case. The bones certainly could be that old."

"Anything about the ethnicity?"

"You're referring to the curly dark hair?"

"I am."

Vitello smiled. "Probably not a Swede, but let's wait for that one. You saw the bullet hole in the forehead."

"Yes."

"I understand that no weapon has been recovered: no guns, no knives, no blunt objects, no firearms, no bullets, no casings. That's unusual."

"Maybe there's a bullet that went through his skull and has buried itself into the ground. Or it could be that someone picked it up after firing the weapon. If it was a revolver, there'd be no spent cartridge."

"Of course." Vitello paused. "I want to show you something on the table." The coroner pointed to the re-creation of the rib cage inside the tent. "The thorax has sustained damage. We'll know more once we get the bones into the lab, but to me it looks like a projectile went from the back to the front at an upward angle. It took out a floating rib and the bottom of the false ribs, traveling up, and exited."

"What kind of a projectile?" Decker asked. "A bullet?"

"It's messy for a bullet."

"Then what are we looking at?" Before the coroner could answer, Decker said, "There were three students who went missing. The first one, Zeke Anderson, had a shattered rib cage and a shattered forearm and hand. I was thinking defensive wound, but as with these remains, we found no evidence of a firearm."

Vitello nodded. "An explosion of some sort would be my guess. If you look here"—he pointed to remaining false ribs—"they have a lot of tiny scratch marks."

Decker stared at the bones. "Am I seeing tiny frags of metal?"

"Yes. The victim was standing with his back toward something that erupted."

"Which came first, then?" Decker asked. "The explosion or the GSW?"

"Don't know," the coroner said. Could be the explosion injured him and the bullet to the head finished him off."

"Weird to murder someone by explosion," Decker said.

"I agree," Vitello said. "The more likely scenario is he was fatally shot first and someone had the grand idea to try to blow him to pieces to hide the bullet wound." A pause. "Or it could have been an accidental explosion that severely injured our buried body and the shot was a mercy killing."

"Yikes. Poor kid, regardless of how it happened."

"Yes, that is cause for empathy," Vitello told him. "Life is funny. Some people die old, some die young, and some should have never been born."

Chapter 21

McAdams hung up the phone. He and Decker were back at the station house after being in the field for over eight hours. There were bags of evidence to be sorted and paperwork to be done. Their desktops were stacked with files, and a card table had to be brought out to hold everything else. He took a sip of cold coffee and said, "The remains were male by the angle of the pelvic bones. Vitello will have more information later on, but he wanted to pass that on."

"Okay." Decker was sitting at the card table, carefully removing the contents of one of the paper bags.

"What are you looking at?"

"These very small patches of material." Decker picked up a magnifying glass. "This could be denim."

"Were Velasquez and/or McCrae wearing jeans when they disappeared?"

"Probably, but that doesn't mean anything. Almost the entire student body of the Five Colleges wear jeans." Another stare. "There's a fiber on the patch." He took out a pair of tweezers, lifted it off the piece of denim, and bagged it separately. "Could be from a sweater."

"Can you tell the color?"

"There's a tiny bit of pigment." He examined it closely. "Maybe red."

"You don't have to bother with the clothes. All the boys have their DNA on file. That should short-cut the process of identification."

Decker put the tweezers down. "We don't know who the fibers belong to. Could be from the body. Could be from the person who buried the body." He stood up and stretched his back. "What do you make of the two being buried so far apart?"

"Murdered at different times?"

"So, you think they were intentional murders?"

McAdams said, "If it was an accident, why hide the bodies?"

"Fear."

"That's an awful lot of work for fear. And the longer you are missing, the more people are going to start looking for you. Maybe just leave the bodies where they are and get the hell out. In any case, it isn't logical to bury one body in one place and then drag another body for two miles through wooded areas and bury it there. The inclination would be to dig a deep hole big enough for the both of them and say sayonara."

Decker nodded. "I'm going to pack it in. What about you?"

"I've got a few more hours left in me," McAdams said. "You like the coroner's explosion theory?"

"A bomb would explain the injuries."

"But not why they were buried so far apart."

"More than one explosion?" Decker suggested. "The blasts went off at different times."

McAdams thought about that. "Maybe that's why they went camping. To make bombs. You'd need a lab for that. But why would they make bombs? They didn't appear to be radicals."

"People have secret sides."

"Even with two explosions, boss, it still doesn't explain why the two boys died two miles apart. Unless there was more than one lab. That's a little far-fetched."

"Agreed."

"You'd think the dogs would have sniffed something out."

"They're cadaver dogs, not bomb dogs." Decker scratched his cheek. "And even if there were trace odors from bombs—unlikely after ten years—the dogs weren't trained to alert with explosives. That's how it is nowadays, Harvard. Everyone's a specialist."

At three in the morning Decker tiptoed into the bedroom. He picked up the pajamas that had been laid out for him on the bed and went into the bathroom to change, wash, and brush his teeth. He crawled into bed and closed his eyes. A moment later, Rina said, "How was it?"

"Long. Let's talk in the morning."

"Sure. Sorry."

"No apologies necessary."

"I'm just saying I'm sorry it was long."

"Oh. Okay. Let's go to bed."

"Of course."

A few seconds passed. He said, "I'm sorry I woke you."

"You didn't wake me. I always have an ear open when you're gone. Do you need anything?"

"No. Let's go to sleep."

"Sure." About a minute passed and Rina heard him getting up. "What do you need?"

"I'm thirsty."

"I left a bottle of water on the nightstand."

"Oh." He slid back under the covers but sat up. "I didn't see it. Thanks."

Rina sat up. "Now I'm thirsty." She opened her water bottle. In the dark she could see his profile. "Cheers."

"Cheers." They clinked plastic. "When I left, the remains were still being removed. DNA will take a couple of days. We'll know soon."

"Do you think it's one of the missing students?"

"I do. The remains are male. And the bones have been there for a while."

"Which one?"

"Don't know. Maybe Velasquez. But I have no scientific reason for that other than Bennett McCrae was stronger and probably more able to bury the other two."

"Why would Bennett kill either one? Max was giving him money, and Zeke was his friend."

"Our thinking has shifted a little." Decker finished the bottle. "I'm still thirsty. I'll be right back."

"Can you bring me another?"

"Sure." He came back a moment later. "This isn't good."

"What isn't good?"

"A man my age drinking at three in the morning."

"You're probably dehydrated. What has shifted in your thinking?"

"We haven't found any evidence of a firearm. And we found some frags in the remains. We're thinking that maybe it was an explosion."

"Like what?"

"McAdams suggested a bomb lab."

"Why would those boys be making bombs? Were they secret radicals or something?"

"I don't think so. But a bomb would explain the frags in the bones."

"True." Rina opened her water bottle. "What about a meth lab?"

"Yeah, you suggested that when we first found Anderson's remains."

"I did suggest that," Rina said. "Wasn't *Breaking Bad* all the rage back then? Maybe the lab exploded?"

"It's definitely a consideration. But from what we've gleaned, none of them were big drug users."

"Maybe they did it for income."

Decker nodded. "Income . . . or for the thrill. None of the students were hardship cases."

Rina said, "Maybe that's where Max fit in. He was the math/science guy. Maybe he proposed the idea to Bennett. Bennett proposed it to Zeke, and the rest is history."

"I could see Max setting up something like that. A chance to prove himself. And I could see Bennett going along with it—for the kicks and money. Then there's Zeke. He doesn't seem to be the type."

"And how well do you know any of them?" Rina said.

"True. The Andersons didn't know that Zeke practiced shooting. They told me that he hated guns."

"Kids that age are a mystery," Rina said. "They think they're immortal. And everything is usually okay. Until something goes wrong." She put down her water bottle. "You want something to eat?"

"No, I need sleep."

"Then let the snoozing begin."

The room was silent. Then Decker got up. She said, "What now?"

"I gotta make a phone call."

"Peter, no one is up."

"I'll leave a message."

"What's so urgent?"

"I ordered a bomb dog. Maybe I also need a drug dog. I wonder if I can borrow a dog trained in both? CBP must have a few of those."

"CBP?"

"Customs and Border Patrol. They use dogs at crossings all the time. Niagara Falls isn't so far from here.

Maybe I could make a phone call. I'm sure they're open twenty-four/seven."

"It's three-thirty a.m. Even if someone answers the phone, you'll probably have to wait until morning."

"Yeah, you're right. Let's go to sleep."

"For real this time?"

"For real." A minute passed. "Unless you want to do something else as long as we're up."

"That might happen."

"Likely or unlikely?"

"Likely." A pause. "Why do you ask?"

"Well, I want to know my odds before I bother going to the bathroom."

Rina hit him. "Go in peace, Old Man. Go in peace."

Some cops made a habit of going down to the morgue. Decker wasn't one of them. Usually he waited for the coroner's report to arrive on his desk. If there were any questions, a phone call could handle it. But the case was old and cold and Decker didn't want to wait for something formal. Vitello said he'd be free around two and didn't object to a visit.

The morgue was located in Hamilton, an area that typified small northeastern towns. Unemployment waxed and waned, but teen mischief was always a staple. Most of the time it was petty crime. But there was occasional spillover to Greenbury and the college campuses, and that was always a problem. Hamilton had two major hospitals, both of them capable of doing autopsies for local police departments. The remains found yesterday had been transported to the basement of Saint Joseph's. The meeting had been called for two o'clock. Decker arrived at ten to. He waited in the car until the appointed time. There was no sense filling one's nostrils with death earlier than necessary.

The crypt was brightly lit and busy. As Decker walked the hallways, the sickly sweet smell of decay wafted through the air and up into his nose. Vitello was in one of the eight autopsy rooms, suited up and standing over the remains. Decker knocked and the coroner waved him inside the glass cube. The room was hermetic and blocked out most of the stink of the rest of the morgue. The remains were arranged anatomically— like a collapsed skeleton—and the bones smelled vegetative, like compost with just a hint of dead-body smell.

Vitello looked up, his blue face mask dangling from his neck. "How's it going, Twang?"

"Not bad, New England. Thanks for seeing me. Got anything of interest?"

"For one thing, I can tell you that our man here was shot at the junction of frontal and parietal bones, and it exited through the occiput."

Decker looked at the cavity. "The entrance hole is pretty round."

"Yes, it is," Vitello said. "I don't think he was moving much when he was shot."

"Did anyone find a slug?"

"I didn't. I don't think SID located anything, either."

"It was an execution?"

"If he was tied up, I didn't find any ligatures at the site or any indentation in his arm bones. The wrist bones fell apart. I'll examine them one by one and write that up in my report."

"Thanks," Decker said.

Vitello said, "Now the killer could have taken the ties with him after our victim was shot, but that requires a lot of forethought."

"How does the bullet hole fit in with the other damage done to the long bones?"

"Like we discussed before, and I'm not saying this happened, but I would posit that our victim sustained near-lethal injuries in an explosion and afterward someone decided to put him out of his misery."

"Then why bother burying him?" Decker said.

"Hide the evidence."

"Then why bother with an explosion? If there was even an explosion."

Vitello shrugged. "Twang, the dead only tell me so much."

Decker said, "And you think the explosion came first."

Vitello said, "I couldn't tell you for certain, but yes I think the explosion came first and then GSW. The shape of the hole, and the cleanness of the execution. Like I said yesterday, when the bullet penetrated the skull, the victim wasn't moving much. With the wounds he sustained on his legs, he would be in a great deal of agony. Someone might have thought a mercy killing was the right thing to do."

Decker said, "Poor kid. He barely started his life and then it's gone." He shook his head. "And then for his parents not to know what happened for ten years?"

"It's a tragedy," Vitello said. "Maybe identifying the body will bring the parents closure."

"You know when closure happens, New England?" Decker said. "Never. It's always an open wound. Sometimes it festers, sometimes it scars over for a while, but the pain never, ever goes away."

Chapter 22

It was close to five in the afternoon, and Decker and McAdams were drowning in work. More and more evidence bags were being brought into the station house from the recent dig. It was only a matter of time before the flimsy card table would sag under the weight. It was already Thursday afternoon. Where had the week gone?

Kevin Butterfield was at the coffee maker renewing the supply of fuel for the rest of the force. He said, "We've searched the area in every which direction, Pete. If there was a lab, we'd have come across it."

"Maybe it wasn't a structure." Decker organized his thoughts. "Maybe this one was a pop-up thing in a tent. Maybe that was the purpose of this camping trip. To make something illegal."

"You can't make meth in a tent."

"Sure you can."

"It requires supplies and equipment."

"Not complicated supplies and equipment," Decker said. "Maybe whoever buried the bodies also buried the evidence of the blown-up lab. The cadaver dogs were looking for bodies not bombs."

"When are the bomb dogs coming?" Butterfield asked.

"I don't know. Maybe never. We're not top priority."

"Coffee ready?" McAdams asked.

"Yeah, which one's your cup?" Butterfield picked up a red mug emblazoned with HARVARD in gold. "Might it be this one?"

"That's mine," Decker said.

"A gift from yours truly," McAdams said. "Mine's the one with Goofy on it."

Butterfield was abashed. "For my erroneous assumption, I will serve. How do you take it, Tyler?"

"A little milk, thanks." After Butterfield poured and handed out the mugs, McAdams said, "I've been thinking about that."

"About what?" Decker asked.

"The buried bodies. Specifically, what you need to bury bodies. You go on a camping expedition to make drugs or bombs or whatever, and you decide to take along a shovel? With all the other stuff, it would be a burden because it's heavy and useless."

"What are you saying?" Butterfield asked. "That someone knew he was going to bury bodies?"

"Or . . ." McAdams stood up and spread out a map of the wooded area on his desk. "Look at this, guys." Decker and Butterfield got up and crowded around McAdams. "Here's where we found Zeke Anderson's remains. And here's where we found the other set of remains. This is where the cops on the original case found Zeke's car. Look at the direction of the lines— from Zeke, to new remains, to the car."

"It's downhill toward the main road," Decker said. "Someone was trying to get help or get back to the car."

"Exactly. But it was dark. He was confused and he got lost."

"Are you thinking that a third set of remains are somewhere on that pathway?" Butterfield said.

"Possibly," McAdams answered. "Or look at this. If you follow the trajectory from where we found the second set of remains and go straight down, you'll hit a trail that does a switchback that leads to the main road about three miles away from Zeke's car. It's very possible that our remaining dude actually made it to the road and hitched his way to civilization."

"How does this fit into your shovel question?" Butterfield asked.

"Suppose that the explosion took place Thursday or Friday," McAdams said. "The remaining camper knows he has a limited amount of time before people start looking for them. He has two days' grace to get rid of the bodies and hide whatever caused the explosion. Once he makes it into town, he rents a car, buys a shovel, and goes to work hiding everything. He can take some time because he knows that no one is looking for them. Once he's done with that, he splits before anyone realizes that he and his buds are missing."

"That takes an awful cool head," Butterfield stated.

"Max wasn't social, but no one ever said he wasn't smart," McAdams said. "Given enough time, he could do it."

Decker said, "Why bury the bodies so far apart?"

"Throw the police off."

"It's a stretch, Harvard," Decker said. "To hitch a ride into town, get a shovel, go back to the hills, bury two bodies two miles apart, and then disappear for ten years?"

"I'm not saying it happened that way. But it could be done, especially if you knew that no one was looking for you." McAdams's eyes returned to the map. "The trail leads out to the main road between Greenbury and

Hamilton. If I were Bennett or Max, I'd go to Hamilton. More resources, and no one would recognize me."

Decker said, "If this was ten years ago, we'd be checking out hardware stores and car rentals and CCTV. I doubt if any recordings survived for ten years."

Butterfield said, "There's a slight chance that car rentals do keep records."

Decker said, "We won't know unless we try. Let's check it out first thing in the morning."

"Will do." McAdams paused. "Am I flying solo tomorrow?"

"If we get the DNA results in the morning, I'll come with you," Decker said. "At some point, someone needs to look over the area for evidence of an explosion. Buttress up our theory."

"It's fine, boss," McAdams said. "I can go to Hamilton myself."

Butterfield said, "I can do the search, Deck. I'm more familiar with the area than anyone."

"You are." Decker stood up. "Okay. Kev, you continue with the search for our third camper and while you're out there, you can search for evidence of an explosion. I'll go with Harvard to Hamilton tomorrow and see if Vitello has finished his report. It should be done. He was working on the remains when I saw him this morning. How are we doing with our search for Bertram Lanz?"

"It's still going on," Butterfield said. "But . . . you know. If he's out there, it doesn't look too promising."

"People can be resourceful," Decker said. "Lanz has overcome a lot of adversity. The least we can do is have a little faith."

The smoke from the grill wafted over the backyard fence to the front of the house. Decker's nose sniffed in the aroma of barbecued meat as soon as he pulled up into the driveway. After parking, he went around to the side yard, opened the gate, and saw Rina wearing a sunflower apron over a pink cotton dress. Her hair had been pulled back into a ponytail, but she wasn't wearing a scarf or a beret. She had earbuds in her ears, and there was an intense look on her sweaty face. The outdoor table had been set for three. Decker crept around and tried to get her attention so as not to startle her. But no matter how hard he waved, she failed to notice him. Finally, he had no choice but to place a hand on her shoulder.

Of course, she jumped. She took an earbud out. "You *scared* me."

"Sorry. I tried to get you to notice me, but whatever you're listening to must be pretty engrossing."

"Just some old *devrai* Torah from an old rabbi."

"Sounds fascinating."

"You're being facetious." Her smile was wide. "It's actually not too bad."

"That's a rousing endorsement."

"He repeats himself a lot."

"Sign me up." Decker looked at the grill: steak and asparagus. "My mouth is watering." It was close to eight in the evening. "I'm starving."

"Salad and drinks in the fridge. You can bring those out."

"You want wine, darlin'?"

"I'm good with sparkling water."

"Then I'm having a beer."

"There's a cold six-pack that's calling your name. Is Tyler coming?"

"He didn't say yes or no when he left, so I'm taking that as a no." He snaked his hands around her waist. "And that's just as well. More food for me."

"How did it go today? Any DNA on the remains?"

"Not yet. Soon, I hope."

"Then you still don't know who it is."

"No, but the bones are old."

"Okay. Any news on Bertram?"

"No." He dropped his hands to his sides. "We found out that Elsie Schulung had a girlfriend. Pauline Corbett. Did I tell you this?"

"No. I've barely seen you for the last couple of days. Could you get me the platter and the tongs from the table? We're good to go."

"Gladly." He gave her the dish and the tongs, then went inside to fetch the salad, sparkling water, and the six-pack. As she doled out the meat and asparagus, Decker popped the top of the can and sipped suds. "Looks wonderful."

"Let the meat rest for a few minutes."

"Your form of torture?"

"Hence the salad." Rina put a heap of leaves into individual wooden bowls. "This is the appetizer. Eat. What about Pauline Corbett?"

Decker said, "You're all over the place."

"No, I'm just able to keep several lines of conversation going in my head at one time. Why is she relevant?"

"I don't know that she is. But her car is missing and she hasn't been seen in about a week."

"She helped Elsie kidnap Bertram and Kathrine?"

"Maybe. We think that there were two people in the car when it came to pick Kathrine up." Decker stuffed his mouth with another forkful of leaves and chewed intently. "We're also thinking that maybe it's Pauline's blood in the kitchen."

"Why?"

"The blood is female. The DNA results from material at Pauline's apartment haven't come back. But we should know soon if it matches. Here's something interesting. Quay brought in a blood expert. She said that there wasn't a lot of spatter or blowback. She thinks it might have been a nonfatal stab wound or an accident."

"Like a knife cut?"

"Exactly." He finished the beer and opened another can. "The blood was found in a kitchen."

"Didn't you say it was a lot of blood?"

"Yes, I did."

"How do you cut yourself by accident that badly to bleed that much?"

"You drop a very sharp knife, and it hits a major vein in the thigh or foot."

Rina's face expressed skepticism. At that moment McAdams came into the backyard. "Am I interrupting anything?"

"Sit, Tyler," Rina said. "I made a steak for you."

"As tempting as it is, I'm going to pass. I'm meeting an old friend for dinner. A guy I went to school with. I just dropped by to give the old man some lab results." He handed Decker a manila envelope that had been opened. "Sent over from the lab right after you left the station. It's Pauline Corbett's blood."

"We were just talking about that," Rina said. "How a person loses that much blood in an accident without hitting an artery."

"You can fall down and hit your head," McAdams suggested.

"That too." After glancing at the report, Decker slid the piece of paper back into the envelope. "We now have a person instead of just blood. What about her car?"

"BOLO went out yesterday."

Decker drummed his fingers on the table. "Did Bertram's parents ever call back?"

"Nope."

"When was the last time we called them?"

"I did a follow-up on the way to the airport on Tuesday. I didn't tell you?"

"No."

"Probably because there's nothing to report. They're still out of cell phone reach. It could be the truth. The secretary said they're mountain climbing in Nepal."

"Okay. Where are we with phone records?"

"Takes time, boss."

"Call up the phone company and bug them."

"Sure . . . now?"

"I'm in the middle of dinner. Do you mind?"

"You're the boss." McAdams scrolled down the contacts of Decker's phone and pressed the phone number.

Decker said, "Can you talk inside? I'd like to eat without distraction."

"Sure." McAdams went inside the house.

Rina laughed. "That wasn't very nice."

Decker cut into his steak. A perfect medium rare. "Ask me if I feel guilty. I don't." He popped the meat into his mouth. "Delicious. This deserves my full attention. Thank you."

"You're welcome."

They ate in silence for a few moments. McAdams came back outside. "They said we're in the line. Maybe another week. Should I call Mangrove PD and see if they have Kathrine's records yet?"

"Sure. Good idea."

"Yeah, I get one every now and then." McAdams's phone buzzed. "Okay. Hold on." Into the phone: "Hey, Spenser. What's up?" He listened for a few moments. "No problem. We'll make it another time. Go save the world." He hung up and said, "My friend is in medical school. He just got paged." A huge smile. He sat down at the table and snatched a can of beer. He popped it open. "I'll take that steak if you don't mind."

"Don't you have to make a phone call?" Decker asked.

McAdams handed Decker back his phone. "You wouldn't want my dinner to get cold. Besides, you're done."

Decker looked at his empty plate, stood up, and threw down his napkin. "Fine. I'll do it."

As he walked away, Rina called out, "Fresh fruit in the refrigerator. You mind bringing it out?"

"Any other requests?"

"How about a smile?" Rina said.

"You want to ask for the moon while you're at it?"

McAdams said, "He's not really mad, is he?"

"He is mad," Rina said. "He was counting on eating your steak."

"Ah." McAdams cut it in half.

"You don't have to do that." Rina pointed to her steak. "I already saved some of mine for him."

"It's fine, Rina. He's a big guy. He's entitled to eat."

"Aren't we two so nice today?"

"Yes, we are. We're just the best."

When the house phone rang past ten in the evening, it was never good news. Rina picked up the receiver, although she didn't know why. It was always for Peter. But this time she was wrong on both accounts.

"Hi. Am I calling too late?"

Rina's heart was beating fast. "Everything okay, Gabriel?"

"Yeah, good, as a matter of fact. She phoned me."

A gush of relief. "That's great! How's your mom doing?"

"We only spoke for a few minutes. She's settled in California somewhere. She said she'd call me when she's found a more permanent home. But she wanted to let me know that she's okay."

"Can I say I told you so?"

"Gladly," Gabe said. "I really do want her in my life."

"I know you do, honey. She's your mom."

"Also, when she's okay, it's less drama in my life. She told me she's got a few possibilities for a job. I told her not to rush it. I have plenty of money."

"What did she say?"

"That she really wanted to find work. She couldn't keep borrowing from me. I know I was kind of be-grudging about writing her a check the last time we met. I feel bad about it."

"She knows you have her best interest at heart."

"I do. Honestly, I was hoping this marriage would work. And I think it did for a while. Poor Mom. Poor Juleen and Sanjay. Divorce is hard. My parents were toxic together, and it was still hard on me. I told her I'd visit them in California once they're settled."

"I'm sure they'd love it. You are a very important person in their lives. How's Yasmine?"

"Stressed."

"How are you?"

"Busy."

"And that's good, right?"

"Yes, it is. I like earning money. I like being independent."

"For sure." Rina looked up and Peter had padded into the kitchen, wearing his PJs and slippers. "Want to say hello to the boss?"

"Love to."

Rina handed the phone to Decker. Their conversation lasted a minute, and then he hung up. Decker said, "Nice that she made contact."

"I'm happy for Gabe. Maybe she learned from experience what not to do." A shrug. "You look tired." When he nodded, Rina hooked her arm under his. "Let's go to bed. I'm tired too."

"No you're not." He kissed her cheek. "But it's nice of you to placate an old man."

"You're not old. It's just the job. I know you don't want to retire, but it's wearing you down."

Decker didn't answer. They went into the bedroom, and a few minutes later it was lights-out with the bedcovers drawn to their chins. He said, "I had a great time in Israel."

That was almost a year ago. "As did I," Rina said. "What brought that to mind?"

"I guess I remembered how wonderful it was to walk everywhere and explore. And do things on my own time. And you seemed so happy. It was really liberating."

"We can go back anytime, you know."

"I know." A pause. "I've been looking at real estate ads—"

"What?" She sat up. "Are you serious?"

"I don't want to sever any roots." Decker sat up and took her hand. "America is my country. I love it and I'm thoroughly red, white, and blue. But I am thinking that we could afford something small. It might be a fun adventure."

"Not a cheap adventure."

"We have assets—social security and my pension— certainly enough to live on. I have a retirement account. You have some money. Not a bad idea to have a second home. The kids would certainly use it."

Rina eyed him in the dark. "You're thinking about the property in Nachlaot that we saw on a whim. The one where you said that you wouldn't mind a project.

And then I said, 'It's not just a project but a total reno.' And it's tiny."

"Two bedrooms, two baths. That doesn't qualify as tiny in my book. The inside has good bones—high ceilings and architectural features. The outside has a small garden."

"It's a weed-choked patch."

"Which you can have fun with." He kissed her hands. "Didn't you say you always wanted a biblical garden? You know the Seven Species."

"Did I say that?" Decker didn't answer. She said, "Yes, I did say that."

He said, "Don't you love the neighborhood?"

"Honey, it's where all the kids hang out. It borders the market and it's loud at night."

"It's filled with action and restaurants, and at my age, who can hear anyway?"

"Stop that," Rina said. "When we left L.A., you said you wanted peace and quiet."

"It's a stone house. All I have to do to get peace and quiet is close the doors. Besides, here may be a little too quiet *all* the time."

"Can I ask where this is coming from?"

"We had a great time there."

Rina sighed. "It's very different visiting as a tourist than owning."

"Why? We're not picking up stakes. I thought you'd be happy."

Rina laughed. "Look at us. You're pushing for Jerusalem and I'm resisting."

"Wonder of wonders."

"That place was a wreck, Peter. If you really want a part-time place, I suggest we call a real estate agent and look at other properties. Maybe we can find something that's in better shape."

"I don't need to see other places. That property is perfect. I could create something beautiful, and the area is great. It's so central." When Rina sighed, Decker said, "Let's forget about it and go to bed."

"I just don't want you in over your head."

"Last I checked I was still an adult male with a cogent brain."

Rina sighed again. "Okay. Fine. Let's call up the real estate agent."

"Don't get mad."

"Now what?" Rina sighed. "You've *bought* the place, haven't you?"

"No, not exactly. We've just been talking price."

"For goodness' sake, why didn't you say something to me?"

"You're mad."

"Of course I'm mad."

Decker took her hand. "I'm wrong. No excuses. I'm sorry."

She shook her head. "How much?"

"I haven't signed anything yet."

"Good for you. How much?"

"Approximately $437,000."

"That's a precise amount for approximately."

"It depends on the conversion rate." A pause. "I told her I have to talk it over with you."

"Well, thank you for that!" A long silence. "That's a sizable chunk from our savings, Peter."

"We don't spend on much, Rina. Our needs are simple. And the kids are all working and independent."

"That's debatable." A pause. "The only reason I'm not murdering you right now is because I'm rational enough to know that you have worked *hard* all your life."

"I have."

"And you have a good pension to show for it."

"I do."

Rina hit her forehead. "I can't believe I'm saying this. Okay, here goes."

"Lay it on me."

"You pay half from your retirement. I'll pay half from my trust fund. Go for it."

A pause. "Really?"

"Really."

"Thank you so much, darlin'. I won't let you down."

"You know we have to get a lawyer."

"I know. The agent knows some people."

"I know a few people who can make recommendations also." She shook her head. "Do you really think you can do a remodel by yourself?"

"Yes."

"You can install a kitchen, bathrooms, air-conditioning, heating, a smart house—"

"I can do it all. And if I hire a few people to help me, so be it."

"Ah, so now it comes out."

"I promise I won't get you involved."

"Peter, you don't speak the language."

"Most everyone there speaks English."

"I mean the *language*. And if we're both going to live there, I'd like to have some say in what's going on."

"It's a total joint venture." Decker kissed her hand. "I hope you have an opinion on everything."

Rina grinned. "You may come to regret that statement."

"I already have."

Chapter 23

Placing the call as soon as the lab was open, Decker waited at his desk, doodling on a blank sheet of paper. It was eight in the morning on Friday. He was always antsy at the end of the week, and maybe that explained why his mind was skipping from topic to topic, landing on each item for a second or two like a fly being chased from a picnic. McAdams walked in, looking dapper: a blue polo shirt, tan khakis, and deck shoes with no socks. He noticed the receiver tucked into Decker's shoulder and said, "Who are you talking to?"

Decker looked up. "You look dressed for lunch at the Hamptons."

"I should be so lucky. Who's on the line?"

"It's the lab. I'm on hold."

"Did they call or did you call?" McAdams said.

"I called." Decker paused a moment. "Tell me why you're going into Hamilton again?"

"To see if one of the students rented a car ten years ago."

A remote possibility. Decker didn't harbor much hope. Someone came back on the line. "Yes, hello. I was asking about the remains that came in with Dr. Vitello a few days ago. We sent them out for DNA . . . yes, to test against Bennett McCrae and Max Velasquez." A pause. "Great. When can I pick it up? . . . I'll be right over." He hung up. "The remains belong to Max Velasquez."

"We sort of thought that. Then it's possible that Bennett buried the other two."

"Or there's another set of bones out there."

"If there is another set and it's Bennett's remains, who buried the boys?"

"Good question. Let's go."

Decker and McAdams were sent from one office to another as various people tried to locate the DNA file. They finally wound up in a pathologist's office, waiting while the doc finished up with a body. While it wasn't an autopsy room, it was located in the Hamilton crypt with its pervasive smell of rotting meat and treacle. Even though the air-conditioning was on, the place was warm. One side of the small, narrow area was lined with shelves containing pathology books, tissue samples, and a jar of teeth; a complete human skeleton was suspended from a coatrack. The other side was the lab—shelves of liquids, powders, and reagents along with a countertop covered with notebooks, scales, microscopes, beakers, vials, calipers, and calibrators. Since it was in the basement, there was no natural light, only the glare of fluorescent tubing strung across the ceiling. There was no place to sit, so both of them stood, shuffling feet and glancing at watches. Twenty minutes of doing a two-step until the doc came in, white coat open and smelling none too fresh.

He looked to be in his sixties, with a short and compact build. His round face was emphasized by a round bald head. He extended a clean hand. "Edgar Ferdinand. Here are the DNA papers and the autopsy report for Maxwell Velasquez. Sorry I took so long. It's been a busy morning."

Decker thanked him and turned to the first page of the DNA report. The material found in the bones was matched to Maxwell Velasquez with 99.9993 percent certainty.

Ferdinand said, "We were talking about the case—Vitello and me—and Vit got me curious. Specifically, the neat little round bullet hole in the head and then the shattered legs. They don't go together."

Decker said, "We were thinking that it could be a mercy killing. Dr. Vitello was thinking that the remains—now we know it's Max Velasquez—that he could have survived for a while with shattered legs. But he would have been in tremendous distress. Maybe someone put him out of his misery."

"Sure, it's a possibility." Ferdinand leaned against the counter. "Vit told me that, in his mind, the shattered chest and leg bones of Zeke Anderson point to an explosion. He also told me that you think it's from a meth lab?"

"It's something we're considering," Decker said. "In the woods there's a lot of room to operate unnoticed."

"Yes, there is. But I think the explosion was more up close and personal. Have either of you ever been in the military?"

"I was in 'Nam." The lightbulb went off. Decker raised his eyebrows. "A *grenade?*"

"It would explain the fragments in the bones."

"What in the world would three students from Duxbury College be doing with *grenades?*"

"I could be wrong," Ferdinand said. "Did you find evidence of a bomb lab or a drug lab?"

"No, we haven't."

391 • THE LOST BOYS

"The woods are hidden outposts for all sorts of outside activities like drug labs and pot farms. It could have been a meth lab. But this is my thinking. Ten years ago we were dealing with two wars: Afghanistan and Iraq. Most of our people came through it okay. But some remain driven by demons. Some can't cope with civilian life. They isolate themselves and live off the grid. For the most part, they're harmless. That is unless they're having a mental breakdown and think they're under attack. For someone with PTSD, the sudden appearance of three strapping young men could look like a threat."

"The boys were buried," McAdams said. "Someone took the time to do that."

"It could be that one of the campers escaped and came back and buried the other two. But none of them were ever heard from again. I'm thinking that if someone launched the grenade during a psychotic episode, eventually he may have clicked back into reality and grasped what he had done. When were the students discovered missing?"

"About four days after they went camping."

"That would have been plenty of time for some misguided vet with PTSD to become rational and bury the bodies."

"How do you explain the one gunshot to the head?" McAdams asked.

392 · FAYE KELLERMAN

"Maybe he brought a gun as well as grenades. Or maybe it was field mines that he planted around himself for protection. Or perhaps it was none of the above." Ferdinand shrugged. "Food for thought."

"A grenade, of all things." Decker shook hands with the doc. "Thanks for your input."

"Hope it helped."

"It helped and it muddled things up."

"Yeah, sometimes the truth is like that."

Walking back to the car, McAdams said, "A maniac roaming the woods." He shook his head. "That'll sure kill tourism. The stuff of horror movies. Not to mention the stuff of panic."

"It was ten years ago," Decker said. "Our so-called maniac could have died. He could have moved on. He could have gotten some therapy and become an up-standing citizen."

"Or he still could be out there waiting for some other hapless hikers to encounter," McAdams said. "Have we found any evidence of someone living off the grid?"

"You know as much as I do."

"On the slight off chance that someone is still se-questered in the hills, we should alert our teams."

"Right. Give Kev a call."

McAdams extracted his cell from a pocket and phoned Kevin Butterfield. After updating him, he hung up. "He'd like more people out there. He'd like to redouble his efforts to find Bennett McCrae's remains, should they be there. And they're still looking for Lanz."

"I'll talk to Mike Radar. Maybe he can round up some volunteers from other agencies."

"Are you going up there?"

"Yes, but first I have to go back to the station to make a death call." He turned to McAdams. "It might be worthwhile to take a quick trip to Cleveland. It's more respectful to deliver the news in person."

"As soon as you call, the Velasquezes are going to know that it's bad news, boss. And you have to call. You can't just pop in on them. What's the real motivation?"

"I'd also like to go to Saint Louis and interview Harriet McCrae again. But Radar's more likely to give me the funds if I say I'll go to Cleveland to talk to the Velasquezes."

McAdams wagged a finger. "You think Bennett might still be alive."

"I didn't say that."

"Am I right?"

"Despite what Ferdinand said, I don't see a lunatic burying three bodies miles apart."

"And I don't see someone like Bennett returning to a scene of carnage to bury bodies. Besides, why would he go into hiding? He didn't do anything wrong if it was a mercy killing."

"That's a very gray area, Harvard. Even if it was a mercy killing, Bennett could have thought that he'd be arrested for first-degree murder. Maybe he was so traumatized by everything that he dropped out. You don't go through something like that and resume your normal life."

"I can believe the drop-out part. But I'm skeptical that Bennett would have had the presence of mind to go back and bury the others all the while *knowing* that there was a maniac on the loose."

"Maybe he didn't go back right away. Or maybe I'm totally wrong." Decker shrugged. "My main concern is finding out what happened to Bennett. I just want to talk to Harriet McCrae. Once she finds out about Velasquez, she'll want to know the details anyway."

"It can be done by phone."

"It can. But I always found interviews in person more productive."

"You're on thin ice, boss. You don't want to imply her boy may still be alive and then get a call from Kev that they found his remains."

"You are absolutely right about that." Decker exhaled. "Let's go back to the station house. It's possible that Radar won't fund the trips."

"I can pay for them."

"I can pay, too, but I don't want to."

"You want company? You haven't asked."

"Sure, I'd love company." Decker smiled. "Someone has to carry the luggage."

"I don't understand why this can't be done with a phone call." Radar was looking at Decker from across his desk.

Decker said, "I can't tease out information over the phone."

"Then you're going on a fishing expedition."

"Sometimes you get a bite."

"And sometimes you get bitten in the ass. I don't want a distraught mother calling me up and complaining about you."

"I can be subtle."

"How much are we talking about?"

"Economy round trip: two hundred sixty-five dollars if I book with an online service."

"There goes the bake-sale money."

"I promise Rina will make more cookies next year."

"It was the rugelach that sold out. Man, that was good stuff."

"It's the cream cheese in the recipe," Decker said. "Yes or no?"

"Go."

"Can I take McAdams with me?"

"Why?"

"I took him with me the first time. I like consistency."

"It's not worth two hundred sixty-five dollars for consistency."

"He'll pay his own way."

"That's not the point."

"He wants to come. I want him to come. If you wouldn't have given me the cash, I was going to pay my own way. If you won't give him the cash, I'll split the fare with him."

"Making me look like a cheap son of a bitch. Especially since the kid took a bullet in the line of service."

"Two bullets actually."

"The second was just a graze wound." Radar scowled. "Yes, I'll give you both the airfare and car rentals. You use your own cash for meals and incidentals . . . oh the hell with it. I'll give you an extra fifty for meals. You go over that amount, you pay yourself."

"That'll go a long way in the Midwest. Thank you."

"You've done a good job with this case."

"Thanks, Mike, but we haven't done anything other than discovering remains, and that was by accident."

"Yeah, you really have done squat." The captain smiled. "Where are you at with Bertram Lanz?"

"Not very far with that one either."

"What about the parents? Have they contacted you?"

"No, and it's been almost two weeks. I don't believe they're out of phone contact. They obviously don't want to contact us or speak to us."

"Any idea why?"

"The only thing I can think of is that maybe they're paying off a ransom that specifies no police involvement. Other than that, I don't have a clue."

"This might help." Radar handed Decker a thick padded mailing envelope. "It's from Germany. It's regarding Bertram Lanz."

Decker took it and pulled out the papers. His eyes scanned the first few pages. "Not surprisingly, it's in German. It looks like a police file." He regarded Radar. "Does Lanz have a record?"

"Appears that way."

"What for?"

"Don't know."

"Then where'd you get this?"

"From the BKA, which stands for Bundeskriminal-something. It's a federal clearinghouse for criminal records. I just went from agency to agency until I got to the BKA, and they sent me a copy of whatever they had. Doesn't your wife read German?"

"Not at a high-proficiency level."

"Then take it to the university and get it properly translated."

"Was Lanz's crime a federal offense?"

"No idea. But if it was a serious crime, it may explain all the blood at Schulung's house. See if you can get it translated before you go to Cleveland. Lanz's case is less than two weeks old. The other is ten years old. Let's get our priorities straight."

"I have packed two shirts already," Decker said. "This is my extra in case I get one dirty." He held them both up. "Which one?"

Rina was sitting on the bed going through Bertram Lanz's file. It was ten o'clock on Saturday night. The weekend had been a sweet reprieve, but come the end of Shabbos, Peter once again turned into Detective Decker. Absently, she said, "The one on the left."

"I like it but the material is a little hot."

Still not looking up. "Then take the one on the right."

"The other one is softer."

"Then I have no answer for you." She finally allowed her eyes to look at her husband's face. "Do you want me to read this or not?"

"Of course I want you to read it. Why would I give it to you unless I wanted you to read it?"

"Then please let me read it. My German is marginal at best."

"Don't sweat it. I'm getting it translated anyway."

Rina plopped down the file. "Then why did you give it to me in the first place?"

"Because I couldn't find a translator until tomorrow."

"You won't be here tomorrow."

"Kevin will take it in. I thought you could give us a heads-up. Which shirt?"

"Peter, you're a grown man." She picked up the file and opened it to where she had left off. "You can pack without me."

She was frustrated. Decker stifled a smile. "I am hassling you. I'm sorry."

Rina didn't answer. She was lost in translation. "*Fahrlässige Tötung. Tod* is 'death.' *Tötung* has something to do with death. Look up *Tötung* on your phone."

Decker turned serious. "It was a murder charge?"

"'Murder' is *Mord*. Look up *Tötung*." She spelled it for him.

"Just a minute." A pause. "It means 'killing.'" He looked up. "He killed someone."

"Possibly. I wonder if this means 'voluntary manslaughter' or something like that."

"That would be . . . hold on." Decker tapped the words into his phone. "That would be *freiwilliger . . .*" He showed her the translation.

"Try the translation for 'involuntary manslaughter.'"

"Okay . . ." Seconds passed. "Aha! You go, girl."

"Did the charge stick?"

"It's an arrest record, honey, not a trial record."

"Of course," Rina said. "Let me see if I can wade through the circumstances."

"Who's the victim?"

"A man named Gerthard Perl. Sit down, please. You're making me nervous standing over me."

Decker sat on the bed next to her. He refrained from the temptation to look over her shoulder. Not that he could understand anything he'd see.

Rina furrowed her brow. "*Krankenpfleger. Krankenschwester* is a nurse. I think this must mean a male nurse. *Krankenhaus* is a hospital. *Er arbeitete . . . er* is 'he' and *Arbeit* means 'work.' Probably means he worked in a hospital. *Und Er ging am Abend aus nach seine Schicht aus.*" A pause. "*Ging aus. Ging* must be part of the verb *gehen*. I think this means he went out in the evening after *Schicht*, whatever that is."

"Spell it," Decker said. Rina complied and he said, "Shift."

"Yes, that would make sense." Rina mouthed the

words as she bushwhacked through the German. "*Schlagen . . . schlogen* is 'to hit' in Yiddish. Okay, Bertram hit this guy. I don't know if it was with a car?"

"Bertram can drive?"

"I can't tell you that." A pause. "I don't see the word *auto*, which means 'car.'" A pause. "Probably means he punched him."

"He got into a fight?"

"Here we go. *Faustkampf. Kamf* is a 'fight' in Yiddish. I bet this is 'fistfight.'"

"He got into a fistfight with the nurse?"

"Maybe." She kept reading. "What's the word for 'voluntary manslaughter' again?"

"*Freiwilliger Totschlag.*"

"Okay . . . he was arrested on charges of voluntary manslaughter in a fistfight. But later the charges were downgraded to involuntary manslaughter. I don't know why. Maybe the nurse threw the first punch." She put the file down. "You really need someone more fluent than I am."

"You've been an enormous help, darlin'." A pause. "It gives me a lot to think about. Where did this happen? I want to see if I can look this up on the internet."

Rina told him the name of the town. "The date of the arrest was October . . . wait, it's probably March tenth. They put the date before the month. It was six years ago. He was twenty-seven."

"That corresponds almost to the time when Bertram Lanz came to America."

"Fresh start?" Rina said.

"I'd say yes. It also could be why the parents are reluctant to contact me. They've already dealt with him before. Maybe they fear the worst."

"Meaning?"

"There was blood in Elsie's house, Rina."

"You think Bertram killed someone?"

"I'd like to find him so I could ask him."

Rina said, "Whatever he did in the past, they called it *involuntary* manslaughter."

"That's not the same as justifiable homicide." Decker thought a moment. "We're dealing with someone with diminished capacity. That's for certain. But that doesn't preclude a temper."

"Why would he kill Elsie's girlfriend? What was her name?"

"Pauline Corbett." Decker stood up, packed the two shirts, and closed his suitcase. "There are thousands of reasons why people commit murder. All Bertram needed was one."

Chapter 24

"I knew you'd be back." Wanda Velasquez was standing in her parlor, facing a picture window that looked out over her lawn. Her back was turned so neither Decker nor McAdams could see her face. "As soon as I heard you found the Anderson boy, I figured Max couldn't be far behind." When she turned, her eyes were wet. "How did he die?"

Decker told her the minimum. "He was shot." Until he had more answers, that was enough.

"Did he suffer?"

Probably. "He didn't know what hit him, Wanda."

"He didn't beg for his life or anything."

"I don't think so, no."

"And do you have any idea why he was shot?"

"Not yet. I'm so sorry, Wanda. The finality is always hard to process."

She nodded, her eyes focused on the detectives. They were sitting on a sofa across from her. "I didn't offer you anything to drink."

"We're fine," Decker said.

"No, it's not right." She started to get up but then began to reel.

McAdams got to her first. He looked around. "I'll get some water—"

"I'll get it—"

"No, you sit. *I'll* get it."

"There's a pitcher of iced tea in the refrigerator."

"I'll be right back." McAdams left the room.

Wanda took in a deep breath and let it out. She mumbled, "He'll probably bring in the everyday glasses."

Decker waited a moment. "Still light-headed?"

"I'll survive." She gave him a weak smile. "I suppose I should call Henry and leave a message. He's in surgery."

"On Sunday?" Decker asked.

"There was an emergency. Sick people don't look at a calendar."

"The man works hard," Decker said.

"Very hard." Wanda paused. "Do you have any idea who shot him?"

"Not yet."

"Ten years ago. It could have been anyone. You haven't found Bennett?"

"No."

"Do you think he did it?"

"I don't know."

"Do you think you'll find his body?"

"We're looking for it."

"Then you're assuming that someone else murdered all three boys?"

"It's a possibility."

"And it's also possible that Bennett shot the other two?"

"Yes."

"What do you think is more likely?" Wanda asked.

"I don't know."

"Was my boy buried?"

"Yes." After McAdams came in with iced tea in three everyday glasses, Decker said, "Wanda was just asking if Max was buried."

McAdams put the glasses on the table. He picked up a tumbler and offered it to Wanda. "Here you go. And yes, your son was buried."

"So at least someone did the decent thing." Wanda sipped her drink. It seemed to bring color back to her face. "Or he buried the boys because he didn't want anyone to find them." A pause. "How were the boys buried? Did they bring a shovel to the camping trip?"

"We're looking into that," McAdams said.

"Why would you take a shovel on a camping trip?"

"Seems odd to us as well."

"But if it was a stranger, why would he take the time to bury them?"

"We don't know," Decker said.

Her eyes leaked tears. "My poor baby."

"Is there anyone we could call, Wanda?"

"To be with me, you mean? No . . . no, thank you. I'm fine. I'll wait for Henry."

"Are you sure? Perhaps your daughter?"

"No, she's working. I don't want to disturb her until I've told Henry. When can I bring back my baby?"

"I'll call you as soon as I know." With that Decker stood up; McAdams followed suit. "I'll keep you up to date, Wanda. And, of course, you can call us anytime. Do you still have our cards?"

"I threw them away."

Decker held back a smile. "Then we'll give you new ones."

After she received the detectives' cards, she said, "I didn't think I'd need them. I didn't think there was anything left to say. But I suppose until the case is solved, there's a lot left to say. You will try to find out what happened, right?"

"We'll work as hard as humanly possible," Mc-Adams said.

"We'll work until there's nowhere else to go," Decker said.

She nodded. "I hope so."

Decker knew she didn't quite believe them. But he'd try his best to make her an acolyte.

On the way to the airport, McAdams's cell jingled. He looked at his phone window. "That's Kevin." He slid right. "Hey, I'm going to put you on speaker. Hold on . . . okay, say hello to the boss."

"Hey, Deck."

"What's up?"

"The translator had to cancel. Some kind of emergency with his family. We're going to try for tomorrow about eight."

"We may even be back by then."

"Then we'll all go together."

"Did you find the case on the internet?"

"No, I didn't. I put in several calls to the police but haven't gotten any callbacks. In the meantime, I've been trying to make sense of the report based on a computer translation and the information that Rina told you. As far as I can tell, lots of punches were thrown. I have a feeling that Bertram Lanz wasn't the only one to be arrested. The file makes it sound like a drunken brawl."

"Was Gerthard Perl drunk? From what we've read, he had just gotten off shift as a hospital nurse."

"I don't know if he was drunk or not. He was certainly in the bar. He might have said something to Bertram that set him off. I don't want to say anything more because I'm using a translation that could be giving me misinformation. How did it go with Wanda and Henry Velasquez?"

"It was just Wanda," McAdams said. "She expected news like this a long time ago."

"Never easy though."

"Never easy at all. We're off to the airport to see Harriet McCrae."

"Can I ask why? We have nothing to tell her."

"I know." Decker paused. "Just making contact."

"That can be done by phone."

"I'm in the area."

"Not really. Saint Louis is out of the way. What are you hoping to find out?" A pause. "Deck, if you think we're spinning our wheels by looking for McCrae's remains, I'd be grateful if you'd let me know."

"If I discover something, I'll tell you. In the meantime, keep digging."

They landed at eight in the evening after an hour delay. After arriving at the hotel, they ate a quick room service dinner, and then went straight to bed. Twelve hours later they were driving to Barney and Harriet McCrae's house near the university. It was deeper into the summer, and that meant soaring temperatures and near 100 percent humidity, even at ten in the morning. As hard as the car's AC tried, it couldn't take the moisture out of the air. The car windows dripped water. Behind the collar, Decker was hot and itchy.

They parked in the circular driveway and walked between pillars to get to the front door. They rang the bell, and a second later the door opened. Harriet must have been waiting in the front foyer. She had on a white, long-sleeved T-shirt, white pants, and sneakers with no socks. Same gold hoops in her earlobes.

"Come in, please." She stepped aside to let them cross the threshold. "I put the air-conditioning on full blast. You two should be comfortable."

Decker breathed in the welcome frigid air. "Set it how you like. We're only here for a short time."

"Which is why I don't mind it cold for a bit. We'll sit in the parlor." She led them into the room, seated them

410 · FAYE KELLERMAN

on a couch, and took a leather club chair for herself. She waited for them to speak first.

"We found Maxwell Velasquez's remains," Decker told her. "I thought you might like to know."

Harriet nodded. When no one spoke, she said, "Thank you for telling me. Is that all?"

Decker smoothed his mustache. "We're still looking for your son."

"I would hope so."

There was no real force behind the words. As if she suspected that they suspected something. Decker said, "We were just wondering if there was anything— anything at all—that you could tell us that would help the investigation."

She bit her lip. "No. Nothing."

"Any kind of a clue or—"

"Nothing." Harriet's eyes moistened. "Bennett was a wonderful boy. I want you to know that."

"That's why we're out there looking for him," Mc-Adams said. "Lots of police power, lots of tracker dogs, lots and lots of people spending time and money on the search."

Harriet wiped her eyes. "I wouldn't expect anything less." A pause. "Until, of course, you all give up."

Decker shrugged. "That's not going to happen anytime soon. Don't worry. We'll keep at it." No one spoke. He said, "Max's remains were buried. We're looking for a shovel."

"Makes sense." Harriet looked away.

"It's been over ten years, but we're sure we'll find it. We have to find it. Both boys were buried. There has to be a shovel somewhere."

"You don't bury people clawing at the ground," Mc-Adams said.

No response.

Decker said, "Any idea why the boys would have brought a shovel with them to camp?"

"Who said they did?"

"The boys were buried," Decker said.

Harriet put a thumbnail in her mouth and took it out. "I told you gentlemen *everything* I knew." She paused. "I'm sorry, I can't tell you more."

"You can't tell us more because . . ."

"Because I don't *know* anything more." She rubbed her eyes. "What do you *want*?"

"Both boys were buried, Harriet." Decker's voice was soft and soothing. "Someone cared."

No response.

"No one's to blame," Decker said. "Just being in the wrong place at the wrong time." First her eyes became wet, then the tears flowed freely down her cheeks. The audible crying came after that. "It's been ten years. I think we all deserve to know the truth."

The crying became sobbing.

Decker said, "Can you take us to see him?"

She wiped her eyes and bobble-headed a yes.

"Can you take us now?"

"It's not close." Her crying had turned to a few tearful gasps. "About three hours away."

"By car or by plane?"

"By car."

"That's fine." Decker stood up. "We'll all go together in my car."

"My car," Harriet said. "He'll panic if he sees a car he doesn't know. He has mental conditions. It haunts him." She wiped her eyes. "He's never been right after that."

Decker thought a moment. "Does he have any weapons?" No response. "Harriet, I need to know."

"A gun." A pause. "Several guns."

"That changes things."

"I will not call the police, Detective. He'll kill himself if he sees the police."

"Then you have to bring him to me. Weaponless."

"I don't know if I can do that."

"You have to convince him to give himself up. You have to tell him that no one thinks he did anything wrong."

"He didn't do anything *wrong*." The tears were back. "I've told him that a million times. He's scared, Detective. Scared and scarred. Nothing you or I say will make a difference."

"Do you know what happened?" Harriet was silent, not about to give anything away. Decker said, "Where does he live?"

"In a trailer in the woods in the middle of nowhere. I wouldn't even know how to tell you to get there. I just know how to get there myself."

"Okay. Do you think you can get him to talk to us without guns?"

"I don't know."

"Because all I want to do is talk," Decker said. "But if he has guns, I can't do that. If you can't get him out of the trailer unarmed, I'm going to have to call in the local police."

"Then I won't tell you where he is."

Decker's brain was reeling. He certainly didn't want to arrest the woman for obstruction. He had been thinking that Bennett was institutionalized, not that he was in the middle of nowhere. It was clear that he was suffering, but that didn't make him any less dangerous. Maybe twenty years ago Decker would have played cowboy, charging forward without any care about personal safety. But he was older and wiser, and with

McAdams, who had already been on the wrong side of a gun twice, he was careful. There had to be a way around calling in the forces. "Harriet, is there a gun shop near here?"

"Why?"

"I'd like to buy some body armor—for all of us. I'm not planning on approaching him if he's armed and paranoid."

"I think it would make all of us feel better." Within seconds, McAdams was tapping his phone. He showed the address to Harriet. "How far is this place?"

"About fifteen minutes."

The detour might give Decker some time to think up an actual plan. "Okay, let's go."

"I should tell my husband. He's out playing golf."

Decker looked at his watch. "It's ten-thirty in the morning. How about we let your husband go about his day in peace."

Harriet nodded. "I'll get my keys."

"I'll come with you." When she looked at him, Decker said, "I don't want you warning Bennett off."

"There's no phone reception where he is. Besides, I know that would be against the law. I wouldn't do that."

She had turned angry. As if Decker had insulted the last vestiges of her son's humanity. "Just being a cop, Harriet," he said. "Just doing my job."

Most of America's swamp region was in the Deep South—from Louisiana's Atchafalaya Basin running east to the Florida Everglades. While Missouri was considered a border state, the heat and the humidity spoke of its southern roots, and it was packed with wetlands and fens that bred mosquitos, flies, beetles, and all sorts of water-skimming insects. Malaria, common at the turn of the century, had been basically eradicated through the efforts of the Tennessee Valley Authority and DDT, but where one disease goes, another comes along. And although Zika was not considered a problem in the United States, Decker didn't want to be a test case. Bites were unpleasant; illness took unpleasant to a whole new level. COVID-19 had proven that point with alacrity.

Along the way, Decker bought some cheap long-sleeved shirts and a pack of undershirts and a big can of spray-on bug repellent at a local Walmart. No sense getting his dress shirt and jacket stained with copious amounts of sweat. He had dressed himself in layers—undershirt, body armor, top shirt—and the heat was seeping into his skin like a slow-spreading fire. He had grown up in Gainesville, Florida, not noted for its cool weather, but this was something different. The air was stagnant with a blanket that was oppressive, thick and unrelenting, similar to the 'Nam jungles in the summer. Except here no one was shooting at him.

Not yet at least.

Harriet was driving, and, lucky her, she got the lion's share of the AC. The two detectives sat in the back, having to make do with an occasional whiff of cold air. Tyler was a steady stream of perspiration dripping from his forehead. His expressive eyes pleaded: *I wanna go home!* Instead, he whispered to Decker, "No wonder they're called the flyover states."

"Sure, just dismiss an entire part of the country," Decker said. "Where's your mettle, Harvard?"

"It melted about twenty minutes ago."

Harriet said, "You two okay back there?"

"We're fine," Decker said.

"Liar," McAdams whispered. "Do we have a strategy going forward, boss?"

"Yeah. Don't get shot." Decker looked out the side window. The natural greenery was dark and wet, the ground hosting patches of low-level stagnant pools and ponds, the terrain heavy with trees: swamp tupelo, locust, sweet gum, hickory, and bald cypress with their knobby knees protruding from the water. The road was paved but barely so, with holes of missing asphalt. Vapor was shimmering off the tar.

Twenty minutes later, as the vegetation thickened,

Harriet turned into a rutted path and parked the car. She killed the motor. "His trailer's up there."

Decker looked over the front passenger seat and out the windshield. "I can't see it."

"Yeah, but he can see you."

McAdams said, "It's stifling in here."

"Sorry." Harriet rolled down the windows. "I'd leave the motor on for the AC but it'll make him suspicious. You can hear everything from up there."

"We're fine without the AC."

"Speak for yourself," McAdams grumbled.

"Let me go up first," Harriet said. "See if I can talk some reason into him. If not . . ." A long sigh. "I suppose at that point, it's your call."

Decker's face glistened with sweat. "Go for it."

Harriet opened the car door. Within a minute she had disappeared among the trees.

"I dunno which is worse," McAdams said. "Getting shot or dehydrating to death. You know, wet heat is way worse than dry heat?"

"I did know that." Decker slid into the front passenger seat, squeezing his big body through the small open space. Once there, he crouched down, eyes remaining focused through the front windshield.

McAdams said, "I got a bad feeling about this. Maybe we should have called the local law enforcement. I mean, what are the odds that after hiding for ten years, McCrae is going to talk to us?"

"Not very good."

"Yeah, not very good." McAdams exhaled angrily. "I know you think you owe the Velasquezes and the Andersons the truth, but is it worth a bullet hole?"

"You're thinking bad juju. Drink some water. Dehydration is the enemy."

He took a swig from a thermos bottle. "It's probably cooler outside than inside."

"Probably. But until we know what's happening, we're staying inside. Sweating isn't lethal."

"That's what you think."

The car turned quiet. Stayed that way for another five minutes.

Decker sat up. "I think I see them."

"Them?"

"Maybe it's just her. Get down, Tyler. I don't know if he's following her or if it's a setup."

He obeyed. "You think she'd let him use her as a shield?"

"Don't know." Decker slid out of view from the windshield. He took out his weapon. When McAdams did the same, Decker said, "You just stay down, okay?"

"And let you have all the fun?" A minute later: "What's going on?"

"She's just walking down the hillside."

"Maybe he isn't inside the trailer."

"Maybe." Decker slowly raised his head so he could see out the windshield. "I want to wait until she's closer."

"Wait for what?"

"Hold on, Tyler. Give me a few more seconds . . ." A pause. When she was around a hundred feet away, Decker said, "Stay down, Tyler. I'm going for it." He threw open the passenger door and used it for protection. He called out loud, "Harriet?"

She stopped immediately.

"Anyone with you?"

"Nope."

"What's going on?"

She looked around. "Can't see you. Come out from hiding. He's not with me."

Decker wasn't sure he believed her. He began to stand from a squat, his eyes scanning the area left to right, right to left. Nothing but trees and brush: the forest hid a lot. When Harriet was around ten to fifteen feet away, he told her to stop walking. "Where's Bennett?"

"Up in his trailer. He said he'd talk to you. But you've got to come to him. He refuses to leave."

"Then we have a problem."

"Can I move? I don't like to shout from a distance."

"Yes, but walk slowly." When Harriet was at the car, Decker said, "You've got to talk him into coming down here, or else I have to call the police."

"He's not going to agree to that, Detective. I can only push him so far."

"Bennett has firearms. You tell me he's mentally unstable. That means I can't go up there. He's got to come down."

"He won't do it." Harriet had tears in her eyes. "Detective, he said he'd talk to you. But he's only comfortable talking where he can see everything. He thinks you're setting him up."

"And I think he's setting me up. If I start up the hill, Bennett can pick me off with a simple scope."

"How about if I stand in front of you?"

"I'm taller than you. And I don't want you picked off either."

"He wouldn't hurt me." She looked up at the sky and wiped sweat from her forehead. "He's rational today."

"What do you mean by that?" McAdams asked.

"It means he knows what's going on. Unfortunately, that isn't always the case." She looked at the detectives. "If we leave now without seeing him, he's either going to run away or kill himself. How long do you think he'd last in this heat?"

"He lasted ten years, running away from what happened," McAdams said.

Decker's head was whirling. "Okay, Harriet, this is what I want you to do. I want you to go back up there. How long does it take you to walk back up?"

"Five minutes."

"We'll come up in ten. We'll have weapons, but they won't be drawn. You keep him calm and away from his guns. If he suddenly gets riled, you let us know."

"Okay. I'm off." She turned around and started hiking upward.

No one spoke for a few minutes as Decker's eyes were glued to his watch. Finally, McAdams said, "I'll walk behind you and cover your back." A pause. "Is this really a good idea?"

"It's a terrible idea, but it's the only one I have right now," Decker said. "She should be up in a minute or so."

"Maybe I should lead. I don't have a family."

"Just because you don't have one now doesn't preclude the future. Just stop talking and pay attention. Let's go."

With deliberation and caution, they started up the hill. Decker was constantly using whatever foliage and trees he could find for cover. Within a few minutes, the trailer came into view, peeking through thick brush. Which meant if Decker could see the trailer, someone looking out the window of the place could see him. But he soldiered on, his eyes fixed on the lodging in front of them. Finally, he and McAdams reached the top of the hill with the trailer about ten yards away. He shouted, "Bennett, we're the only ones out here. I need you to come out so I can see you."

Without hesitation, he said, "I can see you. If I wanted to shoot you, I would have done it already."

"I appreciate that." Decker was dripping wet. "But I'm not going to approach you until I can see you."

Silence.

"Bennett, I'm here to help you."

Still no answer. He could hear Harriet's voice but couldn't make out the words.

"Bennett," Decker said. "I can't stay around waiting. I need a commitment."

Seconds passed. And then a minute . . . two minutes.

Finally, the trailer door opened. The man who stepped out was around thirty, but his face looked twenty years older. He had an uncut beard with gray streaking through the dark brown. His hair was unkempt and sported long Rasta curls. There were wrinkles on his forehead, wrinkle lines that fanned out from the corners of his eyes. Dark orbs were surrounded by red and yellow spots swimming in a sea of white. He wore a long-sleeved plaid shirt and a pair of faded jeans with old boots on his feet. Harriet was right behind him.

"Hands up, Bennett."

"Don't shoot him," she said.

"I'm not going to shoot anyone. I just want to see his hands." To Bennett: "That okay with you, buddy?"

Bennett said nothing.

"Put your hands on the top of your head, Bennett."

The passing seconds seemed protracted. Finally, he complied.

Decker turned to McAdams. "Watch his hands."

"My eyes are glued."

"I'm going to walk toward you now, Bennett. Just keep your hands up where I can see them." Decker approached slowly until he was looking into the tired man's jaundiced eyes. "I'm going to pat you down now. It means I'm going to touch you. You keep your hands up and I'll make it quick."

"I'm not a moron. I understand."

"Just spelling it out so no one gets the wrong idea."

"Go ahead. I'm unarmed."

And he was. Decker said, "You can put your hands down now." Bennett complied. "Thank you for agreeing to see us."

Bennett's eyes darted between McAdams and Decker. "You didn't give me an option."

"Bennett, he's trying to help," Harriet said.

"No, he's trying to solve a case." He addressed Decker. "You found the others?"

"We did."

"Took you long enough."

"Yes, it did."

"Talk to the other families?"

"We did."

"That's good."

"It is good that they have the finality. Wondering is a hard thing. Son, it would help them out if they knew what happened."

Silence.

Decker spoke softly. "Bennett, it's time."

"Yeah." Tears rolled down his cheeks. "I suppose you're right."

Chapter 25

It wasn't the heat or the humidity. It wasn't the hoarding and the piles of clothing and trash and mounds of papers stacked precariously. It was the smell—the stink of decay, piss, and rotted food with a topper of must and mold. There was no running water, as evidenced by a tub of brown liquid—dubiously suitable for cleaning, let alone drinking. Scattered with the trash were empty plastic water bottles. Some had been cut in half and were used for growing greens.

Furniture included a beaten-up love seat, a small round table with a chair, and a mattress on the floor topped with torn blankets. The kitchenette had a sink piled with dishes and a small refrigerator that must have run on a battery-operated generator. Decker heard a background hum. On the opposite side of the trailer was a closed door in the back. He assumed it was the bathroom with a chemical toilet.

Harriet had already pulled out cleaning supplies and a six-pack of paper towels from a cabinet. Bennett said, "I would have cleaned the place if I knew you were coming." He sounded defensive.

"It's fine, dear." She started on the dishes, using bottled water and soap.

Decker had his eyes glued on Bennett. He held his hand over his own firearm. "Where are your guns?"

"Cabinet over the sink."

Bennett rolled up his sleeves and began to scratch his arms. Scabs all over. Decker said, "I'm going to look in the cabinet. I need to do that."

"Yeah, I get it."

Decker locked eyes with McAdams. "Watch him." To Bennett: "What kind of gear do you have?"

Bennett said, "A shotgun, a .38 revolver, a .22 revolver, a .357 Magnum, and two rifles."

"Lot of firepower," McAdams said.

"I hunt. We got wild turkeys and deer and small game. Different guns for different animals."

Decker went over to the cabinet and took out the weapons, one by one, unloading them as he pulled them out. "I'm keeping the ammo."

"I understand." Bennett went over to a section of the living room and lifted a stack of white computer paper with handwriting on it. "This'll tell you everything."

"What is it?" McAdams asked.

"My memoirs. I have a great story to tell. Hollywood should snap it up. Black stars are hot."

"And I will read every page of it." Decker took the papers. Must have been over a thousand pages. "But for right now, I need a condensed version."

"Sure, but you'll be missing a lot of drama."

"That's why I'll read it later."

"I think you'll appreciate . . . what happened that way."

"I'm going to tape this interview."

"Why?" Jumpy eyes.

"Because I forget things—"

"That's why I gave you the memoirs."

"Bennett, I need to tape the interview. It's for your protection and for mine."

"If you have to do it . . ." Eyes still restless.

"Thank you." Decker turned on the app on his phone and pointed to the sofa. "I'm ready when you are."

"You don't want to sit?"

"No, I'd rather stand."

428 · FAYE KELLERMAN

"Why?"

Because I don't trust you and your place is a friggin' disaster. But Decker realized that his height was an impediment to rapport. "I have a bad back." He pulled the chair from the table and leaned forward so as to lessen the impact of his six feet four inches. "Anytime you're ready."

Bennett pushed away papers from a sofa cushion and sat down. His eyes became faraway. "It was a long time ago."

"I'm betting you still remember it in detail."

"Wish that I didn't, but I do."

"Why don't you start on that Thursday, when Zeke, Max, and you were preparing for your camping trip."

"A camping trip that never ended for me."

Harriet was banging around in the kitchen. Decker said, "Would you mind holding off, Harriet. I need to hear what he has to say. I don't want to miss anything."

She stopped and sighed. "I'll clean the bathroom."

"You don't have to clean anything, Ma."

"It'll give me something to do." Harriet closed her eyes. "I've heard the story before."

The implication being too many times. Decker said, "Go on, Bennett. You have my attention."

The man sat back and continued scratching his

crusted arms. "It was Parents' Weekend and we wanted out."

"Who's we?"

"You know. Zeke, Jack, and me, initially. Someplace not too close, someplace not too far. Something in driving distance. I suggested camping. The weather was nice."

A pause.

"We wanted to try the mountain man thing. Zeke and I knew how to shoot, but neither of us had a gun. That's where Max fit in. He had a gun. I used to borrow it whenever I went shooting at the college indoor range."

"You invited him to come?"

"Yeah. We knew he'd say yes even though his parents wanted to see him that weekend. He didn't have a lot of friends. Not that we were really friends." He breathed in, then breathed out. "I told him we were dividing up the labor. I was going to take care of the food. Jack would be in charge of finding the perfect spot: he was a hiker. Zeke would provide us with the car, and he'd pay the gas. I told Max that he was in charge of the equipment, including the gun. He had no idea what kind of gear to buy, so I gave him a list."

"That's a lot of outlay," McAdams said.

"Yeah, I told him to keep the receipts and we'd divide up the cost afterward. We did that a lot with Max."

A breath and more scratching of his arms. "Course he agreed. Then Jack crapped out. His parents were coming in. He was pissed." Bennett paused. "Guess he was the lucky one."

Decker nodded, encouraged him to continue.

"Anyway, the three of us met up Thursday afternoon before the weekend events started." Another faraway look. "Max did his job, including the gun. I got the food. At three in the afternoon we were packing Zeke's car. We figured we'd find a good spot once we were in the hills."

"Did you take a tent?"

"Yeah. A tent and three sleeping bags and backpacks with things like medicine and bug spray and shit like that."

"That's a lot of stuff crammed into a BMW."

"Yeah, it was stuffed. We put the food in the trunk, and the gear was in the backseat with Max. We weren't going too far."

"How did you decide where to camp?" Decker asked.

"Just hiking around." Bennett pointed to the papers. "It's all in my memoirs."

"And I will read it. But now we've got to talk. What attracted you to the spot?"

"It wasn't too far from the public trail, and it was private enough where we could get high in peace." A pause. "That's wasn't the only purpose . . . to get high. But without girls, you've gotta entertain yourself."

Decker said, "Got it."

McAdams said, "You all shared one tent?"

"We did."

"You didn't care about the lack of privacy?"

"You get high enough, you don't care about anything."

"Drugs or alcohol or both?" Decker asked.

"Does it make a difference?"

"I don't know. Does it?"

Bennett sighed. "Zeke and I brought some vodka, tequila, and beer. Max brought the weed and the pills and cocaine and acid. Another reason we invited him. He had money to buy good shit." His eyes misted. "Good old Max."

"What went wrong?"

Bennett's voice turned soft. "It was Thursday night. We'd finished getting the tent up, we'd finished eating. Max brought out some tabs . . . I think he had a pane."

"You mean LSD," Decker said.

Bennett nodded. "Zeke brought out the vodka. It didn't take too long before . . . we got really high." His eyes were staring at the wall—a TV in his mind. "I was fine. Seeing everything in bright colors and slow motion. Zeke was fine. Max . . . I think he was seeing things. Bad things. He was hearing noises. He ran outside. He took the gun . . ."

Bennett swallowed hard.

"Both Zeke and I heard this popping noise." His lips blew air. "Pop, pop, pop."

He stared at the wall. He was covering his ears.

"Then there was this screaming . . . this *painful* screaming." His eyes redirected to Decker. "The stupid motherfucker had shot himself in the foot."

He threw his hands over his face and started to rub his eyes.

"We knew we should get help. But Zeke and I were in warp speed, you know. I couldn't drive. Neither could Zeke." A long silence. "We figured we'd just take care of it when we came down . . . when things went back to normal. I guess we weren't thinking too well. The motherfucker was bleeding."

He puffed up his cheeks and blew out air.

"Max kept screaming. It bothered me, but it was really bothering Zeke. He got angry—weird because Zeke wasn't an angry guy. But things change with shit in your system. He marched up to Max and took the gun, waving it in front of him, telling him to shut up."

A pause. While Bennett was talking, he was gesticulating the action—waving an imaginary gun.

"We were in the tent. I guess Max came inside after he shot himself. He was yelling at Zeke to do something. That he was in pain."

Another pause.

"I was like, watching. I could understand, but I couldn't react."

Couldn't or *didn't want to.* Bennett had turned quiet. Decker prompted, "Go on."

"I'm *thinking.*"

"Take your time."

A minute passed. Then Bennett said, "At some point, Zeke had enough. He dragged Max outside. I heard noises. Zeke had fired off some rounds in the air trying to convince Max to stop screaming. Like I said, we weren't thinking too clearly."

Bennett furrowed his brow. Then he licked his lips.

"At first I thought he killed him. But then Max was still screaming. I wanted to help, but I was like stuck on the ground in the tent. I couldn't move. And all these distorted images are talking to me in this slurred voice . . . whispering. Max was screaming and Zeke was screaming. Then things got crazy."

Decker waited.

"I heard . . ." He tapped his temple and shook his head. "I heard like this really loud boom. Like a fucking cannon going off."

He began trembling as he relived the situation.

"My ears started ringing; my head started vibrating . . . I started shaking. I thought, like: *What the fuck!* Then a second boom!" He cringed. "The air grew warm and stank of rotten eggs. And shit and stuff started falling on the tent. I swear to God, I thought I was dead. I couldn't hear a thing. My head was exploding. I couldn't stand, I couldn't crawl, I couldn't move, I couldn't think. All I could do was shake."

Tears rolled down his face.

"Then everything turned quiet. I didn't move for . . . I don't know. It felt like forever, but it might have only been a few minutes. I was finally able to get to my knees. I peeked outside."

He spread his arms.

"There was this big hole in the ground about five feet from the tent. Like a crater. I couldn't see clearly because everything was dusty and it had turned pitch outside. Had no idea about Max and Zeke. And I was too afraid to turn on a flashlight. Something very bad was out there."

"Did you see anything?"

"No, but I could feel it. Like hot breath on my neck."

Silence.

Then Bennett said, "I finally got the courage to go outside. I dropped to my knees . . . crawling out of the tent . . . on my stomach. My fingers digging up the ground." He clawed his fingers. "My hand hit something sharp . . . like a knife. I look at it, and there's this piece of metal sticking out of it. I still have the scar."

He showed Decker his hands.

"There was shit all over the ground. I pulled out the metal from my hand. I was bleeding bad. Crawling back to the tent . . . to wrap it up." He made a wrapping motion around his hand. Then he stared at the wall. "I heard the moaning. Like this deep, guttural thing."

He stopped talking, his eyes focused on something in his brain.

"Didn't know what the fuck it was. By now, I was back in the tent. I decided to wait for morning. Maybe I'd fall asleep and wake up and realize that it was a bad trip or a bad dream. Of course I didn't sleep. Maybe dozed a few minutes, then I'd wake up shivering. This went on all night."

A headshake.

"When morning came, I found Zeke's car keys in the tent . . . in his sleeping bag. I took them and put on boots and tiptoed outside." His lip started trembling. "Crater still there . . . everything was, like, destroyed! I wanted to run, but then I saw the bodies. Zeke's eyes were open. This look of . . . shock . . . stunned terror in his eyes." He covered his mouth. "He had this giant hole in his chest. Max's gun had fallen out of his hands. I picked it up."

"And Max?"

"He was a couple of yards away. His legs were fucked up, dangling, bone sticking out. Like maybe he stepped on a land mine. He was out, but he was breathing."

A long pause.

"I put him over my shoulder and started walking to the car." Bennett mimicked a slinging motion. "Blood all over my shirt from his legs. When I picked him up, he started moaning, so I knew he was alive." He squeezed his head with his hands. "I still hear it all the time."

Harriet came out and took his hands off his ears. "You're safe, Bennett." She leaned against the wall. Tears were in her eyes.

Bennett shook his head. "I thought I was going in the right direction . . . to the car. I walked and walked but couldn't *find* it. I must have gotten turned around. I began to panic. I was totally fucked up from what happened."

He stopped talking. McAdams asked, "What did you do next?"

"I don't remember too well. I know at some point I put Max down. I couldn't carry him anymore. My back was so fucking sore. I was thinking that I could come back to him once I figured out where I was. I tried to retrace my steps, but I kept getting lost. I thought . . . this is how I'm gonna die. No food, no water, no good-byes. I'd just drop off the face of the earth. All I had was a fucking gun. You don't understand how panicked I was."

Decker said, "I've been through battle. I get it."

"Where? Afghanistan?"

"Vietnam," Decker said. "Go on. You're in the woods without food and provisions. Just a gun. And you keep getting lost."

"I kept walking around and around. Finally, I somehow landed back in camp."

"Any idea how long you'd been gone?"

"Hours." A pause. "It seemed like hours."

Silence.

"Someone had taken all of our shit: the tent and the sleeping bags and the food. Nothing left: no clothes, no backpacks, no money . . . just cleared the place out. I was back to square one. Lost and without any provisions. I was a mess . . . my clothes were soaked and dirty and bloody."

He stopped talking. It took him a while to find his voice.

"Zeke's body was gone, but it was clear what happened.

The crater had been filled up with soil. For some odd reason, the motherfucker left the shovel. Maybe he planned on picking it up later on. But it was all I had, so I took it and headed off to try to find Zeke's car. I certainly wasn't going to stay there."

Sweat pouring from his forehead.

"Of course, I got lost again. And wouldn't you know it? I found Max. He was still alive . . . I heard his heart beat, but he had lost consciousness. His breathing was this weird raspy noise that sounded like static . . . one foot in the grave. I just eased the process."

He made a gun with his hand and fired the trigger with his thumb.

"I buried him . . . it took about two hours, but it was the least I could do." His eyes turned moist. "I must have walked for hours again. Walked and walked and walked. Finally, I found a road. I tried to hitch a ride, but no one picked me up. I looked like a crazy person: tired, starved, and fucking out of my mind. Blood all over my clothes, shivering with cold and carrying a shovel. On top of everything else, it started to rain.

"Another night in nowhere. Must have been Saturday night. But I was better off than before because at least I was on a road. I was trying to find some kind of civilization. A town or . . . whatever. Never found a town, but I began to pass some cabins. One was dark.

I broke in. No one was home. There was some frozen food in the refrigerator. There was canned food and a can opener. There was clothing. My phone didn't work, but the house phone did. I was gonna call for help. But then I remembered I'd put a hole in Max's head. I didn't call the police. I was . . . not thinking right."

"Scared," Decker said.

"Terrified."

"Understandable."

Bennett looked grateful for the empathy. "I was in shelter, out of the cold. First thing I did was eat. Then I showered . . . I changed into normal clothes—too big but better than being too small. Also, I found a warm jacket. After a night in the woods, I was cold. I left the shovel in the house and hit the road, this time looking like a normal person. Walking until dawn. I never did get a ride, but I found . . . a little place where there was a general store and a gas station. In the middle of nowhere, musta been there for years. It was early in the morning. My phone still didn't have any bars, and everything was closed. But I saw a motorcycle that was chained to an iron post. I blasted the sucker with Max's gun, almost blew up my own head in the process . . . hot metal and shit flying everywhere."

Silence.

Bennett said, "I hot-wired the ignition."

"How'd you do that?" McAdams said. "It takes some skill."

"I've been around."

"You knew how to ride a bike?" Decker asked.

"I did." He faced Decker. "I took off and never came back."

"What happened to the bike?" McAdams asked.

"Beats me. I got rid of it pretty soon afterward. I knew that someone would be looking for it." A pause. "I lived off the streets for a long, long time. Big cities like New York, L.A., San Francisco—where they had liberal homeless laws. It took me about five years to contact my parents. Didn't tell them where I was. I didn't want to bring them into my mess. And I didn't want them to bring me to the police."

A pause.

"It was my mother's idea to buy the trailer and hide it out here. Lots of people around living off the grid. She told me where it was. That she had cleaned it and stocked it and it was there if I wanted it. I didn't trust her. But then I became sick . . . real sick."

"A staph infection," Harriet said. "He was riddled with sores, all over. You can see his arms—all the sores and scars. I told him to go to the trailer. I got him medicine and nursed him back to the living."

"I've only been here two years," Bennett said. "You can arrest me, but please don't blame my mom. She's . . . she's my *guardian* angel."

The room fell silent.

Finally, Decker said, "We have to sort this out officially, Bennett. I'll need you to come down to the police station."

"You're gonna arrest me?"

"Yes."

"Murder?"

"Yes, but I will tell you this. I'm not a district attorney, but if what you say is true, there are mitigating circumstances."

"Every word of it is true." Bennett began to tear up. Then he began to sob . . . deep, deep breaths that were as heart-wrenching as they were pitiable. Harriet was crying as well. She held out her hand to her son. He clutched it and brought it to his chest. "You'll stay with me, Ma?"

"I won't leave you, Bennett. Not even for a moment."

Out came a pair of handcuffs. "For your protection and for mine," Decker said. He clamped the bracelets on, but he needn't have bothered. The beaten man followed, as meek as a bunny.

Chapter 26

It took hours to liaison with the proper authorities and to formalize the charges against Bennett McCrae and Harriet McCrae (for harboring a fugitive). His parents seemed relieved by the turn of events. Bennett was impassive as they brought him to his new home called a jail cell. It was cleaner and probably more comfortable than where he had been living.

Then Decker had the incredibly hard job of informing two sets of parents as to what might have happened that awful night. No one was sure, but the consensus seemed to be that some paranoid hermit living off the grid heard the gunshots that had been fired into the air. His brain slipped into a very dark place. Imagining himself under attack, he launched a couple of grenades in the direction of the noise, and then all hell broke loose. Perhaps the next day he was feeling calmer and remorse set in. Hence the burial of Zeke Anderson. It was assumed that he had stolen all the camp equipment. So whatever regret he had felt had been overcome by a desire to grab free supplies. Although there had been an extensive search for the students, no one had ever come across signs of someone living in the woods. Not surprising. All sorts of animals hide in the forests. The students had the misfortune of meeting a very deadly beast. Decker had seen this a few times before when he worked in the North Valley in Los Angeles. Hills hid drug labs, marijuana farms, outlaws and loners, paranoid schizophrenics and vets who never quite made it back into civilization. Most mentally ill people were harmless, but when delusions collided with self-preservation, chaos ensued. One of his past cases had been two dead hikers. The hermit who murdered them was found a week later, huddled and near starvation. Shipped off to Patton State, given proper food and medication, he recovered but lived in constant remorse for what he had done. Just like the pathologist had said.

For someone with PTSD, the sudden appearance of three strapping young men could look like a threat.

All this was strictly theoretical. But Bennett's story matched the crime-scene evidence. If it didn't happen exactly that way, Decker was fairly certain that the recitation had been close to the truth.

The problem was that shooting someone—even someone who was at death's door—was still considered a crime. It was not a premeditated homicide but Decker suspected Henry and Wanda Velasquez saw it differently. To them, a bullet hole in their son's head was nothing less than first-degree murder.

This was not a case where Decker celebrated getting a bad guy off the street. This was not a crime where he felt he could give justice to the parents. This was just an entire day of being a misery sponge to grieving people, and it was exhausting. Back at the hotel room, Decker felt his brain shut down. But sleep was still elusive.

The next day—at one in the afternoon—the two detectives were on a plane headed to Albany. With a long car drive back home, Decker hoped he could stay awake. He regarded McAdams, who looked as worn out as he was. "You okay?"

"Fine." McAdams yawned. "At least no one shot me."

"Thank God."

"Missouri's not going to send him back to Greenbury."

"No. And whatever jail time Bennett gets, his lawyer will request that he does it in Missouri. I don't see anyone objecting to that."

"If he's to be believed." McAdams exhaled. "Did you believe him?"

"He certainly wasn't trying to make himself a hero."

"Or deflect guilt," McAdams said. "He admitted shooting Max."

Decker thought a moment. "He didn't make a lot of eye contact as he spoke. He mostly stared into space. But he's in a different mental time zone than the rest of us." A pause. "Did you notice that as Bennett talked, he acted out his story? Like waving the gun or slinging Max over his shoulder or covering his ears as he heard an explosion. When someone lies, that doesn't usually happen. Because they're making things up as they go along and they don't generally know what's going to pop out of their mouths."

Silence.

"For the most part, I believe him," Decker said. "What about you?"

"His story fits all the moving parts," McAdams said. "A little part of me is still skeptical. Maybe I'll read the memoirs. Where are the pages?"

"Submitted as evidence." Decker gave a weak smile. "I suppose Hollywood will have to wait."

"You never know." McAdams looked at the ceiling of the airplane. "I suppose we can now concentrate solely on Bertram Lanz."

"That will be the next order of business after a good night's sleep."

"I'll second that." McAdams closed his eyes. "Think we'll find Bertram?"

"Who knows?" Decker said.

McAdams said, "Probably not good to speculate right now. I'm zonked. I know you're going to Zeke's funeral. What about Max?"

"Yes, I'm going to go." A pause. "You don't have to come with me."

"I'll keep you company. I'm just wondering why? It's not like you've been at this case for ten years and you're close to the family."

"I'm winding down my time here, Tyler. I want to end it by doing the right thing."

McAdams nodded. "Rina mentioned you buying a place in Israel." Silence. "Are you moving there?"

"Not full-time, no. But I asked Radar for a leave of absence."

"For how long?"

"Six months. Maybe a year."

"A long time."

"Yes."

"When is your leave of absence starting?"

"Next spring after Passover. I doubt that I'll go back to the department."

"If you leave, I'll leave. I've got a law degree, remember."

"I thought you hated law."

"Some law. Not all law. I've been thinking about criminal law."

"Prosecution or defense?"

"Don't know yet."

"Don't be swayed to the dark side."

"It's a constitutional right for everyone in this country to have a defense."

"Yadda, yadda, yadda."

"I could say the same for you. What the hell are you going to do in Israel for six months? I've been there. It's a small country."

"Did Rina tell you that the place we're buying is a wreck?"

"You're renovating?" McAdams opened and closed his mouth. "Don't tell me you're doing it yourself." Decker didn't answer. "You're loco."

"It's not a big job. It's a small house with a small garden in my ideal location."

"What city? Tel Aviv?"

"Jerusalem. Nachlaot, if that means anything to you."

"It doesn't. Are you going to live there while you renovate?"

"Undecided."

McAdams threw his arms up in the air. "At least you know how to shoot a gun."

"It's not a dangerous place, Tyler."

"Sure it's not."

Decker said, "Will you come visit?"

"Will you have a guest bedroom?"

"Yes."

"Internet?"

"Yep."

"An oven?"

"I don't suppose Rina will be doing much cooking with so much kosher takeout. But yes, we will have an oven. Once in a while I'm sure she'll want to prepare a meal."

"Okay, boss. Here's the deal. When she cooks, I'm all in."

A good night's sleep, and the next morning at ten they crammed into Radar's office, the biggest private place in the station house. The captain was behind his desk; Decker, McAdams, and Butterfield were on the other side, sitting in unmatching chairs. A window let in bright eastern light, and Tyler, God bless him, had made a fresh pot of coffee. After concluding the paperwork and putting a solve on the ten-year-old

THE LOST BOYS · 449

case, Decker turned his attention to the most pressing thing on the agenda.

"I finally got the translation of Bertram Lanz's German police report."

"Go on," Radar said.

Decker said, "Here's the deal. Bertram was out with some friends—all of them disabled. The group lived together in a residential home where they were supervised by rotating chaperones, but like Loving Care, they were all independent adults. The gang was out for a night of fun and drinking. They wound up at a bar that they had frequented before so they were known to the owners. Everyone in the establishment was drinking, and more than a few were drunk. A bar fight broke out."

"What was it about?" McAdams asked.

"What most drunk bar fights are about. Some insult where parties not under the influence would usually walk away. Apparently, a bunch of locals threw some derogatory comments at Bertram's group, and the group took offense. Drinks were tossed, bottles were thrown, and the whole thing turned into a big melee. Punches were plentiful, and some of the patrons not involved with the original altercation joined in just for fun. The festivities ended when Bertram threw a punch and Gerthard Perl didn't get back up. The police rounded up everyone, but Bertram faced the most serious charges. I did a little digging and I found out that he pled out. He was put on probation, in his parents' care, for three years. After that, he was a free man. I don't know why he came to the States. I suspect it was to get a fresh start."

McAdams said, "In all of our research on him, we haven't discovered any close relatives over here."

Decker said, "Thinking about the situation, maybe the parents wanted him in an anonymous country. But given the history, we know that Bertram wasn't afraid to use his fists. And his physical therapist told me he was a strong guy. I'm thinking that history may have repeated itself over here."

"He killed Pauline Corbett," Butterfield said.

"There was a lot of blood in that kitchen. If Elsie and Pauline were fighting, Bertram might have come to Elsie's rescue. Or Elsie killed Pauline—maybe accidentally, maybe in the heat of the moment—and perhaps she asked Bertram for help in cleaning up the mess."

"But there is a chance that Pauline might be alive," Radar said. "Until we have a body, we're in the dark."

"Of course." Decker tapped his foot. "Here's what I think: Bertram Lanz, Elsie Schulung, and Kathrine Taylor are in Germany. Maybe even Pauline is with them. I think Bertram's disappearance was planned."

"How do we prove that?" Radar asked. "If they are overseas, we shouldn't be wasting our resources looking for them here."

"I don't know how you verify that other than finding them in Germany."

Butterfield said, "What about Kathrine?"

Decker said, "Yes, I think she's with them. The thing is it's not our business to find her."

"I'm just asking why do you think that Kathrine is with Bertram?"

"Oh, okay," Decker said. "Well, I believe she had the same arrangement that Bertram had with her residential home. She could come and go as she pleased. Her parents told me she had been dreadfully unhappy since Bertram left. Maybe Kathrine viewed Bertram's disappearance as a chance to be with her boyfriend."

"If Kathrine went with Elsie voluntarily, then it's not a kidnapping," McAdams said.

"If she's a legal adult," Radar said.

"She is." Decker thought a moment. "At first, I was thinking about a kidnapping for ransom. Why else wouldn't Bertram's parents call back unless they've been threatened? Now I'm thinking that they didn't call back because the parents were in on Bertram's escape plan."

Radar said, "Before we go any further, what we need

to know is this: Was an actual crime committed—in our jurisdiction?"

Decker threw up his hands. "If the blood we found at Elsie's house was a crime scene, and if Bertram took part in the crime, even after the fact, then we have a reason to be involved in Baniff's territory."

"What's our next move?"

Decker said, "If we think that Bertram is with Elsie and they're all in Germany, someone should contact Interpol. I'm not well versed in international law." He looked at Tyler. "Perhaps this is your cue."

"I'll look up what is needed to involve the agency, but before I do anything, we should find out if they are in Germany."

"Agreed," Decker said. "You know, if they are in Germany, we're going to reach a dead end with credit cards, phones, passports, visas, and other personal effects because Bertram's family is wealthy enough to carry them. They could have even purchased new identities."

McAdams said, "Since it was Pauline's blood in the kitchen, do we look for her? If she's alive, we have no case for anything."

Butterfield said, "Actually, Pauline isn't our case."

Decker said, "Our only case is Bertram Lanz and unless the department wants to give us money to go to

Germany to look for him, I think we're done until we have more information."

McAdams said, "And even once we arrived in Germany, we'd have to work with the local police. The Lanz family is well established and has money. How much cooperation do you think we're going to get?"

Radar said, "Until we have Pauline's body, we have no way of knowing what happened at Elsie's house. And we have no way of knowing what Bertram's role was in all this . . . if he even had a role. He could have just escaped with Kathrine."

"Speaking of Kathrine," Butterfield said. "I'm sure her poor parents would like to know where she is and that she's safe."

"She may have contacted them," Decker said. "I can go talk to them and feel them out."

Radar said, "Kathrine's not our case, either."

"Yes, that's true. But there's at least a connection between Bertram and Kathrine. I don't mind paying them a visit, giving them my thoughts."

"How is Mangrove PD going to feel about that?"

Decker said, "Nothing wrong with talking to them in regards to Bertram's disappearance. I'll make it clear that Kathrine's not my case."

"It's going to look to them like we're giving up."

454 · FAYE KELLERMAN

"Unless of course they've heard from her—and Bertram by extension. At the very least, it would mean we can stop looking for Bertram in the woods, and start looking for him in Greenbury."

Radar paused. "This is what I want to do. Decker, you contact Baniff PD regarding Pauline Corbett's blood and Elsie Schulung's disappearance. Ask them to keep you in contact with whatever developments might come through."

"No problem. Been doing that all along."

"Tyler, you look up international law and find out what we can do if they are in Germany. Also, contact local police in Bertram's hometown in Germany and ask them to look out for sightings of Bertram, Kathrine, Elsie, and possibly Pauline. They may not be cooperative, but we have to try."

"I can do that."

"Kev, where are we on the search for Bertram?"

"It's been a couple of weeks," Butterfield said. "If Lanz is in the woods, we're probably looking for a body."

Radar thought a moment. "Do we still have a cadaver dog?"

"I can get one."

"Do it. We'll continue searching for another few days with the dog. I don't want anyone thinking we gave up."

"I'd like to visit the Taylors and feel them out," Decker said. "I'll tell them what I think is going on. And the rest is up to them."

"Fair enough."

"After the visit, I want a couple of weeks off."

"What's going on?" Radar asked.

"We want to go to Israel. We are looking at a property and everything is simpler if you get a lawyer and sign power of attorney when you're there. Otherwise, I have to go to the embassy. On our way back, Rina and I would like to visit our mothers in Florida."

Radar was stunned. "You're not moving to Israel, are you?"

"No. This will be a vacation home."

"Once you fix it up," McAdams said. "He's doing a reno—by himself."

"What's wrong with a little adventure?"

"No offense meant, but why would you want a vacation home in Israel?" Radar said. "Isn't it dangerous?"

"No more than anywhere else. The country just gets a lot of newspaper space."

But Radar persisted. "May I ask what's wrong with the Caribbean?"

"Something we all can enjoy," McAdams answered.

Decker smiled. "I could pin it on Rina and say it's religious fervor. The truth is, it was my idea. Good weather, good food especially if you're kosher, and I miss living in a city with some street life. Where the property is . . . you can walk anywhere." A pause. "Then I can have some time off?"

"But you are coming back," Radar said.

"Yeah, sure." Decker was looking at the ceiling.

"Two weeks can be arranged," Radar said. "Just sign out the days on the calendar so I know when you're gone." He looked around the room. "Anything else?" Silence. "Good work solving a ten-year-old cold case. That doesn't happen too often. I suppose we have Bertram to thank for that. Having him still a missing person doesn't feel good. But we'll take whatever we can get."

The summer sun shone high in the clear cerulean sky: long hours of daylight with mild temperatures rarely going above eighty degrees. Without the exigency of a case on his shoulders, Decker could actually enjoy the ride. It was the height of the tourist season in the Berkshires, people attracted to the many arts and music festivals on the calendar. He and Rina had gone to Tanglewood a couple of summers back. It was a glorious week of fresh air and wonderful music. As he drove, he thought about the future. Approaching seventy, he knew it was folly to take on a renovation project in a foreign country. And that's what made it so tempting. The unpredictability of it all. A new country, a new language, a new culture, and a new lease on life. It made him smile just to think about it.

As he approached highway 7, traffic backed up, but he wasn't in a hurry. The Taylors didn't seem in a hurry, either.

Come whenever. We're not going anywhere.

It took him around an hour to travel the six miles on the main road to reach the Taylor bungalow. As he was parking the car, Guy and Alison emerged from inside the house and stood at the front door. She gave a wave. Decker got out of the car and waved back. They waited for him and then turned and went inside, Guy holding open the screen door. It slammed as Decker entered the house. Coffee and cookies were waiting for him on the living room sofa table. Alison seemed relatively calm compared to her husband. Guy's deep blue eyes were jumpy.

"Sit anywhere," he said.

"Thank you." Decker was wearing a blue suit with a blue dress shirt open at the neck. No air-conditioning. Although it wasn't that hot, he was sweating. "Thanks for seeing me."

Alison said, "Please sit down, Detective. Can I pour you some coffee?"

"Sure. Just black. Can I use your bathroom?"

"Of course. It's down the hall, second door on the right."

"Thank you." He really did have to use the facilities. But being alone also gave him a chance to listen behind closed doors . . . see if he could detect any movement and hear anything suspicious.

Nothing.

He returned a few minutes later, and his coffee was waiting along with a plate of cookies. The Taylors were sitting together on the sofa. Alison was wearing a loose shift dress with sandals on her feet. Guy wore a white guayabera shirt over olive linen pants.

Sitting opposite them, Decker said, "I'm just here to give you an update. There have been some new developments in Bertram Lanz's case, but no progress in locating him. I don't know what Mangrove PD has found out about Kathrine. They're playing it close to the vest, and since Kathrine is not my case officially, I have to respect how they are proceeding."

Both of them nodded. Both of them said nothing.

"I've actually come to ask you if you've heard from Mangrove PD."

A pause, then shakes of the head.

"This may seem like a blunt question, but have you heard from your daughter?"

Nervous eyes. "What would give you that idea?" Alison said.

"Well, like I told you, it's Mangrove's case. But I have checked in with them. You haven't phoned them or asked for updates. Being a cop for a long time . . . that tells me that maybe you don't have anything to ask because you know what happened to her."

Guy said, "We don't know anything—"

"She's safe," Alison blurted out.

Silence.

Decker waited for them to make the next move.

Alison looked down. "That's all we know."

"You talked to her?"

"Yes."

"And you didn't think about reporting the conversation to the police?"

"She said she's safe," Guy told him. "That's all we know and that's all we care about."

"You know, we've expended quite a bit of energy looking for Kathrine and Bertram. It would have been nice not to spin our wheels."

"We just found out a few days ago," Alison said. "We should have contacted the police. We're very sorry."

A pause. Decker said, "Okay, I'll let Mangrove PD know. Is Bertram with her?"

"We don't know," Guy said.

"Hmm, I suspect you do."

"No, we don't." Guy added, "It was a thirty-second conversation."

"Who did she talk to? You or Alison?"

"She called me," Alison said. "We put her on speakerphone."

"Did you talk to anyone else besides Kathrine?"

"No," Alison said.

"And what precisely did she tell you?"

Alison put her thumbnail to her mouth. "Just that she was safe and not to worry."

"And?"

"That was it."

"No, I don't think so. I think she probably told you not to *call* the police." His response was met with silence. "She still may be in danger."

"She's not."

"And you know that because . . ."

Guy said, "Because she said she was fine."

"She sounded okay," Alison added. "Even happy."

"She was with Bertram?"

"We don't know and that's the truth." Alison shrugged. "But yes, she could be with Bertram."

"And you have no idea where she is."

"No."

"Overseas maybe?"

"I don't know."

"The phone number came up blocked," Guy said.

"We have ways of unblocking the phone number," Decker said.

"It's not necessary," Alison said. "No sense in you spinning your wheels, like you said."

"She told you not to call us, right?"

"Yes."

"And you're not concerned about her safety?"

"I'd be more concerned about her safety if I didn't do what she told us to do."

"'Don't call the police,'" Guy said. "Those were her words."

Alison said, "She was adamant."

"Okay," Decker said. "You don't know where she is." A pause. "Where do you suspect she is?"

"Can I tell you something in confidence?" Alison said.

Decker thought a moment. "Okay. What?"

"She's in Germany."

"Ah. And you think she's in Germany because . . ."

"The blocked number. We actually did hire a tech person to unblock it. He couldn't get the complete number, just the country prefix."

"You know you can get the number by requesting her phone records."

"No authority," Guy told him. "She's an independent adult."

"You think so?" Decker asked.

Alison looked down. "Bertram's parents are wealthy. If she's there with him, we don't have anything to be concerned about."

"Unless she and Bertram were kidnapped."

"I don't think that's the case," Guy said.

"She suddenly decided to go to Germany?"

A long sigh. Alison said, "You said this isn't your case. Let it go."

"If you know for a fact that she's with Bertram, you need to tell me that. Bertram is my case."

"I suspect she is. But I don't know that for a fact."

"Are you sending your private eye to Germany?" When neither Guy nor Alison answered, Decker said, "We'll probably be looking into it, you know."

"But *why*?" Alison was exasperated. "If Kathrine and Bertram are safe, what do you care?"

"Because there might have been a crime committed at Elsie Schulung's house."

"The nurse who worked at Bertram's residential care?"

"Exactly."

"What does she have to do with Kathrine?" Guy asked.

"Maybe something, maybe nothing," Decker said, "but Bertram and Kathrine may be together. And Bertram is our case."

"Bertram wouldn't hurt Kathrine," Guy said.

"He might not, but Elsie Schulung might not be as attached to Kathrine as Bertram is."

Alison said, "Getting the police involved might do her more harm than good. Have you considered that?"

"Of course I've considered that."

"You and I are at cross purposes, Detective," Alison said. "You want to get a crime solved. We want to keep our daughter safe. You go solve your crime, sir, but you're going to have to do it without our help. The only thing that matters to us is our daughter's safety. And like I said, she sounded happy."

"Okay." Decker stood up. "I understand what you're telling me. I'm a parent myself. I'd like to know exactly where Kathrine is before I let go. On the other hand, I don't want to screw up her safety. I'll talk to my captain and get back to you. But I will have to tell Mangrove PD that you've heard from her."

"But not where she is," Alison said. "That was the deal."

"I won't tell them where. Just that you heard from her and you don't want to pursue the matter."

"Do you think that Elsie Schulung is a criminal?" Guy said.

"I don't know. I wish I did." He gave a rehearsed smile. "Thank you for your time. I'm very happy that you've heard from Kathrine. If you need to contact me again, please don't hesitate. Believe it or not, I am on your side."

Alison's eyes moistened. "Thank you." She held out a cookie plate. "One for the road?"

"Watching my weight." Decker patted his gut. "I'll see myself out."

Chapter 27

It took about fifty phone calls, but the family finally decided on a place to eat dinner before Decker and Rina took off for Israel at twelve in the morning from Kennedy. As Decker looked around the table at their five children including a foster son, four spouses, one fiancée, and five grandchildren, he couldn't help but think that even if he died tomorrow, he'd go out a winner.

As usual, the conversation turned lively, then loud. People shouting across the table, kids interrupting, and the usual spillage. Appetizers came and went. Kids started having meltdowns. Right before the entrées arrived, the server came over with two big bottles of rosé champagne and flutes.

"Who ordered this?" Rina asked. "Not that I'm complaining."

"Group effort," Jacob said.

She looked at her son. His blue eyes were twinkling. Everyone looked very happy. She said as much.

"We are happy," Hannah said.

Decker said, "Happy for us or happy to get rid of us?"

"Oh, Abba!" She threw her napkin at him.

"We'll miss you," Sam said.

"We'll miss you, too," Rina told her elder son. "But we're only gone for two weeks."

"You know what I mean," Sam said. "You told us you're planning on going for an extended time after Pesach."

"Six months without being able to complain to you," said Hannah.

"There are telephones," Rina said.

"It's what . . . like an eight-hour time difference," Cindy said. "If I need immediate help on a difficult case, who am I going to call?"

"Or when I need money," Jacob said.

"Or when I need to deflect my crazy parents," Gabe said.

"Or when I need a babysitter," Sam added. "But I must say, it'll be nice to have a place in Jerusalem. Hotels are expensive."

"It's a small place, Sammy," Decker said.

"It'll have beds and cribs," Rina said. "You can use it anytime you want."

Cindy shushed her twin boys. She looked at her father. "Seriously, Daddy, when do you think it'll be ready? Koby and I have a bar mitzvah there next year. We're planning on going with the kids and like Sammy said, hotels are expensive especially at that time of year."

"I have a gig there next year as well," Gabe told his foster parents. "I think it's in Tel Aviv. Maybe it's Tel Aviv and Jerusalem." He turned to his fiancée. "You're coming with me, right?"

"Especially if we have our own place," Yasmine said. "I don't like hotels."

Decker looked at Rina. "Should we be charging rent?"

"Quiet, everyone!" Jacob held up a flute of champagne. "I propose a toast. To the happy couple. May they find peace and solitude in the Holy Land, and may construction go easily and without *gonavim*."

"Here, here!" Cindy said. "What's *gonavim*?"

"Crooks," Koby said.

Jacob was still holding up the flute. "To the happy couple. *L'chaim*."

"*L'chaim!*" everyone echoed.

"One more thing." Jacob held out two envelopes to his stepfather. "For you two. A small gift for all your long sufferings with the clan."

Rina took the envelopes. "This better not be money!"

"Why not?" Decker said.

"It's not money," Cindy said. "Open it."

Decker complied and pulled out two tickets to Israel—business class.

Rina said, "What did you guys do?"

"Go in peace and go in style," Sammy said.

"This must have cost you people a fortune."

"Not so bad between all of us," Koby said. "We just upgraded your current tickets."

Rina had tears in her eyes. "I don't know what to say." A pause. "Thank you, thank you."

"Unfortunately, we couldn't get seats together for the outbound flight at this late date," Hannah said, "but you're together for the return flight."

"Wow, thank you, children. It makes the trip even more exciting." Decker held up his flute. "A toast to all of you."

Just then Gabe's phone rang. He looked at the window. The number was blocked. No doubt it was his father. He often used burner phones, although he had a regular phone with both burner and hush features.

But that was just Chris. Nothing with him was ever consistent.

"*L'chaim*," Gabe said. "I've got to take this." He stood up and walked out of the restaurant. The street noise didn't make it much quieter, but at least his ears weren't ringing. "Hey."

Breathing on the other end. Gabe almost hung up, except it wasn't perverted breathing. It was labored breathing. "Hello?"

"You've gotta . . . get me."

A woman was struggling to talk. Confusion and then the lightbulb. Gabe's heart started racing. *"Mom?"* No response. "Are you okay?"

"No."

"Are you hurt?"

"Yes." She was crying. "They took Sanjay . . . Juleen . . . they're gone. You've got to help me. I'm *dying*."

"Mom, where are you?"

"L.A."

"Where in Los Angeles?"

"Valley."

"Mom, call 911."

"No!"

"You have to—"

"No!"

"You've got to call the police, Mom, and right away."

"They'll arrest me." A long pause. "You need to come get me."

"Mom, I'm three thousand miles away. If you're hurt, you need to go to a hospital. Call 911!" There was no response. "Mom, are you still there?" She didn't answer, but Gabe could hear her breathing. "Mom, I love you. Please call for help!"

"Hold on . . . oh God! I think that's Juleen!"

"Mom?" But she had hung up. With shaking hands, he dialed the phone number she had given him earlier when she had settled in California. It went straight to voice mail. "Why do you *do* this to me!"

He called again. And again. And again and again.

He texted her: *CALL ME!*

Decker had stepped outside, saw his foster son pacing. "Everything okay?"

"No," Gabe told him. "My mother just called me. From what I could gather, someone kidnapped my brother and maybe my sister. She's hurt."

"Your sister?"

"No, my mother. Maybe my sister too. I don't know. My mom can barely talk. She won't call 911. She's adamant about that. I don't know what's going on."

"Where is she?"

"Somewhere in Los Angeles . . . the Valley, I think."

"Her old stomping ground. My old stomping ground. What's her number? I'll see if I can't send someone out there to look for her."

"She doesn't want the police involved, Peter. Besides, she called me on a phone with a blocked number. It goes straight to voice mail."

"Why doesn't she want the police involved?"

"I think . . ." Gabe paused. "I *know* that she took her kids out of India. I suspect she had a court order not to leave the country with them. You know she's divorcing her husband. There's probably a custody dispute."

"If she took her kids out of the country illegally, she could be a fugitive. Hence, no police."

"Yeah. Probably."

"Maybe her husband kidnapped them back."

"I don't know." Another pause. "Honestly, at this moment I'm less worried about the kids than I am about her. She sounds horrible."

"Call her again."

He had already tried six times, but he tried again. Voice mail. He checked his texts. She hadn't responded. He shook his head. "Blank!"

"Does your sister have a cell phone?"

Gabe hit his forehead. "Duh!" He tried that number. Tried it three times. All he got was voice mail. "No answer. I'll text her, but I suspect it won't get anywhere."

"Gabe, let me call the police. Maybe they can ping a location on the phone."

"She insisted no police."

"If she's really hurt, do you think you should listen to her?"

Gabe felt panic in his stomach. "I don't think that'll get you anywhere, Peter. I think both my mom and my sister turned their phones off."

"What about Sanjay? Does he have a phone?"

"No."

"Then I'm out of ideas. You're three thousand miles away and can't get out there for another, what? Ten hours at the earliest. If she's really hurt, time matters."

"I've got a performance tomorrow in Boston. God, this is a total disaster! I need to call my agent and cancel. I certainly can't play with this on my head." He looked at Decker. "Can you come with me to Los Angeles?"

"Gabe, we're about to leave for the airport."

"Right. Of course."

"Do you want me to cancel the flight? I will if you want me to."

"No, no, no. There's nothing you can do anyway." Gabe's eyes turned moist. "I love her dearly. But my mom is a disaster! Devek owes money to bad people. So it could have been them as well. I do think her current husband is even worse than my father."

Decker raised his eyebrows. "Gabe, call your dad."

Gabe turned to him. "What?"

"Call your dad. He's on the same time zone, and he owns a private jet. He can probably get there in a couple of hours. Plus, he knows the Valley as well as I do. That's where he and your mom met. And if she's running from bad people, he can protect her better than anyone. Call your dad."

"He's not going to help."

"Chris just told Rina he was concerned about your mom's safety. Why wouldn't he help?"

"He's been waiting years for her to crash and burn. I think that's what kept him alive all these years."

Decker gave his foster son a skeptical look. "Do you have any better ideas?" No answer. "Do you want me to call him?"

"No, absolutely not." A beat. "Go back to dinner, Peter. I'm twenty-four. I can handle this."

"No shame in asking for help."

"I don't need help." *Even though he did.* "Please. Go back before everyone realizes there's a problem. I'll let you know what's going on later."

"Are you sure?"

"I am." He watched his foster dad go back into the restaurant. With shaking hands, he tried to punch in the numbers that he knew by heart, but he kept making mistakes. In desperation, he looked it up in his contact list under *Dad*. Heart banging out of his chest, he pressed the number.

A lot of the time Chris turned his phone off. Sometimes he used burners. Sometimes he changed his number without telling him. Most of the time he didn't answer even if the phone connected. Christopher Donatti was a very busy man. He didn't like phone calls. He especially didn't like phone calls from his son, who was always managing to interrupt some important business his father was doing.

His oft repeated line: *You're losing me money. This better be good.*

But this time the phone did ring. Which meant the current number he had was still active. Gabe stood there shivering even though it was the height of summer in New York: the cold was coming from within. Trembling like a frightened child as he waited to connect. "Pick up the phone, you motherfucker!" A moment later he heard the line kick in.

"What?"

Thank you, God. "Dad, you've got to help me. Mom called. She's in California. The San Fernando Valley I think, but I don't know for sure. She's badly hurt, but she won't call 911 or go to the hospital—"

"Hold on. Let me go somewhere private." A moment later Donatti was back on the line. "Your mother is on the West Coast?"

"Yes."

"Where are her kids?"

"She had them, but now they're gone. She's in the middle of a messy divorce. She might have taken them out of India without her husband's permission."

"Ah." A pause. "Someone took them back."

"Dad, I know that she wouldn't let them go without a fight, and I think she got a bad one. She sounded in real trouble. She wants me to come and get her, but I'm in New York and I don't know where she is. Furthermore, she called me from a burner with a blocked number, so I can't even call her back. Her regular phone is off." Gabe paused, but his father didn't talk. "I'm hoping she'll call me back. As soon as she does, I'll get more details. But in the meantime, you're a lot closer to L.A. than I am. And you're good at finding people."

Another pause. His dad waited.

Gabe said, "Look, I know you parted on bad terms—"

"She had an affair, got knocked up by the motherfucker, had his bastard child, and then dumped me unceremoniously. Yeah, I'd call that bad terms."

"I've had issues with her as well. I've forgiven her—"

"That's certainly your prerogative."

"She's my *mother*, Chris!" Silence. "You know what it is to lose a mom."

"I'm not moved. Try a different tactic."

"You loved her once."

There was a long pause. Gabe thought he might have hung up. But then Donatti said, "Who says I don't love her still?"

Gabe took in a deep breath and then let it out. This was a battle he knew he was going to win. "Will you help her? Yes or no?"

"Yes, I'll go." No hesitation. "I'm entertaining about a dozen people in my outer office right now. Give me a half hour to get rid of them, gas up the jet, and get a flight plan. If she calls you, *get a phone number.* Also give her my number."

"As soon as I know something, I'll call you."

"And I'll tell you this, Gabe. She'd better *want* my help. I don't have a good track record with your mother. If I don't hear from her by the time I get to Los Angeles, I'm turning around and she'll be your problem."

"Agreed. Let me give you Mom's number."

"I have it. What about your sister? Does she have a phone?"

"She does." Gabe gave him the number. "Both of them are going to voice mail."

"Probably they don't want to be tracked. I'll figure something out."

"Thank you, thank you, thank—"

"Yeah, fine. Let me get going on this." Donatti cut the line and pocketed his cell, running his fingers through his shoulder-length white hair, letting his conflicting emotions battle it out, not knowing what to feel now that the moment was actually here.

For over a decade, he had been formulating his delicious slap of vengeance . . . righteous justice in his mind. He had planted it, nursed it, fed it, watered it, sheltered it from the cold, and given it relief from the heat. He had watched it grow and blossom into something mean and unstoppable. It had consumed his thoughts. How he'd make her *pay* for what she did. And now that his chance for retribution was so close, so, so very close, all he could feel was the rapid beating of his heart, pounding not with revenge but with excitement.

He really, *really* wanted her back!

The thought of sex with her even after all these years was making him pant like a dog. He had had at least a thousand fantasies about it—some benign, some dark and cruel—all of them HD vivid in his brain. To see her face again . . . to feel her body. To hear her *voice*. It was her voice that had haunted him the most. Her voice that had kept him awake at night and dreaming through the days.

The first time she had dumped him was right after high school, after she found out he murdered people for a living. Not his idea of a career, but he had no choice, and at least he was good at what he did. Three years later, when she was at her lowest—desperate and destitute with a child—he had forced her hand, threatening to take Gabe away if she didn't come back to him. Theirs had been a rocky ten-year relationship. Problems, sure, but he never thought she'd have the guts to leave him.

But she did, abandoning him for a second time after getting pregnant by a doctor who had worked in the same hospital as she did. His bad for not keeping a closer watch. She had managed to escape his homicidal clutches long enough to turn his boiling anger into a constant simmer. He was fully intending to kill her. He had wanted to kill her, not with a gun—too easy and too fast—but with his hands: strangling her, watching the life being sucked out, murdering her face-to-face, eyeball to eyeball.

Trouble was, he didn't want her dead.

He had finally, *finally* gotten his shit together, gotten off drugs, weaned himself from cigarettes, cut down on the booze. He exercised and ate a healthy diet. He had reformed while slaving away and had built his own little fiefdom. Lord of the manor, where no one dared to get in his way. He had money, he had sex, he had respect, and, most important, he had the ultimate control over *everything* in his life.

Now that same *everything* was about to blow up in his face.

Even though he just knew it would end in disaster, he also knew that he'd take the plunge into the deep end without a second thought, idiot that he was.

Fool me once, shame on you.

Fool me twice, shame on me.

Fool me a third time, and someone's a moronic dumbass.

He flipped his hair out of his eyes, then walked out of his inner office into the fray he was hosting.

Here we go again.

Here we fucking go again!

At six feet four . . . well, maybe now six three and a half, allowing for shrinkage, Decker had always dreaded flying, cramming his oversize body into seats unfit for someone as tall as he was. The flight to Israel was long, and after he arrived, it took him hours to unfold. This time maybe it would be different.

He beamed as he thought of his children chipping in money to buy Rina and him business-class tickets.

Such a lucky man. He stowed his carry-on overhead in a space reserved for his seat alone. Then he slid into a chair with a footrest. He played with the buttons, and everything worked. He had a bigger pillow than usual, he had a thicker blanket, he had his own TV and flight attendants offering him juice, water, or champagne.

He could get used to this.

Rina came over. She was seated three rows behind him. "Pretty luxurious."

"Unbelievable." Decker sighed. "That was really a surprise."

"We did good with them young'uns," Rina said.

"We did," Decker answered.

"How's Gabe doing?" Rina asked him. "Any word from his mother?"

"I don't know, but he did get hold of his dad. Chris agreed to help."

"Nice, if he doesn't kill her first."

"It's been over ten years."

"Why do I feel that Chris is the type of person to carry a grudge?"

"And yet he agreed." Decker shrugged. "He must feel something other than anger toward her to put himself out like that."

"With him, you never know." When Decker's phone buzzed, Rina said, "Turn that off. We're on vacation."

"It's Tyler."

"It's eleven at night. He can't miss you that much."

"Yeah, this isn't good."

"Don't answer it."

Decker ignored her and clicked in the call. "What's going on?"

"Someone found a body earlier in the evening."

"Where?"

"In the woods about three miles from the diner where Bertram Lanz disappeared. A couple who was camping out decided on a sunset walk with their pooch. The dog started digging, exposing a face and a hand. It's our jurisdiction."

"Where are you now?"

"I just left the scene to call you. No bars up there. I'm going back as soon as I hang up."

Decker's heart sank. "You need me in Greenbury?"

"Peter!" Rina said.

"No, no. We're fine," McAdams insisted. "Coroner should be here momentarily. Kevin cordoned off the area, and we have someone watching the space overnight. We'll do all the forensics tomorrow morning. I'll keep you posted, but I thought you should know."

The flight attendant started making announcements. Decker stuck his finger in his ear and said, "You sure you're okay?"

"We're fine, boss. Enjoy your time overseas."

Right, he thought to himself. "Any first thoughts about the body?"

"Rigor's come and gone, bloat's come and gone."

"Then the corpse is at least a few days old."

"Looks older than that—weeks. There's some de-composition."

"Any insect activity?"

"The nostrils, eyes, and mouth are crawling with maggots."

"Then part of the face was exposed to the air, so the flies could lay their eggs. What about animal activity?"

"No animal activity. Clothes are still intact."

"Is the corpse male or female?"

"Probably female. We're waiting for the coroner for confirmation. The face is messed up."

"Bugs can do that. What about the clothes?"

"Jeans, plaid shirt, sneakers. Looks like a big woman's foot or a small man's foot. We'll know once the coroner arrives. That should be soon."

A flight attendant named Nurit came over to him. "Everything okay, sir?"

Decker looked at her. "Yes, thank you."

She swallowed. "The woman across the aisle over-heard you talk about corpses. I think it's upsetting her."

"Oh, sorry."

"Sorry for what?" Tyler asked.

"No, not you." Decker smiled at the attendant. "I'm a police detective. I'll finish up the conversation." To Tyler: "I have to go. I'll call you when we land."

"Don't worry about it, boss. I have it covered."

Decker hung up. He muttered a sorry to the nervous woman across the aisle.

Rina stared at him. "You're *not* going back."

"No, I am not going back."

"Thank you." Rina sighed. "I hope this won't ruin our vacation."

"It won't." Decker smiled. "I promise. When we land, I'll give you my laptop and my phone. How's that for commitment?"

"I don't need to confiscate your belongings, Peter. Just unplug and promise me you won't let whatever is going on at Greenbury interfere with our downtime." The flight attendant announced that everyone should take a seat. "You have your Ambien for sleep?"

"I do."

"Take it as soon as we take off."

"Will do," he said. "I'm excited, Rina. A new adventure."

"You're very cute." Rina kissed him. "See you in the Holy Land."

Three hours later Rina was sound asleep and he was lying on his back, stretched out in relative comfort with his eyes wide open and thoughts whirling around in his brain. He would probably be sleeping if he had taken the pill, but he chose not to because other things were on his mind.

You can take the man out of the investigation but you can't take the investigation out of the man.

He had promised Rina to unplug from work when they landed. She deserved that. But why toss and turn for hours when the solution to his insomnia was right at hand? Quietly, he stood up and took down his laptop from the overhead compartment. After he booted it up, he looked at his options for buying the plane's internet. At first, he thought about doing a thirty-minute plan. Just a few quick questions and then turn off the noise. But an unknown force led his fingers to choose the two-hour plan. He typed in Tyler's email address.

He wrote: *I'm up. I can't sleep. Tell me everything that's going on.*

About the Author

FAYE KELLERMAN lives with her husband, *New York Times* bestselling author Jonathan Kellerman, in Los Angeles, California, and Santa Fe, New Mexico.